Havens of POMPEII

Havens of POMPEII

Some things always survive

Nicole Louw

iUniverse LLC
Bloomington

Havens of Pompeii
Some things always survive

Revised Edition 2014

iUniverse books may be ordered through booksellers or by contacting:

iUniverse LLC
1663 Liberty Drive
Bloomington, IN 47403
www.iuniverse.com
1-800-Authors (1-800-288-4677)

ISBN: 978-1-4620-1973-1 (sc)
ISBN: 978-1-4620-1975-5 (hc)
ISBN: 978-1-4620-1974-8 (e)

Printed in the United States of America

iUniverse rev. date: 01/20/2014

To my father, Nico, and my brother, Lloyd.
You two never stopped believing in me

Author's Note

Most readers are familiar with the disaster caused by the volcano Vesuvius at the time Titus was ruler of the Roman Empire. Pompeii, a city of about twenty thousand souls situated only a few kilometers south from the base of the volcano, was one of the largest wine-exporting capitals in the empire during the year 79 AD. Vineyards and orchards lined the mountain base, sprouting from the rich soil that blessed the residents with prosperity.

On the morning of August 24, 79 AD, the earthquakes, which had over the years been little more than a growing nuisance, became a continuous vibration. It was not until 1:30 p.m. when Mount Vesuvius hurled a column of pumice and ash nearly thirty kilometers into the air. There was no lava in the eruption, as the magma was too explosive, spitting rock, fire, ash, and pumice into the stratosphere. Due to the strong northwesterly winds, Pompeii slowly became buried in the pumice fall over the next eleven hours. With six inches of ash an hour, many residents fled with what possessions they could while others retreated to their homes where they felt safest. Soon, however, the roofs began to cave in from the increasing weight, killing or trapping those residents still inside. Because of the bizarre atmospheric changes caused by the eruption, by late afternoon there was total darkness, lit only occasionally by lightning pulsing in the volcanic cloud. Terror reigned in the streets. Some residents fled while others took the opportunity to rob and loot empty homes.

At about midnight, the column of the mountain collapsed, sending down an avalanche of superheated gasses, pumice, and rocks moving as fast as three hundred kilometers an hour, with temperatures as high as one hundred degrees Celsius. This flood blasted through Pompeii's sister town, Herculaneum, on the west coast, killing everything that was still alive. Most residents had been on the beach waiting rescue by sea, but in total darkness the erupting volcano made it impossible for ships to approach.

This avalanche was followed by a thicker, deadlier surge moving at a speed of fifty kilometers an hour with a temperature of over four hundred degrees Celsius. By one o'clock in the morning on August 25, Herculaneum was utterly dead.

At Pompeii, three avalanches came down the mountain without ever reaching the city. One came right up to Pompeii's north wall, which no doubt triggered panic in the pumice-covered streets.

In the early morning of August 25, those still alive in Pompeii were trying to evacuate through volcanic debris two meters in depth, which killed many by suffocation. It was not until the early dawn, seven hours after the death of Herculaneum, when a deadly surge in the form of a fourth avalanche breached the walls of Pompeii, killing the thousand or more souls still trapped in their homes or trying to flee.

Since then, the buried Roman city has become the fascination of thousands of people worldwide. The stories around the people who lived there may have intrigued us even more than the disaster itself.

"Nothing can last in unending time.
When the sun has shone brightly, it returns to the sea;
The moon wanes which just now was full;
So the savagery of love's passion ends up as a gentle breeze."

On the wall of C. Julius Polybius, Pompeii, approximately 79 AD.

Chapter 1

April 18

Neapolis. It was a familiar sight; so were the smell and the sounds. The sun was well above the houses, glistening upon the sea. It had been a wonderful journey of leisure and pleasure … but strangely the approach of home offered a different and very strange feeling to both companions.

"What am I doing here?" Valerus asked. "Rome is luxury. What am I doing back here?"

Lucius smiled a little sadly as he walked alongside him. Lucius owned—or lent—his insula in Herculaneum for a good sum, which was worth the district in which the flat was situated as well as its view. Lucius was an old friend to Valerus going back many years to the start of Valerus's career. He had gone to Rome for the sole purpose of helping and escorting his companion south, leaving the Jewel of the Empire to return to the southern outskirts. He was the seller of exotic perfumes, thus his build was thinner than most men as he did not spent much time out and around. For this reason he wanted to make the most of what remained of the trip.

Valerus felt two ways about it, though. There was indeed some relief and satisfaction to return to the place where it had all started, but it also represented the end of the road from which there was no turning back. Perhaps, he tried to believe, the south did hold promise to a gladiator, but he knew from experience that Rome was the place for professionals while the south belonged to the trainees.

He stopped for a moment to rub his left knee—the faint scar was still visible across it, even after all the months that had gone into its healing.

Lucius regarded him suspiciously before speaking. "Are you going to start training again, Valerus?" he asked in a tone that suggested he already knew the answer.

Valerus didn't answer.

"I saw you packing both your swords as well as your visor. Are you planning to start again?"

Now Valerus shrugged. "Maybe."

There was a crowd in Neapolis, the type of crowd Valerus did not come across often. The main square was packed with people, stalls, platforms, musicians, and performers. There was no real surprise for either Lucius or Valerus. Neapolis often had festivals—even at odd times of the year.

"What a coincidence!" Lucius said brightly. "You wanted to return with a gift for your parents ..."

"I cannot afford a gift," Valerus said under restraint, as if he had repeated it a dozen times over. "Nothing of quality, that is, and I don't want to go into my savings. I would rather approach my father with nothing than to bear him an insult of cheap slaves."

"A gift may be appropriate. It may make your parents more patient with you."

"I do not believe anything could make them pleased about any of this," Valerus confessed. "They took me in because it would be humiliating if the rumor got out that their son was sitting in the streets. They paid a lot of money for my training. This fighting incident is now going to be used against me … like some debt I owe them."

Slaves were on display; cloth and imported materials were fashioned for the public. Egyptians were selling their latest perfumes, papyrus scrolls, and parchments. An entire platform was filled with dancing girls with veils soaring in the air above their erotic movements.

Valerus wandered by uninterested while Lucius stopped to admire them for a while. Most wore their hair loose to catch the sea breeze, which carried their perfume through the air. Lucius was touched by an uncontrollable desire.

"Valerus!" Lucius walked quickly to catch up when his voice was drowned by the crowd. "Valerus," he said again when he reached his side. "Come on," he begged his companion. "One dancer. Let's get one together."

"And do what?" Valerus said with a frown. "A few more hours and we'll be home."

Lucius caught his breath and held back for a few seconds. He wanted to take hold of the opportunity.

"One more night away from home. You don't want that?"

This got Valerus to stop.

"One night away from home … with a dancer. Together we can make that. It is barely a few hours walk to Herculaneum, as you said. Any slave can manage that."

Valerus thought for a while. It had been a while since he had been with a woman. Slowly a smile rose from the corners of his mouth.

Lucius punched the air. "Yes! For tonight we shall be emperors!"

❧

"*Twenty thousand sestertii!*" Valerus blurted. "That's daylight robbery!"

"It's not too bad a rate for the quality," Lucius informed him.

"For one dancer? No! Let's have a look at the others."

"What others?" Lucius grabbed him by the shoulder. "We have looked at all the slave traders. All that are left is Cephys and Arandus. And if you think this one is pricey …"

Valerus was already by the exhibition of Cephys. Their prices were high along with their fine setup of dancers, labor slaves, and gladiators. All the women were very much to his liking. Valerus had to admit that Cephys sold quality compared to some of the others.

Six young women were dancing their display, veils streaking against the blue sky over their heads. And their clothes were extraordinary. Valerus could suddenly feel how long it had been: short veils across their waists, those revealing tops, and the bracelets on both their wrists and ankles, which added a new instrument to the music they were dancing to.

Three more dancers were taking rest in the shade of the display's awning, sharing a small flask of water.

"Interested, master?" A man approached Valerus and squatted on the edge of the platform by his head.

Valerus casually pointed to the dancers. "How much?"

"Cheapest, two thousand denarii," he said and continued quickly when seeing the young man's expression. "But I am sure we can come to a good bargain."

Lucius was by Valerus's side the next moment with a hand on his shoulder as an unspoken request for him not to comment. "What bargain would that be?" he asked while avoiding Valerus's gaze.

"I'll give you that one for half price." He gestured with his head.

The two men looked at the woman he was referring to. She was resting under the awning. She had the lightest features of all the women there, with light brown hair and shockingly bright gray eyes.

Valerus chuckled. "Why do you want to get rid of her so badly?"

The man shrugged. "Honestly … not much into smiles, that one. Not good for advertisement … not good for my business."

Again they looked at her. It was true: there was no smile on her face and no erotic sparkle in her eyes. All the other dancers were at least putting effort into their display. Makeup did not suit this one either, not with that gaze in her eyes, and Valerus could see why they were desperate to get rid of her even at half price. She appeared to be mere background to the others, especially the attractive redhead who was cooling herself with some water.

"I won't pay more than twenty-five hundred sestertii for that one," Valerus said from the corner of his mouth. The denarius was a valued currency: four sestertii to the denarius, and Valerus would not soon part with it.

The seller scratched his beard thoughtfully. "Well, she is bad for my display, yes. I think I could let her go for nine hundred denarii then. Not much chance for getting more out of her."

"What's the catch?" Lucius asked suspiciously.

"Well, she comes with two more. I cannot break up the trios, as are my rules."

"And I take it they do not go for half price."

The man sucked on his teeth. "Hispanian trained … now all the way from Rome. They are top quality. I could let them go for eighteen hundred denarii each."

Valerus broke into laughter. "Thank you very much, sir." He hushed Lucius away. "But we are not interested."

"I could even take them down to fifteen hundred denarii each," he offered hurriedly. "Good prices for the slaves I offer."

Valerus and his companion were already taken by the crowd.

"Valerus!" Lucius struggled to break free. "Those slaves are Hispanian trained! That is a dream offer for three dancers."

"He's bluffing! They are probably rejects from Octavianum! Besides, I think none of them is a *true* bargain."

"Virgins or not, this is Cephys Slave Traders. He sells only the best to the best!"

"And where do you expect me to get that money? I only have four thousand denarii left in my savings, and that counts my entire income for the past six years. I still would like to live on that before becoming completely dependent on my parents. Buying those slaves will leave me with one hundred."

"I have six hundred denarii on me."

"What?" Valerus could not believe it. "How did you ever manage that?"

Lucius was about to say something and hesitated, but Valerus had known him for too long to be bluffed by his expression. "No." He shook his head. "You don't still gamble, do you?"

"I made a good little fortune in Cumae."

"You said you were going to get fresh horses. I gave you a thousand sestertii with which to get a decent pair."

"I was, Valerus, I really was. But some snobs pulled me in for a roll. I couldn't resist."

"And you got six hundred off of them, yes?"

"Actually five. The rest was received from a few deliveries."

"What? Perfumes?"

"I told you that it was a good market."

Valerus moistened his lips and looked at Cephys's display, barely visible beyond the crowds. Six hundred denarii made a difference as it was enough for the average male slave … but for a dancing girl?

"What do you say?" Lucius was still smiling. "I'll pay five hundred and you the remaining."

"And what's *your* catch?"

"All I ask in return is that I can take one dancer for a period of time."

There was another moment's thought. Valerus looked over his shoulder again. "Will you take the 'no-smiling' one?" he asked hopefully.

"That's not fair, Valerus. You are getting two."

For the first time, Valerus smiled. "All right." He put a hand on Lucius's shoulder. "But if that redhead is in the bargain, she's mine."

Chapter 2

The redhead was in the bargain, much to Valerus's delight. She was perfect, erotic, and prepared to do whatever her master commanded with great pleasure and enjoyment. He did not have to impress or charm her; he needed only to command.

They had taken a room of two beds in a little inn that faced the sea near the docks, and they gladly allowed the dancers to join them upstairs.

Valerus had—with pleasure—settled on the bed with the redhead, known as Alia, lying beside him while Lucius had accepted the brunette, Ursalus.

"And this, my charming lady," Valerus, his arm wrapped around Alia's back, laughed as Lucius offered his woman a sale, "is the Rose of Gaul." He uncorked the small bottle. "Take a sniff of that."

Ursalus sighed when catching its fragrance. "I should wear that every day when around you, master."

"And you certainly will." He re-corked the bottle and carefully set it on the bedside table. He paused to look across the room a moment before looking to his companion. "What is keeping that slave you sent out for the wine?" he asked. "Taking her time?"

"Oh, she'll be around." Valerus stared at the woman lying beside him and clasped her hand tenderly. "In no hurry, are we?"

"We should trade every now and again." Lucius leaned across his bed. "Just for the different flavors."

"Yes, we should." Valerus gasped delightfully when Alia's hand reached far down his *chiton*.

Just then there was a gentle tap on the door. Giggling due to her resistance, Valerus pushed Alia's hand away. "Enter." He nearly laughed when she playfully fought to get to him again.

The third slave entered the door shyly, saw the activities at hand, and averted her eyes. In one hand she carried two ivory cups and in the other an amphora of Pompeian wine.

"Ah, bring it over, woman!" Valerus waved to her, carefully sitting up a bit. "We have wasted enough time waiting for you."

"What is her name?" Lucius asked his companion.

"Flaria," Valerus replied uncertainly.

"Her name is Flavia." Alia rested her hand on Valerus's torso. "She does not talk much."

"Nor does she smile."

It was true. Flavia did not speak to the other dancers; there was no need to. They were obsessed with their clothes and the size of their breasts; erotic points expected of a dancing girl. Flavia had never indulged in those activities; few men were ever keen to take her unless there was no other choice. Her breasts and pubic hair had never developed to her age, and many men were put off by the scars she still carried from Seianus, a reminder of him she knew she would have to keep for the rest of her life.

Melani was her first decent master and a very wise one at that. She had taken her in when she was eight. She had been part of a cult that was greatly frowned upon by people, but this did not stop her from preaching to the children about love, forgiveness, and tolerance. Since then, her masters had been good and her life had not too much to complain about. Separation was part of the procedure. When Melani was forced to sell them, she made sure all three siblings went to a good home together. But Flavia always knew there would come a day when she would have to leave the comfort of her siblings; and it was so when she and her sister had first been sold from her brother … and now she from her sister.

Flavia looked at her new masters reclined on their beds, each with a woman and each with an empty wine goblet waiting to be filled. She listened to the two men laugh. They were worse than drunken men because they were sober. She poured the wine in silence, first for Lucius and then for Valerus.

The man stared when taking the cup from her. When Flavia tried to move away, he firmly grabbed her by the wrist, pulling her closer. She did not resist; it was no use to disobey the master … for the moment at least.

"I have seen you before!" Valerus exclaimed, sitting up and pushing Alia away. "From where?"

Flavia shook her head and dimmed her gaze respectfully. "No, master. I do not believe this is true."

Valerus's frown deepened. He recalled tears to have come with that gaze.

"Hold on." A smile began to extend across his face. "You are from Rome, correct?"

Flavia nodded uncomfortably.

The smile on the young man's face had now become a grin. "Ah, yes!" He leaned across the bed and pulled off the extra blanket folded at his feet. Then, still on the bed, he rose to his knees and threw the blanket over the young woman's shoulders. Then he lay back. "Come on. Wrap yourself in it … use it as a hood."

Realizing that she was shaking, Flavia did as she was told. Having no other option, she wrapped herself in the blanket, pulling up a corner to shadow her face.

"The woman in the slave cart!" Valerus laughed.

It was then that Flavia remembered having seen him before as well. It was on her entry into Volturnum, locked in the back of an oxcart. She distinctly remembered his face because she had looked directly at him, which slaves never did to their superiors; it was an unspoken law. The look in his eyes had been of a spoilt, well-fed rich boy, and Flavia at that moment could not help but feel envious over his life.

"You must have made very few stops for having reached here before us." Valerus was still chuckling.

"Two," Flavia said coldly between their laughter as she pulled the blanket off her. "Only for fresh oxen."

Valerus smiled at her. A lot of men had smiled at her like this in the past without effect.

She turned toward the door, desperate to make her escape before anything else was said.

"Slave!" Valerus called just as she was to leave. She looked at him over her shoulder. "Come here." He waved her over. "Enjoy me."

Flavia shook her head. "Pardon me, master." She spoke honestly but a little fearfully. "I am tired and will be comfortable in the stable yard."

Valerus's jaw hung open when the door shut behind her. Suddenly switching emotion from pure luxury to rage, Valerus pushed Alia aside and got to his feet. He gave no one a second glance as he fastened his girdle, straightened his chiton, and threw his toga over his shoulder simply to be reminded of his rank. Then he followed after her, down the stairs and outside into the stable yard. The sun had nearly set to the west and slaves were tending to the last few horses that had come to the stalls. Valerus felt slightly out of place among them; this was no place for his kind.

When she saw him, she jumped to her feet, hands held in front of her and eyes to his feet submissively. She was well aware that she had insulted him by turning away, by not feeling honored and choosing a straw bed in the stables rather than alongside him. She could see on his face that the humiliation was nearly choking him, and she did not know him well enough to know how he was going to react.

"*Flavia*, is it not?" He was standing right in front of her now.

She nodded.

He brought her head up by her chin. She trembled when she looked into his eyes. There was the glisten of insanity, which she recalled seeing in Seianus—not as strongly though.

"You disobeyed me," Valerus whispered, putting his mouth near her ear. "I cannot have that in a slave." He tried to kiss her neck.

She backed away hurriedly, not taking her eyes off him.

"And again you disobey me."

Flavia shook her head desperately. "I can't do that which you ask me to do," she whimpered, "master."

Only now did the young man smile. "You mean you have *never* done that?" He was aware of his own excitement. It was very rare to come across a virgin in the category of dancing girls, and this was an unexpected surprise he was looking forward to exploring. It was obvious that the trader who had sold her had not known of it, otherwise Valerus would never have gotten the woman for the price he did.

Now realizing she had made a terrible mistake, Flavia backed away from him until she came into contact with the wall. Valerus advanced on her, seeing now that she had no space left to go.

He was on her very suddenly, his hands up on the wall above her shoulders and his body pressing against hers. "I will ignore this," he whispered, catching the scent of her hair, "if you will take this opportunity to your advantage."

Flavia tried to get past under his arms, but he blocked her.

"I trust that you need some training," he said before kissing her.

Flavia screamed an inner scream, trying to use her hands to push him away, but he was pressing up against her so tightly that it hurt. Then she felt his tongue in her mouth and forgot that she had to obey his commands.

With what she could, she brought up her knee and got him in the groin. Valerus winced and staggered back only a few steps before Flavia brought up her hand and slapped him across the face.

The rage was swallowed by surprise. Valerus stared at her, his hand on his red stinging cheek. Flavia had the look on her face of one truly defying her superior.

In his rage and humiliation, the young man clouted her with the back of his hand and while she still had her head turned grabbed her by the shoulders and pressed her against the wall.

He had never touched a woman like that before, even a slave, and though he felt a terrible guilt when seeing the tears coursing down her cheeks, he felt it his every right to discipline her.

Some stable boys returned to their work when Valerus looked their way. Besides, it was no business of theirs what a master did to his slaves.

Valerus looked at the woman, his face barely an inch from hers. "That was only a warning, slave. Trust when I say that I can inflict upon you far worse things."

She wanted again to push him away, but he took each wrist in one hand and held them above her head. He was stronger than most men, a strength she had previously recognized to come from a fighting career—a soldier perhaps.

She brought up her knee again. This time Valerus stumbled back and for some reason, which was strange to her, he crumbled completely, as if his leg could not hold up his weight.

Valerus rolled aside with a short, painful cry, and when he looked at her she realized that there was blood seeping through his fingers. He had landed in a grooming case, in which one of its contents had been a hoof pick; it was sharp on the end to remove even the smallest stone from the frog of a horse's hoof.

Fear curled up in her face when she watched Valerus remove his hand from his cheek to stare at the blood. She knew that the penalty of striking the master could well be her life. A long bloody scar ran from his ear to halfway down his cheek and the look he threw her could just as well have come from those bad memories she carried.

The stare he gave her was far longer than necessary before he looked at the blanket she had laid across the straw. Fury stricken, he grabbed it and threw it at her. "Sleep in the stable yard!" He growled as his hands returned to his cheek. "But share it with a horse! I refuse to pay for your lodging." He then stormed away only to stop and turn back to her. "You will be severely punished for what you have just done!"

"And who will punish you for what you tried to do?" Flavia asked, using the same tone.

Valerus grabbed her wrist with a bloodied hand. The young woman gasped when he pulled her to him. "*I* own *you!*" He hissed in her ear. "I paid nine hundred denarii for you, and that I consider a robbery! You will be punished for your lack of respect!" He pushed her away so hard that she stumbled. Then he left, gently tapping the scar on his face.

Flavia watched him go, trembling without control. Once he was out of sight, she fell back against the wall, buried her face in her hands, and cried.

Nine hundred denarii ... her life was worth less than the coins in a man's hand.

Chapter 3

April 19

Storm clouds came up over the night and the journey to Herculaneum the next morning was set in the rain. Lucius and Valerus each took a girl with them on their horse, keeping them dry with their cloaks, while Flavia was left to follow on foot. Valerus had clearly stated that the cold rain could teach her some manners.

But Flavia took the opportunity to observe both men, especially Valerus. Early in the journey she noticed the scar that ran up Valerus's upper calf and across his knee to the inner thigh, and it seemed to cause him distress. After a while she watched him pull a second padding beneath his knee and he fastened it around his lower thigh to keep it in place. She came to the conclusion that he had suffered an injury and had learnt over time different procedures for dealing with the pain.

But she felt nothing for him, especially after yesterday's incident. In fact, she regretted not having struck him on the old wound rather than having slapped him.

Flavia's clothes were soaked through and her feet were bruised and freezing on their entry of Herculaneum. The rain had diminished to a light drizzle, but the wind was still icy. She had wrapped her shawl and veil over her bare arms, for what good it did.

She watched Valerus bidding farewell to his companion, who appeared anxious to get home and to a fire. There was some kind chatter, a few laughs, and finally a short manly embrace. Lucius set off on foot, leading his horse, which carried Ursalus. Flavia envied Ursalus's luck and wondered if she was ever going to see her again.

Valerus turned to look at her over his shoulder. His hair had been flattened down by the rain. He too was on foot … and he appeared even more dangerous than when he was on horseback.

Flavia bent down to rub her feet a little, trying to return the life into them. When she looked up, Valerus was still staring at her. She moistened her lips and pretended not to notice.

Finally Valerus looked up at Alia and smiled for the first time since they had entered the city. "My father owns a villa outside of town with a beautiful view of the ocean. You will love the garden."

Alia smiled to him sweetly. Valerus's eyes turned from her to Flavia, who was still in the process of rubbing her feet.

"That's enough of that, Flavia!" he bellowed to her mockingly. "We want to get home."

Flavia got anxious when they reached home; her new master lived in a luxurious villa home. It frightened her: the rich were usually good people, but with what she had ended up with it did not appear so; there were always exceptions, and oftentimes those exceptions were harsh.

The villa was large and marked only the home of a wealthy man having done well in his life. They stepped up onto the columned portico from which Flavia could hear the ocean and feel the breeze whip her hair.

A slave had opened the door, and another went to take the reins belonging to the horse of his master. As Valerus stepped inside, he was met by his parents who greeted him warmly, pleased for his presence after so long.

Flavia shook her head. The man had been a false image; he lived with his parents. However, this meant that she had some chance that the family was not as cruel as Valerus had introduced. She heard him call Alia inside but deliberately left Flavia in the cold wind and rain a little while longer.

She saw his parents' reaction to Alia; they smiled and greeted her kindly into their home, fascinated when she announced that she was trained in Hispania. Only after this did Valerus call in Flavia with a wave of his hand. Sheepishly she took the step and entered the door.

The couple appeared less impressed by her.

"And this is Flavia," Valerus introduced flatly.

"Where did you get them?" the older woman asked.

"Cephys."

"Oh, Valerus." The woman walked up and took Flavia by the shoulders. "You shouldn't treat Cephys's girls like this. They are worth their weight in gold."

Valerus was about to protest in regards to Flavia but then recalled that she had not yet lost her virtue. This did indeed make her more valuable than she appeared.

Flavia took a quick glance around; the atrium was a welcoming entrance that opened to the rest of the villa, lined with fountains of satyrs and Amorini. There was a damp trickle in the air.

"They are for you." Valerus looked at his father and nodded. "I am truly grateful for you to have called me home."

For an instant his father looked at the scar on his son's leg before looking up at him again. "You have made us old with your career, son," he confessed and embraced him again.

When he looked at the dancers again, Flavia dimmed her gaze respectfully.

"I am Pedius Cascus," the man said to both of them, "and this is my wife Rectina."

Both dancing girls gave a smile.

"I am certain that you will find our household most comfortable. The first day you will be accompanied by one of our supervisors who will gladly show you around. Do either of you cook?" he asked with a sudden smile.

Both Flavia and Alia nodded.

"Do either of you know how to work with animals?"

"I do." Alia raised her hand.

"Fantastic!" He turned to his son. "You got us some fine quality, son."

"It's quiet," Valerus said as if noticing it for the first time.

"Your sister is in Neapolis, hunting for a fine *stola.*" Rectina informed him.

Flavia did not listen to a word they said. Certainly she was looking at each of them, but her focus was mainly on Valerus, who was standing beside his father. She could feel his eyes boring into her every now and again … she began to tremble when realizing that his mind was focused on some revenge as to what happened in Neapolis. This was confirmed when Valerus leaned to his father and whispered in his ear. Pedius threw her a look. She felt herself stiffen in fearful apprehension and noticed how Valerus was enjoying it; he was scheming something. She wished she could get into the man's head and know what he was planning.

"Tell me, father," Valerus suddenly spoke aloud. Flavia could feel the sweat begin to form on her brow. "What would be the punishment for a slave refusing to obey his or her master?"

Flavia swallowed, avoiding both the men's gazes.

Pedius was taken aback but replied, "Two lashes would be my discipline."

"What about a slave striking the master?"

Pedius sucked on his teeth. “Severe … very severe. I would not go less than seven lashes. Maybe even ten. Some would sell them off to the arena after that.”

Flavia felt her heart give up on her for a beat or two. She could not believe that she would ever end up like her mother … not after life had given her a second chance. She risked a glance up and noticed Valerus smiling at her. She could not believe that someone actually took pleasure from her fear.

Rectina gazed at her son suddenly and stepped up to him. “What happened?” she asked as she ran her fingers across her son’s cheek where the hoof pick had cut him the previous day.

At once Pedius stared at the slaves. He only glanced at Alia an instant but could not consider her. Then he grabbed Flavia’s wrist and pulled her to him. “Was it her?” He demanded to know. “Did you strike the master’s son?”

Valerus stepped in, gently taking Flavia’s wrist into his own hand. “No,” he shook his head. Flavia’s mouth dropped open for a second before she shut it and returned her gaze to the floor. “It was not her, father. That scar came from a little accident that occurred on the road.”

“Ah,” Pedius stepped back to gaze upon her.

Valerus looked at Flavia, and the little smug smile on his face said it all: *You owe me …*

Flavia returned a hard, cold stare which said, *I owe you nothing …*

⁂

The villa was exquisite, larger than most others Flavia had served in. They walked along the ambulatory, which was open to the large beautiful garden, fountains, and large swimming space. Two male slaves were tending the shrubbery while two dogs took shelter from the rain under the pillared roof. Across the peristyle were the statues of female water carriers whose expressions stood out beneath their glass eyes.

From the main reception room the house opened to a smaller garden, though just as well tended and beautiful. Windows lined the upper story; some vines had found their way up the pillars and framed them beautifully. The villa and the gardens were decorated with bronze statues, some even life size of athletes.

The slaves' quarters were larger than what Flavia had been used to but still in the dark—they always were—with little source of incoming light. In her previous home she had shared a room, half this size, with three others. It was large to the standards of slaves but tiny to the rich. Now she was offered a space shared with Alia, who was far more social than herself, thus out in the gardens with the others.

She looked across the room at the mosaic décor and felt the tears stinging her eyes. She would have preferred the company. She discovered that she was frightened … nothing was stopping Valerus from stepping into the room while she was asleep.

The worst part of it was that she knew she was fighting a battle that was impossible to win. Valerus was the son of her master now and she had struck him. There was only his decision standing between her and a leather whip …

… and the world of entertainment.

She collapsed on the thin mattress and unwrapped her small bundle of clothes and scarf. She owned three *tunicas*, five now since her arrival to the villa. Three were sleeveless and the other two had sleeves for the winter. Along with them was one childhood dress, which she had outgrown years ago. She kept it for the sentimental value; it was the one Melani had given her the day she was sold.

What was Valerus's game? Every master had some individual form of pleasure concerning his slaves. Thus far Flavia had had the emotionally abusive, the violent, the caring and lastly, the loving and understanding. Valerus did not appear to be any of these, and her fear fell strictly on the idea that he enjoyed watching her fear. So far he had done well. Flavia dreaded the days to come, wondering what more he was going to do. For the moment, despite the fact that he was her master, he had her in the palm of his hand. All he had to do was reveal a secret and she would be flogged.

Ten lashes! She had—at most—endured five, and that was when she was barely seven. It was a long time ago. And if they saw her previous scars, she would be sold off good and cheap. God only knew where that would take her.

Being sold cheap was the fear of every slave, dancing girl, cook, or hard laborer. Cheap prices meant cheap masters offering little in the lodging and food department. Flavia herself had nearly been starved by a previous owner.

But Valerus was not someone to do that. No, he had other ways that Flavia knew would become far more dangerous if she was not careful.

The night was long. Flavia spent most of her time listening to others coming and going. She heard Alia being introduced to the other slaves. She was tired, having walked the better part of the journey; her legs ached.

As she dozed off, she could hear people murmuring in the corridors and thought of what tomorrow might bring.

She was a slave, an object, and the men of the house could do what they wanted with her.

Frightened by her own images, she sat up and leaned against the cold stone wall, clasped her hands together, and prayed. This was a secret very few knew. She was not a part of the local or even common belief. There was a wisdom she had been converted to in the early years of her life. Melani had secretly introduced her to the teachings of a man who had come from the east in the kingdom of Judea. Melani told them many stories and also confessed that the reason she had saved the three of them was because she believed in the teachings of this Hebrew stranger.

Melani had called Flavia and her siblings to her one afternoon only a few weeks after they had been bought. She sat them down on some blankets near the fireplace and then settled between them. She smiled at them and rested her hands on her round belly, heavy with the coming child. "Are you frightened?" she asked.

"No," Flavia said. "Not anymore."

"And why is that?" Melani asked her.

"You saved us," Torus said as if reminding her.

"Ah yes, of course. Listen to me, all of you." She put her arms around them. "I saved you; I love you despite the fact that I did not even know you at the time. It was not so much pity and compassion as it was love."

Flavia frowned at this. How could she love them without even knowing them?

"Can I tell you stories?" she asked kindly.

They all nodded without a word.

"There is a place, a long way from here, where there is little more than desert. From this land was born God's son who taught the people to forgive and to love."

And Flavia had been captivated. She became far more intrigued by Melani's stories than her siblings and spent many late nights listening to the stories of the stranger from the desert kingdom of Judea. There were little ways anyone could tell whether the stories were fiction or fact, but Flavia wanted—no, *needed*—to believe them. It gave her some hope for the world, realizing that it was more than she could see here. Melani had taught her to pray and meditate. Most importantly, though, she informed the siblings not to announce their faith publicly, especially as slaves. It was a new faith that was very rare to come across, but she could not believe that a man who loved so much could have been wrong. Mankind was cruel and in the stories Melani shared with them Flavia saw a flicker of hope. It was this faith that raised her standards, and ever since, her life had been decent with few complaints. After four and a half years in the dancing profession, she was still a virgin, which had to be a miracle.

And Valerus knew that … and he was playing a game. This frightened her. She thought it unfair that she believed in things she could not control. The Hebrew had said that to be an outcast was to be a disciple of God, but what was sin? Was an outcast one who committed it or who was involved in it? As far as Flavia could tell, she could not control her fate or her actions to the commands given.

Finally she got up and stepped into the small corridor, which was lit with at least a dozen lanterns. There were noises coming from the kitchen and there were murmured voices from the other rooms.

Flavia caught the breeze coming in from the peristyle; it was fresh and chilly.

"Hey!"

Flavia nearly jumped out of her skin when the guard called to her. She spun around to the heavily armed man making his way toward her. "No slaves out after dark," he said, "unless you have other duties."

"I'm just dying for some fresh air," she told him honestly.

To her surprise, the man smiled kindly. "You're the new girl, aren't you? The one that came in with Valerus?"

She nodded but said nothing.

The guard was large but not heavily built. He was blond, but his eyes were dark, nearly black in the dim light. He could not have been older than forty to Flavia's guess.

"I'm Marcus," he said while smiling again, "captain of the guard."

Flavia could not help but smile at the name of her previous master. It was pleasant to hear his name spoken again. "And you work here?"

"Pedius often has watchmen patrolling the grounds. I am here to inspect before and at daybreak." Marcus looked over his shoulder to where the voices were coming from and then back at her. "Still not *that* late," he said to her. "How about a tour?"

Marcus took Flavia on a tour around the villa, which was finer than her first impression had let on. It reminded her a lot of the home of her previous master, though this peristyle was far larger. There was a small library, much to Flavia's fascination and delight, and the *tablinium* overlooked the large ornamental pool of the garden. She was much of a reader after she had received lectures from Melani as well as the dancing academy, but as a dancing girl and its demands she had little time for it. Shelves lined most of the walls as well as a couple or so more in the center of the room. There was a desk near to the room center, crowded in scrolls, parchments, and leather-bound documents, which Flavia thought wisely not to touch.

The two of them stepped out onto the outer terrace; Flavia felt as if she was on a ship. The ocean stretched out ahead of her, the small waves gently lapping on the walls below. The clouds had cleared and an ocean of stars was set well above them, meeting the ocean ahead and setting the horizon.

"Come," Marcus said as he lightly touched her arm, "we can't be here too long."

The smaller peristyle was beautiful, which no doubt stated the importance and health of her new master. A small fountain had been built in the center where the two paths crossed. There was a whistle as the wind gently rocked the cypress trees.

Marcus explained to Flavia the importance of gardens, especially to the people of Herculaneum, and how the masters ate and children practically grew up in them. It was the garden that made the home, and a slave who poorly tended it was considered useless.

"Can you tend a garden?" Marcus asked her.

Flavia shook her head.

"Well, what is your profession then?"

She took a deep breath and shrugged. "Dancing girl."

Marcus was obviously surprised and looked her up and down as if trying to believe it. Flavia was beautifully built; her waist was small, but her hips were well shaped. Even below the wool tunica he could easily tell that her breasts were well set. Her pale brown hair was reaching for her hips and there was no mistaking that her smile would always be radiant. For these reasons, someone had taken the time to train her in the art of erotic dance, but there was something very defiant about her that did not match the description of her occupation.

"I know." She nodded, having seen that look on many people before. "I'm not the average type."

Marcus smiled, clearly amused. "Well, then." He looked back over the garden. "This is where you will be performing most days."

That was a pleasant thought. She recalled the previous locations of dance and orgies, crowded space so that the heat allowed wilder frenzies and never gave the perfume a chance to escape. The peristyle would be a positive change.

A light filtered across the grass. She glanced to the source and noticed a lamp up on the second floor. There was a dark figure looking down at them from the window. Flavia recognized the posture he held.

"Tell me," she asked Marcus softly, "is Valerus a violent man?"

"The boy? I wouldn't say so. Not unnecessarily violent. He was trained as a gladiator but stopped fighting after a serious injury. We are all waiting to see what his next profession is going to be."

Flavia looked at him and frowned. "He used to kill for a living? Really?"

"*Kill* is a harsh word. Occasionally I'm sure he must have. He's quick with a sword, that boy. I'll give him that."

She looked up at the figure again, which had disappeared into the room. The light was still there but faded. "So what happened?" she asked, looking back at Marcus.

"Valerus had this … dream of fighting in the games in Rome. This dream made him take the challenge of a professional gladiator who had come from Germania. It did not go well for him; he was down, nearly losing his leg. Of course Pedius was very upset and somewhat ashamed; many doubted that Valerus would ever stand in the arena again."

"I did not notice a limp."

"Best surgeons … hardly a scar. But I've been told that he tends to buckle unexpectedly. I believe he can't put his full weight on it."

The light had gone out upstairs, and the peaceful darkness reigned again. There was a second—barely a fraction of a moment—when Flavia noticed she was feeling some compassion for the man. She knew what it was like to lose your very dreams.

Valerus sat in the dark, rubbing his hands across his left knee. It was aching again, which caused a lot of distress. Valerus's mind moved to a place well into the future; so far he could not comprehend how he was ever going to make it … in his condition at least. It would only have been a few more years and he would have been fighting in the *amphitheatrum* itself.

His last fight had left him cripple and extremely weak in the left leg. Though the surgeon assured him that it was temporary, taking eleven months to heal fully, Valerus had the uneasy feeling that he was going to keep some of it for the rest of his life.

That *retiarius* had been good; Valerus had to admit in a spit of rage. A slender agile man who wielded his net like a dancer's veil. Valerus had been lucky that it had been the dagger that hit him on the knee and not the trident. The battle had come to an end when the retiarius was ordered to show mercy over his fallen and cripple opponent. The audience had been so moved by the battle that the emperor had permitted both of them to leave the arena with their lives.

And that was the end of the dream; his *lanista* had him released from his oath, a rare occasion. He had taken the advice of the surgeons. First it had been four full months of rest: no work, no riding, and no fighting. Seeing that his career had come to a temporary standstill, he could not live alone either. Moving back into his father's villa had been his last choice, a decision he was forced to take as he could not afford a personal slave in his insula. Now, a year since the incident, Valerus took his health into consideration and had to confess that he could not look after himself anymore.

He knew the injury would be the last leg on his journey, which would force him back to Herculaneum and the family. It had been humiliating to friends and family—especially to his father. It had been a long fight without a coin falling into his pocket. He had tried fighting amateurs in small stadiums on the outskirts, but even those hosts were reluctant to take him on due to his injury. After those many months, the money ran tight, forcing him to return south to the family's support—a family he had barely seen over seven years of travel, training, and fighting.

And Herculaneum was small. It was not the city for a gladiator or one seeking the fame. Valerus had been taught in Herculaneum's small amphitheater, but had traveled to Pompeii for the fighting audience. Herculaneum was the holiday suite to many people who owned land along Vesuvius. It was the city of farmers, stewards, or wealthy men under retirement. No place for a young man of twenty-five.

The surgeon was right that the injury would hardly leave a scar, but Valerus knew that it was not properly healed; it never would be. It was a terrible reminder … like a broken dream branded into his leg.

But it was not over as far as he was concerned. He was going to get back into the arena under the shock and surprise of all his onlookers. He would surprise his parents and amaze the emperor when he heard about Valerus's history when he fought in the Colosseum. He was going to get there; its construction was nearly complete, and with it was Valerus's desire to fight and stand among the best.

He did not know when he fell asleep, but his dreams were twisted and meddled that night.

A loud thud in the room woke Valerus with a jerk. He sat up, looking around, trying to get his eyes accustomed to the darkness. There was a strong wind outside snapping the curtains. The wind moaned through the trees. He didn't look at what it was that had been knocked from his table, instead he leaned forward and pulled up an extra quilt that was neatly folded at the end of the bed and pulled it over him, lying back, grateful for the warmth. The moaning wind and the flapping curtains kept him awake for what felt to be hours. He turned on his side, trying to get comfortable when he heard a rumble and felt the earth beneath him begin to shake.

Not again. He had forgotten about this.

He threw a pillow over his head and to his relief the earthquake was light and short.

Chapter 4

April 20

Dawn was promising; strangely everything that had worried Flavia the previous day was distant and dreamlike. She washed up before getting dressed. Her new master—or *masters*—had ordered fresh clothes for their servants. Most households had different designs and occasionally different fabrics for different tasks which the slaves were entitled to. Of course dancing girls, when in their element, had erotic clothes, which hardly covered up anything at all, but for the day's simple side work she had been given a very ordinary brown wool tunica that reached to her ankles and fastened around the waist with a length of cord.

It was clean and fit her surprisingly well, meaning that, to her standards, it hid her figure.

She followed Alia and the others to the kitchen where other slaves had prepared a nourishing breakfast of flatbread and fig jam. It was a luxury which Flavia had not gotten since leaving the home of Melani so many years before. Despite Valerus and his frightening interest in her, it was obvious that the family tended well to their slaves.

Three women were gathered by the kitchen table, each wearing the same plain wool tunica as Flavia had been given, except for one who, to her surprise, was wearing breeches.

She sat on the wooden bench by the table between Alia and a woman she had never seen before. She nodded kindly her way, and she responded with the gesture. She had to be in her late twenties or early thirties with hair that matched Flavia's.

"You are Flavia, the dancing girl." A chirpy, happy figure appeared by the table in front of her. She could not have been any older than Flavia, but she looked far more mature. Flavia estimated her to be from the far reaches of Hispania. She had a large and definitely strong upper body with the blackest hair Flavia had ever seen. It was also shorter, barely past the shoulders, which was something Flavia seldom saw in the dancing profession. Her well-built legs indicated that she had been riding a lot in her life. Having grown up in a society where horseback was the fastest means to travel, Flavia had learnt a long time ago to notice the small indications of someone who did.

Flavia, on the other hand, had the typical thin legs of every dancing girl. She had never been allowed to ride a horse—or any creature—which had been a disappointment in her teenage years.

"You came in from Rome?"

She nodded.

"Can you believe that I have never been there?"

Flavia was genuinely surprised. "Really?"

"I'm Alaine." She laughed. "Pleased to meet you!"

The other women around the table were looking at them, giggling as Alaine jumped up to offer Flavia a helping of jam. "Oh, I'll get to go," she informed her as she set the jar down in front of her. "Only a matter of time. My reputation is growing; I have ridden-in Pedius's personal stallion, no problem!"

Flavia smiled. She had been right, and she congratulated herself for that. Flavia may never get to ride, but of course Alaine would never pass for a dancing girl. She was too heavily built to pass into the world of erotic dance.

Not that it was anything to be proud of. Flavia would have much rather been a rider; at least it would have kept Valerus's attention drawn to other things.

"So?" Alaine slapped her hand on the table with a huge grin on her face. Flavia stared as she waited for her to continue. "What's it like?"

Flavia glanced toward Alia, who turned away to speak to the others.

"Oh, she can't tell me anything!" Alaine shook her head. "All she talks about is the fashion, the dance, and men. No! I want to hear about the streets, the arches … the horses."

"Um …"

"Anything!"

Flavia thought frantically of something to tell the desperate woman … anything. "It's big." She shrugged. "Lots of horses, beautifully fine ones." That was all she could say on the subject of animals. Horses were just … things of transport that passed her on the street. She did not know anything *about* them. Breed? Size? Flavia was proud when she could tell whether they were male or female.

Alaine laughed loudly. "Well, when you're done with your chores you ought to come out to the stables with me. Pedius's horses are really worth seeing."

Flavia looked around at the others gathered around the table. "I did not even know I had any chores for the day," she confessed softly.

"Everyone has chores," the slave beside her spoke. She had fair features including pale skin, much like hers but she spoke with a strange broken accent which Flavia could not place. "I'm Helen."

She introduced herself quickly. "I run most of my chores in the kitchen with Luci. She's on her day off. You may be a dancing girl, but everyone here pulls weight and helps each other out. The master hates the idle. So when you're not dancing, and it's not your day off, you will be doing whatever chores you fancy or do as you are told."

Flavia nodded; it was the same in most homes she had been in before. In many ways it was a peaceful life, provided you did not get sold to the wrong person. Of course that was not a slave's decision at all.

Helen was not a hard person, though she sounded as if she could be. There was a gentleness to her voice that put Flavia at ease. Slaves in general seldom had brawls among themselves; it just was not worth it. Slaves got enough shouting from their masters and sometimes the guards, thus, when in each other's company, peace reigned. Flavia was always pleased about this.

"You can help with the laundry until tonight." A washerwoman suddenly spoke for the first time from beside Alaine. She, like Helen, was lighter in feature with blonde hair. She was a little overweight, Flavia noticed, and probably several years older than her.

"Tonight?"

"The party for Valerus's return. Obviously your service will be asked for."

Flavia felt the nausea return to the pit of her stomach. Another dance …

"I have been dying for some help since two days ago," the woman continued hurriedly, as if expecting the others to cut her off. "I started to take the sheets from the master's room to laundry and barely got through a third of it before yesterday's rain …"

Flavia took her chance when the woman was forced to catch her breath, smiled, and said, "I will help you."

"I'm Cotti." She reached across the table and clasped Flavia's hand firmly for a second. "It's so wonderful to have you around."

Flavia caught sight of it just as Cotti sat down again; she was not overweight as she had first thought. Instead Flavia noticed that Cotti was pregnant, at least four months. It was only the second time she had met a pregnant slave in the household where she worked, and it was heartwarming to know that the master had allowed it.

A party tonight, a dance. Wine, men, strangers, and ... Valerus. What was he going to do next?

⁂

Valerus slept later than he had intended. He propped himself up on his elbows and looked out the window and over the peristyle. It was a typical spring day: birds were in the cypress trees outside and the rain of the previous day had left behind clear skies and a wonderful smell in the air.

He swung his legs over the end of the bed and rubbed his face. Then he moved his feet, trying to get some life back into them.

He heard voices from outside and suddenly seemed to remember the previous day. Paying close attention to what was being said, he went over to the window and saw two washerwomen crossing the ambulatory with bundles of laundry in their arms. In fact, as he watched them, he realized that one of them was not a washerwoman but a dancing girl.

Ah yes. The one who had struck him ... *the virgin.*

He smiled to himself, fancying his thoughts for a moment, before turning into the room and calling for an attendant.

⁂

Flavia was folding sheets as Cotti brought in a second bundle of clean laundry from the washers. She dropped it into the basket by the bench. They had been to the Herculaneum laundry, which the *domus* used for the larger pieces, such as most of the bedding. Having returned from the washers, Flavia had joined the women in folding and sorting the family's bedding.

"Do we press the sheets?" Flavia asked, having noticing the large iron press.

Cotti took a quick glance at it before shaking her head. "No. But the master's togas, tunics, and *pallas,* yes. I always ask one of the men to come in and help me work it."

Flavia studied the contraption for a few more seconds. "Looks heavy," she agreed before continuing with the folding. There was silence for a few seconds before she frowned. "I have not seen any of the men slaves around today."

"Most of them are down in the docks or in the vineyards. Pedius owns several fishing boats and a few acres. Of course he never fishes himself, but it's a good source of income." She was about to leave but then stopped near the door. "Some are very cute," she informed Flavia with a smile. "You will meet Procimus tonight." She blushed when having said his name.

"Oh ..." Flavia grinned. "Is he the ... the father?"

Cotti put her hands on her stomach. "No, unfortunately not." There was a tinge of sadness in her voice. "He was sold just after I learnt of the pregnancy. Pedius did not stand for it. He does not approve of slaves becoming pregnant in his house."

"Oh." Flavia felt the disappointment. She had hoped that the master was one of the softer ones who cared well for his servants and organized the weddings for them. Sadly this was not the case.

"I really loved him," Cotti told her. "I still do. Harolde was his name. He was sold in Surrentum. For the first nearly two months I got letters from him on a weekly basis. Now, nothing."

Flavia wanted to ask whether she thought it was due to an accident, the master, or if he had been sold to the world of entertainment, but felt she could not ... or rather should not. The pain in Cotti's eyes was very distinct, pressing her onto different ground. "Is Pedius letting you keep the baby?"

Now the tears glistened in her eyes. "I …" She began to shake her head slowly. "I don't think so. He said he cannot afford keeping a slave who is raising a child on his time and expense. Either I go, or the child goes."

Flavia was shocked. "As in … die?"

Cotti shrugged. "If Pedius decides to keep me … We have to admit that I am useful in the house. The baby will have to … go."

Flavia was tongue-tied about what Cotti said. There was no reassurance she could give; she had no right to make any decision. Thus, all that came out was very weak: "I'm really sorry, Cotti." It was nearly a squeak.

Cotti shrugged and swallowed her tears. "Ah, well, you will meet Procimus tonight."

Flavia laughed softy. "I look forward to it," she agreed, but her mind turned to other things.

Who are these people? How can they decide who lives and who dies? Who ever gave them the right? How can anyone be condemned and punished for having loved? These thoughts brought her back to the teaching Melani had introduced her to, and there was suddenly a peace as she thought about life as the Hebrew had lived it.

She was left alone for a while, setting the folded sheet on the pile of others and picking up the next. A shadow fell over her. She caught her breath as she spun around.

"Are you Flavia, the dancing girl?" the large man asked her.

She noticed the sword at his belt and nodded obediently.

"Master Valerus is asking for you. I will lead you to his room."

Flavia realized that she was trembling as she followed the guard along the passage and up the stairs to the second level. The door to the bedroom was open and the guard went about his duties as she stepped inside. Valerus was, to her relief, fully dressed and in the process of fastening his sandals by the bed. She walked to the center of the room, purposefully avoiding his gaze. In many ways, she hoped that he would not notice her at all.

She then noticed a sheathed sword on his bed.

"Ah, Flavia." Valerus said with a smile as he stood up. "Thank you for coming."

"I obey you, master." She dimmed her head, hoping that he would realize that she was here for no other reason than the fact that he had called for her.

"You ought to," he said as he took up his sword and made his way across the room toward her.

She watched as he fastened the weapon to his girdle.

Is he going to start killing again?

For a second, there was a pang of relief when he simply walked past, but, as she let out her breath, he suddenly had her by the shoulder, spinning her around to face him and pushing her back until she was up against the wall. She caught her breath when he blocked her escape as he had done before.

"I have a command for you now that you *will* obey," he whispered, his mouth by her ear. "Just nod your head."

She did so, more out of fear than obedience.

"Good," he continued. "Tonight there will be a little get-together down in the peristyle. Your service will be expected. You understand this?"

Flavia took advantage of the brief pause to nod her head frantically. She could feel his breath on her neck and the heat of his body up against hers. It was terribly uncomfortable. She fought the urge to push him away when he suddenly continued.

"After your second performance," he said, "you will leave the crowd and come back up here. You will light a lamp so that I will see it from the garden. Then you will wait for me." She suddenly felt his hand reach down to fall on her inner thigh. She shuddered.

"And I am going to train you in the places you have never been before."

She turned her head away from him when his hand came up even higher. He watched her for a few seconds trying, ineffectively, to hide his smile.

He let her go and left the room without another word, leaving her to dwell on the command he had given.

Flavia felt the tears stinging her eyes when hearing his footsteps fade along the passageway outside.

She stayed where she was against the wall, trying to fight the panic that was welling up. She blinked away her tears and wondered how she was going to avoid this command. She knew that some day it would come to this—when a man would get to places she tried so long to protect—but she had always viewed it as far away, in some distant future. Of course she had always believed that it would have been because of love, not command.

Valerus walked with reason and determination. He had been gone from Herculaneum for over four years, but everything was so familiar, as if he had left only yesterday.

Cornelius was a lanista, a gladiator trainer and combat referee. His school was exactly the way Valerus remembered it, except that the tree by the entrance was slightly taller. The gates were open and the dust hung in the air where gladiators were in practice. There was a distinct smell in such a place that Valerus had always found pleasant, and he took a deep breath as he walked into the atrium.

Cornelius was an old man who had trained Valerus in the first few months before he left for Pompeii and then later for Rome. Herculaneum was not best known for the gladiatorial combats; the amphitheater was small and used more for training and the occasional spectacle. The real fighting was in Pompeii and other larger cities in the vicinity.

Valerus's old teacher appeared to have aged over the years of his absence. The trainer had had high hopes for Valerus and had kept close track of his progress. He had been a gladiator himself, and then a bodyguard to Pitus for at least eight years, before he was freed from the fighting profession. Since then he was the trainer of gladiators in Herculaneum, Pompeii, and Neapolis.

Valerus approached him confidently and with a smile. He was supervising two *mirmolles* in combat with wooden swords when he suddenly recognized the young man coming toward him.

"By all the gods!" He threw up his arms. "Valerus? Can it be?"

Valerus clasped his hand and shoulder in friendly gesture. "It's good to see you again, Cornelius." He chuckled. "It's been years."

"You did well for a while there." The old man tapped the side of his nose. "Heard you got to fight in front of the emperor himself."

Valerus sucked in a breath of air. "It didn't end well." He shook his head.

"Well, you are alive and you were freed from your oath. A rare occasion. Having fought in front of the emperor puts a good mark on your name."

"That's why I am here. I am prepared to sell myself off again."

Now the old man's expression changed completely. His smile faded for one and his brow wrinkled in concern. "You want to fight again? But you can't … you are …" He stopped and swallowed awkwardly.

"I am *not* a cripple!" Valerus snapped. "I can ride, walk … I am nearly as I was."

"Nearly. When you were at your best you were nearly killed. You are a good lad, Valerus, only a few years older than my grandson, and I don't want to be the one to watch you die in your first fight."

"You first trained me as a *meridiani* and *ordinarii.* In Pompeii I became a *thracian;* you will recall how popular I was."

"With the girls, yes … most definitely."

"And when I got to Rome, I was trained in the fighting art of a *myrmillo.*"

"Ah," the lanista raised his hand to silence him. "And there lies your weakness. A myrmillo fights the fisherman, and it's been proven that the retiarius is what you can't stand up to."

"I can still fight as a thracian and meridiani; none of their armor puts any distress on me."

"It's not about what you fight as, Valerus." Cornelius opened his hands to him. "It's about the crowd and the demand. People like to see the fisherman catch the fish or the fish swallowing the fisherman. That's what entertainment is: giving the people what they want.

"I am not concerned with your ability to hold a weapon," he continued. "The public does not pay to see you hold a *gladius.* They pay to see a fight. I want gladiators that can hold the arena longer than ten minutes. Your weakness had always been the retiarius, Valerus." He shook his head. "I am to believe it was one of them who brought you down and caused you your injury."

The young man swallowed when recalling his adversary. The trident carriers were always a challenge and difficult to get around. They were armed with a dagger, a trident, and a net but wore very little armor other than a visor and perhaps a metal *galerus* on the left arm. But they had a good choice between attack position and preferred weapon. They moved fast, the net especially. Valerus would never forget how it came for him.

Cornelius grasped his shoulder kindly. "I don't think it's wise, Valerus. Don't sell your life away. At least give that wound of yours time to heal properly."

"It may never heal properly." His voice was suddenly hoarse as he tried to hold back emotion. "But I want to fight! There is honor in it."

"And women!" The old man smiled—one of the few times he

did. "As a thracian especially." The trainer looked him up and down. He had a great deal of compassion for the young man, but he could not bring himself to take him on again. No money was worth his reputation, and he was known for his impressive displays. He could not afford a loose end on the fighting grounds.

"Sorry, Valerus." He nearly cringed at Valerus's expression. "But no. There is no place for you in the arena as yet. People don't pay gladiators who had been at their mercy."

Flavia did not know how she got through the rest of the day. She felt the sting of nausea in her stomach and thus did not eat. By late afternoon she was shaky and weak from hunger. She continued to help with whatever chores were available to the extra hand; she would have done anything to keep her mind from wondering about the immediate future.

At dusk the guests began to arrive. Flavia heard their greetings to the couple and the laughter coming from the gardens. She helped in the kitchen as long as could, hoping that she would not be missed.

Alia came past the door, stopped, and stepped inside. Flavia nearly threw up at the sight of her in her full dancing outfit, a thin veil wrapped around her arms. Her ankles and wrists were decorated with bracelets and bits of wool.

"Flavia!" she scolded. "You're not even dressed yet! The master called for us nearly an hour ago."

Flavia pretended to have been distracted by other things and threw her a genuine look of surprise. She ran past her and into the back atrium, following the back passage to the servant quarters. Once she was in her room, though, she got dressed at her leisure. She stood by the piece of polished metal she used as a mirror and did her hair, tying it above her head as she had been taught so that it fell down the sides and framed her face. Someone had put makeup on the table for her, but she ignored it as she began to slip the long green veil through its rings attached on the back of her short linen dress and her fingers. She had a second outfit, which was far more erotic and in demand. It was two parts: a short top and skirt. For tonight, however, she disregarded it completely and used the thin, tight tunica instead.

There was an urgent knock on the door.

"Coming!" Flavia called out and adjusted her hair one more time just to kill time before going over and opening the door.

Marcus was standing where she thought Alia would have been. He smiled to her kindly. "All the dancing girls are out in the peristyle already," he informed her. "You had better hurry."

Flavia slipped past him and he trailed behind her hurriedly. "Have they started yet?" she asked, still fiddling with her hair.

"Just waiting for Valerus to turn up …"

Flavia spun around to look at him before he had even finished saying it. "Waiting? For Valerus? Isn't he here?"

"No. Should have been back hours ago."

There was a moment of relief; maybe it was not going to happen.

But it was, she knew, if not tonight then another day. As long as she lived under the roof of Valerus, she knew that his command was inevitable.

She went out into the peristyle where no fewer than twenty people had gathered around the swimming area and fountains. Braziers and lanterns had been lit to greet the night and wine was being passed between the guests by male slaves who Flavia had never seen till this moment. She wondered if Procimus was there; it would be pleasant to meet the man who Cotti admired. She reacquainted with Ursalus who had come with Lucius. By the looks of it, things were going well with her, which it always did, due to her constant eagerness to satisfy any man in any way.

She met Anneria, Valerus's younger sister; Flavia was surprised how different she was from her brother. She did not acquaint with slaves and merely viewed them as property. She never thought of touching a slave. How Flavia wished Valerus was more like his sister. She was treated as grandly as the mistress of the house; very dark featured with a hard-set face. Flavia admired the way she had made up her hair.

She looked up at Valerus's bedroom window. It was still too light to expect to see any lamp lit, and there was some dull hope that he would not make it back before the dancing.

High hopes. Valerus returned even before Flavia was up for her first round, and seeing him nearly had her knees buckle out from under her. He appeared angry as he walked the corridor alongside the garden, his hand resting casually on the hilt of his sword, but he passed his weapon to Marcus, who was watching the performance nearby, and then came forth to greet friends and family.

Flavia shrunk back behind the slaves and behind the corner of the wall lining the fountain. She sat alone in the dark for some time, trying to slow the race of her heart. She was so frightened of the man, so frightened of the immediate future … and there was nothing she could do to change her master's wishes. Valerus was her master and she had to obey him.

It was not fair. She thought back to the teachings Melani had told. He had said so many things about the body being the temple of God; that no one could own another and that one was to love your enemies.

How could she, Flavia, in her position do or be any of those things? They were all well for someone who had the freedom to choose, but what freedom did *she* have? She was nothing more than a tool, an object to the people around her, and though she knew that she had a right in the face of God, she knew she was powerless to the wealthy who had bought her at the fair.

She wrapped her veil tightly around her hand and bit her lip in apprehension. She did not want Valerus to touch her or come near her. She had always prayed that the first man to ever touch her would be one she truly loved and who truly loved her. She did not want it to be a game, a form of relief. It just didn't seem right despite what many of her colleagues had said of it being enjoyable. It was not the fact that it was enjoyable that made it right. It was the reasons and the intention of it that marked its power and righteousness.

But she was powerless and this was going to happen; it was inevitable. She should have known it was going to happen this way since the first time a man looked her way.

Why did she have to be beautiful? Why had she been trained to dance?

To satisfy—that was her only purpose. And Valerus was not going to stop at watching her performance.

He was staring at her when she looked his way again and she felt the chill run down her neck. He was expecting … waiting for her to do as he had commanded.

She turned her head back to the darker shadows of the garden but could feel his icy stare on her, cutting into her soul and preparing a beating.

Maybe she could talk to him. Maybe she could tell him of her faith and what she believed.

Clearly she overheard Melani's strict caution in the back of her head. She looked over her shoulder again; Valerus was now in conversation with a companion, laughing at something he had said.

While his attention was turned, she rose from her place and left the garden. Valerus saw her the moment she stepped off the grass; she could feel it. She walked the lonely corridor, which was so empty compared to the gathering outside, and followed the steps up to Valerus's bedroom.

She sat down on the edge of the bed, feeling for the second the softness of the wool blankets, and stared into the dark. "Light a lamp," he had said, "so I can see you from the garden." She could ignore the command and say that she had forgotten, but what good would that do? It merely postponed the inevitable.

What was the use? She may as well continue and get it over with. It finally came to this: the fear and apprehension of this moment was developing into a need to get rid of it entirely and forever.

She went over to the table and lit the lamp, allowing it a few seconds to catch a bright flame before moving it over to the window. Leaving it on the sill, she went back to the bed, sat down, and waited.

The waiting was the worst part; the seconds passed slowly. How would He have dealt with the situation? God's son had never been in this, but He had been beaten as well as crucified. He had simply allowed them to do as they wished. She remembered how Melani had praised His surrender and faith in God, letting go completely of the ego mind and focusing on what was needed, not what He wanted.

She was not strong enough to do that, she realized, especially when she heard the approaching footfalls; they were steady and moving with intent. She wrapped her scarf around her waist out of fear.

Valerus stepped into the room, carefully shutting the door behind him without even meeting her gaze. He did not move. Flavia watched him from her place by the bed, wondering what was making him hesitate. His conscience?

He looked over to her suddenly and smiled. It was, she was forced to admit, a reassuring smile: kind and somewhat compassionate. He pushed himself away from the wall and walked up to her but stopped halfway.

"Watching you dance tonight," he began by telling her, "I realized for the first time what a beautiful woman you are. Tell me your name."

Flavia frowned at him. "You already know my name, master."

He shook his head slowly. "I know dancers are often given assumed names, something which fits more to their profession and the society in which they are based. Flavia is not the name given by your mother or siblings. Even if you say it is, I believe that you are hiding it from everyone, including yourself."

Flavia's jaw had dropped open. No, Flavia was not the name given to her by her mother. Melani had called her by her name as well as the dozens of pet names she had for the children. However, Melani had christened her with the name Flavia, stating that a Roman name would help her in the future, which it really did as it had for her sister and brother. For this Flavia took her name to be her real one. The name Anabell was a distant memory, which she felt no bond to anymore; in fact, the only emotion linked to that name was hurt. Though she could have given Valerus the name of her mother, she stuttered in an effort to respond as she did not know how he would respond when he discovered her true nationality. The man had seen straight through her.

Valerus came up, put his hand on her shoulder, and clenched it gently. "You don't have to tell me." He smiled again.

Flavia relaxed, but only slightly. "What are you playing at, Valerus?"

It was not often that a slave—no matter his or her position—called him by his name. It was official for them to call him as their master—nothing less. He decided to let it pass for now and took her hand. "Lie down," he whispered, and gently he pushed her.

Flavia resisted and slipped from his hold. "I don't want to."

Valerus shook his head and turned back to the room. "There is a quality of a dancing girl that you are yet to learn, Flavia." He was at the window now, looking at the gathering below. The dancing girls were serving wine to the guests. "It's very important; it will keep you in a proper household." He pinched out the tiny flame of the lamp and looked at her. She hadn't moved. "A dancing girl is meant to be erotic in more ways than one."

"I know that!" Flavia snapped. "You think I have not seen it? You think that I am stupid enough to believe that it's only about the dancing?"

"How old are you?"

Flavia shook her head angrily. "What does it matter? You want me to do something that I don't want to."

A dawning realization came to Valerus's face, nearly a disappointment. "Oh, are you … do you prefer female companions?"

This statement made Flavia even angrier. "No!" she growled. "God, is that the only reason you think a woman would not want to?"

Valerus's smile returned and he moved toward the bed, his hands clasped behind his back. "Ah," he said as he nodded once. "Then I think it's only because you have never experienced it." He sat down on the opposite side of the bed and leaned on his elbow toward her. "You don't know what you're missing."

"I don't, do I?" She got to her feet and began to pace a small area. "What am I missing? I have seen what girls like me become: an instrument that is only there for the enjoyment of others. They are dull, like living dead, doing only what they are told to do. They have no more conscience, no more morals, will, or mind of their own."

Valerus got to his feet and started around the bed toward her.

"At least I do! I have some standards and I want it to be that way. *That* is what attracts you to me! Now you want to destroy it! Look at those girls down there! Look at you! It's all about the comfort, the security, and the pleasure. What is real? Is it you? Or is it only the comforts that make you feel alive?"

He suddenly grabbed her by the arms; Flavia did not even realize that he had been close enough. He pressed himself against her; she could feel his erection and tried desperately to push him away.

"That's enough talking for now," he whispered, and then he bent forward and kissed her. He was too strong to fend off and Flavia felt herself cringe under his pressure. When he withdrew, he smiled but still held her tightly. "Just relax." He shook his head and ran his hands down her arms. "If you're going to be this wound up, it's going to hurt."

"I don't want to!" Flavia gathered her strength and pushed him back a couple of feet. He, however, had a firm grip on her wrist and pulled her along with him.

"Stop it, slave!" he said softly but harshly. "Or you may see the worst of me yet!"

She struggled uselessly in his grip.

"Would you prefer it to be some stranger?" he asked her suddenly. She stopped and caught his gaze. "Or would you prefer it to be my father? In public? Truly, you ought to consider yourself lucky that I got to you first."

Flavia stared at him; some tears that she had been holding back finally began to well into her eyes. She realized then as she had before that it was inevitable. What was happening here and now could have happened years ago or was going to happen the next day. She ought to consider herself lucky having held out this long. Despite the fact that she was but a slave obeying the command of her master, Valerus was far more gentle and kind than others who had tried to have their way with her.

His grip went slack on her wrist and then ran down to clasp her hand. "Come, Flavia." He gently pulled her toward the bed. "If you refuse it so much, then why postpone it?" He sat her down on the bed and settled beside her. Shaking his head, he brushed the tears that ran down her cheeks. "I have done this before." He tried to reassure her. "Most women have never complained or even commented about the pain. In fact, they said it was rather pleasurable, even the first time."

"Of course they would. You are their master."

"Stop with the commentary." He leaned forward to kiss her again. Flavia turned her head aside, but Valerus merely shifted his weight and kissed her neck instead. She felt the tickle of his tongue on her skin and smirked disapprovingly. It was somewhat enjoyable to feel it, but another part of her cringed. It felt wrong, and that was something she could not deny.

She let him have his taste of her, trying desperately to accept the happenings, but she was aware of how time slowed suddenly. His breathing was coming in fast and she felt his hands on her shoulders, pushing her back onto the bed. For the moment she complied with nothing more than a twitch of hesitation. There was something strange she noticed: as much as she knew that she did not want this to happen, her body responded positively; *it* wanted it to happen. Valerus's hands, moving faster now, ran down the profile of her body, making her shiver. Then he kissed her shoulders and her throat. She gasped when his one hand slipped in under her veil to cup a breast.

It was enjoyable, she had to admit, but it was wrong. It was a temptation of flesh, she knew. This was not something she wanted; it was what some older instinct wanted. She fought off the temptation, knowing that it was the weakness of mind that caused sin. It was to deny one's self.

She got her hands under Valerus and threw him off. The only reason she had managed that was because he had not expected it. She rolled off the bed and was suddenly looking at Valerus from the middle of the room.

Valerus moistened his lips before brushing back the inky black hair from his eyes. "That was the second time you've disobeyed me," he told her calmly. "Disobey me a third time and the punishment will be harsh."

Flavia shook her head. "I can't do this!" She wanted to make a dash for it, but Valerus was not going to let himself be humiliated.

He was after her within the instant and grabbed her by the arm and threw her up against the wall.

"Enough of this!" he growled, holding both of her wrists back with tremendous strength; one Flavia could not fight. She whimpered and tried to break free, but this time he was more prepared for her resistance. "Do you prefer me or the lash?" She felt his breath on her cheek. "You had better make the decision quickly, slave!"

His hand had got in under her tunica; she suddenly felt its coldness running up her inner thigh. The fear and the anger of the forceful treatment gave her a sudden strength and she freed her arm with a fast yank and slapped the young man hard against his ear.

It was as if he hadn't felt it, but he was aware of it. With his free hand he grabbed a lock of her hair and rammed it up against the wall. The yank on her scalp brought a scream from Flavia's lips and she froze, unable to resist him.

"Slave!"

It was only a few seconds later when Flavia realized it was not she who he was addressing but rather a male servant who had been confined to the house for moments such as these.

"Master?" The male slave bowed before him, trying not to show any distress by the manner in which Valerus treated the woman.

"Take this girl out to the back terrace!" he snapped. "Give her a good thrashing!"

Blood drained from Flavia's face. That was another major difference in the classes of the different homes she had come to know during her life of moving from one household to another. People like Seianus cared nothing about decency and exploited their violence and discipline in the open in front of family members and guests as well as other slaves. He always appeared to get some satisfaction in hurting and humiliating his servants in front of others.

The higher class, however, was more careful. Brutality on slaves was a poor and very undesirable act to be openly exposed. It represented poor maintenance and a lack of respect from the *lower* classes and slaves. For this reason, discipline was kept in tight control. Any disrespect or denial of command was dealt with privately and away from others, though some disciplinary punishments were often to be viewed by other slaves as a warning. Most households had used pantries, basements, garden sheds, or, in some cases, the back terraces.

When Valerus spoke again, his voice was softer but far more threatening in tone. "Maybe next time you'll think twice before refusing me!"

Chapter 5

April 21

Lucius arrived at the public baths later than he had intended; Herculaneum was always so busy at this time of the day.

He paid the entrance fee of a quarter *as,* tipped the servant who took his clothes, and entered the steam bath with the towel flung across his shoulder. Valerus was already seated on a marble bench on the other side of the room, his body glistening with vapor and sweat outlining every muscle. Across the left knee, though, was a long, faint scar, which guaranteed him some discomfort. He merely nodded when he saw his companion. More than a dozen other men were in the steam room, their conversations were muffled in low voices. Lucius sat down near his companion, back against the wall, and brought up both of his legs to rest his elbows on his knees. There were a few seconds of silence. Valerus had been sweating for a while, Lucius noticed. His breathing was short and fast.

"Long day so far?" Valerus began.

"How are the new girls?"

Both of the men had started simultaneously. They looked at

one another until Valerus decided that Lucius's question was more important.

"Flavia? Ha! She got a good thrashing last night!" Valerus's tone said far more than his words, though. There was a smirk in the way he spoke and perhaps even some enjoyment. There was, however, some concern also. Lucius inquired and Valerus replied simply, "Spoke to the discipliner this morning and he said that it was not her first." Valerus's eyes were shut. "He says that she had been scourged before, probably dating back to childhood or as an early teenager."

"Is that really a problem?" Lucius felt this somewhat irrelevant.

"Previously beaten slaves are like buying chewed meat: bad for your health and frowned upon by guests." Now he opened his eyes and looked at him. "Can't have it; it's like a branded slave. If my father finds out, it could put a black mark on my name. Whipped slaves … it's a mark for trouble imprinted on them."

"What are you saying? Are you thinking about selling her off?" Lucius made a quick mental calculation on how much he could afford to pay for her if this was the case.

"I was wondering if she ever mentioned anything. Did she say anything about her previous masters and why she was sold?"

The man quickly thought back and shook his head. "Not that I can remember."

Valerus stared into the vapor hanging thickly in the air in front of him. He knew that this was likely to put a black mark on his name if his father ever found out. It was considered an insult gifting family and friends with branded slaves, no matter whether they were whiplashes, bruises, or tattoos across the forehead. It was going to cause problems. Of course his ordering of the lash on Flavia last night had been his right, and he felt she deserved it not only for that moment but also her future. A whipped slave seldom ended up in good homes. Valerus wondered how Flavia had ended up in his.

"You should talk to her," Lucius said to him. "If it is that much of an issue, you should inquire."

Valerus stared at him for a second before responding. "One-on-one with a slave?" he asked coldly. "I don't do that! I don't get personally involved with servants. They are objects and property for our convenience. You don't form a bond with them."

"Would you like me to talk to her then?"

It was a sincere offer and Valerus could not understand why he did not take it up. It could bring a bad reputation to anyone who asked personal details of a slave's life. "I cannot ask that of you." Valerus shook his head. But his father was going to find out and what then? The very least Valerus could do was tell his father why and give an acceptable explanation other than the fact she was disobedient and that he had purchased low quality.

He would have to talk to her, Valerus knew. It was something very much to his disliking, talking personal with a slave, but in the future it would protect his own reputation and his position in the domus.

Someone hammered on Flavia's door later that morning when some of the slaves were entitled to a short rest. Flavia was resting with a pillow beneath her stomach, naked with the lash marks open to the air. Someone had made a kind effort to lay a cold wet cloth across some of the streaks.

The knock came again before the door opened enough to fit in a head. "Flavia?" It was a man's voice, and when he saw that Flavia was naked he pulled away again respectfully. "Flavia? Valerus is calling for you."

Now she raised her head and looked at the man over her shoulder. It was the slave from last night who had handed her over to other servants for the beating. Though she had, for a moment, hated him, she knew that he was merely following the commands of his superiors, as she to ought to have done. Her eyes were red as if she had been crying, but the look therein was raw rage. "What does he want?" she asked coldly.

The slave glanced inside again. "I am in no position to inquire."

Flavia sat up and winced. There was the tinkle of bangles and she realized she had not even removed them after last night's dance. The man came in to help her before she was waved off. "Leave it! I'm fine!" She took a few seconds to catch her breath before taking her wool tunica and carefully slipping it over her head.

"We have been introduced," the man said as he tied a piece of cord across her hips. "I am Procimus. I believe you have already heard of me."

Flavia returned his smiled. "Yes. Cotti speaks fondly of you."

The man blushed. He was young looking; in fact, he appeared younger than Cotti. He was well built, though, proving that his labor was something far more suited for men, probably working in the shipyard.

As they slipped out into the main hallway, Flavia suddenly had the recollection of last night's performance as well as the thrashing that followed. But her prayer afterward had been so comforting, so soothing. It was as if everything had slipped away during the time and all the trouble appeared dreamlike and unreal. That was peace. It had felt so right to walk away from Valerus last night; it was right to have him think about what she had said to him and that she *did* prefer the lash rather than him. It was not fair! No one had the right to command someone the way he had commanded her last night.

Now everything was very real and frightening again. She was going to be sold; she knew it for sure now. And, as Valerus had said, it was not going to be a wealthy place. She thought of Seianus and winced. She would much rather have Valerus be the first instead of someone like him. At least Valerus had been gentle … to a point.

What good was it, all that Melani had taught her, every story she had told? What was the point in the end?

"Sorry about last night," Procimus confessed as they continued. "I'm just following commands. It has been a while since the master ordered a thrashing."

Better the lash than having to sleep with him, she thought bitterly. Better the lash than the other forms of punishments masters gave to their slaves. She had already experienced the whip in her childhood and seen slaves left to die in the street after having had their eyes, tongue, ears, and lips cut from their faces, but it had been so many years ago. Mostly she remembered the sleepless night that followed because of the stinging pain and the nightmarish images.

At least she was not being sent to the country.

She felt the tears grow in her eyes just as Procimus clasped her tenderly on the upper arm. "Here you are," he whispered compassionately, having stopped by the bedroom door. "I'll be around." Then he left her there with her own fears and thoughts.

Flavia took a few seconds to catch her breath and compose herself. She knew that if Valerus was going to have his way with her, it was going to be now. Her entire body ached and she would not be able to resist him to the extent she had previously.

So this is it, she thought bitterly. *Finally it comes to this.*

She pushed open the door. Inside Valerus stopped his pacing in the middle of the room and regarded her critically. She saw the anger in his gaze when the recollection of her disobedience the previous night filtered through.

"Take off your tunica," he commanded, and he pulled a chair from his table by the window.

Flavia watched as he turned into the room and settled down. She did not move and hoped he would reconsider. It had been nearly five years that she had lived in this routine of erotic dance and orgies. Some men preferred to watch, Flavia had learnt early in the career, and though it was better than to get physically involved, Flavia hated it nearly as much. To her, there was little difference between the dancer and the prostitute; the main difference was that a prostitute got paid.

Valerus had his eyebrows raised when he caught her attention again. "Off with it, slave." He waved an open hand to her.

Reluctantly, knowing she had no other choice, Flavia undid the thong around her waist and quickly glanced around before setting it on the floor at her feet. Then she reached up and pulled her tunica off over her head. This time, before she set it down, Valerus took it from her hands and set it on the armrest by his elbow. He leaned forward over his knees, looking her over with quiet satisfaction.

"Stop trying to cover yourself." He smiled when she did this. He waved to her again. "Turn around."

Flavia did not like that; turning around meant that she would not be able to see him, and there was no telling what he was going to try to do. She stuttered in an effort to protest verbally but knew it was a losing battle. She did as she was told.

Valerus studied the red streaks across her back and then the paler, more faded maroon bruises beneath them. The discipliner had been correct when he said that the earlier scourging she had received had to have been brutal.

"I have some questions I need answered." Valerus got up from his place. Flavia looked at him over her shoulder. He had gone over to the table and was pouring himself some wine. She blinked back her tears of relief when realizing he was not going to force her into anything as yet, but there was concern over what his questions were.

The man looked at her, spinning the contents of his goblet absentmindedly. "You have been beaten before, Flavia, and there are questions that need answering."

Flavia sighed, shook her head, and turned to him. Her eyes fell on her tunica still on the armrest of his chair. "Can I have my clothes, master?"

"No." Valerus retook his seat and took a sip of wine. "You have a beautiful body and I am enjoying it. Something to look at while I listen to your story."

She twitched with rage, never having worked harder at resisting slapping a man as that moment. She twitched in an effort to control herself before deciding to break the tension by turning to her life's memories. She had so hoped that they would not have to come up. She had tried so hard to forget about her childhood that now being asked about it made her cringe. She still remembered and all too well.

Valerus smiled at her tortured expression. "A beaten slave could cause problems; you already have. You need to tell me when and especially *why*."

"I must have been about seven when I fell into the hands of Seianus," she said quickly, desperate to get it over with. "My master was insane. He enjoyed hurting people."

"What did you do to provoke him?"

This question made Flavia terribly angry. It sounded as if she was being accused of causing her own beatings, that she was responsible for her mother's demise. She felt accused of falling into the hands of a madman, a choice that was never part of a slave's life. "Nothing!" She shook her head instead. "I was seven. I did not want him to have my mother killed in some cheap arena. I merely cried a lot, and he could not stand the whining coming from me and my siblings."

For the first time Valerus appeared compassionate. He set down his goblet and the amused smile was lost when he frowned her way. Flavia was aware of the slight tremble in his voice when he spoke next. "Was your mother killed then?"

She nodded. "Three wild boars tusked her to death." Her eyes were getting glassy. "I was forced to watch it. Are you going to tell me that I was wrong to hate the man?"

There was a pregnant pause before Valerus slowly shook his head. "No, I would have hated him just as much."

"He enjoyed beating his servants, the children especially. I got five lashes when I cursed his name. Those are the scars you see." There was venom in the last sentence before she continued. "They were hard, biting into me far deeper than yesterday's beating. I was only a child then, half-starved."

"You have siblings?"

"My sister was twelve at the time. I am the middle child. She had been beaten and raped repeatedly. My brother was a little more favored due to him being male, but he was clouted a few times as well."

"How did you end up here then?"

Tears ran down Flavia's cheeks as she was forced to recall her life during that time, but Valerus saw the smile reappear when talking about Melani.

After their mother's death on the outskirts of Rome, Flavia and her siblings were sold off to the world of entertainment where they were meant to meet their mother's fate. Melani had simply been passing through the area when the sight of the three children in their chains caught her eye. How she managed to have Seianus sell them to her was still a mystery Flavia had stopped trying to learn. Melani was six months pregnant with her first child but took them in like she would have her own children. Slowly she rebuilt the children physically and mentally but especially had them rebuild their faith through the truth of one man.

When Emperor Nero committed suicide two years later, Melani and her husband, along with their slaves, moved to Verona.

Here they lived peacefully for another two years until the birth of Melani's second child. At this point she was forced to sell the children and made sure that they stayed together going to a good home.

This was Drusillius, the second master Flavia felt worth remembering. He too was a good man living in Verona, though he did not take as much personal interest in the children as Melani had. He owned property in Arelate and for four years they lived between Italy and Gaul until Flavia and her sister Alesia caught the interest of a dancing instructor from Hispania. They were sold to the dancing academy near Segovia. Her brother Torus stayed behind, and that was the last she ever saw of him.

For two full years the two sisters learnt the art of erotic dance and proved to be very good at it. From there they were sold to a small household near Lugdunum, her first return to Gaul as a dancer. Eighteen more months passed when the family fell into financial trouble and was forced to sell them to a colleague in Rome named Marcus Socandus. He was a good man, Flavia told Valerus repeatedly, but he had always hoped Flavia would become more like her sister when it came to sex and the art of pleasing a man. He was respectful and never made any such approaches on her as Valerus had done, but after eleven months he got impatient and sold her to Cephys: House of Slaves, and she ended up in Neapolis where he bought her.

"Why were you sold from your last home?" Valerus had to ask.

A dancer was meant to please a crowd in more ways than one. Flavia's refusal to a man's gestures had caused disturbance before. Her previous master, Marcus, tolerated it to a point, but the last occasion had no doubt been the limit. A man had made a pass at her when she offered to fill his cup. Then, drunk and built on sexual energy, he grabbed her by the wrist and pulled her down to him. Flavia brought up the amphora and drenched him in the wine until he let her go, splattering and cursing.

Valerus smirked, knowing she was telling the truth. "You never mentioned your father or how you became a slave to begin with."

Flavia was dreading this. "Some of the villages around Londinium were uprising against Roman invaders. Fighting broke out and the empire tore it down. My siblings and I, along with my parents, were taken after the conquest."

"Your father was a British soldier?"

Flavia shook her head. "No. He shoed horses. He had nothing to do with the fighting. He was taken by some Roman soldier while we were taken into Gaul. I never saw him again."

"So you were not born to a slave?"

Once again she shook her head. "I was three at the time. My mother was pregnant with my brother."

"What was your father's name?" Valerus asked, guided to ask her from a compassionate point of view. For this he was unsettled when Flavia started sobbing.

"I don't know," she said tearfully. "I can't remember. My mother seldom spoke about him; I think it was too painful."

That was her life story, and Valerus had listened intently to her every word.

This was the obvious fear of any slave, the fear of being sold from a good home. It was frightening to have to leave what was familiar, knowing that there was no control where you were going to end up. Flavia's greatest fear was ending up with another Seianus, but she truly believed that the worst was over now and that the world could not harbor more than one man as cruel as he.

To the slaves, a stable family meant regular meals and good lodgings. Money was important: as Flavia had well learnt from experience, the richer the family the better you had it as a slave. Dancing girls were a luxury and thus ended up in the richer households, but Flavia hated the dancing, which was Valerus's greatest surprise yet. She confessed to him how small it made her feel; how demeaning it was for her to be looked at by men who only had sex and pleasure on their mind. She did her best, though, as a dancing girl was more likely to end up in good homes than any other slave.

Flavia saw—and sensed—that he was taken by some different emotion then. The beauty and excitement of her naked body seemed to fade from his stare as he suddenly averted his eyes. Flavia wondered if a man like Valerus could actually have a conscience as he was portraying.

Finally the silence reached a limit and Flavia felt cold and alarmed. "May I have my clothes now, Master Valerus?" she asked him pitifully.

Without a word, the young man took up her tunica and held it out to her. She took it from him and slipped it over her head.

"Off with you." Valerus waved her away as she picked up her thong. "Go about your duties."

Chapter 6

April 22

Flavia went on her daily tasks the following morning with as much enthusiasm as she could muster. Valerus had drifted away after yesterday's conversation and he made no more demands of her that day or the next. She did not question this but merely enjoyed it. She joined Helen in going to the bakery in the morning to pick up a fresh loaf and helped prepare a breakfast before the family was up. Afterward she followed Cotti across the city to the laundry. It was fairly easy to find it following the smell; ammonia reeked in the air before they even reached the street. From there the washerwoman took her on a quick tour across the city, taking a detour past the theater on the north edge of town. There was a troupe of performers rehearsing their lines and they were told to leave earlier than Flavia had hoped.

"Ever watched a play, Flavia?" Cotti asked her as they made their way home.

She shook her head. "No, as frightening as it is to believe. I know Melani wanted to take me on several occasions, but I was young and paranoid of the crowds."

"Melani? A previous master, I take it?"

The name had come out so naturally that she was only now aware that she had never mentioned the woman's name to anyone in Herculaneum. She smiled and nodded, pleased that Cotti had been the first.

Back at the villa she helped with the chores, both in the house as well as in the garden. It was a strange change of events, she thought as she cleaned algae from the fountain. The fear of Valerus and his advances had faded away and she did not see him at all that day. Perhaps he had a conscience after all. The way he had listened to her and kept any comments to himself proved to her that he had felt some of the hurt of her childhood. He let her go without pulling her to his bed.

It was a famous inn, attracting rich guests even from Rome. Its mosaic floor was a fine art on its own, and Valerus studied it closely. He was dining alone, reclined on the terrace where there was a good view of the bay. Many guests were enjoying the spring breeze coming in off the coast. Beyond and above the rustle of Herculaneum waking up to the morning was the cry of seagulls fighting over the scraps from fishermen returning to the beaches. He took opportunity of the distant sounds to still his mind a bit.

The story of Flavia's life haunted him and he did not know how to react to it. He had pity for her and felt an urge to repent his actions. On the other hand, he had every right to command her and he had not done anything wrong from viewpoint of the Roman society. This was precisely why he did not want to get personal with his slaves; the moment you did, it brought out certain feelings, which none of them deserved.

Yet he felt that perhaps Flavia did deserve it; he had considered apologizing to her but then it was not his place. He had no dealings with slaves; they were objects and property. It would be frowned upon to view them as anything more.

He had never ordered a lashing on a woman before. Strangely it felt very wrong to him despite the fact that Flavia well deserved it. He could not let her get away with it; let it happen once to one slave, and next you were dealing with an uprising.

The young man got angry thinking about it, feeling humiliated by the way he had so easily let her get away from him. But the real guilt came from the fact that he had truly admired her by the way she stood her ground. No one had ever done that to him or ever shown such determination and self-respect. It was, he had to admit, strangely attractive. She was right about what she said about the dancing girls. They all appeared so much the same, like objects simply following command with no will of their own. He was attracted to Flavia in this respect, realizing that he had tried to turn her into something he had so much of already only for an hour of pleasure. She stood out of the crowd not because she was disobedient or because she was rude in the face of her superiors, but because she had showed no doubt that what she was doing was right. It was a fascinating quality Valerus had seen very little of in his life, and not only among slaves.

There were certain places you stood in society. A slave was not meant to be disrespectful to his or her master in the same way that the master would never be seen dining with his or her servants. Valerus would not be seen dead by the docks despite his father being the head of the business. It was not his place to mingle with slaves or their place to stand up to their master. And yet Flavia had done it, and it fascinated Valerus to have witnessed it. He was also a little dumbstruck and bewildered. No woman had ever refused him before, and he was not entirely sure how to handle it. He could have her whipped, as he had with Flavia, sell her off, or he could simply force her. Yet none of the options available and familiar felt appropriate in this case; the whipping for one had not brought him any satisfaction at all.

❧

Flavia went to the kitchen where a slave Flavia had never seen before was busy by the oven while Helen worked dough on the counter. This slave was the youngest Flavia had seen in the household till now. She introduced herself as Luci, being barely fourteen, and Flavia had the sensation as if it was a new household all over again. They were preparing bread, eggs, and pie while a boar roasted over the fire by the hearth. Luci was busy chopping vegetables.

"It's a large meal for a small family," Flavia mumbled as she took a knife to help her.

Both women threw her a look. Flavia noticed and wondered what she had said wrong. Finally Luci turned from the oven. "You do know this family, don't you? You've been here a while."

"No," Helen said as she shook her head. "She's the dancing girl that came with Valerus."

Realization dawned over the younger woman's face. "Oh, yes. I remember now. Sorry. But then you have seen the crowd that night after you first arrived?"

Flavia thought back to the gathering, but it was all a little fuzzy. The best she could remember was the fear she had of Valerus and his oncoming plans. Lucius had been there, and so were several others as well as a few teenagers.

"That's ..." She hesitated. "All family?"

The two looked at each other and then nodded. "Mostly," Luci said.

"But they don't all live here, do they?"

"No, but the family has close bonds. They often join for *cena.*"

"I know the mistress had a baby ..."

"Rectina's sister, actually," Luci said kindly. "She is three months now. The baby is often brought here to be looked after by Rectina and myself."

Flavia smiled at her. She said it as though she really enjoyed the work. "So living in the villa, there is ...?"

"There is Rectina and her husband Pedius. Then there is Valerus and his younger sister."

"Anneria." Flavia felt she needed to show that she knew something of the family.

"Also staying in the villa," Luci continued, "is Pomponianus, an old friend to Master Pedius. He came here for surgery and needs a few weeks to recover. He's getting better; walking by himself a lot now. Another week or so and he ought to be well enough to take the journey home to Stabiae."

Flavia shook her head; that was a man she had no idea lived in the villa. She had never even met Pomponianus.

The idea of Valerus as an older brother was a pleasant thought. It almost made him appear more human ... more gentle.

"You'll see them when dinner is served tonight," Luci whispered to her.

"Do we do the serving?" Flavia asked anxiously.

"No," Luci answered from the hearth. "The men do that."

Flavia continued her work in making the salad as she thought of the sudden change of events. Valerus suddenly appeared far more human and less threatening; why this was she could not exactly decide. Perhaps it was because he had a sister.

At dinner, Luci crept up behind the curtains with Flavia close behind her. Carefully she drew the corner aside and peered though.

"All part of the household *familia,"* she whispered and craned her head a bit. "I can't see Valerus. He must be behind Pomponianus."

"Here, let me see." Flavia pressed past her and looked out.

Two male slaves were doing the serving. The family was reclined on their couches, neatly lining the opposite sides of a long low table. A fruit bowl was neatly placed in its center and was surrounded by goblets in the process of being filled.

The family was engaged in friendly chatter. On Pedius's one side was his wife and on the other was his friend from Stabiae. Flavia could see by the man's posture that he had had trouble with his back. Anneria, who Flavia estimated to be in her late teens, was resting beside an empty couch.

"Valerus!" Pedius bellowed suddenly. "Cena is waiting! I'm not going to call again!"

"Still a small family for such a large villa." Flavia shook her head without turning from the family.

"It was huge … at a time," Luci said. "Aunts, uncles, and grandparents. It has been emptying out rather quickly over the last few years."

Flavia looked back to the banquet, wondering what it was like to have it every day without exception. The slave's ration was mostly small things that would not be missed from the kitchen along with the leftovers mixed into stews.

Valerus stepped into the room suddenly. "Sorry, Father," he began to say, and then he saw Flavia through the curtain. It was so quick that Flavia, as she jumped back and out of view, was not entirely sure whether he had actually seen her.

Desperately she turned to Luci. "Valerus saw me!" she said harshly.

The young woman shook her head. "Don't worry about it. He's never done anything to us."

Flavia stared at her as if she was trying to pull a prank, but her expression was completely innocent and sincere. Flavia was impressed that gossip was not as big a sport as it had been in previous homes. Gossip among slaves was like twigs in a fire; it took off fast and spread quickly to the next. Because a slave saw practically everything in a household, there were few or no secrets among them. For this reason, she was astonished that her lashing had not reached everyone yet.

Flavia looked at the small slit in the curtains again and heard Valerus's voice engage in the conversation.

It suddenly reminded Flavia of her own siblings and the wonderful meals they had shared with Melani and her husband. Though it only lasted four years and it was nearly eight years ago, it was still one of the fondest memories she held.

The three cooks shared a meal of stew in the kitchen after the masters had been served. Slaves were not expected to eat while their superiors did, but instead ate only when their chores had been completed.

After the courses had been served, table cleared, and cutlery cleaned, they sat around the kitchen table and shared stories of their lives that were worth telling. Flavia listened more than spoke, realizing how easy Luci had had it. Luci for one had been in Pedius's home since she was five and had never known the masters Flavia had in her earlier years.

There was a knocking on the main door. The sound of it traveled through the corridors with an echo. Flavia heard it being answered, for a second convinced that she could make out Valerus's voice, but sound was so muffled traveling through the house.

She turned her attention back to the women present but all the while tried to hear beyond them. Soon she could not contain her curiosity. She left the kitchen and gingerly stepped into the hallway where nearby the two men were in a friendly discussion.

"You surprise me, Lucius." This was Valerus speaking, "You? An actor?"

"The money's not bad," Lucius announced.

"Well, I'm not going to be paid for sitting in the stands, am I?"

"Come on, Valerus." Lucius's voice nearly sounded pleading. "We need bystanders for the theater. We are rehearsing and we need critics."

"What about Ursalus?"

"A dancing girl? All she knows is erotica. She would not appreciate the acting art."

"You ought to take Flavia," Valerus said quickly without thinking. "Nothing erotic about her, I can tell you."

Lucius raised his eyebrows. "You will let me have her for the afternoon?"

Valerus's jaw snapped shut. For a second he stood his ground before shaking his head stiffly. "No. She gives problems. I'd rather you didn't."

"Are you prepared to be the bystander?" He sighed. "We need a small audience, Valerus. *We need critics.*"

Valerus made an effort to shrug. "What about your helper, Protia?"

"Someone needs to man the shop."

"I'm sorry, Lucius," he said softly. "Theater is not my thing; you know that. It's all make-believe."

Lucius smiled and shrugged, obviously disappointed. "Well, ask around," he said, and with that he walked off, seeing his own way out and shutting the door after him.

Valerus ran his hand through his hair, wondering why he disapproved so much of the idea of Flavia going to theater. Valerus refused to give Flavia a chance for theater after her behavior …

Then the emotional war took place again. Perhaps he ought to gift it to her. He knew it would likely clear his conscience.

But no. It was not his place to decide such things. All three dancing girls belonged to his father and he really had no authority over them.

Flavia had heard the conversation between the two men and her thoughts rotated around the Roman theater. She had never watched theater or attended a play, even under the roof of Melani, and suddenly the thought was very encouraging. Of course Ursalus was going to have first choice, but even then Flavia felt there was some hope of joining her. Real theater and a real acting show. Would Valerus let her go? Would Pedius accept it? No, probably not, but Flavia felt she needed to make sure that this was the case.

She left her room that night, past the time when most slaves were expected to have retired. From there she slipped into the corridor and followed the wall to Valerus's room. Marcus was patrolling the ground and simply smiled at her on approach. Loyal to his position, he escorted her the rest of the way, passing her a lamp to light the way.

A dim light flickered beneath Valerus's door, proving that he was still up. Marcus gently tapped on the wood.

"Come." A voice sounded from the other side.

The guard stepped in and bowed respectfully. Valerus was lying in bed; there was an instant of awkwardness when Marcus noticed a figure wrapped in the sheets beside him. The young man lowered the parchment he was reading to his chest. "What is it, Marcus?"

He had barely asked the question when he saw Flavia materialize behind him. She was carrying a lamp in the palm of her hand.

"Leave us." Valerus nodded to the man.

After Marcus had left, Valerus pushed his reading aside and sat up. His sheets fell away leaving his chest bare. The lamplight outlined every muscle on his body and for a second Flavia considered viewing him as attractive. That was until she too noticed the figure in the bed beside him. She recognized the thick tuft of red hair that belonged to Alia. She had to smirk; Valerus was like all the other men she had known.

With a sigh, Valerus rested his hands in his lap and looked at the slave girl. "Yes?"

"I am sorry to disturb you so late, master." She began by apologizing.

"It's all right. What do you want?"

Flavia hesitated, not knowing how or where to begin. The lamp she carried began to flicker in her hand as she trembled.

"Speak, woman."

"Is there any possibility I can join Ursalus to the theater, master?"

"What?" Valerus was on his feet suddenly. He was wearing loose fitting drawers and Flavia could not help but notice the vague scar on his left leg. "You are asking me if you can have a day off at the *theaters*?"

Flavia lowered her head.

"You are unbelievable! You disrespect and disobey this household and then ask for a day at the theatre! By Vulcan! Who do you think you are?"

"I am sorry, master!" She still did not look at him. "But I have never witnessed a play before. The acting profession has always fascinated me and this is a rare opportunity for a slave."

The man had his mouth open, not knowing how to respond to her last comment. On the bed Alia murmured sleepily and shifted her position.

"I would love it and enjoy it utmost." Flavia finally looked at him. "I would like to know if there is any possibility …"

"You cannot ask me these things, slave! You have no authority!

In fact, I do not even own you; you are the property of Pedius! Why not speak to him?"

"Will he listen?" she asked with her eyebrows raised.

Valerus gave a short sharp laugh. "He'll give you a few stripes."

The silence that fell on the room was heavy; Flavia nearly felt choked by it. She should have known the conversation would be one sided; Valerus was not a man to negotiate with. "Sorry to have taken your time, master." She bowed shortly.

"Wait, wait." Valerus went after her just as she reached the door. He turned her to face him and clasped her shoulders tenderly. "I will talk to my father in giving you a day off. How about that?" His voice had suddenly gone soft. "Then you can visit the theater on your own time."

Flavia could not believe what she had heard; it was not like Valerus to make such an offer. Yet it was not much of an offer either. Flavia was looking forward to her day off to join the other slaves down by the docks and stables, not to mention that there was no telling that her day off would match with Lucius's rehearsal.

"Well?" Valerus shrugged.

Flavia was not keen, but refusing this offer may condemn her to no free time at all. She put on a brave yet false smile and nodded. "Thank you, master."

She returned to her room, feeling somewhat put down by the whole affair.

After she had gone, Valerus returned to his bedside and glanced down at the woman sleeping beside him. The sensation that came over him was so sudden and abrupt that he had no control over it: he did not want the woman there anymore. "Enough, woman!"

Alia opened her eyes and blinked at him. "Would you like me to please you, master?" she asked as she tucked her arm in under her head.

"No." Valerus gestured his head toward the door. "Get out."

Alia sat up. "What's this, master? Have I displeased you?"

Valerus's eyes turned to the door and he felt more displeased and humiliated than ever to have the dancing girl in his bed. "Just go." He shook his head, not wanting to try to explain what he was feeling; he did not know himself.

After she had left, he blew out the lamp and lay back again, staring up into the darkness of his room. For a second there was some unidentified humiliation on his part that Flavia had seen Alia in his bed. It was only after he pushed the feeling aside that he felt the odd smile on his face that he frowned to, wondering what he had found amusing. Perhaps it was the strength and determination Flavia had shown him.

Or perhaps it was the realization that she had come to his bedroom willingly.

Chapter 7

April 29

Flavia continued on her daily chores without a word of protest. They were fairly simple after all; she picked up fresh bread at the bakery in the early morning and helped prepare a fine breakfast for the family. She helped with most meals other than the times she was sent to deliver and pick up laundry. It was one such trip, when the shadows began to lengthen, that she saw Lucius by the nearby stalls buying some low-class or cheap jewelry. He was dressed so strangely that she had to go up and see if it was him.

He was dressed in a long white robe, like a Greek would be. He was also wearing a wreath of imitation gold on his head. He was wearing makeup.

"Lucius." Flavia was giggling, "Why are you dressed this way?"

His shoulders sagged and he sighed. "Full dress rehearsal, one of three."

Flavia felt the excitement boil out of her, feeling the same interest she had for theater as a week back. "Lucius, that's wonderful!" She hopped up and down. "That explains the …" She swallowed the laughter coming up again. "The outfit."

"You can laugh!" Lucius announced. "It's meant to be funny! I'm Augastus the madman—who never knows what's going on."

"What's with the jewelry?"

"Oh," he looked down at the few strings of beads he held in his hand. "One actor playing a woman needed more items to … uh, hide that fact that he is not a woman."

Flavia laughed. "Will I get to see it?" she asked hopefully.

His smile faded slowly. "I am allowed to invite someone to watch, as we need some public feedback before we go for the whole of Herculaneum. But," he shook his head, "I cannot decide when you have time off."

Flavia's face fell; it was so distinct that Lucius felt a little taken aback. "I can talk to Valerus," he said quickly so as not to have to see her face fall any farther. She smiled and he returned it automatically.

"I would really appreciate that." She chuckled.

Flavia returned to the villa, skipping every now and again and swinging the empty laundry basket. It was all so exciting. She had never seen actors on stage before, and suddenly the future looked bright; there was actually a large possibility that she might get the opportunity.

Chapter 8

May 9

Days went by without much change of routine. Flavia turned to Cotti to help with the laundry. It was terribly monotonous. She acquainted herself with the dogs, which spent most of the day playing and sunning themselves in the garden. She did find it strange that she saw so little of Pomponianus. Sometimes, in the early afternoon, he would be reclined by the pool's side but would be gone again when the heat got too much.

On one day she accidentally walked into Luci who was carrying a baby in her arms. It was the first time she had gotten to see Rectina's niece and was truly impressed by her beauty. Still a baby, she was well draped in linen and wore a gold bracelet on the left wrist.

"How old is she?" Flavia asked.

"Nearly four months now. I'm taking her for a little walk and then to her mother for feeding."

"Her name?"

"Aleen, though I keep calling her Ali." She winked at Flavia.

"You really love children, don't you?"

Luci laughed. "Oh, yes. I've always hoped to have one of my own."

Flavia remembered what Cotti had told her regarding Pedius's views on slaves bearing children and doubted she ever would. She smiled to her and went on to collect the laundry from the master's room.

Sadly she was not told to take the laundry out to the cleaners that day. Thus once the laundry was collected and separated by color, Flavia left it near the slave's quarters where the washer was sure to see it.

As she was heading back to collect the sheets, Valerus stepped out of his room with Lucius.

The moment Lucius saw her, his face lit up. Valerus simply watched like an idle onlooker as the two engaged in conversation. She noticed Valerus's look of disapproval when seeing her.

"You have persuasive friends, Flavia," he said to her rather bitterly. "Speaking to my friends to get your way."

Flavia did not respond to this. To break the tension, Lucius rubbed his hands together excitedly. "Well," he said. "Tomorrow is the last full dress rehearsal, and I got permission to get you out for a few hours."

Flavia's face turned to him completely and lit up. "Lucius, thank you!"

"With Valerus accompanying you, of course."

Flavia looked at Valerus and thought how strange it was not to see a smile on his face, no amusement and no expression of having conquered her yet again. Instead he looked disrupted, bothered, and awkward. He was a gladiator, after all, and she could not believe he had any fascination for staged plays. Her first thought would have been that he was accompanying her simply to once again announce his status and his dominance over her, yet his expression did not seem to correspond to this.

Flavia shook the bewilderment from her head when Valerus stepped back and looked her up and down. "You have been given the day off; it begins at dawn and ends tomorrow evening by sundown. Your chores will return as normal the morning after. I will escort you to the theater, however, and I expect you there on time. It starts in the *decima.*"

She got through the rest of the day, somehow, and slept little that night. Above her, in the larger master bedroom, Valerus too was sitting up in bed, rubbing his hands together as if in sheer anguish. He did not understand why he disapproved so much of Lucius getting so close to Flavia. Despite her being attractive, she was still a slave and a problem one at that.

But there was something about her that propelled him. The feeling was very different from anything he had ever had, including with women he claimed to have loved. Flavia's effect on him was powerful and felt so much more real. Was he really attracted to the slave?

He thought about this and confessed that he was. Flavia was different from anyone he had ever met before. For a slave, especially, she was outgoing and particularly stoic. He smiled when remembering how she had resisted him in the stable yard a month before, which was just as strange. Why did he find that attractive suddenly?

When he slept that night, he dreamt of dancing girls …

Flavia was up early, ready to make the most of the morning off before the theater. The air was crisp as she stepped outside for the first time as a free person—almost free—at least for a day.

She took the road toward town and down toward the stable yards. She had never walked this road before, but well recalled

Alaine giving her enthusiastic directions. Soon the smell of bedding and straw became very apparent and so came the sound of horses.

It was smaller than Flavia had pictured, but it did make it easier to find a familiar face.

Alaine was rubbing down a large gray horse, running her hands down the length of its legs. Flavia approached gingerly. She had always felt uncomfortable around horses; they were all so large that it was difficult not to feel intimidated by them.

"You are up early," Alaine chirped when seeing her from the corner of her eye. "I thought dancing girls always slept in."

"My day off," Flavia announced as the woman turned to her. Alaine was wearing a tunica beneath a long *pallium,* which was neatly draped over her body. Alaine looked so different from the first time Flavia had seen her. She was large and strongly built but not in the sense of obesity, just large. "So," Flavia said as she pointed to the stallion, "this is the master's horse?"

"His personal stud!" Alaine nodded happily. "He's a big baby, really. A pushover when you know how to handle him." She patted the horse's neck. "His name is Elysium, the place where good men go."

Heaven, Flavia thought. Heaven did not work like that. It was not only for the so-called "good" people but for the people who felt, in their deepest heart, they deserved it. You could have been a murderer, but when you truly began to consider your actions, even on your death bed, things could change very suddenly.

Remember us, oh, Lord!

Today we will be in paradise together ...

Flavia smiled; it was the voice of Melani saying those words, and it had always been a special part of the stories she told.

"He is Andalusian with a small touch of Barb. Impressive, isn't he?"

Flavia was at a bit of a loss. It was like she was being spoken to in a different language. She did not know the horse world as Alaine did, but she did her best to show an interest. "Does Pedius use him for breeding?" she asked.

"Often, and what a price he can ask. The serious breeders may pay up to four thousand sestertii for a single mount."

Flavia studied the stallion again, finding it hard to believe that so much could be put into an animal. She felt a little degraded when realizing that the animal was far better looked after and treated than she was. She was certain that Elysium didn't get any whippings.

"You ride often?"

"Every morning," Alaine told her as she picked a bridle off the nail. "Except on my day off, then Marcus would take him out. He needs his daily run otherwise he gets a bit hyped in his stall."

"Can I come with you?" she asked.

Alaine slipped the bit into the stallion's mouth and then the bridle over the head and halter. She fastened the buckles before replying. "Up until the beach. From there I always take him for a good run."

"That would be perfect," Flavia agreed. "Cotti told me to get down to the docks to see Procimus at work."

"Yes, the shipyard." Alaine threw a blanket over the horse's back and flattened out the creases. "Fascinating really, but I would not go there on my day off."

Flavia frowned at this. "Why not?"

The woman sucked on her teeth. "Harsh conditions. Oh, Pedius's slaves are well kept, but there are many in Herculaneum who have a hand in the fishing industry. Not all of them take much effort in the well-being of their servants."

This made Flavia hesitate slightly.

"Well, come on." Alaine leapt onto the horse, which merely shifted its weight slightly. "I'll escort you down."

⁂

They followed a small earth track on the edge of town which led to the beach, passing through a thick patch of shrub and trees before being hit by the cool sea air.

The shipyard was easy enough to find once you got down to the beach; in fact, along the city itself, there were only lines of small harbors, shipyards, and storage rooms for boats and slaves. Fishing was early work and, by the time Flavia was on the beach, most boats had returned, making the sand open to clusters of slaves sorting fish.

This was a place for slaves; Flavia very much doubted that any master, especially of the higher class, came down here. Nor were there many women, Flavia noticed. Conversations fell quiet when she walked past groups and occasionally there was a comment on the edge of her hearing.

She must have walked for a quarter of a *mille passuum* before finding Procimus. He was on the beach beside an upturned boat, his feet and calves covered in wet sea sand. The boat had been lifted and set on a tripod on either end, making easy access to the places to be repaired.

Procimus saw her coming up but made it quite clear that he could not let go of whatever he was doing. He was working on the wooden hull. A hammer was laid beside him.

"Bad time?" Flavia asked as she went to sit next to him.

He still did not look up from his work. One hand was held in a small opening on the side of the hull while his other was pressing hard on the wooden frame. "Difficult repair, this," he muttered, completely engrossed in his work. "Some idiot hit the reef. I warned him about the low tide."

"Can I help?"

"No, no. One-man job this, really. Let me just get this … ag!" He shifted his position until his legs were extended beneath the boat. "I just need to get this flap …"

Flavia inched away, leaving the man to his work. She walked up to the storage rooms a short way up the beach, listening to Procimus curse and spit under his breath behind her.

The air was cool the moment she stepped into the shadow of the stone building. Its small archway entrance made it strangely welcoming. A small fire was lit in the one corner, over which hung a small pot. The contents were boiling.

"Ey! 'eave 'e pot!"

It sounded like it came from someone who was trying not to move his mouth while speaking. She turned into the shadows and saw a hunched figure sitting by yet another upturned boat. This one seemed to be in the birth of creation as the wood was bright and fresh. The owner of the voice was holding a hammer and chisel in each hand, obviously in the process of carving.

"I'm sorry," Flavia said to him. "I thought this was my master's district."

"Who yor mashter?"

"Pedius."

"No; 'ot him. 'efinately not 'im."

Flavia stepped forward until a dim light fell on the man from the crack in the beams. She held her breath, expecting the worst when remembering Alaine's warning.

He was middle-aged to Flavia's observation, going bald and with a freshly but badly trimmed beard. He appeared to be from Germania; his nose certainly told it. When he smiled at her, she noticed his blackened teeth. It was no surprise that he stuttered; it hardly seemed that he had any good teeth left at all.

"Sorry," Flavia apologized again. "I didn't mean to trespass."

She made the gesture to leave before the man waved at her desperately. "No, no. No nee' to go. 'tay, pleas-se. I get little comp'ny." He tried to get up, staggered, and fell back again with an agonized groan. Flavia went to help him to his feet. He stood crookedly like a man who had had his back bent separate ways. “Ah,” his hand went to his back. “Hurt …”

Flavia did not recognize the accent, but it was not that he spoke badly; it was just becoming obvious that his bad teeth were giving him terrible pain. “Can I get your pot?”

“Boilin’ ye?”

“Yes, it is boiling. Shall I get it?”

“Pleas-se …” He took a few short steps and then sat down again in the sunlight, slowly and with great effort.

Flavia took the small cloth hanging from the nail and gingerly removed the pot from the fire. A wooden spoon poked its head out of it. She got a good look of the contents and assumed it was more water than anything else. Once in the better light, she saw it did contain some bits of fish.

A poorly made fish stew. Flavia shook her head as she set it down beside him. He took a few deep breaths before pulling the pot nearer to him. Flavia saw how scabbed and burnt his fingers were, causing complete ignorance to the heat coming from the metal. He took a small sip of merely fish-flavored water. “Wan’ some?” He offered her the spoon.

Flavia shook her head. She had not had breakfast, but she could not come to take the man’s food. It was obvious he had little of it.

He took another spoonful of water.

“What is your name?”

He shrugged. “I repair boat-es,” he replied simply.

“How long have you been working here?” she asked him, beginning to witness the horror of the situation.

He shrugged but did not answer her.

“Does your master look after you at all?”

The man laughed. “Don’ know wha’ he looksh like.”

Flavia blinked, truly surprised and horrified by it. She thought of bringing something from the kitchen for him; they always had a lot of leftovers, and there was always something in the larder that would not be missed.

She returned to the villa and came back with a loaf of bread she kept concealed in her tunica. The repairer then, though very grateful, explained to her that he could not chew anything harder than stewed fish because of his teeth, and so Flavia spent the better part of the morning soaking the bread in the stew and feeding it to him a spoonful at a time. It was obvious to her that he never got enough to eat, and that the little he did was only a merciful token from some of the fishermen.

When she left later in the morning to meet Valerus, she felt terribly guilty. Here she was off to enjoy the theater while the repairer sat in his lonely chamber, carving wood and lifting beams. Flavia knew there were many slaves who lived the life she had experienced in her childhood, but seeing it offered a very different kind of feeling.

Love as I have loved …

Would He have left a crippled old man to go to the theater? Of course not; He would have healed him.

Flavia did not have that gift. She cursed herself and her inability to do as He had. Melani had made His miracles sound so easy, so effortless.

Yet, as she reached the villa, there was suddenly room for praise. She was pleased in what she had done and began to scheme ways of getting extra food to him. Her chores began in the morning, yet, if she left before the dawn, she could get something out to him. Marcus was sure to turn a blind eye if she explained the situation and asked him to.

Valerus was waiting at the theater entrance when she arrived, and his presence returned her to the here and now. He was dressed in a plain gray tunic with a white toga and over his shoulder he carried a small bundle.

She looked down at her own outfit and felt a little plain, wishing that she had something a little more fitting for the occasion. He appeared uncomfortable to be seen in public with her. Flavia knew she was pretty but her clothes were very obviously those belonging to a slave. She obviously observed that Valerus did not like it.

He did not say anything, but his eyes did fall on her feet, which were covered with beach sand. She wiped them off hurriedly when noticing his stare.

"You seem to have enjoyed your morning," he announced.

Flavia laughed but did not comment. She felt good for the deed she had done, but the repairer's face haunted her still.

It was soon forgotten, though. The play was hilarious and kept Flavia and the small group of onlookers in laughter. Lucius was an excellent actor as he played the role of a forgetful madman, always getting the wrong impression from the actors around him. Flavia's cheeks were wet when her laughter expired and turned to tears.

The play lasted for at least an hour until the audience was offered an intermission while the actors prepared for the next act. Flavia ran down the theater steps to the stage where Lucius was in conversation behind the painted mural. She waved to him and he came forward on her gesture. He was carrying his blond curly wig in his one hand. "You are so good at this!" She shook her head. Her jaw hurt from all the laughter.

"Thank you." He squatted down on the edge of the stage to be more level to her.

She laughed again when she reached out to touch the wig. "How did you get so good so fast?"

"Comedy is easier to play than drama. Most can do this."

"I couldn't."

"Have you ever tried?"

She thought for a moment he was going to make her an offer to try acting, but he didn't. After all, she told herself later, it was not really his decision.

She returned to her seat beside Valerus and sat down a little farther from him than before. The look on his face was clearly of disapproval.

❧

It was just past sundown when Valerus and Flavia finally walked back to the villa. Over his shoulder he carried a small leather bag in which he carried a spare cloak in case of rain. The afternoon had been strangely enjoyable, he had to admit. Flavia had a beautiful laugh, which rang in his ears like music; it was his first time to see her truly happy. He was also aware that he felt lighter in her presence. The play had certainly made him feel a little better about what he had previously done to her.

"I hope you enjoyed it," he said distantly as they reached the portico where he stopped. He admitted that he would not have enjoyed it had Flavia not been there; he would not even have gone to begin with.

"I've never enjoyed anything more." She smiled at him. "Thank you, Valerus. This was really special."

It was the first time she had said something like that to him and genuinely meant it. Valerus had to smile at this, feeling that he had achieved something without really aiming to.

There was silence as the two entered the villa and stopped together in the atrium. Here Valerus turned to her completely. "What about a roll of dice?" he asked her hopefully. "I've got a fine ivory set."

"I don't gamble." Flavia chuckled. "What do I have to give, after all?"

Valerus looked her up and down and smiled, amused by the

images that fed his imagination. "I suppose you are right." He gave in but would not admit defeat. "A friendly roll, perhaps?"

This time when Flavia smiled Valerus felt something come over him; he had never felt anything like it before and could not place it, but it was pleasant and left him feeling warm and strangely happy.

"Good-night, Master Valerus," she whispered.

He watched her disappear down to her lodgings and smiled oddly despite his disappointment.

Chapter 9

May 11

Flavia woke up the next morning feeling as if she was still bound to yesterday. She relived the play, smiling at some of the lines Lucius had thrown to the audience, and then relived her earlier visit to the horses and docks.

She jerked up into a sitting position. Alia was sleeping soundlessly beside her. Just as well. She did not want anyone to know about her dedication to a poor slave; rumors went around too fast among slaves.

Quietly, Flavia pulled on her tunica and then threw a mantle over her shoulders. She slipped from the room and snuck into the kitchen.

It was deserted. It was still too early for anyone to be working. She slipped into the larder and scavenged through some of the shelves, digging in the far back for any scraps she could get. She pulled out a small packet of flour and a handful of oats. It was not much, but the oats ought to be a good treat in stew, even with his bad teeth.

The sun was barely reaching for the horizon when she stepped outside. The wind was coming in from the sea and was pleasantly cool.

"Flavia?"

The woman jerked at the sound of her name. She spun around and saw Marcus seated on the steps a short way away, peacefully enjoying the early hours of dawn.

"Marcus, you frightened me."

"What are you doing up so early?" he asked suspiciously.

"Uh …" She felt the weight of the foodstuff she carried and stuttered in an effort to reply. She looked into his kind eyes and saw no reason to hide it. She confessed that she was smuggling food to the docks. On his question as to why, she told him the story of yesterday's encounter.

Marcus smiled when she had finished and then waved her off. "I will turn a blind eye. But please don't get caught, or it will be both our hides. Be back before the family is up."

"I will be running."

She got back when the first sunlight touched the rooftops. She slipped back into her room and found it empty. Alia had already left for her chores and Flavia saw no point in trying to catch a few more minutes of sleep.

As if only remembering now, she quickly brushed the sea sand from her feet and smelt her hands to learn if they left any scent of fish or oats. Then she switched tunicas, slipped on her sandals, and stepped out to greet the day.

It was like every other, yet the good deed of the morning and the memories of the play yesterday kept her in a particularly good mood. She hummed to herself as she fed the dogs and helped slaves around the house. By afternoon she found herself in the garden with Luci along with the two dogs playing around the fountain.

Flavia helped trim the shrubs and bring in good soil from the mountainside.

Things were very different around at the villa now; very different indeed in regards to Valerus. Flavia had no idea how she was expected to behave. She did not know if Master Pedius knew about the theater. She worked hard the following day, trying to make her escape in chores and the things expected of her. She steered clear of Valerus, not getting into close proximity of him at all.

Valerus was the short-tempered spoilt brat of the house. Flavia was a survivor; she had gotten through conditions the norm would not have managed. She was hard, direct, and oftentimes without fear. Slaves such as her did not get into the good homes—or at least were not meant to. For this reason, Valerus had noticed her … she stood out. Flavia knew this to be true, but she could not help it. She could not cover herself to be someone else as her sister and so many others had done.

Hard, direct, and oftentimes without fear …

Yet she could not deny that it was pleasurable to be in his company, even enjoyable.

Flavia got by as if in a dream. Lucius was not seen for several days and she did not know how to behave in front of Valerus anymore. She tried to be respectful, especially when the family was present, but it was becoming so difficult to be anything but casual around him.

Valerus never called for her or spoke to her after the theater. Occasionally she would catch him watching her from some corner only to wander off when she looked his way.

It was a very strange and somewhat uncomfortable feeling; she felt as if she was being stalked. She was extra careful when slipping from the house in the early morning to see the repairer, and it was becoming obvious that Macrus was getting a little anxious with her new routine.

After three days Cotti passed a remark in the kitchen, demanding where all the food had gone, and Flavia stopped for several days straight, giving things a chance to settle down.

Concerning the food, things did return to normal and nothing was said to the master, but Valerus continued in his odd behavior. He began leaving the house for long periods of time. Lucius called on him twice to find that he had been out since the morning.

No one had ever behaved this way toward her; most people were crude or very direct in their intentions. Leaving the house and wandering the beach was something new, which Flavia could not relate to or understand.

But then she was also spending time on her own. She avoided Valerus as much as he did her, and she kept to herself. The other slaves took interest in her; there was a change over Flavia, which the surrounding people could see far more clearly than she could. Even her style in dance was less when Pedius demanded it for the family. She watched Valerus come and go during the performance, avoiding meeting her gaze entirely.

May 16

Nearly three days had gone like this when Valerus suddenly called for her in the late afternoon on a Saturday.

Valerus was leaning against an ambulatory pillar, his arms folded across his chest, watching her work in the garden with Luci and Alia. He was dressed in casual wear of a chiton and sandals; there was not even a sword at his belt as she had usually seen on him. It appeared as if he had been there a long time watching her. With her eyes to the ground, she greeted him with a nod.

The man looked in Alia's direction before back at her. "Come up," he gestured with his head.

Flavia obliged respectfully and followed after him. He walked out along the ambulatory for a while before heading up to his room. Once inside he stopped, sighed, and looked to her.

There was no smile on her face as she regarded him.

"I can't sleep at night," he told her honestly. "I roll dice in the lamplight."

"I can't either." She shook her head. "The theater made such an impression on me."

His smile became a little sad; it was not exactly what he was hoping to hear. Instead he turned to the flask on his table. "What do you say to some wine?"

Flavia could not believe his offer; no slave was offered wine during chores, but some masters did test the faithfulness of their servants by putting them through tests. It was for this that Flavia declined his offer.

He appeared disappointed as he poured himself a goblet and sat down, and then he gestured to her. For the first time Flavia noticed that there was a second chair by his table and again the thought that he was testing her came to mind. She went forth and sagged to her knees near his feet. Valerus nearly choked on his wine. "Not on the floor, woman! Take a seat."

This was the first master since Melani who invited her to sit at the superior's table to share wine. She felt a little out of place when she sat down on the chair and looked across to him.

Valerus laughed as he sat up. "Please, make yourself comfortable." He pulled an amphora toward him. "Again, may I offer you some wine?"

This time Flavia nodded, sensing a genuine kindness from him. He poured her a goblet and passed it over to her. She did not take it immediately; she kept wondering whether this was some kind of disciplinary test. Past masters had tried to test her faithfulness, and thus far she had never failed.

Valerus appeared truly genuine as he pushed it gently into her hands and sat back. "Relax," he said. "Seriously."

Flavia smiled and lay sidelong, picking her feet off the ground and tucking her tunica under her. She propped herself up on the armrest and tried the wine.

Valerus watched her; there was a twinkle in his stare that anyone would have noticed. "How is the wine?" His voice came out weakly, as if his mouth was on automatic while his mind traveled elsewhere.

Flavia licked her lips, nodded, and set the goblet down. "Very good." She smiled. "From around here?"

"Pompeii." Valerus shifted his weight in an effort to get comfortable. "My father has some friends in the trade. They always supply the family with more than we can use."

She took the goblet again and smelt the rim. It was sweet scented, as though it had been treated with spice, but then she had heard of the richness of the land.

"Don't get the wrong idea about me."

Flavia looked up at him, wondering why the sentence struck her as so important. She frowned. "What?"

"Me." Valerus shook his head slowly. "I'm not a violent man."

Flavia pulled herself away from him and pushed back her hair. This she had trouble believing. He was a gladiator; he had killed for a living and he had had her whipped. His statement made her wonder why she was putting up with his advances.

He sighed. "It's just … I'm not used to the lesser races disrespecting me."

"Lesser races?" Flavia smirked.

"Please hear me out," he said. "We are a rich family, the Cascuses. My father had done well in the Roman senate, and now with him being an aristocrat, well, there are rules about respect and obedience."

"Valerus Cascus," Flavia said as if to herself. It was the first time she heard the entire name being said.

"Valerus *Claudius* Cascus." He introduced himself fully.

"Claudius? There was an emperor with that name."

"Who invaded Britain."

Flavia lost her smile when hearing the name of her home and remembered what the empire had done to her family only a few years later.

Valerus did not notice her expression and continued by saying, "Thirteen-year reign that ended twenty-five years ago; same age as myself and barely two years older than Lucius."

Flavia was genuinely surprised to learn that Lucius was so young; he looked older, but in a positive sense. Valerus looked young; he could have passed for eighteen. She would easily have believed that Lucius was the older of the two, especially in the way he behaved. Lucius appeared mature while she could not view Valerus as anything more than a spoilt child.

"I am not a violent man, Flavia," he repeated, this time leaning over to her. "There are just rules in the domus, which you don't seem to oblige to."

Flavia was aware that he was avoiding eye contact.

"When I lived alone it was one thing, but now back home with my parents things are expected, from you as well as from me."

Flavia set down her goblet slowly, keeping her eyes fixed on him while his were turned to the floor. "Are you trying again to get me to …?"

"No." His head jumped up suddenly. "I am just trying to say that what you have seen coming from me is not how I usually am. I am just trying to fit into a society that threw me away."

Those words softened her. Flavia looked into his dark eyes and noticed something she never had before: pain. Automatically her eyes fell on his left knee. She saw the faint remnants of a scar, which ran from the cap to midway down the calf. She looked up at him and felt forced to ask, "Does it still hurt?"

He shrugged. "Sometimes, in the winter especially."

There was suddenly compassion from her side. Valerus appeared to have been badly broken after that fight, both physically and in mind. Flavia wondered if he still had any faith left in whatever gods it was he worshiped. She knew what it was like to have a dream—a future—destroyed by one incident or, as it was for her, one person. She had always put herself in the poorer position of being a slave, but here suddenly she felt differently. This was not a time to argue which of them had a worse life, but instead to see the familiarity and equality therein.

"I know what it's like to lose a dream," she told him. His eyes were downcast but he looked up at her when she spoke. She smiled at him. "I really do. I am a slave, after all. Dreams and goals to us are simply ways to pass the time."

He smiled at this, causing Flavia to lean back in her effort to control the strange feeling coming over her. "Then we have something in common." He looked into his goblet. "You are a brave woman, Flavia, to say that to me after the life you have led."

She was about to speak when he turned to her and continued by saying, "Your life story has haunted me ever since you told me. I find myself wondering what it must be like not to have any choice … in anything."

Flavia shrugged sadly. "You get accustomed to it."

For the first time they made eye contact. Flavia was aware of the faint hidden smile on his face and could not decide if it gave her a comfortable or distanced feeling. Suddenly, like a snap to her psyche, Flavia saw how attractive he was. His years of fighting had put a fine build on him and his inky black hair framed his face, matching the cool shade of his eyes. His skin was darker than hers, like a deep yet perfect tan. This was such a surprise to her that she felt for a second she had to take a step back to view him completely.

The shock of this realization caused her to reel back a bit then take up her goblet to avoid any questions.

For a few seconds he watched, until he smiled and reached into the small leather pouch that was tied to his girdle. From it he removed a small leather string. At its end hung a little pendant of green polished shell. He held it out to her. "I got you this."

"Why?"

She saw the terrible debate commence in his stare and regretted having asked it. So she took the small pendant from his hand and ran her fingers over it, watching the light catch it and create beautiful colors and patterns over its surface. Then she looked back at him. "Thank you."

"You don't know me," he said quickly. She saw the truth of his words in his eyes and heard it in his voice. "What I've done and who I am are not the same people."

Flavia could not believe what she was hearing. No one but Melani had ever given her any gifts or pieces of jewelry or tried to apologize; and he was trying to, but pride held him back from saying it too obviously. Melani had taught her the power of forgiveness and the importance thereof. Indeed some anger and pain were associated with the incident, but how could she refuse someone who repented? "I forgive you," she said, and then she added automatically, "be at peace."

His smile appeared puzzled, but she said nothing of it.

Chapter 10

May 23

Flavia and Valerus formed a strange bond over the next week, which even Anneria commented on one night at the table. Pedius regarded his son with a strange expression, which Valerus could not place, but he did not comment on it. Rectina threw him smiles and odd winks from time to time. But these events were merely background to what was happening in Valerus's life currently. Flavia had become a close companion, which he was pleased with. They played in the garden and fountain when they thought no one was looking and shared wine in the kitchen after the family had retired. They talked a lot, something which Valerus admitted not to have done often with anyone. Some stories he told her came from childhood and others were more recent. They compared life situations and lessons that came over their years and found similarities that brought them even closer together.

This strange turn of events was well discussed around breakfast when all the slaves were gathered. Valerus knew his place and did not join this meal but waited it out in the gardens or the baths. Lucius was also noticing a difference in his companion as well as in Flavia whenever he saw her at the villa. They both appeared so much more at ease. He did not interrogate his friend, but his imagination began to make its own assumptions.

Flavia also had to face her challenges as rumor spread among the slaves. It was getting out now that the master and dancing girl were often seen together. Luckily she shared her room with Alia who rejected the statement when it was said that Flavia often spent nights with him.

The rumor was never blackened, though, and the looks and teasing that she got were never done with bad intent. A lot of jokes began to pass among the slaves, but none affected Flavia in the manner she had dreaded.

And Valerus made it so much easier for her. Heavy duties for women were oftentimes replaced by the men. One afternoon Flavia walked in on Luci trying to work the large press on her own. At once Flavia went up to help her when Valerus, who had been trying the whole day to catch Flavia alone, stepped in. There was little said as he helped the women press the master's tunics and togas.

"What was that?" Luci asked Flavia once he had left.

"You can't work this press by yourself, Luci. You are going to hurt yourself."

"I already have." Her hand went to her back. "It won't make much difference now, would it?"

"Still, instead of questioning Valerus's action, you ought to be grateful." Then she smiled at the girl. "Come on." She took the freshly pressed outfits from the counter. "Let's get these folded, shall we?"

Flavia snuck out of the villa early one morning to Marcus's dismay. He watched her leave and shook his head. Flavia had a good heart, no mistake, to go up against the master like that to feed a poor slave, but he wondered if it was truly worth it. The Roman punishment on slaves was very severe and the fact that each master had a right to do as he please made Flavia's actions even more worrying. Marcus himself had already been ordered to publicly humiliate and execute slaves who had stolen and disobeyed. He hated the thought that one day it may be Flavia.

Valerus came up behind him; the guard leapt when he politely cleared his throat. "All well, Marcus?"

The guard swallowed and nodded without a word.

"When do you go off duty?" He was draping his toga across his shoulders.

"Only later this morning. I am expected to inspect the guardhouse at first light."

"Must be an awful routine."

"We do what we must, Master Valerus."

Valerus passed him by. The morning was still and pleasurably warm as he made down the steps and into the city. Herculaneum had its routines as did any other town. Urine was needed for laundry and occasionally the dying procedure, so the collection thereof was three times a day; morning was the north and west districts, midday the mountainside and center, and in the later afternoon the south and central again. For this the carts were already busy loading along the coast when Valerus reached there. He did not cross the wall into the working district but instead kept to the higher class part of town. Bakery stalls were being opened and there was the fine smell of bread from the ovens.

Mostly women and slaves littered the streets this time of the morning, purchasing breakfast for their masters and families. Many households had their preferred bakeries where they could place orders to their requests, thus there was a lot of chatter and haggling as he walked on.

He turned east up the main road where Mount Vesuvius was

looming its shadow over the town. For some unexplained reason it stood out today. Valerus had lived most his life here and the mountain had always been some background to the world in general. Today, however, it loomed. It was a blessing though; it was, after all, the mountain that had blessed the earth with fertility.

He walked on until reaching the east end of the city where he continued to follow the road past villas and vineyards. Olives were grown further along the mountain slopes and the soil that scattered over the flagstones from passing carts was as black as the night. The smell of it intoxicated the air the farther he went.

Valerus was not entirely sure where he was headed, but then he felt no need to know. The open air cleared his head from all the spinning images and thoughts he had had since last night. Flavia was part of every single one. In some strange way he did not feel it was worth it. Many people of his status, himself included, frowned upon having any form of relationship with a slave. It was not a good impression to other people, especially if you were respected and well brought up. Slaves were very different from the upper class. Some households treated their slaves like family, but Pedius had never done that—there were too many to begin with.

Valerus made a mental calculation of how many slaves his father actually owned. Two men worked down at the docks and occasionally around the house with another for serving and for the heavier work women had trouble with. In the house were two cooks, a washerwoman, and one who looked after Father's horses. That was seven slaves—ten when he counted the three dancing girls as well. That was a specialty that was a positive bonus for a family: entertainment. Of course he had dozens more working on the vineyards, but they were supervised by a steward appointed by his father.

But it all cost money; slaves needed feeding, clothes, and lodging. Valerus sometimes wondered how his father managed. Even as a senator and aristocrat, Valerus could not contemplate how much money that actually brought him. The very villa they lived in had belonged to Julius Caesar's father-in-law, and that alone labeled wealth.

He stepped off the road and followed a footpath along the lower edge of Vesuvius.

Of course when the family was hit with financial trouble, the lower of the slaves and the less useful were sold, sometimes at a rock-bottom price depending on the desperation. Dancing girls were a luxury and thus well looked after but the first to be sold in a crisis due to their inconvenience. It was never certain as to when financial trouble would strike. At the moment, Valerus had about six hundred denarii left from his previous career, and it was not going to last, nor would it be enough if he ever decided to buy Flavia from his father. This he wanted to do without second thought; he wanted her under his name.

Rome was the center of wealth; Valerus recalled his life there before the accident; he had lived among its people. If the emperor—or Rome—had the slightest tremor in finance, the surrounding provinces were the ones to feel the quake, and it shook them like the earthquake had seventeen years ago.

Valerus sat down beneath an olive tree, using his cloak to protect his clothes from the rich black soil from which it grew. He stared out over the bustling city and to his home set against the sea. Here, in the shade, the wind was cool and reaching for nippy, but his thoughts distracted him for the moment.

He ought to be fighting again. He had been thinking about leaving for Pompeii and trying to start a new career there, but something held him back. Lucius had started going for theater, which was a good source of income all the same, but Valerus found it stale and somewhat boring. The true excitement was the fight, the raising of swords and tridents. It was not to sit in the audience and watch. Valerus thrived on the adrenaline, the blood rushing through him when an opponent came at him fully armed and shielded. It was those moments that made him feel alive, as if he was soaring above all the mundane life he had grown up in.

Until now, at least. He had felt that every time he was with Flavia. There was uplift in his way of thinking where he felt the rest of the world fall away, leaving only what was tangible and real. His lust for battle was being drowned; he could feel it. His thoughts turned to her and what it could possibly be like if she felt the same for him. He knew why he held back the things he felt; she was a slave and he the master. It was enough reason for them never to engage in conversation again. But he wanted to, he admitted. He wanted to touch her and kiss her in a manner he never had before. He wanted this so much he nearly felt choked. Why was he holding it back if he wanted it so badly?

He looked at the scar on his calf, knee, and upper thigh; it was hardly visible and strange to think that it had barely been a year since his injury. He had walked with a pair of crutches for just over a month before beginning to put any weight on it. Now he could walk nearly as well as he had before. In the winter it had been terribly painful and since the warmer months of summer it tended to buckle. It was terribly humiliating at times. At a touch, it tingled, like small bee stings. It was sensitive, at times waking Valerus up in the night as it brushed against the sheets of his bed. It seemed to put women off. But he considered himself lucky, perhaps not with the women, but he had made it out alive. Now Flavia had appeared, just at the right time when his life appeared lifeless and dull. The gods were strange in the way they worked.

There was a light tremor, followed by a deep low hum. In the distance a dog howled just before the ground vibrated slightly, rose, and fell beneath him. Valerus sat unmoving, allowing the phenomena to pass. It was not a completely unusual occurrence; Valerus had grown up with it for many years, but it always surprised him on some deeper level.

It was merely a few seconds before the ground settled again. More dogs howled, but, other than that, the earth was still again—like the dead; not even the birds were singing.

On his way back to the villa, he went to the temple to give his gratitude for his life so far. On a large scale, he really had little to complain about.

⁂

Flavia was helping Helen in the kitchen when Luci ran in out of breath but obviously pleased. "Heard the news?" she panted.

"What? Why are you so out of breath?"

"Pliny is back in Misenum. Rectina heard it from Gaius a few days ago!"

Helen appeared excited, her mouth dropping open and jumping to Luci with open arms. Flavia, however, stood still, gazing at them in bewilderment. "Who is Pliny?" she asked them when their excitement had diminished to a point where they were able to take notice of her again.

"The uncle of Gaius."

Flavia shook her head. "And who is *that*?"

"Gaius Plinius Caelcilius Secundus!" Luci squealed happily.

Flavia shook her head. "That's a mouthful," she said as if to herself.

"Gaius," Helen said more calmly and laughed shortly. "He is a fine example of a man!"

"And remarkably good looking," Luci interjected. "It's so exciting! He was here last year for a couple of weeks."

"And he is so special because ...?"

"He's just a good man," Helen answered. "Decent, noble, and fair. He is studying law and I've heard him to be a good poet. A trait we as slaves don't get to see often."

"And he is coming here?" Flavia asked.

"I assume he will. Pliny, his uncle, and Rectina have known each other for years and they have frequent correspondence. She invited him for a visit, along with his nephew! It's so exciting." With those words, Luci darted off to announce the news to the others. Flavia threw a knowing glance to Helen, who shook her head as she returned to her cooking. "Madly in love, that's the word," she announced kindly.

"I saw as much." Flavia smiled for the first time in days. "False hope, though."

"Oh, I would not say that. Gaius really is a good, decent man, and he won't let status stand between him and a good woman."

This would have been an appropriate time to think of Lucius, Flavia thought afterward, but for some unexplained reason it was Valerus that slipped into her mind.

"Pliny has close ties with the emperor and was now made prefect of the fleet in Misenum," Helen explained. "Obviously Rectina is most thrilled. I am looking forward to seeing him again. As for Luci, well, I hope she is not disappointed. I don't know how young Gaius feels about her."

"How old is this man?"

"I gather around eighteen. Luci saw him the first time when he was sixteen and she twelve."

"Anything happen then?"

"They had a long chat one night alone in the atrium. Luci did not get back in until after midnight. She never said what happened, but there have been rumors."

Flavia was getting dressed into her evening gown. A small lamp was burning on the table between the two beds and a cool breeze was coming in from the sea through the small window overhead. Alia had come and gone several times, hurrying to finish some of her chores, thus, when the door was opened, Flavia thought nothing of it as she brushed out her hair.

"Can I brush your hair for you?" Valerus asked.

Flavia spun around to the sound of his voice, startled at first and then overjoyed. She passed him the comb and then sat down on the bed. He followed, sitting behind her, and gently began to run the bristles through her long fine hair.

"Alia comes and goes," Flavia warned him kindly.

"I am the master," he commented casually. "I can be wherever I want to be."

Those words began to gnaw at Flavia's heart, and, as she felt him behind her and the brush running the full length, she felt it necessary to ask, "Do you ever make it down at the docks?"

She felt him hesitate for a second before continuing. "Oftentimes, yes. But not, I suspect, to the area you are referring to."

"Where the slaves work." She nodded slowly. "Ever been down there?"

There was no reply, which was an answer in itself.

"The conditions in which some of those slaves work is frightfully inhumane."

Valerus sighed from behind her. "It's not my business how masters treat their slaves." He shook his head. She turned around to look at him over her shoulder. He smiled compassionately. "Nor is it yours."

"I can't believe people don't care. How can one man decide how another ought to be treated? How can one man chose who lives and who dies?"

"The rules of the world, Flavia." He made an effort to continue but she turned to him fully.

"Doesn't it bother you, Valerus, when slaves are treated so badly that death would actually be an improvement?"

"My father taught me to handle slaves well; after all, the good ones don't grow in the fields. I respect slaves to a degree that I will not subject them to starvation and excess brutality as one of your former masters did. No, this household will not stand for it. But slaves are property, and what is owned can be done with as the owner pleases."

"What about me then?"

"I am not your master." He smiled.

"It just doesn't seem fair." She shook her head.

"Sometimes the world is not fair, Flavia. There were times I was forced to kill people who I really felt did not deserve it."

"But you did it. You went against what you believed and felt to be right."

He could not comment on that statement. She sighed and took his hand. "Why is it that the good men perish and the evil linger?" she asked dreamily, thinking again of the stories Melani had shared with her.

"Well, I am still here," Valerus said as if hopeful. "Surely that must count for something."

She smiled at him, his black hair hanging over his brow and the spark in his eyes from the candle lit them up even more than they already were. "I do appreciate that, Valerus. God has truly blessed my life with that."

For a second he appeared questioning, but instead of saying what was on his mind, he cupped her face carefully in his hands. She stiffened, wondering what was going to be his next move. He placed his hand on her neck and gently pulled her closer. He did not give any indication of forcing her, thus she felt no reason to resist. A shiver came up her back when their lips touched and then numbed her legs when he pressed even closer to her. His kiss did not have the same effect on her as the previous time; instead of the familiar urge to resist, there was something very familiar and comforting about it. There was no heat flash, no ache in the gut, and certainly no urge to resist him.

She did not, however, want to give him the wrong impression. Forcing herself, she pulled away from him, gently. She felt the soft suction just as their mouths parted and stared at him with round-eyed disbelief.

Valerus did not move, nor did he say a word. He simply stared at her while trying to catch his breath, his hands still holding her firmly but gently.

The feeling that came over her was unexpected, leaving her dizzy when she realized that she was attracted to him; she wanted him to touch her. She did not give into it though, as she did not trust his gesture no matter how much she wanted to. She rubbed her mouth with the back of her hand. "What was that?" she asked.

The young man opened his mouth but not a sound passed his lips. Then he shrugged and shook his head. "For the moment, I don't know. Can we try again?"

The magic died away and suddenly Flavia felt terribly alarmed. She did not know what was happening in the man's mind and felt certain that she did not want to know.

No, she did, and that was why she stayed where she was, watching him and waiting for some kind of explanation. In the far reaches of her mind, which she was not even fully aware of, she wanted to have him kiss her again. The feeling had left a tingle on her lips and an odd weakness in her knees. It was strange; she had never experienced these feelings before—not for anyone.

He hesitated for only a moment though, and then they both leaned into each other at the same time and kissed. It was gentle, so unlike the last time. He did not pull her to him or apply any unneeded pressure; it was merely soft, warm, and comforting. She invited him, to her own surprise. She never thought she would ever bring her mouth to any man who wanted to kiss her, but with Valerus it was a wondrous feeling that left her shivering comfortably.

"Will you take me to the docks on your day off?" Valerus whispered between two kisses.

Her eyes were still closed, embracing the feeling while she could. She merely nodded and said nothing more. For the moment, words were completely pointless. The kiss was passionate but very uncertain as well. Valerus's previous actions, when he had made his intentions quite clear, were certain, definite, and without a doubt. From that, she knew how to react. This moment had been the complete opposite, and Flavia was bewildered by it. No man had ever kissed her in that manner before, and though it was a little uncertain and awkward, it felt real because of it.

A sudden rumble interrupted the kiss. The earth began to tremble, moving away from beneath them. The surprise pulled a scream from Flavia's mouth. Valerus instinctively pulled her to him protectively, aware that it was a tremor far more evident than the one earlier that morning.

She clenched her teeth and tried to rock with the movement. She tried to control her panic by clinging onto the young man, trembling as much as the ground did. The earthquake only lasted a few seconds, but it seemed like minutes to Flavia. The quake of earlier that day had left her frightened and trembling. This time, however, she felt out of harm's way at the feel of Valerus holding her.

The earth settled. Flavia was scared to move, as if it would start again if she did. Also the feel of Valerus holding her was too good to want to move away.

Finally she summoned up enough courage to look up at him. There was bewilderment and terror in Flavia's gaze and Valerus smiled in an effort to reassure her. The air was still and she heard some insects beginning to chirp again in the distance.

Helen suddenly rushed into the room. "Flavia, are you all right?"

She stopped when seeing the two in each other's arms. "I'm sorry, master." She bowed awkwardly. "I did not know you were here."

Flavia stared at her and gave quick short nods. Helen looked from her to Valerus. The young man appeared more uncomfortable than she did. Finally he nodded down to Flavia. "Are you sure?" he asked her worriedly.

"Yes," Flavia finally muttered, looking up at Helen again.

"It's always been here." The woman looked up at the walls, "But it is getting stronger now."

"Two in one day," Valerus said as if to himself.

"I've never really gotten used to it." Helen shook her head.

"I don't think I ever will either," her master commented.

Chapter 11

June 1

Gaius's coming was seen throughout the house. All the working slaves were put to work, their leaves and off days canceled when the guests were to arrive. Pedius, being a fair man of dignity, did give them their rest before that. Many slaves got their day off over the next week; Flavia was off for only an afternoon and took the opportunity to head to the beaches. She visited the repairer, who was asleep at the time, and left him to rest and instead got acquainted with Procimus. Cotti too was there and the three of them enjoyed the sun and sea, swimming along the shore in the gentle waves of the beach. The weather was cool, making the gentle spray from the sea enjoyable.

By late afternoon, Flavia decided to enjoy the sunset. She left the couple to themselves and walked southward along the beach. On the edge of the city she came across hoof prints in the sand and followed them, watching how the waves slowly washed them away as the tide began to rise.

When the bustle of the city was faded into the background, Flavia turned westward and settled into the sand, tucking her tunica in under her. The sun was just about to touch the horizon when the sound of hoof beats rose above the crack of waves. She looked up and saw two riders come toward her. She recognized Elysium but not his rider. The other was Alaine riding a horse she had never seen before—brown with a long black mane and tail.

They had seen her, for they had turned from their inland direction and were coming up to her. On their approach, Flavia realized that the stallion's rider was Valerus. It was the first time she associated him with horses in a positive way; he looked good on a horse. It also surprised her; she did not think he was able to ride a horse any faster than a steady walk with his injured leg. He was without a blanket and she could see the strength he exerted in his grip on the horse's sides as he pulled the animal to a stop.

"Hello, Flavia." Alaine greeted, trotting the energetic horse in large circles around her. "Enjoying the sunset?"

"Very much." She smiled up at her but avoided the man's gaze. "I thought you only rode in the cooler mornings."

"Oh, usually." The woman quickly looked at Valerus and then back at her. "But this little devil here needs a good running and is impossible on his own. Valerus wanted a ride, so it all worked out perfectly."

Only now did Flavia look at the mounted man. He was having a little trouble holding the stallion as it fought him, pulling its head down and yanking it from side to side.

He did not move on the creature's back; his posture and position barely slipped. She had never realized how well he had mastered the art.

"Well, I'm off," Alaine announced. "This one is going to need a good cooling off before I turn him in." She gave the animal slack on the rein and it headed home at a steady trot.

Flavia returned to face the sunset and Valerus watched her as he held back the stallion, keeping the rein tight in his hands as it struggled to follow the other.

"What are you doing out so far?"

"Enjoying the sunset," she replied with a smile but did not look at him.

Valerus looked up to where she was looking. The sun was a deep red, shimmering a reflection across the water that gently shattered where the waves built. The sun was a quarter down now.

He slipped off the horse's back, took the lead rope which he had been using as the left rein, and walked toward her.

Flavia heard his approach and felt stiff and rigid, wondering what she was going to do if he sat down beside her.

He didn't. Instead he stood beside her, also looking out over the ocean. Elysium yanked at the rein and Valerus disciplined the stallion with a sharp yank.

"I haven't seen you around much lately," Flavia said. She would have said anything to keep him from being so quiet.

"Strange turn of events," he confessed. She looked up at him, expecting him to be looking at her. He wasn't. Her eyes turned back to the sinking sun. "There remains a tingle on my lips." *Then* he sat down beside her, bringing his arms up to rest them over his knees.

She was terribly aware of his presence. She heard the rhythm of his breathing and saw the small movements of his hands and chest in the corner of her eye. She momentarily thought his arm was coming up to rest on her shoulders and she sagged with disappointment when he merely brushed the hair from his face.

"And what are you doing?" he asked her again.

"Thinking," she said.

"What about?"

She looked his way, her hair whipping up in the breeze. "Do you ever think beyond the ocean, Valerus?"

"What?"

She looked back to the sunset. "Out there." She pointed briefly. "Do you ever think what's out there?"

"The end of the world." he said sarcastically.

"No, Valerus." She shook her head. "More like … another world. Undiscovered and unexplored."

"I doubt that very much, Flavia."

"Use your imagination a moment and pretend with me," she pleaded. "Try and imagine it: brand new."

Valerus admitted that it was a pleasant thought, and the more he looked at the sun setting ahead the more he wished it was real rather than imagination. He turned back to the woman beside him. "Where do you get these ideas, woman?"

She shrugged. "From all the time I spend alone, I guess."

He inched closer to her and then with one hand took her by the side of her face again. She came closer just as the stallion suddenly pulled away, dragging Valerus a few feet before stopping again. Flavia laughed as he sat up, pulling the horse his way and spitting sand.

"I think he's getting impatient," she told him.

"He must learn." Valerus rubbed the sand from his face with his sleeve.

"I miss you around the house," she said with genuine disappointment. "I miss talking to you."

He stared at her for a long time and then suddenly changed his posture. She studied him; his shoulders came up as if he had made a decision. "Remember when I kissed you last?" he asked her.

Flavia felt the heat wash over her, from head to toe, leaving her dizzy. How could she forget? It had been one of the strangest yet most wonderful things she had ever experienced.

She nodded slowly, wondering whether it was appropriate to say something more, but Valerus continued without waiting for her to comment.

"You asked me what that was and I said that I didn't know. I keep trying to figure it out, but then I wonder if I ought to."

Flavia looked around wildly for something to turn her attention to. The sun was nearly down now but was suddenly background to what the man was telling her. "What are you saying, Valerus?" She shook her head nervously.

"Flavia …" Valerus raised a hand to her cheek, considered it a moment, and lowered it again with a sigh. "I think I'm falling in love with you."

It came out so fast that Flavia was taken aback. There had always been some kind of stability in her life, something keeping her grounded; her master and the rest of the world. Now suddenly she felt like a drifting boat with no tug of an anchor. She looked his way, her mouth gaping in an effort to comment, but nothing came to her, not even a sound.

Valerus shook his head and looked to the sunset. "I think that's what it was," he said dreamily. "I dream of you at night. I am prepared to take up any profession simply to earn the money I need to buy you. That is not the behavior of a sane man."

"Buy me?" she asked with her jaw hanging open, but that was a point that was not as important as when he said he loved her. She merely needed to turn her attention somewhere before she lost complete focus on the moment as she would try to work it all out. She had to say something; this was an appropriate moment. But what? Did she love him? No? Yes? She didn't know. He was the son of the master. What place did she have to say anything?

He looked her way. He was expecting her to say something, but she couldn't. It had all been blown open so fast. In a peculiar way, she was not entirely surprised by this, but now that the moment came she was at a complete loss. No master or guest had ever said he loved her … at least not in the way Valerus had just done.

Nothing passed between the two of them. The man was watching her mental debate for a while before he said, "Well, that's a weight off my shoulders." He got to his feet and brushed the sand from his breeches. "Sorry if I stole your sunset." Valerus remounted his horse and without a word turned him homeward.

Flavia looked to the sun; it was gone, sunk behind the horizon and leaving nothing but a bright glow.

The moment had passed … maybe forever.

Chapter 12

Flavia sat alone in her room while Alia was finishing her chores in the atrium. Flavia was rubbing her hands together. She had let one of the dogs in for the company, which was now dozing on the carpet between the two beds. Its mere presence comforted her; at least she was not alone.

Did she love Valerus? What kept fighting against her feelings was that there was no reason to love him. What had he done to deserve it?

Valerus loved her; the thought that he was playing a game with her in this respect had never even crossed her mind. He had said it and left it there, and it was her turn now if she chose to join.

But did she love him? This was what racked her mind even after Alia came to the room. She knew she thought of the man a lot, she thought of not saying a word to him and seeing where it led, but that also felt not to be an option. She might lose him completely if …

There was her answer, right there. Flavia saw it had been sitting in front of her all along.

She drew the covers back and got to her feet. The dog woke up and looked her way as she carefully picked up the lamp. The glow of the tiny flame led her out into the main passage. She walked for a while before meeting Marcus in his usual place by the murals.

"Evening, Flavia." Marcus nodded in greeting. He had become so used to seeing Flavia out in the strange hours that it was more a routine to see her than a surprise.

"Hello, Marcus. All quiet?"

"Except for you." He chuckled. "Where you off to this late at night?"

"Valerus," she replied. "I need to speak to him about a few things."

"I believe the young master has already retired," he said as he took the lamp carefully from her palm. "Master Pedius has been strict with my orders that no slave be up after hours unless called by their superiors."

"Well, there you have it." Flavia took her lamp back. "I think Valerus would want to see me."

"I can't." He shook his head. "Pedius made it very clear. You don't want me to get into trouble, do you? I have turned so many blind eyes to your behavior that you will have to grant me this moment."

Flavia felt a tinge of guilt thinking of all the help and trust he had offered previously. But then there was an undying urgency in her gut that pushed her to persist. "He called for me," she lied very convincingly. "*Please* let me go."

He was at a loss. He was holding her by the wrist now and felt the tension mount. "I did not hear Master Valerus's voice," he told her honestly.

"Now you do." A voice rang out clearly through the corridor. Both looked up and saw Valerus standing in the hallway in a sleep shirt, also carrying a small lamp that flickered in the incoming breeze.

Marcus released Flavia instantly on seeing him and bowed shortly. "My apology, master," he said as if to them both before returning on his rounds.

The woman watched him go, suddenly feeling a little vulnerable without his presence. She looked back at Valerus and stuttered, "I … I just wanted …"

"Let's not wake up the domus." He waved her over. "Come to my room and we can talk there."

She followed after him like the dead, her little flame trickling small spirals of smoke. The night was pleasantly warm, bringing the air in from the sea. Even the sky was clear, but everything was suddenly background to the mere fact that she was going to have to ask Valerus some questions that he had no need to answer. She was, after all, the slave and he was the master. He needed to do nothing.

She walked into the room. To her surprise, he was not settled on the bed but instead on the chair on the other end of the room. His lamp flickered on the table beside him. "I'm sorry to disturb you this late," she began respectfully.

He waved her into silence. "What is it you want to tell me, Flavia?"

"What you said to me earlier," she began, taking a few steps toward him. "Did you really mean it?"

The man raised his eyes for a moment as if considering her question and then answered. "Yes, I did."

Flavia frowned at him. "You love me?" she asked, shock framing her words.

"I think so," he replied. He was so casual about it that it was difficult for her to believe him. "I have never felt this way for a woman before; I don't know what it is."

I've never felt this way for a master before … not even for any man. Is this a game? Is this like a sport to him? What is he playing at? What was I thinking?

She felt the panic rise; what was he thinking of her? How gullible did she appear to him now?

"Again I apologize," she whispered and tried to make her escape.

Valerus was up fast, slamming the door shut before she had even reached it. She looked at him as he leaned against the hardwood, his one hand raised up above his head. He took a deep breath and turned to her.

"That's not the reason you came to me so late in the night." He bore down on her. She stepped back as he drew closer. He followed. "That was not the reason you tried to get past the guard. It was not to ask if I merely meant it, was it?"

She was forced to stop backing away when her ankles knocked against the chair. He was barely a few inches from her now; she could feel his breath on her.

"Why are you here?" he whispered.

She trembled, not knowing how to say it. It was not him that made her nervous, but rather how she was going to tell him … what she felt.

Then what did it matter; she was but a slave and what she said would mean nothing if Valerus was beyond her bounds. She felt the strength surge though her and fought herself as it accumulated in her throat. "I think I love you," she said quickly.

The young man stepped back and looked at her from the tip of his nose. "You think?" he asked and then laughed suddenly but softly. "Then we have met an impasse. We both think and neither is certain. What then are we to do?"

Flavia wondered whether she was supposed to reply to this question, but then Valerus continued: "Strange place this world … where the gods never make it clear as to what we feel, see, or even desire. It becomes a very strange illusion indeed that keeps us guessing as to what is real and what is not."

"This is real." Flavia heard her own voice trembling. He looked at her. "I know what I'm feeling, Valerus, I simply can't explain it. The question is, as you said, should I try?"

Valerus walked up to her, reached out, and touched her shoulders with his palms. "And what are you feeling, woman?"

"I care about you. I spent the whole evening wondering why that is. I have no reason to feel this for you—nor at times do I feel you deserve it. Yet there is something about you that makes me *want* to love you." Her eyes met his.

"But?"

Her eyes went glassy. "There are things about me you don't know, Valerus, and which I cannot tell you; I don't think I ever will. I don't want to tell you because … I don't want to lose you."

"Here," he took a step forward and pulled her the rest of the way until they were up against each other. "Let me try something." He leaned forward and found her lips with his. He pressed her to him and there was no resistance on her part at all. He increased the pressure, but only slightly.

They pulled apart by an inch. She had her eyes closed, buried in the sensation that washed over her. Valerus still had his eyes closed when she opened hers and slowly he came forward again to press his brow against hers. His eyes opened a slit. "There is something about this …" He confessed with a sigh. "I could do it all night without wanting anything more."

She had to agree with him; there was something in the air around them. She felt it grip her and hold her perfectly still to wait for the next moment. She did not want to resist the urge she had to feel him close to her and allowed herself to lean in a little.

Neither moved. Flavia felt extremely comfortable in his hold; his hands were on her hips now and his breath gently warmed her face. She could not move even if she had wanted to. His closeness was suddenly very enjoyable and for an instant—only an instant—she hoped he would draw her to his bed.

He didn't. Instead he straightened up and looked at her. She was only a little shorter than him. His eyes were large, glistening in the lamplight, and Flavia caught herself trying to look at every small detail and curve of his face as well as his body.

He kissed her again, unable to resist, this time a little more passionately than before but not as long. Then he stepped back and took her hand. "I think it better if you leave now. I don't want to keep you from your rest."

"And all this?" Flavia asked, shaking her head. "What was all this?"

"This was real."

Chapter 13

June 8

Days went past that consisted of hiding in the corners. Flavia worked hard on getting her chores done, hoping to join Valerus when he was reading in his room in the later afternoon. Like the first time they ever had a decent conversation, they often shared wine at this time, recapturing on events of the day.

Now, however, Pedius was around the house more often than usual, demanding the completion of chores and the cleaning of the two guestrooms. Valerus struggled between his own routine, that of Flavia's chores, and especially his father. Instead Valerus would watch Flavia from his window when she was down in the garden, and at the table he asked for the dancing girls to feed his entertainment. Flavia did so, loving the looks he threw her when she spun her veil.

By sundown, however, as the family was reclined for the evening meal, Valerus did not have the heart to call for the dancing girls again. He had watched Flavia on numerous occasions running across the house that he knew how tired she must be.

"It's all settled then," Pedius announced to his family. "Pliny will be here within the next couple of days with his nephew Gaius.

No slaves are to leave the house from tomorrow until after their departure."

Valerus looked up over his goblet of wine. "How long will he be staying?" Valerus asked cautiously.

"As long as they wish. Gaius needs a lot of time in our library."

"It will be good to see young Gaius again."

"Hardly a boy anymore." Rectina reached for the olives. "I've heard he's grown into a fine young man." She caught her daughter's look and winked. "Just a year older than you now."

"Mother, please."

Valerus turned to his father. "I may have to ask permission for one of the slaves tomorrow," he said quickly, nearly desperately.

"Only a few hours then," he told him disapprovingly, throwing him that same strange look. "There is a lot of work around the house that needs to be done."

Flavia and the other slaves were gathered in the kitchen after the family had finished the meal. She had watched Valerus leave the table and he had thrown her a wistful look, which drew her to him, but her hunger from the hard day's work put her off from seeing him, at least for an hour.

"He's coming!" Luci bobbed up and down on her stool. "I'm so excited."

"Yes," Cotti reached for a small bun. "Apparently Anneria is looking at Gaius in a different way as well."

"But not the same as Luci here." Alaine shook her head. "Besides, I saw the way Gaius looked at Luci the last time he was here."

"That was two years ago."

"Love does not change."

Flavia listened to them from a far-off place, nibbling the bun she had dipped in honey. As much as she needed to eat, she wanted to see Valerus. It was so strange, really, but the last couple of weeks had been the best in her life; playing in the gardens, the sips of wine in his room. It had all been so magical that every moment away from him felt boring and lifeless.

"Isn't that right, Flavia?" Alaine pushed her in the ribs.

She looked up at them and shook her head. "What? Sorry, I was somewhere else."

"With Valerus, perhaps." Cotti grinned.

"How's that going, by the way?" Alia demanded with a smile from across the table. "Has he kissed you?"

Flavia rolled her eyes but said nothing. It was such a typical question to be asked by a dancing girl. The most common one was …

"Have you seen him naked?" This was Ursalus asking. "What does he look like under those clothes?"

The room held its collective breath, waiting to see what Flavia was going to say. Instead it was answered by Alia. "Fantastic!" she announced and threw Flavia a look.

Flavia felt her heart leap into her throat when recalling that Alia had pleased Valerus sexually, more often than once she was sure. It was a lingering thought that surfaced at the most unexpected times and in the most unpleasant places. For one it was like having a hole punched in her chest. The other was in her heart; for a second it completely threw her off and she did not think she could look him in the eye again.

"You have never seen something like him!" Alia continued, now turning to the others. "That body of his … it belongs only to the gods! You ought to do yourself the favor, if he allows it." This last sentence was directed to Flavia, who felt the rage and especially the jealousy boil out of her.

It took her a few seconds to get her vocal cords under control again, and that was her first mistake. She was so angry at them—dancing girls had no morals and thought nothing of a relationship that did not involve some sexual activity. She had seen Alia—and many others—in the pleasurable company of others, and it bothered her how easy women made it for men to get the impression that they were nothing but objects of relief.

"No, I won't ask him that," she said bitterly, but her hesitation caused a few to snicker. "We are close friends, maybe a little more, but not to that extent, and neither do I want it to be." She got up and left.

Once she was gone, Helen turned to the others, Alia especially. "Cut her some slack! What she and Valerus do is none of your business!"

"This is just so unusual." Luci shook her head.

"She's right." Cotti supported the comment. "I have been here long enough to know that Valerus has had women, and a lot of them. I find it so strange that he has taken such particular interest in Flavia. I mean, it's not that she isn't pretty, but …" She looked at Ursalus and then Alia. Their profession and dedication to men as well as the dance had made them terribly attractive. "But there are such finer specimens to choose from."

The two dancers smiled simultaneously, but this was broken by Alaine who shook her head. "Has it ever occurred to you that Valerus may be looking for something a little more stable?"

"With *her*?" Alia asked coldly.

"There is more to love than the physical appearances," Helen interjected their discussion. "You may never have learnt it, but obviously Flavia and Valerus are both good pupils to the concept."

June 9

Valerus got Flavia from the house only by the later afternoon of the following day. It was the first time he was out in public with her, and it felt peculiar. He was not the type to be seen walking with a slave.

Though it was common for masters to escort new slaves across the city, it was strange to have to fight the urge to hold her hand.

Flavia walked beside him but not too close. She could feel his apprehension; obviously he had not thought all this through, and he was getting stares from people he knew.

He walked eastward toward the mountain. A slave cart passed them by and Valerus saw how the young woman tried not to look its way, but it was nearly impossible. Valerus looked up and saw the lower-class slaves: unhealthy, scarred, and obviously undernourished. Among the older men was a boy, barely twelve year of age, looking out at them through the bars. It was clear that he was from the northern African region; his skin was dark and his hair was short.

Valerus could not turn his eyes away; before knowing Flavia, they would have been slaves, nothing more. Now he saw the fear, the uncertainty, and the lack of all will and ambition to live. He had never noticed this before; it was the first time he noticed the awful horror of his own culture; all the killings he had done were in support of it. In the past those people were probably the same he would have met in the arena. He turned to look at Flavia, who had her eyes to the ground, trembling slightly. After the slaves came a trail of gladiators followed by a second cart carrying a cage with a large wild boar, the largest Valerus had ever seen. Its tusks could have reached twice the length of his hand. It paced nervously at the endless rattle beneath its cloven hooves and grunted at the passing people.

Again Flavia moved away, turning to Valerus's other side. He felt her grasping unconsciously for his hand, seeking some unspoken comfort. He complied by taking her around the shoulders and pulling her to him.

They took the dirt trail once they were outside the city and followed it for quite some time without saying a word. Once they reached the first lower slope of Vesuvius, which was more like an individual hillside scattered with vineyards and cypress trees, he noticed for the first time that tears were running down her cheeks.

"You all right?" he asked as he turned to her, concerned.

She nodded and quickly wiped her face dry.

Valerus nodded slowly. "Bad memories? I saw your reaction the moment they came into view."

"Did you see the fear in their eyes?" She shook her head.

Gently he pulled her to him and held her close. Shame was suddenly a large factor of his life.

She turned to the landscape, pressing the side of her face against him. "It is beautiful here," she whispered weakly, forcing herself to see the beauty again. She had reason to be grateful despite the cruelty of the world.

The late sun was shimmering over the ocean and the fertile green earth appeared as a wonderful contrast. Clouds were building to the north and the scent of wet rich soil engulfed them, joined by the scent of blossoms.

For the first time Valerus was completely aware of Flavia's presence: her smell, the sound of her beating heart, and the feel of her hands holding him. He didn't move but instead became drunk on the moment, intoxicating himself completely. For a few moments he could smell nothing but her unique scent and hear nothing but the soft thud against her chest. There was a pulsating effect coming up from her hands, giving him a warm and pleasant shiver.

As the intensity slowly dispersed, he found herself thinking: he had never felt this way with anyone before.

She pressed tightly against him and he put his arms around her to hold her even more closely. It was so comforting, so real. Time appeared to fall away as they stood on the mountain's slope together. Far in the distance were the calls and cries of the city, but they were so distant; it was as if hearing them from a dream.

"Flavia." His voice pierced the silence like a call across a deserted street.

She looked up at him. There was no smile on his face but a simple look of peace reflecting from his eyes into hers. "Yes?"

He started to say something; he drew in a breath but not a single word passed his lips. He caught his breath, leaned forward a bit, and kissed her hair. "I've never felt so whole," he whispered.

To the east, Mount Vesuvius regarded the two of them with a watchful eye.

⁂

Duties were hard that evening, driving Flavia as well as the other slaves to near exhaustion. The peace of the afternoon trip gave Flavia far more strength than the other slaves were capable of. Valerus did not eat that evening, too captivated by the afternoon past. Flavia came in to serve the wine and was surprised when the young man refused by gently placing his hand over his goblet and smiling kindly.

Pedius regarded his son from across the table and gently cleared his throat to get his full attention. "No wine, Valerus?" he asked, surprised.

Valerus smiled. "Not tonight, Father." The walk with Flavia had left him feeling drunk on happiness and especially peace. Nothing—no wine—could ever compare to the feeling. Also he was looking forward to sharing a glass with Flavia later.

"I think that's a first," he said simply. Anneria threw her brother a look he had never seen before.

⁂

There was no way Flavia was going to get any sleep. Valerus hung on her mind—everything about him. She did not have the courage to get undressed, fearing that his smell that had rubbed off onto her clothes would be gone in the morning. Between her fingers she gently played with the shell pendant Valerus had given her.

How his image crowded her thoughts.

Alia was already asleep beside her; her breathing was deep and regular. Flavia slipped the pendant over her head, blew out the tiny flame from her lamp, and rose out of bed. She gently pulled the door open so as not to make a sound.

A guard would be on his rounds, and, seeing that Marcus had left, she decided to stay in the shadows. Marcus was a good man; he always turned a blind eye when she snuck out in the mornings to see the repairer, but now she had to do him the favor by not letting the men under his command see her.

The wind made an eerie howl in the larger rooms as she walked along the corridor. It sounded as if a storm was brewing.

She reached Valerus's room with nothing more that the glow of a lamp around a corner. She stood by his door, first considering to knock, but then thought it inappropriate. There was no light from the slit underneath, but she was not going to take that as an excuse. For all she knew, Valerus missed her just as much, but of course did not want to join her in the room with Alia.

The woman made Flavia uncomfortable; always reminding her that she had been far closer to Valerus physically than she was—and probably ever would be. Alia was an erotic dancer and Flavia knew that there were far more reasons for Valerus to ask her to join him in the evenings. This gnawed in the back of her mind whenever she was around her. For this same reason, Valerus was a little reluctant to be in the same room with her—especially in the presence of Flavia.

Slowly she pushed open the door. The dark walk from the slaves' quarters to his room had sharpened her night vision to see the room in clear detail. There was a shuffle of blankets and a figure sat up in bed at the sound of her entry.

"Flavia?" A sharp whisper came from him.

"It's me …" She grinned and added, "master."

Valerus's figure pushed the sheets aside and swung his feet off the bed. He did not get up though, and she approached a little reluctantly.

"What are you doing here?" he asked.

She stopped and replied, "I miss you."

Valerus smiled in the dark, reached out, and gently touched her cheek. "I miss you too," he confessed. "I can't sleep thinking of you."

She observed the bed; it was large, probably large enough to accommodate four people if they squeezed. She felt it almost unfair that he slept alone.

He noticed her gaze and grinned. "Will you sleep here with me tonight, Flavia?"

Her smile was lost; maybe she was not ready for the consequences of her decision. She wanted to be with him, but she was frightfully aware of what it could lead to. Besides, Valerus had made his intentions clear in the past.

But how to say no when she knew she would never get to sleep other than beside him? She stuttered for a second, desperately looking for the answer that would not be a lie but also not the reply he was hoping for.

The young man shook his head. "That was a mistake, Flavia," he said as if reading her mind. "I won't do it again … not without your permission, that is."

Flavia could not believe that he had picked up her emotion so easily. "Really?" She was aware of a little twist of disappointment.

"Really. Just feeling you beside me will be all the comfort I could ever want tonight."

Chapter 14

June 10

Flavia rolled over and stretched out her arm. There was no one beside her. She had never woken up to feel anyone beside her, thus for a few seconds she thought nothing of it. Then her sleepy mind began to wonder what she was doing in a bed so large that she could reach out to begin with.

She opened her eyes. The bright sun of morning filled her vision and for a second she could see nothing else. She sat up, squinting in the hazy morning.

Valerus was sitting on the stool near his table, patiently watching her as she woke up. The moment she focused on him he smiled. "Slept well?" he asked.

Sleepily, she rubbed her eyes. "It's late," she said.

"Reaching for noon."

"What?" Flavia jumped out of the bed. "There is work to be done! Pliny and his nephew are coming today. What if questions are asked?"

He was on his feet and walking toward her before she had even said half of it. "Don't worry. I told them you were running errands for me."

She sagged onto the bed in relief.

"Besides, Pliny's nephew arrived early this morning. His uncle is arriving in the later afternoon."

"He's already here?" The panic relit.

"They will be a while. He's gone to see the vineyards."

She sighed again. "Are you good friends with him?"

"Not so much as my mother is with Pliny the Elder. Oh, young Gaius has great potential; already a respected lawyer and a fine poet. Nothing to get too excited about, though."

"Not a fighter, is he?" Flavia asked a little more sarcastically than she ought to have.

Valerus maintained his smile and opened his hand for her to take it. "Come with me," he said. "I have something to show you."

He led her out into the peristyle where the dogs greeted him enthusiastically. For the first time Flavia saw Valerus greet them in the same manner she previously had; he got down on his knees and rubbed them down kindly and smiled up when Luci approached them.

"How's your little helper?" he asked her.

She simply nodded. Valerus got up again and Flavia glanced over his shoulder. There was somebody else helping her, tidying the garden from last night's wind: a boy with dark skin. Valerus could not help but smile as Flavia went forward with her mouth open. On her approach, the boy turned to her, nodded respectfully, and returned to his duty to pick up fallen leaves.

Flavia could not believe it; it was the boy she had seen in the slave's cart the previous day. "What? How?" She shook her head.

Valerus came up behind her and laid his hands on her shoulders. "I bought him. I went out this morning."

She looked at the man. "You bought him?" Her eyes were becoming glassy with tears. "Why?"

"This household treats our slaves well in comparison to others, wouldn't you agree? My father is going to have him sent to work as a fisherman with the others."

She started to cry, a reaction he had not expected. He took and held her gently, aware that there was another slave present.

"What about the boar?" she asked him suddenly.

"What?"

She looked up at him. "It was a wonderful gesture to have bought the boy, but what about the wild boar?"

There was a sarcastic laugh on the man's breath as he shook his head. "What am I going to do with a wild boar, Flavia?"

"Take it back to its home."

He frowned. "Didn't wild boars kill your mother?"

"Not that one, and even if it was, it can't be blamed. It's just an animal, but it was taken from its home. What chance does it have? Did you see the look in its eyes? The fear?"

Valerus had not thought of it like that at all. He had seen the fear in the boy's eyes—and in the people. Flavia had made him feel what it was like to be a slave on the market. But they were just, well, animals—beasts brought in for sport, or occasionally when there was a gladiator shortage.

Did you see the fear in its eyes?

He shook his head. "No," he said, "I don't think I did."

Flavia looked back at the boy, pleased and grateful at Valerus's kind gesture, but then also upset that the wild boar had no choice to its life; it was going to die. Perhaps its fate was first to kill before it was killed itself by some armed fighter.

"I didn't think you were on good terms with wild boar," Valerus said honestly.

She did not look back at him when she spoke. "Why not? How

can I blame the boars for what happened to my mother? I have seen how they tease, taunt, and hurt the animal before they set it loose, to get it angry and aggressive. How then can I blame it? It's not the boar that kills; it is men that coax it to kill." Now she looked at him, smiling for the first time, but sadly. "What good will it do to hate the boar? God never meant boars to be put in an arena surrounded by a cheering mob. There is a reason God planted them in the woods and made them fearful of men."

The frown on Valerus's face was very distinct now. He took her by the arm. "Come with me," he said, "I think we ought to talk more privately."

⁂

They returned to his room together and Flavia noticed the look of her hair in the polished metal near Valerus's bed. She gasped. It was not that she was embarrassed by her looks, but a dancing girl was expected to be seen somewhat differently, and as a slave she had to keep to the master's expectation.

Not that Valerus minded. He shut the door after him and sighed. "Flavia?"

"What?" She desperately tried to tie her hair back with copper clips.

"What exactly do you believe regarding gods and the afterlife?"

The question caught her completely by surprise. She froze what she was doing, staring at her reflection and feeling the fear boiling in the pit of her stomach. Slowly, nearly fearfully, she looked at him over her shoulder. "What?" Her voice trembled.

"This must be the third time you refer to God instead of the gods. I'm no philosopher, nor do I study much in the lines of religions of the world, but as far as I know, only the Jews are monotheistic, worshiping one individual God rather than a collection thereof."

She looked back at her reflection, desperately thinking of what she could say in response. She knew that most Romans were not in favor of the things Melani had taught her, and again her strict warning repeated itself in her mind. She remembered the gruesome stories of what happened to believers such as her under the rule of Nero.

Valerus began to walk toward her, his hands clasped behind his back. Flavia listened to his approach, feeling panic replace the fear.

"I think that in these regions there is only one culture that worships a single God." He put his hand on her shoulder and gently turned her to face him. He saw the fear in her eyes as he had in the slave the previous day. "Christian?" he whispered.

Flavia cringed under the sound of his voice, but she said nothing. Valerus let out a long sigh and turned from her. "You are a Christian, then." He shook his head. "You were the ones who tried to burn Rome to the ground fifteen years ago."

"We would never do something like that!" Flavia snapped. Her voice was so forceful that he spun around to her. For a second she hesitated before continuing. "The teaching of Christ was to love, forgive, and treat others as we want ourselves treated. Why would we ever want to burn a city and kill thousands of people?"

"I was nearly killed in that fire as a boy."

There was a brief silence before she said, "We had nothing to do with it! Nero was only looking for something to accuse us with!"

Valerus was rubbing his eyes vigorously, as if trying to decide how to deal with the matter that had suddenly sprung at him.

It was not that Christianity was sacrilegious and needed severe condemning, but there was a lot of tension about the new growing faith and in many regions interrogations and executions had taken place. Some towns were known to harbor more than a hundred Christians, and these were in the process of being invaded by soldiers as well as Roman priests in the emperor's effort to gain control of the situation.

One man, one God.

"You do not approve of what I believe, do you?" Flavia asked.

He turned to her again. "It's just one man ..."

"Then why are you so threatened?"

"Threatened?" His voice rose for an instant but he gained control of himself before he continued. "It's just somewhat of a ..."

"Disappointment?"

"A surprise." He took her hand. "I have never thought of meeting a Christian here."

"A Christian slave for that matter. It's been difficult concealing it at times, yes, but I felt that if I lived by the foundations of what He taught, I did not need to do anything else."

To her complete surprise and astonishment, he smiled. "That explains your love for animals; for your fellow humans—slave or master. That's why you have held out, so desperately, to remain a virgin."

She tried to read his expression but could not. What he said along with the look on his face did not match with what she thought his reaction would be. It appeared as if he was actually accepting it.

"It's what makes you who you are, Flavia."

She blinked at him. "What? You're not going to give me away? Sell me to the world of entertainment?"

"Why would I do that?" He shook his head and laughed shortly. "I have never wanted to be with anyone more than I want to be with you. I am not going to let the fact that you believe in one man—one God—stand in the way of how I feel."

Her mouth was gaping open, suddenly feeling as if all the air had been sucked out of the room. She suddenly felt complete, having told him the greatest of her secrets. When she finally managed to utter a sound, it came out as a hoarse whisper. "How do you feel?"

The smile he gave her then was one she had never seen before. He took her face gently in his hands. "I love you," he said, and then he kissed her. He could taste the salt of her tears but could not pull away to give her her moment to speak. He loved her and he had admitted it to her as well as to himself. There was nothing left to hide behind: no mask, no sword, and no religion. Just as Flavia, he had a strange sensation of being naked—completely exposed to that around him where anyone and everyone could see into the farthest reaches of his soul.

He had never felt more alive.

Flavia left the room first. Valerus waited for a few minutes before following, and when he stepped out he walked into his sister. She had her hair tied back in curls and the stola she wore dragged delicately behind her. Surprised, he stepped back and greeted her more formally than was usual. She shook her head when he tried to slip away and then called to him. Valerus stopped and looked back.

"And what were you doing in that room with a slave girl, big brother?" she asked him mockingly.

"What business is it of yours, Anneria?" He shook his head.

She approached him slowly and then grasped his arm. "Walk with me." She smiled sweetly and practically pulled him to follow. "I think there is something you ought to tell me."

He followed where she led him without a word. She took him past the atrium and walked up the ambulatory that surrounded the peristyle. "What's this about, Velli?" she asked him.

The man gave her a puzzled frown. "What?"

"You have been giving eyes to a slave, Valerus. Even mother is noticing."

"Father?"

She laughed. "I don't think he notices anything."

"Is this another subject for your gossip conversations?" he asked coldly.

"What do you take me for?"

"What I always have."

"Come now, Velli." She grasped his arm as he tried to walk away and admired the feel of his strength. "You have eyes for that dancing girl."

"I have eyes for many."

"This is very different. I can see the way you look at her, how you always ask for her to dance. She has spent the night … willingly."

Valerus shook his head. "Stop, Anneria!" he hissed. "It's none of your business."

Anneria grabbed him on his effort to escape. "Tell me …"

"Enough!" He jerked his arm free. "I would appreciate you not making any assumptions in front of the guests. Family reputation, you know?"

Chapter 15

Pliny the Elder arrived when the day was drawing to sunset, carried by his servants as he read from some scrolls. Marcus was in the kitchen with the three dancing girls, Ursalus having arrived earlier that day from Lucius, along with three male servants and the two cooks. Pedius had had a long talk with the night guard who was now passing the news on to the staff.

"Pedius wants to make a good impression!" he told them all. "No sloppiness! These are dear old friends and the master will not tolerate any slack this evening. Are the dogs on their chains?"

Galen nodded before Marcus gestured to Flavia, Ursalus, and Alia. "You three, the master wants the best; everything from your clothes to the dance and the eroticism. No master or guest will be left unsatisfied tonight." He then turned to the cooks. "You have gotten the menu for this evening's cocktails and meals. All wines will be the best vintages from the cellar! As for the servers …" He looked at the three men. "Neither glass nor any plate left empty. Tonight you will be serving emperors."

As he continued his extensive command to the cooks, Flavia, Alia, and Ursalus made their way back to their rooms. "The best," they had been told. Flavia would have to get out all her bangles, the large gold-plated earrings as well as the leather ankle bands. Once in the room, she first changed into her thin short top and her skirt. Then she went to the metal disc she used as a mirror and began to do her hair.

She wanted to look her best, and it was not for the guests. She kept thinking of Valerus and wondered what he would think if he saw her at her best. Dancing, since then, had meaning, and she enjoyed it.

She leaned over her knees and brushed her hair over her head, tightening it before clipping it with silver studs. She felt it gently before coming up again, satisfied by her reflection.

Behind her, Alia was in the process of making a far more elaborate hairstyle by braiding it into a pattern that softly framed the top of her head. She was wearing her dance outfit of red top and skirt with an orange veil. Ursalus wore yellow with a white veil and Flavia, as was her usual preference, wore a pale green with a darker green veil. She straightened her top in the mirror while listening to the woman cursing behind her in her struggle to clip her hair into place.

Flavia applied her makeup with great care, gently lining her eyes with charcoal and then adding only a dash of saffron and chalk powder to the corner of her eyes and lips.

She liked that; she smiled at her reflection and looked back at Alia, who appeared to have finally gotten her hair sorted, but she was still fiddling with some loose strands.

As Flavia began to dress herself in jewelry, Alia spoke from behind her. "No guest is left unsatisfied tonight," she told her as if quoting. "You do realize what that means?"

"Of course I do. I have been dancing as long as you have."

"And yet you are still a virgin."

Flavia said nothing to this. There were a hundred things she could have told the woman; everything from her dislike to men's view of pleasure to how little respect she had for people like Alia. She kept her mind to herself though and did not say a word of it.

"Valerus is very patient with you," Alia continued. Flavia froze when she heard the man's name. "You do know that it won't last, not after tonight."

Flavia sighed and looked at her reflection. "What are you saying, Alia?"

"Well," the woman said with a shrug, "he is going to demand things from you tonight. Wine and eroticism do things to a man. He will command and you will have to obey."

"He would not do that," Flavia said, though there was a hint of uncertainty in her voice.

"Flavia," Alia said as she walked up to her, suddenly concerned. "You have seen what wine does to a man. You can say whatever you like about Valerus, but he is still a man—a very fine man." Her eyes suddenly went dreamy. "You ought to treat yourself to seeing him in the nude. What a man …"

Flavia rolled her eyes. "Where are you going with this?" She could not stand the memory that Alia had once pleased Valerus in such ways.

"He's just a man." She shrugged. "Like all the others. They have wine, they become intoxicated, and they want to be pleased. And that is what we do, Flavia. We tease and give them that. Valerus fancies you, thus he will not turn a blind eye. He will command, and unless you want to be sold off cheap, you had better obey."

Flavia stared at herself as Alia went back to work. She thought about what the woman had said. Flavia had seen and experienced what the effect of wine had on those people she performed for. Most men became innocently jolly, fondling any woman—or even occasionally other men—when they had been intoxicated. Most women had been no better. But there had been the occasional violent outbursts, especially on her refusal to recline with them. She had been flogged once for rejecting a guest's merger attempt.

She looked at her hair and then her makeup and outfit. Suddenly she felt it was too much. Perhaps Alia had a point. Valerus may very well intoxicate himself, and there was no telling what he would do or how he would behave in front of her and the other guests. Most decent and higher class families were well mannered when it came to celebrations, parties, and orgies, but after the wine most became like all the others.

Making sure Alia did not see it, Flavia took a cloth and carefully brushed some of the makeup off her face. Then she stopped and thought over her actions.

What was she doing? A little makeup was not going to make any difference. If the family was going to drink, she would rather have Valerus make the motion than any other.

She tossed the cloth to the ground and slipped on her bracelets. As she fastened the leather bands around her ankles, she noticed the shell pendant Valerus had given to her lying on the table. She took that too and slipped it around her neck.

⁂

The gathering was lively and happy; the outside garden made a wonderful place to dance and perform, especially in comparison to her previous venues. The night was cool with a breeze blowing in from the mountain, carrying the light scent of earth. Braziers had been lit along the walls and by the pillars while the tables that had been brought out carried lamps of all sizes. Music, lyres, flute, and small drums were keeping the atmosphere lively.

As before, the dancing girls were performing on the flagstones by the fountain with the view opening to the ocean. Flavia looked at the gathered crowd; the whole family was present. Valerus's sister was in conversation with Gaius the younger. She could not see his face in the shadow, but he was of average height with dark hair against the night sky. His uncle was with the older family members, Valerus included.

Luci met with Flavia when she took a moment to catch her breath after a dance. She appeared to be upset.

"No luck?" Flavia asked as she took a short drink of water.

Luci shook her head. "None. At least he recognized me."

"That's good. It's a start."

Luci appeared downcast.

"Hey," she said as she gently took the young woman by the shoulder, "it's only been the first day. Besides, he is reacquainting with old friends. He will have to notice you in the days to come."

She smiled. "You really think so?"

"He'll be here for a few weeks. You can be sure of it."

Alia sat down beside her suddenly. "Your turn," she panted. "I need a short rest."

Wine was going around; Flavia saw how the servants were struggling to keep up with the filling of glasses. She was keeping her eye on Valerus, who was in the process of emptying his third glass.

And he had hardly looked her way! This was upsetting. When she danced, he would look up, perhaps smile at her before turning back to the conversation. This was bothering her to a point where she no longer wanted to dance. It suddenly felt empty again.

When the meal was served and the family and guests were reclined to receive it, Flavia got her first good look of Gaius. Average height, as she had estimated earlier, but not as darkly featured as she had thought. His hair was brown while his eyes could nearly pass for gray. He was not, to Flavia's standards, very attractive. He was rather thinly built for a man of his age.

Her stare went automatically to Valerus. Now that was a fine build, she had to admit. He had worked hard on his body to match the skills needed in the arena and now he had every reason to be proud of it. For an instant she thought of what Alia had said about seeing him without any coverings—to see him fully. *Of the gods?* Perhaps she was right.

Pliny the Elder was stout, bearded, and strongly built. He was also very modest and consumed wine slowly and with great care and dignity. Flavia could not see any trouble coming from him.

Valerus was staring at her when her thoughts reeled away and she returned to reality. The dance she was performing alongside Ursalus was coming through automatic; her eyes focused on the man watching her. The others were consumed in food and conversation, but Valerus stared without a smile.

Ursalus suddenly chose the moment to move among the guests, throwing her veil across Pliny's face before drawing it up again. The old man smiled, suddenly very focused on her. Flavia cursed internally, knowing that it was now expected of her as well. Then she smiled and went up to Valerus. Teasingly, she threw her veil around his neck and leaned over him. There was a light smell of wine on his breath. He made no reaction except for smiling. It was a smile, though, that said a dozen things. It said, *I want you.* It also pleaded: *Don't tease me like this. You don't know what you're doing.*

Flavia heard it all in that single moment and withdrew. For a second she forgot the dance before remembering herself and continued, rejoining Ursalus in her place by the fountain. Valerus had noticed her broken step and frowned her way.

Alia stepped up to relieve her, and she had her top off. She smiled at Flavia who simply threw her a look in return as she took a short drink.

Valerus was automatically and momentarily focused on Alia as she began her dancing, but his eyes shot around her to the movement behind. He frowned. Flavia was slipping away into the shadow cast by the fountain. Why?

He shifted his position and saw her sneak along the ambulatory wall, throw a quick glance his way, and disappear into the villa.

Valerus was dumbstruck, wondering why she chose to leave the performance. He looked at his father, who did not appear to notice.

Gaius had; the young man was looking from where Flavia had disappeared to Valerus.

The young man shook his head. He had his own thoughts and fantasies as to what this could mean, but he was well aware of the wine he had indulged in as well as the fact that Alia was coming forth with her breasts exposed.

Valerus tried to distract himself by reaching for the apple flatbread when a flicker caught his eye. Turning his head slightly, he noticed that someone had lit a lamp in his room. He spun back to the food in front of him, catching his breath sharply. He tried to think of what else this could mean other than the obvious. Flavia was alone up in his room and she *wanted* him to know.

His thoughts were so muddled that he could not think straight. He looked at those around him, but they were too preoccupied with the meal and talk to notice anything he had seen … all but young Gaius. He was smiling from his place and raised his glass in his direction. Then above the din, the young man said to him, "What are you waiting for?"

It was an automatic reaction that owed nothing to thought. He pushed himself up from his place and left, brushing past Alia without so much as a glance. His walk was urgent but dreamlike; he had no mental thought between the garden and to when he opened the door of his room.

Flavia was sitting on the bed, clasping her veil in her lap—a little nervously, he noticed.

He shut the door after him and leaned against it, trying to get a grip on himself. The woman on the bed simply smiled and then got to her feet without a word. Valerus held his breath when Flavia undid her top and slowly let it run down to her waist, revealing her rounded breasts. She stopped there like an unspoken plea for him to participate.

She appears so shy, he thought. She was no doubt ready for the moment as she was initiating, but he could see she was a little anxious. This was all new to her and, strangely he had to admit, new to him as well.

Valerus walked up to her slowly, fighting himself in every part not to grab her and throw her down. With the other women it had always been so fast, pleasurable, and wild. He enjoyed it that way. Now suddenly, in this room alone with Flavia, he wanted time to slow down a little. He did not want to rush it. He wanted to feel her and experience the very core of his pleasure with her; he was becoming conscious that it was not so much about him anymore. For the first time he was aware that he was not alone in the room, that there was someone else who he wanted to please just as much as he wanted himself pleased.

He stood in front of her, trembling slightly in his effort to restrain himself. He kept his eyes fixed on her for as long as he possibly could before they lowered to her exposed breasts. They were smaller than what he had previously liked, but suddenly perfect.

He reached up, very slowly, and cupped them in his hands. He let out a sigh. He had dreamed of this moment, but even his fantasies did not compare. He wished he had been more prepared for it.

Flavia had her eyes closed, biting her lower lip as if in complete awe. Their foreheads came together. Flavia swallowed.

"I've never wanted anyone more," he whispered.

He kissed her, slowly and gently, wanting to show to her that he could control himself. She pushed the toga off his shoulders, let her hands in under his tunic, and pulled it up to touch his bare chest. There was a tickle of short chest hair and it was curiosity to want to see what lay beneath his garments that had her continue.

He helped her remove his tunic, dropping it to the floor as he stepped out of his sandals. Then Valerus had that same feeling as before, as if he was completely exposed and naked for the first time in his life, where anyone could look at him and see everything that lingered in his soul. Yet he was comfortable in Flavia's presence. He wanted her to see him fully and completely.

Flavia circled him as if still partaking in the dance, running her hands across his torso and then his back, feeling every part of him, every muscle and every texture of his skin. When she came around in front again, she kissed his chest. He had short hair and very little of it. It felt as if he had removed the hair at some stage, probably when he was still a fighter. Just like the dancers, gladiators too had an image to maintain.

She raised her eyes to look at him. His posture as well as the hunger in his eyes had not changed at all. His breathing was heavy, as if he could not get enough air into him.

She sunk down onto the bed and pulled him after her. He obeyed, suddenly a slave to her every demand. She kissed him. "Would you like me to …" she said, but he cut her off.

"Do whatever you want," he gasped.

She kissed him again. Nothing in her life had ever felt so real, so alive and so very right. There was no twist of guilt as he pushed her back into the pillows. He laid half his weight over her and cupped a breast, shutting his eyes for a few seconds to drink in the moment. Her skin was slightly pale while his was dark like a perfect tan. It made a beautiful contrast when they came together. The green pendant he had bought for her was well set between her breasts. He took it between his fingers and rubbed the smooth shell and then looked at her.

"Did your deity ever experience this … this complete peace?" he asked her.

Slowly she nodded, unable to believe otherwise. It was a wondrous moment, which she never wanted to have end. She loved this man; she would not have come this far with someone whom she did not.

He pulled her top out from under her, undoing the last of the knot and tossing it aside. Her short skirt he left for now, allowing

Flavia to get completely comfortable with him. He simply smiled and planted a few gentle kisses on her cheeks and then her mouth as his hand moved down her hip and then her thigh. He felt her tense slightly when moving inward.

Flavia was completely focused on the movement of his hand, feeling every other part of her slip away. When his hand came to her inner thigh, there was a brief shiver which pulsated. Then he reached her soft mound of pubic hair. At this moment she took him around the neck and pulled him down to her. She kissed him, running her hands down his back and feeling the muscular curves of his body. She was aware of how much she wanted him; there was no man—no other person—who she momentarily thought of. It was Valerus—only him. She felt urges she had never experienced to this intensity before.

Valerus rolled over, undid his *subligaria*, pulled the underwear out from under him, and turned back to her. Her gaze first went down before back at him. He saw the fear spark in her eyes and decided to run the moment a bit longer to get her comfortable again. Her eyes went down again and her gut twisted. This was not going to work! How could it? How would he fit into her?

He kissed her eyes and then her neck, taking his time to reach her navel with his tongue. Carefully and slowly he undid the knot of her skirt and unwrapped it. Then he worked his way up again, kissing her breast and throat before coming to her mouth again.

She shivered under his touch; he sat up a bit and ran his hands in circles around her breasts until her eyes shut again and she dug her head in the pillows.

He was frightfully aware that he had never done this; he had never really taken the time to please a woman. It had always been about his pleasure and his release rather than that of his partner. He was not entirely sure where to go from here or for how long.

Flavia pulled him to her. He sighed softly as he gently rolled over on top of her, supporting his weight on an elbow. His other hand ran down again to her thigh and then back to cup her pubic hair.

"Valerus," Flavia began, her voice trembling.

"I won't do a thing if you don't want me to," he said honestly.

She looked at him a little bewildered. "I want you to do it," she said after a moment.

Without a word he brought up his weight again and entered her, carefully. He saw her hold her breath and proceeded slowly. He had seen from experience that the first time had hurt other women. Despite them saying it hadn't, he had seen it in their eyes. With Flavia, he did not want to hurt her, but he was uncertain if that was at all possible. At least he knew that she would not lie to him.

He reached a shallow depth where he felt a barrier. For a second he looked at her, and, when she smiled at him, he kissed her gently before breaking through.

She gasped.

He stopped; every muscle tensed. He regarded her expression and then asked, slowly and deliberately, "Do you want me to stop?"

She considered it, but only for a second before nodding gingerly. It was painful, like a tearing sensation in her loins. She felt him back off and exit her. She saw the tortured look in his expression—his urge to finish what had started—but she was not going to doubt what she was feeling. It was painful and she knew she would not be in the moment with the pain present.

He rolled over and lay beside her, his breathing still heavy in an effort to calm himself from the experience. Flavia, feeling a little guilty to have stopped what she first began, asked. "You all right?"

Valerus chuckled and moistened his lips. Finally he looked her way and nodded. "I will be."

She gave him an apologetic smile.

"The most amazing experience in my life," he announced as if to show that he was not disappointed or upset. "Don't worry about me. I don't want it to be uncomfortable for you."

She ran an imaginary circle on his torso, allowing herself to admire his body.

"You *do* have a magnificent body."

Now he laughed. "If it means anything," he told her, "so do you." He pulled her veil out from under her and gently brushed her cheeks with it. "I prefer you without makeup, though."

Chapter 16

June 11

They slept together that night as the gathering went on below them, lulled asleep by the music of lyres and flute. When the dawn reached, it was Valerus's turn to wake up alone. Flavia had slipped out only a short while earlier as her place in the bed was still warmed by her body.

He rolled over with a sigh and rubbed his eyes. What a night! Despite the fact that he had not come to relieve his urges with her, no evening had ever been more memorable. It had to be love; how else could he explain the fact that just having been with her the way he had surpassed the pleasure he felt in orgasm a dozen times over?

He lay with his hands behind his head, staring up at the ceiling and enjoying the peaceful morning for a while, remembering the smallest details of the previous night.

Finally he got up and got dressed, picking his clothes up off the floor where they had been left last night. He pulled on a fresh tunic, barely reaching his knees, and draped it with a toga before making for the door. Flavia was bound to be helping with the cleaning up of last night's banquet.

There was a commotion in the corridor. It sounded to be coming from a man, definitely his father. His voice echoed across the hallway, making the words difficult to understand.

He followed it and became increasingly aware that it was coming from the directions of the slaves' quarters.

A frightful image met him when he turned the corner. Flavia was standing with her hands folded in front of her. She had had time to change from her dancing outfit to her plain working tunica, and in front of her was Pedius, red in the face and scolding her harshly. Flavia's gaze was set to the master's sandals, holding back all the things she wanted to say to him.

"What's going on?" Valerus asked as he went up to the two of them. Flavia's face brightened slightly from anguish to relief on seeing him while Pedius became crimson.

"You!" Pedius pointed a finger at him. "Did you command this woman to your room last night?"

Valerus saw Flavia's pleading stare and nodded. He could not, after all, tell his father that it was in fact Flavia who invited *him*. Obviously it was going to get her in even more trouble than she already was.

"Is this your slave, son?" he asked angrily.

Valerus had to go against everything he felt and knew to be right and answer simply, "No."

"Damn right! I am her master and what I say is law! She left halfway through the banquet, leaving the other dancers terribly lonely. Even Pliny commented!"

Valerus swallowed. "Sorry, Father. She was only obeying my command."

"Never again!" Pedius bellowed, stamping a foot on the ground like a spoilt child. "Do you understand me? Never again!" He turned to Flavia. "I am your master! You will do as *I* say. He …" he pointed to Valerus, "he is my son. My command stands above his. Understand?"

Flavia nodded without looking up at him.

"Look at me!" he shouted. She obeyed. "Do you understand me?"

"Yes, master," she said loudly as she nodded.

"Good." He turned to Valerus. "And you … you and I need to have a serious talk as to where you stand in this household."

"Of course, Father." He caught Flavia's gaze for a second before following him.

The morning was not meant to be like this, not after the night they had shared. It was so contradictive that both of them felt as if one of the two experiences had been nothing but a dream.

It could not have been the experience of last night; that had been too real, too tangible, and too wonderful to even consider having been anything less.

⁂

Valerus entered the atrium after his father. For a while he watched his father pace back and forth, letting him simmer until the raw rage had died away. Finally the old man looked at his son; his eyes narrowed. "You forget your place here, Valerus," he said much more calmly than before.

"I have overstepped my stay here, I believe."

"You are my son," Pedius said to him. "Your presence here is something to be grateful for. Your mother certainly is. Seven years of fighting, four being in far-away theaters, has made her grow old."

The young man chuckled. "It is good to know that mother takes my injury as a blessing," he said bitterly.

"She does. I am sorry, Valerus, but she really does. It brought you home alive."

"But now I am a cripple and of no use."

"Don't say that," Pedius said quickly. "You can ride very well and walk."

"But not fight, run, or put honor on your name. For this reason I was forced to give up my insula as well as my life in Rome."

"I am not disappointed or shamed by you." Pedius went right up to him. "You are my son, my flesh and blood. I do not blame you or feel any less for you. You will just have to readjust to a life you appeared to have forgotten how to live."

It was true; he had forgotten how to live it. He had been an independent man and a bloodthirsty fighter for nearly seven years. It was a shock to have to return to the closed atrium, the rules, and, worst of all, the broken dreams.

"You need to find a new profession," Pedius continued. "Something you have an interest and passion for."

The young man smiled when he automatically thought of Flavia. He could not stop himself. She was there, plaguing his mind with images from last night, maybe even more than he had actually seen and experienced with her.

"I heard that Lucius is doing well in theater." Pedius smiled.

Flavia was in the library, dusting the shelves and cleaning the master's table. Every now and again she would read from one of the scrolls as she lined them on their shelves or in their cases. Some were Greek text while others were in Latin. Flavia had been tutored by three of her previous masters, including the dancing academy, in the languages of Latin, Greek, and Hispanian. Gaulish she had picked up during her stay in Arelate, but she could not read it.

Reading did not present much chance to a dancing girl, but Flavia tried her best to slip it in when she could, at least to keep her in practice.

She thought of the incident earlier and hoped that Valerus had not gotten a scolding because of her. Then again, Valerus was a man and she was only a slave. Of course most of the blame would be put on her; she had, after all, disobeyed the master.

There was still a slight pain, but the night had well been worth it. Despite the fact that it had hurt, it was not a pain she had ever endured in her life; this one she actually felt good about. It did not leave a guilty feeling or a nagging sensation that she had just lost something she could never have again. Instead she felt as though she had gained something very special, which could never be lost.

She heard Valerus come into the library; she could tell it was him by the pace he walked. He came up behind her and wrapped his arm around her stomach, burying his face in her neck. "I didn't mean to get you into trouble," he whispered and kissed her.

Flavia reached up and touched his cheek, feeling the faint stubble of a beard. She looked at him and smiled. "It was worth it."

Valerus cradled his face in her neck and she was surprised at how whole she felt. For the moment she was with him and that was the only thing that mattered. The troubles of earlier she would face another time.

"Valerus?" Flavia whispered.

"Ah?" He shifted back a bit to kiss her shoulder.

"What will we do once all this is resolved?"

He grinned. "Aren't we doing it right now?" He ran his tongue lightly across her ear.

Flavia felt, for a second, a little unsettled. She wanted to ask the things that sat on the edge of her thoughts but then it nearly felt as if they were being watched.

There were footsteps, and when Valerus looked around he saw Anneria looking at them around the corner. The anger that boiled from him, drowning his expression, made her flee. Valerus went after her, not once looking back at Flavia who he left behind.

His sister was so nosey and he knew that word would be all over Herculaneum after one night. He caught up with her in the atrium, grabbing her by the arm and pulling her to him. She was smiling mischievously, pleased that she had caught him-red handed in what he had tried to deny the day before.

"What are you doing?" he demanded to know angrily.

"You can't deny it now!" She laughed. "I saw it with my own eyes!"

"What stops me from disciplining you like I would a slave?"

Anneria pulled a sarcastic face. "I'm your *sister*."

This only enraged him even more. "What's the matter with you?"

A knock echoed through the house and that moment the young man appeared to remember something. He let her go.

"Lucius," he said as if to himself before the slave Galen appeared behind him.

"Master Lucius is here to see you, Master Valerus," Galen told him respectfully.

"I forgot I was meeting him this morning."

"What a shame." Anneria shook her head. "The dancing girl will be so lonely."

"Will you shut up?" Valerus spat.

She was already making her way to the garden.

Flavia listened to the confrontation; sound traveled far in the villa. She then heard the brief voice of Lucius before that too disappeared. Her memory of Lucius dwindled. She had not seen him for many days now and there was an apprehension in seeing him again. She knew he had feelings for her and she wondered how he would take the news if Valerus told him. Had he already told him? Valerus had not said anything to her. Maybe that was why she saw so little of Lucius now; maybe he felt awkward to be around the two of them together.

She finished her duties in the library and then left to go to the kitchen to see if Helen needed any help. On her way, she saw

Gaius walking the ambulatory along the peristyle, nose buried in a document. He was barefoot and in nothing more than a long tunic. Yet he had definitely been out; his feet were covered in beach sand while his hair had been tangled by the breeze.

"Morning, Master Gaius." She greeted him.

He merely smiled, stopped, and studied her walk with amused interest. She stopped as well when noticing this and regarded him carefully.

"How was it last night?" he asked suddenly. He was grinning.

"What?" Flavia tried to appear baffled by his question.

"Last night. You called Valerus up to the bedroom." He looked her up and down. "Your walk is a little awkward. First time?"

Flavia could not believe it. How could a man seven years younger than Valerus be so observant and so knowledgeable of the earlier events? It was as if he was looking at the two of them through a perfectly clear glass, knowing everything that had happened and how.

Flavia would have expected to feel overstepped and uncomfortable, but Gaius asked it with such innocence that it was nearly impossible to feel any of those things. For this reason, Flavia chuckled and brushed the hair from her face. "Yes, Master Gaius. It was."

"I am pleased Valerus has found someone so special. Any future plans?"

"Not as yet."

"Pity." His smile appeared to belong to a small boy. "I will watch the two of you with great interest." Then he turned and walked away.

Flavia watched him for a while, still intrigued by his observation and skill in awareness. Luci was right when she said he was an amazing person; he really was. Flavia was taken by the young man's smile and words so well that his appearance changed from average to very attractive. It was truly amazing how a character influenced that.

The kitchen was deserted when she got there, but the clean dishes and cutlery were piled along the stone basin. She took her time to pack it all way, drying the ones that were damp, before going to see if there was anything left to be cleaned or picked up in the garden.

That too was empty, except that Gaius was reclined in one of the couches of last night. He had a few scrolls beside him and was reading with interest and a sense of peace.

Flavia went up to him, still intrigued and impressed by this man.

He looked up and smiled on her approach. "Do you have any knowledge in the art of poetry, Flavia?" he asked her suddenly.

Flavia shook her head and was about to settle on the grass when she remembered herself and asked, "Can I get the master anything?"

"No, but please," he said as he opened his hand, "have a seat."

She settled on the grass beside the couch. Now, for the first time, she noticed an inkwell with a reed pen beside him. She was impressed. "You are a poet, Master Gaius."

"Only as a hobby."

"That's right. You are studying law."

"No, I *am* a lawyer. A lawyer does not study law. Lawyers learn how to speak."

"That explains your success in poetry. Is this all your work?"

"Most of it. I am working on a little something for a girl I know."

"Luci?" The name slipped from her mouth faster than she could have controlled it.

Gaius frowned. "Luci?"

Flavia was genuinely surprised by this. For someone who had noticed the relationship between Valerus and her without any apparent effort, it was difficult to believe that he had not noticed Luci's liking to him.

"Luci," she told him, "the girl who helps with the cooking and looks after the children."

"Oh, yes, of course! We first met two years ago. She told you her name was Luci?"

"It isn't?"

"Lucinda. Beautiful name. I wrote a verse regarding it." He fumbled through some papers and extracted one. "So a midnight sun wanes in the ocean as a mirror of her heavens," he read. "So does the name be dark in depth but a mirror to her outer havens."

Flavia smiled and nodded. "That is beautiful. Have you read it to her yet?"

"Do you think she would be interested?"

"Oh, yes. She does not stop talking about you. Have you not noticed her? She's been trying to catch your eye ever since you arrived."

"I don't believe I have." He neatly stacked his papers. "I've been too focused on you and Valerus. Talk about an odd couple."

"Why so odd?"

"I never saw Valerus as the type of man to accept a slave as his love. It just comes to show how the gods play games with the lives of men."

She smiled at this.

He suddenly looked very serious. He asked her then, in a steady tone, "Do you love him?"

She hardly had to think about it, and nodded.

"Don't forget to say it. There is nothing more painful as to tell someone you love them and not having it said back."

⁂

Valerus sat alone on the marble ledge, feeling the sweat run off him. It had been two days since he had last visited the baths and the heat gave him time to think. Lucius was a little way off, nearer to the steam bath itself, while he sat alone, separated from the people in his own world.

The previous night felt hazy, like a vivid dream; he could still feel the excitement and clearly see Flavia in the nude, ready to receive him. And it seemed too good to be true. What had he done to deserve something like this? He had killed man and beast with the simple goal of touching glory, and even that had been a waste of time, energy, and hope. Why had he killed so much? The young man began to question the very core of his lifestyle and passion.

He thought of what Flavia had said to him regarding the wild boar and then about him going against what he believed when killing a defeated gladiator. What right did he—Valerus—have to a woman like Flavia? In a completely unselfish way, he knew that he had her, he loved her, and there would be no more trying, convincing, or fear on her part. But it felt so incomplete. He wondered what he had missed. They had confessed to each other how they felt. They had kissed and embraced. They had made love … to a point. What was missing? Guilt on his part that perhaps he did not deserve her?

He had never been in love before. Valerus knew now, with all the women he had had, that it had always been about sex—the pleasure and the release. He had never felt two ways about never seeing the woman again after the night. In Rome he had had many orgies and many women at once. Yet, with Flavia, he wanted no one; no onlookers, no more women, and not a single thing to come between the two of them that would rush the moment. Last night made him aware of something, and that was that he was in love with Flavia. He wanted no other.

Valerus shook his head. *It's not fair*, he thought. She should not have been the one to get in trouble over last night. It was not her decision, after all.

No, it had been her decision. She had left and lit the lamp in his room, knowing full well that he would see it from the peristyle. It had been she who had initiated last night's encounter.

There was a nearby hiss and more steam rose into the air. He looked up and noticed Lucius's figure coming toward him slowly. The young man sat down a short distance from him, lying his towel down on one side.

"Lucius," Valerus's stare kept straight ahead as he spoke. His voice was muffled like a whisper; in the heat it was too much effort to speak any louder. "Have you ever been in love? Truly, madly, and completely over your head?"

"I don't think to that extreme," he confessed in the same soft voice. "There were times I thought I was, but after one night it just died away for both of us."

"Ah."

Lucius regarded his friend for a while and then smiled weakly. "It's Flavia, is it?

Valerus sighed as the tension drained out of him. "How did you know?"

"I noticed it. You address her by name. You even asked her how she was doing. I thought Valerus Cascus does not get personal with slaves."

The young man laughed. "She's pleasing." He shrugged casually. "Strong mind of her own. Somewhat fascinating, really."

"Don't get personally involved, Valerus." This reaction came as a surprise to him. Lucius had seemed to accept that his companion had gotten close to one of the servants, but now suddenly he appeared to disapprove of it. Lucius was shaking his head. "Don't get personally involved with something you have no control over. She belongs to your father and he can do with her whatever he wants. You are working yourself into a corner of hurt."

Valerus said nothing and sat back, suddenly blatantly aware of what Lucius was saying. He was right, for one thing. Valerus had tried to have his way with Flavia before, something now he would not even consider. But his father still had every right to demand it of her. The thought made him cringe internally. His father had full authority over the property that was rightfully his.

He rubbed his chin thoughtfully as Lucius continued to speak, but his voice was mere background to the thoughts and realizations dawning. He had no control over Flavia's fate, none whatsoever, and if his father saw signs of her beatings, both recent and past, he might not tolerate the quality. Could Valerus afford a slave like Flavia? Did he have enough in his savings to make an offer that did not border on an insult? And he wanted her; he wanted to buy her and make her his property.

He frowned. No, he wanted to free her, not have her be anyone's property. It was her free spirit he wanted to maintain.

When he looked at Lucius again he felt opportunities and options filter through. "What can you tell me about the theater, Lucius? Does it pay well?"

Chapter 17

June 12

Flavia got up early, long before anyone else, and started getting dressed. She wanted to go see the repairer. It had been days since she had last been out to him and there had been a lot of food left over from the banquet that no one would miss.

She managed to slip out without Marcus spotting her and headed for the beach. The dim glow of dawn was on the east horizon like a hazy dot rising from behind the hills. She would have to be back before the glow changed from pale gray to bright yellow.

The beach was active in the early hours; slaves were launching their boats for their morning catch. Procimus was gone already when she came past the shipyard; so was the boat he had been working on.

She approached the small chamber and noticed a glow coming through the thin sheet that was being used as a doorway. Carefully she pulled it aside. Inside water was boiling over the small fire; the repairer was huddled beside it with a thin wool blanket wrapped around him. He smiled on Flavia's entry and waved her over.

She went to sit alongside him, unwrapping her bundle and extracting the vegetables and bits of bread. He nodded with great satisfaction when she removed some lamb. It had been well cooked and soft enough for him to chew with his bad teeth.

"How are you this morning?" she asked kindly.

Without a word he tapped the side of his jaw. Flavia looked at him compassionately when realizing what he was trying to say. "Are your teeth sore again?"

He nodded.

"I wish I knew what I could give you for the pain." She shook her head. "I don't know what can help that."

He waved a hand her way, letting her worry and helplessness pass like water. He turned to the food she had brought him. It was then that Flavia noticed the bruise above his right eye. She carefully ran her fingers across it. "What happened here?"

"Board hit me," he said, hardly moving his jaw as he did.

"Your master did this, didn't he?"

"Master 'on't come here."

"Well, someone on his behalf, no doubt." She reached for the cloth and carefully dipped a corner in the water. She tapped it on her cheek to test that it was not too hot before gently running it across the blackened skin. "Why did he strike you?"

"Not finished." He gestured to the boards behind him, which he was in the process of carving.

"How can he expect it with what he's been feeding you?" Flavia snapped angrily. "What people are these? They are not people! Where is their love, respect, and compassion? Don't they see you? Don't they understand you are a person as they are?" None of these questions expected any answers; Flavia was simply getting rid of everything that boiled inside her.

"Christ never wanted this!" she spat. "He tried to make people see! What good did he do? The world is still hateful! No one cares. I mean, just look at you! We are all born equal! *What gives them the right*?"

The repairer said nothing as she continued to spill out her anger and frustration while she dabbed his bruise. In the meantime he carefully stripped the lamb and tossed it into the pot along with most of the vegetables. But he listened to every word, aware that there was a small glow in his blackened world that he had never seen before.

Flavia didn't know how long she released her vexation verbally, or what exactly she said, but she was suddenly very aware that the glow of the sun had already touched the ocean. She was also feeling a little better. She sighed and looked at the man in front of her.

"I have to go. Sorry. It upsets me when people are treated like this." She absentmindedly stirred the stew and smiled. "I will try and be back in a few days. Things are very busy at the moment."

He gently grabbed her wrist as she got up. Flavia felt for the first time how hard his hand was from warts, callouses, and burns. "Tell me more of Him, you come?"

Flavia shook her head. "I'm sorry?"

"You come," his hand went to his jaw with a wince. "Tell me more? Christ?"

Flavia blinked, aware suddenly that she had mentioned the name to him. She was not meant to do that; Melani had strictly warned her not to. But then, what harm could it do? He was no more than a slave in a shipyard who obviously needed to hear of His teachings. She nodded. "I will tell you His story."

Flavia hurried back to the villa, following the beach as far as she could to avoid the morning traffic. Then she turned up the path toward the stables that would be—perhaps not the shortest—but the quickest route back.

And suddenly Valerus was there. She nearly slammed into him when she turned the corner of the stalls. He grabbed her as she tried to reel away and she laughed when he pulled her to him. He was smiling as he held her, unable to let her go. The surprise of running into her had been so pleasant.

"You frightened me!" She shook her head in relief.

"What are you doing out so early?"

"Enjoying a walk before the chores begin."

"You are lying to me." His smile turned into a grin. "Keep to the truth, Christian; it's what you're good at!"

She caught her breath. "I went to see a friend down by the docks."

"Oh, another man." It was clear that Valerus was in a playful mood and was going to say anything to keep it that way, perhaps even pull Flavia up with him. "You sneak off to see other men. Perhaps you are not as innocent as you announce." He pulled her to him.

"Valerus." She laughed, drawn into his mood, and took him on either side of his face. "I love you. I know I should have said it a long time ago, and I'm sorry if I held you in doubt, but I was just frightened ... with the Christianity and all. But I say it now: I love you! I have never loved anyone more."

"Oh, woman!" He took her into his arms in a tight, nearly desperate, embrace. The doubt had suddenly washed away and everything was pure and clear to him. "And I love you," he said to her softly, "more than anyone before you!"

She kissed him, holding him by the neck to pull him down to her. He took her by the waist, feeling the sudden excitement surge through him, and it was not only sexual. He suddenly felt complete. He kissed her, again and again, pushing her back until she was up against the wall.

He stopped to catch his breath and looked into her eyes. "By Jupiter, Flavia!" He breathed heavily. "What you do to me ..." He kissed her and picked her up, feeling her wrap her legs around his waist; it was more than he had imagined and hoped for.

He carried her into the nearest empty stall, smelling the fresh straw hang in the air. He laid her down gently with him over her, kissing her neck and ear while his hands found her hips.

She didn't say anything. It had been so spontaneous and sudden that there was nothing she could say. She definitely did not want to protest, because she knew she wanted him to take her, right there as she was. It was such a new feeling that she was desperate to explore it, and yet with Valerus it was as if she had known it her whole life. She raised her chin to give him access to kiss her throat, which he gladly obliged to.

"Valerus!"

"By Vulcan!" Valerus raised his head and hissed under his breath.

"Was that Alaine?" Flavia asked.

"I told her we'd be riding this morning!" He spat, obviously greatly disappointed to have arranged it.

"Are you here, Master Valerus?"

"I think it best she doesn't see you." Valerus got up and she followed. He kissed her and held her face in his hands. "Forgive me?" His breathing was still coming in short, sharp breaths.

So was hers. She kissed him back. "I will see you back at the villa later then."

Valerus glanced out the stall door. Alaine was nowhere in sight, but he could hear the clinging of tack. "I'll get Alaine out of the way. You can slip out then."

"It's probably for the best," she said as she fished straw out of her hair. "It's getting late and I have chores to run."

Flavia returned to the villa quickly. She was late and was worried it would be noticed.

On her approach she saw Marcus standing on the steps by the portico entrance. He was dressed in civvies and had a small bag slung over his shoulder. The moment he saw her he waved urgently for her to get out of view. At that moment Pedius appeared and stood by him. Flavia ducked out of sight, pulling in behind a small wall.

She tried to listen to the conversation, frightened that it was something regarding her. She heard something regarding Valerus and then about breakfast … then there was silence. She peered over the top and saw Marcus making his way toward her. Pedius was not to be seen.

"You really ought to be more careful," Marcus scolded kindly. "Do you know how much trouble we can both get into if he had seen you?"

"You did not see me leave this morning," she told him.

"Of course I did. But I was not going to make a scene. Now I expect you to get inside before they notice you're gone. The master is going to start having you watched, so watch your step. You ought to be grateful that you did not run into Valerus. He left early as well."

Flavia smiled at this. Then, being careful as to who was around, snuck back into the villa.

Valerus returned earlier than expected—far sooner than a good long ride could have been. He joined the family and guests for breakfast and tried the rest of the day to get some private time in Flavia's company. It never happened. The house bustled with the guests and even at night the dinner ran late.

June 15

For three days it continued like this until Valerus finally caught Flavia alone in the corridor around the garden, carrying clean folded sheets across her arms. He waited for her to return, and when she did, now free from her burden, he took her by the wrist and spun her around, pressing her up against a pillar. "It's difficult getting you alone these days," he whispered to her.

"It's so busy." She shook her head. "You've seen how we're struggling to keep up."

He placed his hands on the pillar just above her shoulders and leaned against her. Flavia bit her lip as he came in slowly and kissed her neck. "How about we finish what we started in the stall?" he asked in her ear.

"I have a lot of chores to complete," she said a little uncertainly.

"Is that so?" He did not move from his place.

The woman dimmed her head a little and then said, in a frail voice that was so unlike her, "Your father is keeping an eye on me."

Valerus frowned. "What?"

She looked at him. "Marcus told me that I am being watched, at least for the next week or so; to make sure I run my duties and that you do not interfere with my master's orders."

Automatically Valerus looked up and glanced around. There was no one in sight other than one of the dogs lying on the cool flagstones beside a pillar. The incoming breeze whispered through the trees, but that was it.

"Why didn't you tell me?"

"Your father has become very strict after the incident," she continued. "I really have to watch my step for a while, Valerus. Please understand."

He stepped back, letting his arms fall to his sides. "Of course." He nodded.

It was at this moment, as he watched Flavia hurry off to complete her duties, when he realized he would have to buy her. He wanted her so much, yet his father stood in the way. He had considered telling his father the situation, but chose against it. There was no knowing what his reaction would be. He may very well be lenient and give her to him without any regret, but then he was just as likely to sell her off as quickly as possible—a chance Valerus was not prepared to take. Also there was a risk of Pedius discovering her Christian faith. If that ever occurred, Valerus would not vouch for her life, nor was his father going to listen to any plea.

He wanted the woman, and not having her plagued him. She was so close—she was right there—but he could not have her the way he wanted. He made the decision that moment to visit Lucius, to talk business.

Chapter 18

June 16

Pedius was not taking any more chances regarding his position in the household. He had been well brought up and had studied many years in Rome's university, and later he held a position in the senate. Since his involvement in the political system, he had been head of the household. He did not tolerate disobedience or lack of respect. Valerus had grown up under his strict discipline and thus had taken up the traits of his father. Living in Rome had made Valerus an independent young man who did not take command, but merely gave it.

Now the two worlds of father and son had collided, and there was a question rising about authority and who was master of the slaves. Pedius was the rightful owner of all the slaves the villa held and his wife was an equal to him. They were the dominant ones. Anneria was next in line, having lived in the house since her birth. To Pedius, Valerus was a familiar intruder, taking command and behaving as if it all belonged to him. Of course he was his son—his firstborn—and there was a certain degree of love and respect for his own bloodline, but there was a sense of superiority: the young man did not respect him. During the course of the days, he watched Valerus, who soon appeared to notice and began leaving for longer periods of time. Once Valerus was gone, Pedius's attention turned to Flavia, and he had her watched very closely, making sure she did everything as she was told to.

Gaius the younger also watched the goings-on from his place, shaking his head when he saw Pedius stalking about to see what the slaves were up to. This was going to cause problems for the young couple if they were not careful, and even though they were, things were beginning to heat up.

"And that's it?" Valerus asked Lucius. "They give us the lines and we just have to memorize it?"

"What did you expect? We don't write the act. We are just the actors."

They were sitting in the apartment above Lucius's stall; a single lamp was burning on the table between them, casting shadows on the walls behind. The small insula was set along one of the busier streets where Lucius had made his parlor of exotic perfumes on the ground level while his lodgings were on the floor above it.

"That's all you have to do. You get paid per act as well as per show. Once you get into the higher positions, you get paid per watcher."

Valerus rubbed his hands. It all sounded unreal; he could not believe that people actually did these things out of choice. Everything was make-believe; none of it was real: wooden swords, fool's gold coins. What was the point? Entertainment? He wondered where the excitement was.

"And there is good money in this?" Valerus asked him.

"Very good! The better you get—the higher up the ladder you go, the better."

Valerus took some time to think about it. It was not his dream occupation, for certain, but for Flavia anything was worth getting money in his pocket. How much would his father ask for her? A dancing girl from Hispania? He had paid nine hundred denarii for her. His father would not accept less. As she was part of a trio, he doubted that her price would go anywhere below a thousand. He still had six hundred denarii left from his previous professions. He only needed a few more hundred before he felt comfortable in making an offer. Lucius had said theater, especially in the beginning of an actor's career, paid anything between ten and twenty denarii for a play, and it took at least a couple of weeks of rehearsing and preparations, if he got the part, that is.

It would only have to be for a couple of months, he thought. He could dedicate himself to it completely for that period of time. Afterward he could make the offer, and if Flavia ended up as his, they could work something out together.

"I spoke to my agent." Lucius broke him from his thoughts. "He would be most grateful if you could give some swordplay lessons to the other actors. There are some combat scenes in a performance he is writing and he would like it to be as professional as possible."

"With wooden swords?"

"It's theater, Valerus. Besides, he is prepared to pay a good sum."

"How much?"

"Two denarii a session."

Valerus nodded, biting his thumb nail in thought. That was not a bad deal. Besides, he enjoyed swordplay. It was a passion of his and training generally took place with wooden swords and lances in any case.

"Can I ask the reason for your sudden desperation to earn some money?" Lucius asked him.

Valerus looked up, his hand dropping to his lap. Lucius studied his expression and nodded slowly. "It's for Flavia, is it?"

The young man sighed. "I just need to cover my debts. I still owe you more than three hundred and fifty sestertii and a few hundred denarii more for Flavia's freedom."

"My debt is not as important, and I will let it go for half the price if I can get one of the girls every now and again. Of course I would like it back over time, but no hurry. He carefully poured some oil into the opening of the lamp.

"It's late," Valerus announced.

"We will go over to the theater first thing in the morning. You're welcome to spend the night here. How about a few rolls?"

"I can't afford to gamble, Lucius."

"Friendly rolls. Just to keep the flame company."

Chapter 19

June 19

Flavia did not see Valerus that following day or the next. She listened to the family's discussion around the table that night and heard that he had taken to the theater with Lucius. Gaius was hardly surprised by this, and Flavia met him in the atrium after the table had cleared.

"Valerus is getting impatient with your master, it appears," he told her with his knowing smile as he admired the murals. "He's getting desperate to win ownership."

Flavia shook his head. "He does not like the theater, he told me that!"

"A man can do many things when he is in love."

She blushed and smiled at this. "I love him, Gaius. I miss him so much. My dancing and chores are so empty without him."

The young man put his mind at ease suddenly and took her by the shoulders. "Sit back and enjoy your time alone."

Flavia walked through the house that evening, around the ambulatory again and again. Valerus was going to take weeks if not months to get anything out of the theater that would come close to affording her.

⁂

Valerus stepped around the two actors who were partaking in a mock combat. The scriptwriter, Aurleus, was watching from nearby as the man ran through the simple yet professional motions of swordplay. The morning heat was getting to all three of them; already Valerus was stripped to his waist and his brow was running with sweat.

"Here," Valerus took the wooden sword from the one actor's hand, "hold it up high, like this, when you fight. You will have more control and strength over its movements." He swung the weapon to the opponent, years of experience suddenly kicking in as the actor parried over his head. "Hold your hands farther down and you become more agile." Like a full strike, Valerus swung around, turning his wrist and bringing the wood down to strike the man on the hip. He stopped barely an inch before impact.

The armed actor looked up from the sword at Valerus. "You've been fighting long, have you?"

"A few years." Valerus handed the wooden sword back to the actor standing behind him.

There was applause. When he turned around, he saw Aurleus walking toward him, applauding softly. "Very good," he announced. "I like your style, Valerus. I wish I had five more of you."

"These people have never held a sword in their lives, Aurleus."

"Which is exactly why I need you. Damn the acting, Valerus. I will take you on as a fighting coordinator and instructor for my actors. I will pay three denarii a day for the next three days. That's nine denarii for this play alone, which is what the average lecturer gets a month. What do you say?"

Valerus glanced at Lucius, who opened his hands to him and shrugged. He looked back to Aurleus. "Serious?" he asked.

"Absolutely. What I want in this is professional, not a mockery of the fighting profession. I want soldiers to watch it and feel as though they are watching the real thing."

Valerus said nothing. It would never be the real thing; no soldier or gladiator would feel the same for a fight when watching it take place on a stage with wooden sticks. The reality of it was in the metal blades, in the awareness that it can hurt you— kill you. There was a rush of adrenalin, and in that moment you felt so alive.

This is not real, he thought bitterly as he took the wooden sword from the second actor and weighted it in his hands. He ran a series of small moves, demonstrating the motion of attack and defense, parrying the actor's weak and slow attempts dozens of times before he stepped back and waved in his partner.

Someone was applauding from the stands. Valerus looked up along the empty seats of the theater and saw one solitary man watching them, applauding a few more times to get his full attention.

"Excuse me," Valerus said as he passed the wood to the actor and left them to practice. He took the steps and walked along the stone seats to the mysterious onlooker.

On closer approach, he recognized young Gaius. He was dressed in a white linen chiton with, draped over his shoulders, a wool toga which he was using as a hood. "Take a break, Valerus. Sit down. We need to talk."

He looked down at the stage for a second before sitting down beside him. The theater echoed with the clatter of wooden swords.

"What's this about, Gaius?" he asked to fill the silence that followed. "I'm busy."

"Flavia misses you." His eyes did not turn from the stage.

Valerus frowned at him. "How did you know?"

"I am not a fool, Valerus. You should know. The two of you make it very obvious; the way you sneak about, light lamps to call each other around." He laughed.

"Who else knows?"

"Only myself and a few of the other slaves." Slowly he shook his head. "Your family appears oblivious to the happenings … although the women of the household are suspicious."

"Why are you here?"

"I think you ought to come to dinner tonight. Your parents would love to have you around. It's been two full days since you've shown your face."

Valerus shook his head. "I need to work. It's important."

"I know … trying to earn enough to make your father an offer. Don't worry," he added quickly when Valerus threw him an urgent look, "I haven't told him anything. But please, join us at supper tonight. You'll enjoy it." As a closing statement, he threw back his hood and walked out from the stands.

Valerus watched him go, baffled but strangely curious to see what the young man was up to.

Flavia and Alia were helping Helen in the kitchen that evening, mostly in the carrying of wood. Luci was sitting by the table, holding a piece of papyrus paper that Gaius had given her earlier that day. "He wrote it himself," she said dreamily. "It's a description of my name. He is one of the very few who knows me as Lucinda."

"Yes, you told us that a dozen times over," Alia said from the counter where she was chopping vegetables.

Flavia smiled and looked at the young woman. She was turning the paper over in her hands, her mind clearly in other places. "Read it to us, Luci," she said kindly, encouraging the feeling.

"I can't read," she said. "But he read it to me."

"Give it here." Helen wiped her hands and took it carefully from her. "As a midnight sun wanes in the ocean as a mirror, so does your name be dark in depth but a mirror to your outer havens."

"Nice." Alia nodded, yet there was an edge of bitterness in her tone.

"That's beautiful," Flavia said.

"It really is." Helen passed it back to Luci, who cradled it like a baby. "Especially coming from him. What a romantic."

Flavia smiled to herself. Poetry was romantic—sweet words on paper. Valerus had never done that, but with him she did not feel she needed it either. Being with the man she loved and who loved her was enough of poetry for her, for the moment at least.

Valerus's voice rang through the kitchen. Flavia's head shot up from her work. She had not heard or seen him for two days.

Alia threw her a look. "Your lover is here," she said teasingly.

"Stop that!" Flavia sneered and went to the door to peer out. He was there, along with Lucius and talking to Rectina who had come to greet him. He did not see her as they left for the atrium together.

Flavia ambled back into the kitchen. It was torturous, really, to be so separated from him. A month ago it would have been a relief. In her experience, she had enjoyed being alone even from fellow slaves. Now it was lonely; it was even lonely in the presence of the others. It was with Valerus that she finally felt that she had room to breathe.

Valerus did not know why he had joined the family for cena that evening. Flavia was nowhere to be seen and he knew, as they spoke, that there was a rehearsal going on which he would have been paid for having been part of.

Gaius was reclined on the couch beside his uncle and smiled his way, nodding his head in a reassuring manner.

They ate as the sun set and the first stars began to appear

overhead. Their conversation was empty and terribly boring for Valerus. He declined the offer of wine and kept looking in Gaius's direction for explanations.

By the end of the meal, Pedius reached over the table and took his wife by the hand. "Well, Anneria is dying to know," he said loudly for the family to hear. "Gaius and his uncle have convinced us."

Anneria beat her fists in the air. "Yes!"

Valerus was well aware that he had missed something. He waited for the conversation to unfold.

Pedius looked at Pliny and smiled. "We will join you to Stabiae for a few days."

"Stabiae?" Valerus was taken aback. "Why?"

"Pomponianus has fully recovered and wishes to show gratitude," Pliny the Elder informed him. "He has invited us for the market entering over the weekend. Fabric from all across the empire along with slaves, wine, silk, and ivory. Something you don't want to miss."

Gaius was the only one to see the expression change on Valerus's face. He smiled, but only internally.

"Go without me," Valerus told them. "I'm too busy for day trips."

"Two days," Gaius told him.

"We were thinking of going by boat," Rectina said to him. "We have one of Rome's finest naval admirals with us."

"No," Valerus shook his head, "at the moment I can't afford it."

"Theater going well, son?" Pedius raised his glass to him.

Yes, it was the theater that was keeping him in Herculaneum, he reminded himself strictly. *To my father, it's the theater … not a woman … not Flavia.* He looked toward Gaius, who threw him a wink.

Gaius turned to his uncle. "If we go by ship, let us go for three days." He told them, "Let us spend the last back in Baiae and let us try the wine."

"What, nephew?" Pliny shook his head. "We just came from the area. Why return?"

"The wine is excellent. Apparently they prepare some with spicing. It's worth it."

Valerus stared at the young man, baffled by his sudden over-keeness to get the family away from the house. Gaius looked his way and then back at his hosts. "Let us take three days; you can join my uncle and myself to visit the town."

"I heard it's terribly crowded this time of year," Rectina informed them without much persistence.

"It is; but for good reasons." He looked at Pliny. "What about it, uncle?"

Valerus looked to his father, hope suddenly twisting in his gut. If he agreed, it meant that he would have the house to himself for three days … alone for three days. He threw a quick glance at Gaius, who merely smiled at him.

He knew! The young man knew everything. He remembered the banquet when Gaius also knew Flavia's intentions. He was playing a game with the crowd before him, sweet-talking them for Valerus's own advantage. Why? Why was the man so keen to help them?

Pedius looked at his daughter and then his wife.

Rectina grinned. "I think a long trip would be good, for me especially. It's been so long since I've been out of the house."

"Very well. Anneria?" The oldest daughter looked up from her place. "Will you be joining us?"

Valerus now turned to her, just as hopeful.

"Of course!""

Valerus gave an internal cheer, suddenly slipping into a different world, which he was looking forward to so much more.

Then came the tremor. At once all their gazes went to the walls and then the roof. Pedius knew the procedure of quakes and was the first on his feet to beckon his guests. "To the peristyle, everyone," He told them. "It ought only to be a moment."

They had barely made it out to the gardens when the tremor

died away. They took some time to talk around the fountain before merging back into the villa, all but young Gaius who stayed behind, observing the night sky from one of the hedges. With one hand set on his hip, the boy's gaze was fixed on the stars. Obviously his observation came from years of study. Valerus came out to join him and noticed his stare was like a crazed man fascinated with time and eternity.

Valerus stood in the shadow of a tree. "What are you playing at, young Gaius?"

The man frowned but didn't shift his gaze. "Who says I'm playing at anything, Master Valerus?"

"You coaxed my family in to leaving for three days. Why?"

"Why? Don't you want to be alone with her?"

"Of course I do, but I ..." He stopped, realizing he was standing in the peristyle, a place where sound traveled to many rooms of the house. He walked up to the young man's side and, with his voice much lower than before, said, "I want to know why."

"Do you see that star there, Valerus?" he asked while pointing. "The bright one, reddish, below the moon?"

Valerus looked carefully and then spotted the one he was indicating. "Venus."

"Goddess of love. She wants people to love and unite. There are many poets who use her in their documents, as well as philosophers."

"Still," Valerus put his hand on Gaius's shoulder. They locked gazes. "I need to know *why*."

"Isn't it simple? You are seven years older than me and you still haven't gotten it. Love, Valerus. I like to see it in people. I like to study its pattern. We all look for that perfect match, and yet the perfect match always raises more complications, testing its worth. So far you have both been successful students." He smiled at Valerus now. "I would like you to see me as Diana's little helper. I am going to give the two of you a three-day break; an opportunity to get out together."

"Why?"

"I just told you why."

"But what's in it for you?" Valerus shook his head.

"To see the two of you happy." He turned to face him completely. "Why do you keep putting some form of wealth on everything? The world needs more unconditional acts, wouldn't you agree?"

Valerus said nothing but stood in awe of this young man who was so much wiser than he. "I am pleased about you," Gaius continued. "Flavia is making you see what real worth is. It's not the money; it's not the adrenaline to kill. It's love, Valerus. Nothing has ever been simpler."

Chapter 20

June 20

Valerus did not need to look at his sundial to know he had woken up late; the sun had already lifted over the villa roof. He swung his legs out of bed and sat for a moment, rubbing back his hair. The sleep stung in his eyes.

Slowly, dreamlike, he reached for his tunic, which a slave had neatly folded beside his bed. This made him smile, knowing it was likely to have been Flavia, and this thought shot a bolt through him—three days alone! Gaius had well arranged it. Had they already left?

He jumped up and pulled the tunic over his head. He cursed as he looked around for his girdle and found it rolled up in the blankets of his bed. He must have been moving around a lot last night to have turned the sheets like he had.

He stepped out into the corridor; everything was quiet and appeared deserted. He walked slowly, becoming increasingly aware of the cluttering sounds coming from the kitchen. Two women were working there, cleaning and packing and engaged in friendly conversation. Flavia was not among them. He stepped inside and addressed the two slaves. "Morning."

Both women turned. Alia and Helen bowed and spoke together. "Morning, Master Valerus."

The young man took another look around, just to make sure he had not missed anyone. "Is Flavia in the vicinity?"

"I think she's weeding the block," Helen answered.

He nodded and smiled at the two of them. "Thank you," he said and left.

Alia threw Helen a glance. "I don't like this," she said to her. "He's too obsessive."

"I think it's wonderful." Helen turned to her work.

"He is going to hurt her. Relationships always end like that. Mark my words: Flavia will be crying within the week."

The villa had been built many years ago northwest of the township as a gift to Julius Caesar's father-in-law. Over the years it was well managed and kept in authentic look despite all the additions built to it. It was situated down against the waterline with Vesuvius well visible on the eastern horizon, making both views exceptional. The earth was rich, which made it an everlasting job to keep the weeds growing up between the flagstones. They lined the entranceway, eastern wall, and south side of the villa where slaves were able to walk and renovate the walls. Valerus seldom walked along the outside to the south, but here, all along the flagstone path, was remnants of Flavia's work: weeds having been pulled up and piled ready for collection.

Flavia was on hands and knees just around the corner to the south, pulling weeds from between the flagstone cracks. She was barefoot and he saw her feet from under her dress; they were muddy.

"Morning to you." He smiled when she spun around to him. "You should not be working in the dirt." He shook his head and helped her up.

Flavia cracked her back and sighed.

"I gather the family has left?"

She nodded. "Early this morning. Gaius was keen to leave."

"We owe that boy a lot," he said as he took her by the hips and gently pulled her to him, "don't we?" There was a moment of thought before he took Flavia's hands and studied them, turning them about. They were blackened by dust and dirt and blistered on her fingertips from the hours she had spent.

"Your father gave me a lot of chores to complete," she told him. "No excuses."

Valerus sighed. "It will be done. I can help you now. Later this afternoon I will have to visit the theater. Aurleus is expecting me."

"Aurleus?"

"I haven't told you, have I? I am the new sword coordinator and fighting instructor for actors." He opened his arms proudly to her. "Clean fighting. Not a drop of blood."

Flavia laughed.

"Would you like to join me? It will be for a couple of hours."

"I was hoping you'd offer me the chance. I would love to see you fight."

"I don't fight." He shook his head. "I may give a few tips and pointers, but it's mostly the actors that do the work."

"Will Lucius be there?"

"Most likely. He's playing a minor role in act two."

"I have not seen him for so long."

For a second, only a second, Valerus felt that he did not want Lucius anywhere near Flavia. His protective sense over her was so astonishing that it surprised even him. He wanted no man to look at her, touch her, or smile in her direction. He had seen what some men were capable of; in fact, he remembered the things he had done when he got intoxicated at orgies. These memories frightened him. Though he was certain that he would never do that to her, or any woman after having known her, he knew that other people in the world were capable of worse things. He recalled one dawn in Rome when he had left his insula early for training and came across a woman's body cut up in the gutter. Soon after the city guard arrested a man younger than himself who had killed many women over a period of a few months. Valerus wondered what pleasure he had found in it.

But then he had found pleasure in killing in the arena, whether it was man or animal. He had cheered bloody sports when he watched them from the stands.

He looked Flavia in the eyes, having that same naked feeling as before. His entire life was laid bare and he saw all the errors, all the mistakes, and all the wrongs of his life. Blood sport was distant and dreamlike in her presence; what had once been his only reason to live was now replaced by the woman standing in front of him … and a Christian at that!

And yet he felt terribly protective over her. In many ways—as Flavia had once said—there was very little reason why they had come together. A master and slave: a Roman and a Christian. Who would have believed it?

He did not question these things with the thought of getting answers. Instead he helped Flavia with the weeding. By the time they had managed three quarters, the afternoon sun had reached a station in the heavens that made Valerus anxious to leave. He got dressed in a summer tunic of linen and wrapped it over with a white toga.

When he met Flavia, however, he felt overdressed. She was wearing nothing more than a sleeveless tunica of coarse wool and a pallium of a darker color. It reminded him of the status gap between them. Thus he lost the toga and replaced it with a wool mantle.

They walked along Herculaneum's streets together, though not hand in hand. There was still some apprehension on Valerus's part to do that. His father was a well-known and respected member of the community, and things were bound to turn foul if rumor stretched that he, Pedius's son, was seen in public holding the hand of a slave. In truth, it was not Valerus's fear of reputation that caused his apprehension, but instead that his father may hear of it. One thing about Pedius was that he was unpredictable. Valerus remembered all though his life how he could never seem to catch a steady rhythm in his father's decision making; he went one way and then another. This affected Valerus more now than ever before; he had to play his role very carefully and would have to make very sure he could predict his father's actions well enough before making any sort of indication of his intentions.

They came by the markets when Valerus stopped to look around. *There is a way to end all that,* he thought. He did not want Flavia to get the wrong idea when he behaved differently with her in public.

"What are you looking at?" Flavia asked.

He nodded to some stalls on the street corner that were selling fine fabrics, everything from wool to linen. "Maybe I ought to get you something more appropriate." He smiled at her. "Something more fitted to your beauty."

She laughed but said nothing. In some small way she took what he said as a joke. Valerus knew that the tunica and pallium she wore were all she had had known in her life, the plainly colored ones usually of a dark brown or gray. Slaves were not permitted to wear the stola as their masters did, just as the men were prohibited to wear thin togas of natural colors.

"Then again," Valerus nodded to the open street, "I think the sestertii is more valuable to buy other items." He grinned down at her.

The rest of the way to the theater, Valerus became acutely aware of the dress coat of other women, especially of the higher class. They wore the stolas draped in a palla, and theirs were linen and finer, lighter fabric. He recalled seeing a linen dress of blue and white of his mother's and thought what an appealing color it would be on Flavia.

He looked down at her plain tunica and wondered if she would ever fit into something which was so unlike what she had known; this one did not even have sleeves but was merely fastened on her shoulders. Her most colorful outfit was the one dancing outfit she owned—the one of two parts. The other was linen white and, though beautiful in dance, still plain to the public eye.

❧

It was twilight by the time they left the theater and headed home. The crowds were diminishing and, once they took the road out, Valerus reached down and took her hand. He kissed it; there was a glint in his eyes which she had recognized a few times before. Then he turned on the road leading southward.

"Let us go along the beach," he said hopefully. "Let's enjoy the cool air."

She did not respond to his proposition but instead had him guide her down the main road and down the steps to the beach. Flagstone paved the small sidewalk where other couples were enjoying the evening. They walked all along the city wall until the path dissolved into the sand of the beach, and still they continued. At one point Flavia stopped to remove her sandals and soon Valerus did too.

The sound of the city was falling behind, as were the lights and passing couples. Soon only the stars lit their way as they walked hand in hand, quiet and without sharing a word. Flavia said nothing as she was completely focused on the moment and her excitement about the man's next unexpected move.

Yet Valerus did not stop; he continued walking until the city behind them was merely the flicker of lights and a dark silhouette against the horizon. His own thoughts were pushing to new ground. Most of it was a distraction as he tried to focus on anything else rather than his desire and want of her. His first intent in bringing her here had been to make love to her, far away from the distraction of society.

Now, suddenly, it felt strangely frightening. What if she did not want it here? It would only be her second time and may still be painful. He shook his head and sighed. He would much rather have Flavia initiate it; that way he knew she was ready and prepared for him.

Finally Valerus stopped to look across the ocean to the west. Some fishing boats were still out near the horizon, their small lamps illuminating the water in long broken shapes.

Flavia came beside him, taking him around the waist as he laid an arm across her shoulders. For a long time she looked out with him before gazing up to regard his expression. There was no way anyone could read anything on his face; it appeared lifeless and distant as he was fighting himself for control and preparing himself for disappointment.

"Daydreaming, Valerus?" she asked and looked out again.

He looked at her as if suddenly noticing her presence but said nothing.

"I used to daydream a lot when I was younger," she confessed quietly.

"Your new world. I have been thinking about it a lot lately." Valerus smiled. "What I would like to think of it is: no money. No possession. Freedom to have what we want and love."

Flavia met his stare; they looked at each other for a while before Valerus opened his hand to her. "And what about you?"

"I imagined what the creatures would look like."

Valerus smiled for the first time. "Tell me," he whispered.

"Giant deer, larger than a horse, with massive horns. You could ride them if you got on their backs. Then there are birds the size of trees; you can make leather with their hides."

The young man chuckled.

She laughed in return. It was such a beautiful sound that drew him closer. He moved in and kissed her. She reached up and encouraged his kiss as much as she dared. He responded, but ever so gently, moving his hands from her shoulders, down her sides to her hips. He sighed for a second when their mouths parted, but it was only for a second before they came together again. He heard Flavia's heavy breathing and wondered if he ought to take it another step. He pressed against her, taking her by the upper arms to keep her from slipping away.

She took him around the neck and leaned into his ear. He heard her draw the breath to tell him something, but not a sound passed her lips. He felt the excitement mount in him and was suddenly fearful that he could not hold back this time.

Then, feeling her breath in his ear, he heard her whisper: "Come on, then."

It was the way she said it that had Valerus drop and forget all his plans and hopes. There was a break of tension, which suddenly gave him room to breathe again. He stepped back and removed his mantle, laying it out flat on the sand. Then he took Flavia's hand and they settled down together on the cover.

He touched her cheek gently and then kissed her, letting his hands slip to her thigh. The he came up and cupped her breasts as he pushed her back, settling down beside her with a sigh.

Flavia felt how his hands ran across the length of her body and could not believe how much she wanted him this time. The pain had been a lingering nuisance, both physically and as a memory, but suddenly all that was gone and she wanted to feel him inside her again—all of him.

"Flavia." It was a moan that crossed his lips as his face buried into her shoulder. "I'm not sure what to do."

The woman grinned to herself, took his hand, and put it over her breast again. "I like that."

He sat up a bit, lifting his weight onto an elbow, and ran his other hand to her hip, holding her gently. "And this?"

"Yes, I like that." She chuckled softly.

He kissed her cheek and then nibbled on her earlobe. Flavia arched her back for a second as a tingle of excitement rushed down her spine. “Yes!” She laughed and took him into her arms again. She kissed him when he looked her way and then felt her hands reach down to unfasten his girdle. As it slipped off he decided to pick it up a pace. He stood up and pulled the tunic off over his head. At his feet Flavia had removed her pallium and he bundled the pair of their clothing on the edge of the cape. He settled down beside her again, pressing himself against her.

To his surprise she suddenly removed her tunica, exposing her full body to him and the heavens. He looked her over for a second. The dim moonlight and the fact that she wore no makeup made her so much more beautiful than the first night they had been together. Suddenly she was real, beautiful in a natural setup. Valerus had never had this before; he had never had a woman without makeup, without lamplight, without perfume, and without a good dosage of wine. This was real to him.

She rolled up on top of him. Valerus did not protest but was genuinely surprised when she straddled him. “And this?” he asked, his voice a little hoarse with the growing excitement.

“Just a game.” She grinned and came down to kiss his mouth and then his torso. The hair on his chest had been removed again recently; she could feel the tiny pricks of those which had begun to grow. She came up again to kiss his shoulders, feeling the bulk of his build under her hands and lips.

It was no surprise that he had had many women before her. In the past men of such a build were a threat to her; they frightened her with the knowledge that they could easily force her in doing what she was now doing freely.

Now she wanted to do this and she removed his subligaria to act out her growing urge. Valerus’s figure drew and excited her. Earlier, when she had watched him on stage coordinate a dance with a weapon, she had wanted him to take her. She loved the way he put his strength under control and used it to please her rather than hurt. It was the thought that he could hurt her but didn't that excited her most.

"By Juno!" Valerus breathed heavily. "I want you!" Then he reached up, took her arms and rolled over, pushing her to the ground until he was on top of her. He held her there for a moment, just to regard her beauty, before letting her arms go free again. He lay over her, kissing her as he sought for passage. She opened up to offer it to him, but as he entered he felt that tingle of fear again. She was not used to this and, even though he wanted her more than any other woman before her, he did not want to hurt her for it. He stopped where he was, his hands coming on the ground above her shoulders to support his weight. A part of him wondered what actually stopped him; he could easily get it done in a few short moments. It was her pain, not his. What was holding him back?

He loved her. He did not want to hurt her. He felt he could undo all his wrongs by not giving into the physical ecstasy now. He wanted to please her, have her experience the same things he had always felt.

She was staring at him, wondering what had changed his mood so suddenly. She wanted him completely this time, not just partly as it had been before. It was not out of guilt to want to have this happen but instead to satisfy the yearning she had for him.

"Valerus, please don't hold back." She shook her head. "Please …"

"I don't want to hurt you, Flavia." His voice sounded on the very edge of oncoming tears in his effort to restrain himself.

"You won't. You can't." She moved her hands down to his waist to guide him into her. "Please," she whispered when the hesitation returned.

Valerus put his weight down on top of her and kissed her

passionately, desperately wanting to work through the forces that so suddenly held him back.

Her hands ran along the profile of his body and then to his shoulders where she wrapped herself around him.

It gave Valerus the strength he was looking for. Kissing her again, he entered slowly but continued until he was in her completely. He stopped to look at her then, marveling at the moment. Her eyes were closed but there was a smile on her face. He pressed against her and kissed her throat and shoulders, trying to savor the moment for as long as he could. He tried to get his hands everywhere at once, wanting her to feel the sensations he so often had.

He heard her gasp a few times before she suddenly threw open her eyes and gasped his name, feeling a sensation she never had before, coming fast and very unexpectedly. Valerus did not rush it as before, but instead drew back and took his time. He started again, kissing her across the shoulders then taking her into his arms again, moving slowly and enjoying every moment. He did not want the moment to pass, but when that tremendous ecstasy reached a peak, it was very sudden and unexpected, even for her, and drained that last bit of his energy completely. He lay over her, his breaths coming in huge gulps.

Flavia still had her arms and legs around him, clenching him to her like a child. She did not want him to move … ever. She had never felt anything remotely to what she felt that moment. There was pleasure from the beginning to the end, from the time they were fully clothed to when he was inside her. Even now there was pleasure as they lay naked against each other, feeling their hearts throbbing rhythmically. But Flavia had felt a peak of intensity, and even though it had only lasted a few seconds, no experience could ever compare.

He rolled over and lay beside her, resting one hand on her breast. "By all the gods, Flavia!" He gulped for air and kissed her cheek.

She said nothing for a moment, still drunk on the feeling and the intensity of the passing moment.

"Flavia," he said as he sat up a bit, "I didn't hurt you?"

She shook her head slowly, staring at him with round-eyed fascination. She did not know that a man could make her feel such things. Other dancing girls had always talked about it, but she could not believe that any of their experiences had ever matched to what she had with the man she loved. If she had known the feeling was like this, she would never have stopped him the first time.

She took him by the neck and leaned into him. "Valerus." She pressed her brow against his. "I've never felt anything like it."

They did not move but stayed instead as they were in embrace, head against head. They listened to each other's breathing coming down and the heart slow to its normal rate. Then they finally embraced and lay together for much longer still.

Chapter 21

June 21

Flavia woke up with Valerus's arm flung across her hip. They were both naked but back home sharing Valerus's bed. The sun had barely risen; it was Flavia's usual time to get up to begin her chores, but suddenly none of that felt important anymore. She shifted her weight slightly and felt the man snug up and press against her.

Flavia tried to think of how the teachings of Christ related to this feeling. She wondered if He had been in love; if He had shared this same experience. Had Christ been married? Melani had always believed He had been married and had told them some stories regarding His children, but she never went into much detail, claiming that silence was needed to protect His offspring.

Others she had heard refused to acknowledge it; in fact, she herself could not—did not—want to believe that such a great man would fall for the temptation. She had seen what *love* was from the view of a dancing girl; she had seen what sex was. She did not want to believe He ever gave into that. She could not compare Christ with any of those people.

But now her entire perspective had changed. Was this temptation?

Loving someone? Wanting to be near to him? There was a world of difference between what those people did and what she had experienced with Valerus last night. Now she discovered that she wanted to believe what Melani had told her; she wanted to see Christ as a man who enjoyed the pleasures of being in love and having a family. She could not believe that either of them had acted on any sin last night. It could not be; it had been too wonderful.

And they loved each other, which was the biggest reason Flavia could think of; in fact, it was the only one, because she knew that nothing loving could ever be of sin. That had, after all, been His most important commandment to mankind.

"You're awake," a voice said behind her when she shifted again.

She glanced over her shoulder. "I thought *you* were asleep." She smiled.

"I was." He sat up and stretched shortly before coming down beside her again. "I just cannot move when you're sleeping."

A few minutes passed in which neither spoke. Finally Valerus moved away and she rolled over onto her back. He leaned over her carefully. "What shall we do today?"

"We could bolt the door," Flavia said teasingly.

He laughed. "I will have someone cover your duties, Flavia. Today it's me and you, our first and last full day together, at least for a while. I am not going to have it wasted with you doing your chores. No … today is ours."

Flavia scavenged through the pantry, digging into the back of the shelves for anything that was dust covered and that no one would miss. Valerus stood in the doorway, keeping watch for anyone who may approach. He had dressed especially simply for the day; a master in a white linen chiton and toga down at the docks was bound to draw attention. For this reason he was dressed to fit in with a gray tunic of light wool and a darker wool pallium. He looked at the small basket Flavia had filled with a loaf of stale bread and some grain. Now she was moving to the larder, taking a little salted pork from its hook.

Valerus shook his head. "How long have you been doing this?"

"For a few weeks," she confessed as she sifted insects from the expired grain. "But I don't take food out to him every time."

He was relieved by this. It was not so much that she was technically stealing, but the punishment for theft was rather harsh for slaves; he did not want to see her get caught.

"How did you manage to get it out of the house without being seen?"

"I would leave early." She did not say anything more, aware that mentioning Marcus could get him into some trouble. But Valerus seemed satisfied with her reply.

"Why?" He shook his head as she jumped off the stepladder and picked up the basket. "I mean, you are putting yourself at terrible risk, and I for one don't want to see you whipped," he swallowed, "again."

"It won't happen," she reassured him with a smile. "No one misses these things. Besides, after you meet him, you'll understand why."

⁂

Valerus had Flavia lead the way; he had not lived in Herculaneum long enough to know the routes used by the slaves. He felt out of place as they entered the lower-class district of the city; he had grown up to know the social differences among slaves, himself, and people like his father. Some took no notice while others regarded him suspiciously. Some slaves working in the shipyards had never seen their master and took their commands from stewards, guards, and other slaves who were considered more valuable. It was known that some masters spied on the work of their slaves by wearing a simple outfit and lingering around as one of them. For this reason, Valerus noticed slaves completely engrossed with their work as he followed Flavia past them.

Even the repairer was busy; they could hear the sound of a striking chisel as they neared the tiny entrance to his lodging as well as his work place.

Flavia stepped in under the thin drape and Valerus followed her after a quick glance around. He felt as if he were part of some criminal act by delivering stolen food to a slave that he had no right to feed or even get near to. Slaves were property and some owners took their possessions very seriously indeed.

The inside of the shelter smelt of smoke and wet timber. Flavia put down the basket by the hearth and went straight toward the next room where the noise was coming from while he inspected the small fireplace and thin sleeping mat. The slave appeared to have nothing more than a thin sheet with which to cover himself, at least until he noticed a blanket folded up on a shelf a little way up. He frowned and felt the fabric. It was a blanket from home; he knew it. Sometimes he had seen and felt it on his own bed despite it being mostly for the laborers.

He could not protest Flavia's generosity when he looked around though. There was little; no, there was nothing. He saw a mat, a blanket, a pile of collected driftwood, and a worn pot. That was it.

Valerus shook his head, wondering why some men allowed their slaves such conditions to work in.

There was some muttering from the next room followed by a groan. Flavia came through the archway with the repairer's arm over her shoulder for support.

It had been many years since Valerus had seen a slave in this bad a state. He knew it happened; some people could not afford a slave but were too stuck up to work themselves. Others simply did not care. This slave was about the age of his father, cripple, and obviously in tremendous pain. Valerus had met and fought many different races in the arena, and he could tell this one was of a Germanian origin. When he opened his mouth to utter a few words, he saw the state of his rotting teeth.

"Valerus," she said as she smiled to him, "this is the repairer I told you about."

"He does not have a name?" he asked as he stepped forward to take him from her.

"He won't tell me. Either he does not know or does not want me to know."

"Pleased to meet you, sir," Valerus greeted a little gingerly as he helped him down on the mat beside the fire.

The slave pointed to him and looked toward Flavia. "He yours? Married?"

"No." Flavia shook her head and Valerus saw her smile. He returned it before she got to the contents of her basket.

"We got you some salted pork," Valerus informed him as he settled down into the sand opposite. Flavia extracted the meat as evidence.

The repairer shook his head. "No good," he said.

"He can't chew this on his own," Flavia informed him. "I chew it for him or I mix it into a stew."

"You chew it for him?" Valerus could not believe what he had just heard.

"That's right," Flavia said coldly in response to his tone. "It's what I was taught to do: be of service … help others. Don't you think the world lacks that?"

He blinked at her but found no way to respond or comment. Instead he watched as Flavia carefully cut a piece of meat and began chewing at it. He watched her feed him, so carefully and compassionately, taking her time to make sure that the meat was soft enough so that it would not hurt him.

Valerus was so taken by it, so in awe, that he could not turn away. He had never seen this dedication, this love for a stranger that made someone help to such an extent. It had his thoughts draw to all his pleasure, conveniences, and wild orgies. And all the time he had those things, in the world somewhere, someone, was serving another not because of a command and not because he or she was being paid, but instead simply because.

After a while she took the pot, which Valerus automatically offered to fill. On his return, Flavia placed it over the small flames of the fire and got it to a boil. Then she began adding the bread, grain, and what was left of the meat.

"You promised," the repairer said suddenly.

Flavia leaned back from the fire. "Promised what?"

"That you tell me stories. You promise. About Christ."

Valerus felt the air being sucked out of him when Flavia spun to him and moistened his lips a little nervously. It was coming out again—the reason why they should not be together—and it always affected him the more she spoke His name.

It was out of respect that she turned back to the slave. "I don't think that today is best," she began by telling him, but Valerus interjected.

"No, please do." He waved his hand in her direction and made himself more comfortable. "Perhaps I too ought to hear the teachings of this one man."

Flavia disapproved of his tone; he could see it at once. For a moment she appeared like a slave again acting under the command of her master, but this dispersed quickly and she began telling them both stories.

⁂

Valerus could not believe when midday reached and passed so quickly. He was engrossed and completely captured by Flavia's storytelling.

She had a supernatural way of telling them, locking the listeners in complete awe and fascination. The repairer was resting on his side, picking at the cold stew, while Valerus was sitting opposite, cross-legged with his chin on his fists.

Every now and again Valerus would shake his head slowly, a gesture Flavia did not take well to as she interpreted it as ridicule.

However, Valerus was not thinking such things—not even close. He tried to imagine the power one man had to have done the things Flavia told them. Did this man have no fear? Was he a messenger from the gods? Or God? How did he heal people like that? How could he love so much and so unconditionally?

"Oh," the repairer said as he sat up a bit. "It late! Must work!"

Flavia looked out the entranceway and saw how the building shadow had shrunk; in fact, the sun was creeping in.

"No," Valerus said as he waved his hand, "finish the story, Flavia."

Flavia was truly taken aback by his words. "The story of Christ does not finish, Valerus." She shook her head. "And why are you so taken when He was only one man?"

His stare went to the glowing ambers, but he said nothing. There was indeed some guilt in the fact that he had given in to listening to her preaching, but there was even a greater guilt when he accepted the fact he had been completely captivated by the story. He had never thought that His story was so fascinating; he had always thought that Christ was some individual who merely preached and created His own followers. He never would have believed that He actually caused miracles in the way Flavia told them. Healing the sick? Casting out demons? That was all believable in a way, but raising the dead? Only the gods had the power for that. Could a mortal human do that? He supposed He could if He was a descendant of the gods, like so many heroes before Him. But they had been warriors, fighters. Their honor was led by killing and their own strength over mankind. Christ was the opposite; He was weak in the sense that He did not use any weapons—only the sound of His voice and the touch of His hand.

Maybe it was not true; maybe they were just stories made up in the moment to form a new superstitious cult.

But maybe it wasn't.

He looked up at Flavia, who was regarding his expression closely. He suddenly saw a different person then, no less beautiful than the previous Flavia, but suddenly he understood her. He knew now why she served; why she cared and especially why she loved. In her stories, Christ had said that anyone who loved could perform the miracles He had. It was true, Valerus realized. Flavia had changed the life of the repairer simply by caring for him. She had even changed Valerus's life, all through love. It really was a miracle, he realized. She changed people's lives in the same way Christ had.

"I need to work." The repairer struggled to his feet.

Flavia made an attempt to help him up when Valerus was suddenly past her, pulling the man up gently from the mat. He nodded gratefully as he was helped into the next chamber. Valerus watched without a word as he settled down by the boat boards and picked up his hammer and chisel. Valerus watched for longer still as the repairer began to work; suddenly Valerus was overwhelmed to sit down beside him and help … to work alongside him. He glanced around, wondering if there was a second pair of tools, and then realized that, with the surroundings and possessions he owned, it was hugely unlikely.

He returned to Flavia who was storing away the pot of stew for the repairer to finish later. She turned around as Valerus stepped up to her. His face was bleak and filled with remorse. She frowned and took him on either side of his face. "What is it?"

The young man moistened his lips and shook his head. "How did He do those things?"

"Faith." She smiled and then walked out of the room. He followed her down to the water.

"Yes, but I mean … raise the dead."

Flavia laughed. "Don't look up to Him, Valerus." She told him. "He told the people that we are all His siblings. We are equal to Him."

"*He raised the dead*, Flavia."

"He changed people's lives by loving those people. Am I doing anything less by helping that slave?" She pointed to the archway.

It was true. She was—technically—not creating any less of a miracle than Christ had. He realized that that was what he was attracted to the moment he had bought her; she radiated what she had learnt, and it pulled people in like it did him and Lucius. The difference was that he fell in love with her and her unique trait.

He took her hands into his but found no words to say. He simply stared at her, thinking of all the things she had told him that day.

"Flavia!"

The two of them looked up across the water. There was a small fishing boat a little way out to sea; it contained Moe, Procimus, and the Numidian boy Valerus had bought nearly two weeks before; he was looking well.

Procimus was waving her direction. Flavia returned the gesture but Valerus merely watched on as the boat made its way to the beach toward them.

"Are you a fool?" Valerus heard Moe hiss to his companion as they docked. "That's Master Valerus! You're crazy."

"Oh, get off it!" Procimus jumped into ankle-deep water. He bowed shortly and respectfully in front of Valerus. "Master."

"Hello, Procimus," Flavia greeted him.

"Can I interest you in a boat ride?" he offered with an open hand.

Valerus looked up to Moe who was trying not to meet either

of their stares. The boy sitting beside him smiled oddly, not having forgotten the man who had bought him but well aware that he was still his master.

The boat was large enough to accommodate six, maybe seven, fishermen. It had been years since Valerus had gone fishing, and not with the household slaves. It was not something expected of someone like him.

But then he was with Flavia and he saw the excitement in her eyes at the man's offer. Then, to Valerus's own surprise, he thought of the stories Flavia had told him, including all the time Christ too had spent on a boat with the "lowly" community.

They got onboard together. Procimus pulled in the mooring rope as they got out to sea and laughed at the way Valerus looked so out of place and uncomfortable.

"Relax, master. You appear so tense."

"Valerus," Valerus said.

Moe, who had been sitting quietly in the back of the boat, looked up from his thinking. Both the men were staring at him.

"Do not call me your master," Valerus told them. "I am Valerus. Call me by my name."

The two slaves looked at one another and then back at him. "Very well," Procimus nodded. "Valerus."

The boy sat down alongside Flavia and was smiling broadly at Valerus when he looked their way. Then, slowly on the rocking boat, Valerus stepped forward and settled on her other side. He took her around the waist and kissed her cheek.

The two men watched, fascinated and somewhat horrified at their open affection. Procimus had never seen this; he never thought he would.

But the tension was quickly dispelled as they got into their duties. Shoals were located and fish were caught, both men helping teach the slave boy the tactics of the trade. Flavia and Valerus helped hauling fish into the boat, jumping about as their smooth scaly bodies rubbed up against their legs. Valerus too was laughing; it was his first time fishing since he had been a boy, and he discovered how much he had missed it. It suddenly erased all his memories of the arena and his passion for blood sport. With Flavia it made an even bigger impression on him. They laughed and worked together, something Valerus had never done with any woman before.

As the afternoon reached for evening and the boat started making for land, Flavia, Valerus, and Moe began sorting the fish, setting a few aside for the repairer. Procimus was steering toward home to the port of Pedius and where he was expected to be.

They pulled in by the dock just as the sun sank beneath the horizon, swallowing the last light of the day. Valerus helped the men carry the fish and nets out onto the wooden platform while Flavia picked at the fish that had been set aside for the repairer.

As she made her way toward his chamber, thinking of how she was going to prepare it for him, an agonized groan caught her attention. She looked up and saw, in the fading light, the slave against the outside wall, hunched over his knees with his hands over his head. Standing in front of him were two men, both of whom were armed and bearing leather clubs. One had raised the club over his head to strike down at the repairer, who let out another cry.

Dropping the fish and feeling the fury propel her, Flavia sped toward them. She did not speak; the raw rage had her forget about words. She merely growled as she rammed into the nearest man at waist height, throwing him to the ground.

The second man was standing over them and raised his cosh. It came down hard and heavy over her head. She cried out and clenched at the place it had struck her. The man raised his cosh again for a second blow when someone, far stronger than himself, grabbed his wrist and twisted it up behind his back. He groaned as the unseen attacker rammed him against the wall.

"That's no way to treat a lady!" Valerus hissed with his mouth by his ear.

"You have no authority here!" the man breathed as he was pressed up even harder against the stone. "Slave!"

"I'm no slave!" Valerus, strengthened by his anger, twisted him around and threw him aside so hard that he collapsed at his feet.

Then he quickly turned to Flavia who was already up and fretting over the repairer. He was bleeding on the side of his head and Valerus saw the glisten of tears in his blackened eyes. Then he looked at the two men. The one Flavia had bore to the ground was still clenching at his cosh; the other, however, had lost his, but Valerus was well aware he had a sword tied at his belt.

"What are you doing?" Valerus demanded from them. "What has this poor man done to deserve such brutality?"

"He had not finished the work his master put him out to do." Both men picked themselves up off the floor. They were well dressed but not in the togas of the higher society. It was obvious that they were messengers, runners who took their command from their masters to other low-ranking slaves. As Valerus had suspected, masters seldom came to this area.

"How can he with what you've been feeding him?" Flavia roared.

"He is a thief," one of the men snapped and pointed to the stew pot which had spilt over. "We don't feed him that!" He jumped to the repairer and picked him up by his tunic. "Where did you get it, you thief?"

Valerus grabbed the man by the shoulders before Flavia could react. He spun him around before the second man threw out his fist. The blow caught Valerus on the nose.

He stumbled back, clenching at it. Blood seeped from between his fingers. He turned and looked at the men again. "The food comes from my home!" he growled, looked at the blood on his hand and then up at them again. "I am the master of this woman, and your actions towards her and myself I find disgraceful!"

"Our master will not tolerate your actions, master or not! This is not your jurisdiction!"

Valerus wiped the blood from his nose and then shook it from his hand. "Show a bit more compassion to this old man," Valerus said to them as he went to help Flavia to her feet. "And I may choose to ignore this." He pulled Flavia up and carefully brushed the sand from her clothes. Then, not waiting for her to say a word, he pushed her out toward the beach. He knew that he had no right to his actions—none at all. The man was not his slave. Slaves were property of the master and they could be dealt with as pleased. Valerus knew he had overstepped his bounds, as had Flavia.

Both men gritted their teeth in anger, having been violated by two trespassers. Then one of them jumped and grabbed Valerus by the arms, pulling him back.

Valerus, seeing the look on Flavia's face, threw back his elbow, striking his attacker in the chest. He bent over and loosened his grip. Valerus struck with his elbow again, hitting him full in the mouth this time.

He stumbled back then bent over to pick up his cosh. Valerus saw the movement in the corner of his eye.

It was instinct; seven years of fighting took over at his point. Valerus grabbed the hilt of the sword carried by the man in front of him. In one motion, without even looking around, he pulled the sword from its scabbard and swung it around. It met resistance, which yielded slightly as it cut the attacker across the neck.

Blood sprayed across Flavia's face. She clenched her eyes shut, not wanting to witness the horror that was being bestowed in front of her.

There was suddenly a thud that was followed by a second's silence. Then came the sick raw sound of a body hitting the ground and when she risked opening her eyes she saw the attacker's body farther away on the ground between her and Valerus. His head was near her feet.

She gasped and jumped up, pressing up against the wall in complete disgust and shock. The head looked her way; its eyes open and frozen with that last wave of surprise and terror. She felt her chest fill up with stones, cutting off her breathing. Then her breathing came suddenly in huge racking sobs.

Valerus did not move from where he watched her. The sword he still held was hardly bloody; that was how fast it had happened. The second man behind him was cringing against the wall fearfully and whimpered.

Slowly, still disbelieving what had happened, Flavia looked down. Blood speckled the skin of her arms while her face was cold and sticky. She looked across at Valerus; his figure was blurry with her oncoming tears while the repairer wept by his place against the wall. Then she fled, running out and disappearing down the beach.

Valerus watched her go and then looked down at the sword in his hands. The body was slumped, bleeding heavily into the sand. He had just killed this man! He had decapitated him … just like that. In front of Flavia. This was a nightmare, yet he tried to understand why now it was so horrific. He had killed people before; this man had been holding a weapon; despite it being a cosh, it was a weapon none-the-less.

But this was not a game! This was not in an arena nor was his opponent a fighter at all. Valerus was not even in a position to have tried to defend a slave that was not his.

He dropped the sword as if it had burnt him, looked at the man still cowering a short way behind, and then left after the woman.

A crowd was beginning to gather; already slaves were milling around to try to see what all the row was about.

"Flavia?" Valerus called, but his voice was drowned in the rising din.

Chapter 22

She was gone. Valerus scanned through the gathering crowd, desperately trying to catch a glimpse of her. The night had fallen and the stretch of beach was lined with small fires flickering in the breeze.

"Flavia!" he called again and then tried to run in the direction he assumed she would have taken, but instead he staggered and fell. He winced as his hand went automatically to his knee. Here again, of all times, he was reminded that he could not run. He carefully got up and instead walked the way she had gone.

His action had been so stupid of him, he thought, but what was he expected to have done? He did the first thing that came to him, which was to protect her at all costs. He would have killed both men had they tried to hurt her again.

His violent outburst had been sudden and unexpected; like it had always been on the sands of the arena. People didn't see it coming from him. Most times Valerus did not either.

He did not want to kill anymore; that occupation was gone, dead and burnt. Since having met Flavia the world had changed for Valerus, and the thirst for blood was drowned in her compassion, love, and ability to serve. Especially after today, after Flavia had told them the stories of Christ, he cursed himself for his own actions. It was just sudden; his fear in the moment of losing Flavia or seeing her get hurt in his presence was unthinkable. His reaction had been so spontaneous that he had no control over it.

And it was going to cause problems, he knew. He had killed a man, destroyed property. Serious things were going to come out of it. It may have bordered on self-defense, but it had all occurred on private property.

For the moment, however, he knew he would have to find Flavia. She had never witnessed that brutality so close at hand. It had taken her many years to get over the images that haunted her regarding her mother's brutal end, and now the incident of today had no doubt opened up the old scabs and planted fresh images, both real and imagined.

He found her a long way down the shoreline, past most of the slave chambers where many of the boats were docked in neat rows. He noticed her figure in the dim light of the early night; she was hunched on her legs in the water, desperately rubbing her arms and dress. He watched her splash water against her face and rub that down as well, violently scratching in an effort to get the blood off her.

As he approached, he heard her breathing, gasping, and sobbing. It didn't appear as if she was winning the battle, the way her washing motions became more desperate. At first he did not want to interfere, but soon it became apparent that she was imagining the filth of blood on her dress, arms, and face. She was hissing between her teeth, scratching at herself with her nails.

"Stop it, Flavia." Valerus shook his head. "You're clean as you are."

"You killed him!" she shouted and continued to scrub frantically.

"He had his cosh …" he said softly and shook his head, realizing how ridiculous it was. He had decapitated a man who was armed with a cosh? Valerus had killed him while he stood in one place.

She did not hear him as she was in the process of wiping her face again. He began to approach her, stepping into the water and ready to take her into his arms.

"Don't touch me!" Flavia screamed at him.

The man stopped but did not back away. Instead he watched her for a while longer before making another attempt to go up to her. This time she jumped to her feet and spun around to him. He was closer than she had expected and pushed him back several feet. "Don't touch me!"

He was bewildered and sorry. He opened his arms to her submissively. "I didn't know what to do, Flavia." He shook his head. "I thought they were going to hurt you."

"You killed him!" she screamed, tears racking out of her trembling body. "You cut off his head! Right there! *You killed him*!"

"I didn't want anything to happen to you."

"Nothing did!" She turned around toward the dark ocean and walked a few steps toward the horizon until she was nearly knee-deep. Then she spun around again, running a shaking hand through her hair.

"Flavia, please …"

She threw her one hand out to him, took a second to catch her breath, and then said, "Don't speak to me! Don't ever talk to me again!"

Valerus was taken aback by her outburst, unable to believe what she had just said. He looked momentarily toward the light farther up the beach. There appeared to be a lot of activity going on now. He looked back at Flavia, who was on her knees again in the water. He did not know what to do, how to react, or what to say to her. He was sorry? That sounded so fake, so unable to make any difference. More than anything, he wanted to take her into his arms, but it was clear that she would not let him.

Slowly he shook his head. "Let me walk you home," he offered at least. "It's dark."

"Go away, Valerus!" she screamed again above her tears. "Just be off!"

This caused him pain, the worst he had felt in all his life. He felt the sting of tears, and the hot, heavy weight that settled in his chest, as if he was ready to die that very moment in that very place. The world fell away at her words, and the ruins it left behind left him broken, trapped, and with no more reason to want to live.

❧

Valerus did not go home while Flavia was on the beach; he could not. Instead he made himself as comfortable as he possibly could be among the boats and tools and watched her from afar.

Flavia could feel him watching her, and for this she did not move. She did not want a man like him near her. He had killed the man … just like that. Certainly he carried a cosh, but that was it. He was probably going to chase them off the property.

What was it like for Valerus? Like a sport?

Weakly, exhausted from the ordeal and terribly cold, she rubbed her arms down again. There was no way any blood could still be present, but she still saw it glow in the moonlight.

Moonlight?

She glanced to the heavens and saw the half moon aglow over the ocean to the west. It was getting late and she knew that the family was returning tomorrow. She would have to get up early to complete the tasks expected of her.

She looked down at her open hands. Valerus: what was it in the man that she saw? He was a killer; at first Flavia had truly thought she could have gotten it out of him, but now she realized it was a waste of time. It was what and who he was. He killed and she served. Why had God made two people like that fall in love? It was not right, it could not be right. It had to be a mistake.

Her eyes returned to the stars overhead and then slipped to the horizon. She felt ashamed for having told Valerus of her dreams and thoughts regarding the new world. Then she had wanted to share it with him, hear his ideas, and have him become a part of it. Now she felt as if he had stolen it from her. What would he do with such stories and fantasies? Would he kill that too?

Suddenly she was angry. She felt terribly betrayed and hurt by Valerus. He had no right to do what he did; not to her, to his servants, or the man he had just killed. He had no right to do any of it!

She beat the water with her fists a few times and then watched patiently as the water settled around her. How could she go back to the villa now? How could she ever be as she was? Valerus knew so much about her now; she had even preached to him of Christ a few hours ago! How would he deal with her now? There were so many things he could do to her—so many horrible things that it was not worth imagining.

The fear twisted her in the gut, knotting her up and making her feel sick. She was still a slave. Maybe it was better that the family was returning tomorrow. That way Pedius was master again, and Valerus would once again be forced to shrink into the background.

Valerus followed Flavia back to the villa at a distance. Marcus was on the portico, engaged in a soft conversation with one of the men under his command. He was genuinely surprised when he saw Flavia step in from the dark into the light of his lantern but then unwound when Valerus followed.

Not a word was exchanged as slave and master entered the villa together. Valerus shut the door and turned to Flavia who was no longer there. In the distance he heard a door shutting softly.

He leaned against the heavy woodwork and sighed. He had really messed that up; he could not have done a better job of it. Worst was he knew it was going to cause a stir with the law, socially as well as politically.

And it hurt. He had never felt anything like it before. His heart ached terribly and he felt as if he would never eat again. He thought of Flavia's teachings earlier in the day and wondered how they related. Despite the fact of what the man had done to the repairer as well as to Flavia, he did not deserve it. Besides, Valerus did not have any right to trespass or interfere in what did not belong to him. That slave is the property of someone—whether he be cruel or not made no difference. The best they could have done was simply leave the property. Everything would have been settled that way.

He considered going to talk to Flavia but then it was late and the house was quiet with sleeping members. Plus he knew that Flavia shared a room.

He walked to his own room like a dead man, not knowing what to think anymore and suddenly not having anything to look forward to the following day. It was a shock to him. The last few weeks he had been eager to get up in the mornings. Now he wanted to sleep and never wake up again. He did not want to have to look Flavia in the face.

June 22

Valerus tried not to wake up the next morning. He was aware of the day noises reaching his waking consciousness but tried to erase them with a dream. Soon the birdsong was too evident to ignore and he was forced to full wakefulness.

He got dressed slowly, stretching time as much as he could. He put on his toga, taking extra care with the way it fell over his body. Then he combed out his hair and ran his hand across his jaw, realizing he had missed a shave the previous day.

Thus he shaved, taking longer than he ought to and slowing even more when tackling the area under the nose.

Finally he stepped out into the corridor. Alia and Ursalus were making their way toward him with baskets at their hips, collecting the dirty laundry. He greeted them a little coldly and marched on, feeling their penetrating gazes on his back.

There was talking in the kitchen. He looked inside and saw the slaves Helen and Luci working with some vegetables. Flavia was seated at the table, her back to him, softly chatting to the two of them. Valerus tried to listen in, but the sound of the cooker drowned out nearly everything.

He stepped in and made his presence known with a gentle cough. All three of them spun around to him; he saw Flavia's gaze just as quickly hit the floor rather than meet his.

"Flavia," he spoke gently, for the moment not acknowledging the other two at all. "Can we talk?"

"No," she said flatly.

Valerus was aware of the other two staring at him, watching in anticipation as to how he was going to react to that remark. Valerus found himself in a situation he had never been in before; he was being disrespected and disobeyed and he could not bring himself to punish her. What made it worse was that other slaves were present and he was frightened of their reactions if he allowed Flavia to get away with that remark.

He looked from them to Flavia and then up again. "Everyone out!" he commanded with a tone he thought to have left behind after knowing Flavia. It was the tone of command that allowed no disobedience.

Flavia too made an attempt to leave with the others but he stepped up and put his hand on her shoulder, pressing her down into the seat again. Helen and Luci left quickly, and, once they were out of the room, Valerus walked around the table to sit down opposite her.

She kept looking at her hands, which were clenched on the tabletop.

"Flavia?" His voice was as she had known it over the last several weeks, but she could not bring herself to look at him.

"Flavia, please talk to me."

Now she looked at him for the first time. He saw the redness around her eyes that confessed that she had been crying.

"Please don't do this." He shook his head. "What happened yesterday was … Well, I thought they were going to hurt you. I had no control over it."

"No control?" She frowned. "What if I had been standing in his place?"

"The blade would not have touched you."

She turned her head away.

"Please, Flavia." He reached for her hand. "Forgive me."

She pulled her hand away and looked squarely at him. "You killed the man, Valerus."

"He was armed."

"With a cosh! He had merely picked it up."

Valerus tried to speak in defense when she continued. "Does he forgive you? Does his companion? Will his master forgive you? Did he have a family? Will they forgive you?"

Every question she asked cut him deeper until there was nothing but the dull throb of open pain. He felt like dying that very instant so that he would not be humiliated in the fact that he could not answer a single one of them. But then an answer came; it came suddenly and so automatically that, like yesterday, he had no control over it. "If they were like you they would." He clasped her hand. "If they were believers in the Christian faith …"

"You know nothing of Christ!" she snapped at him and yanked

her hand back. “Yesterday proved it! You know nothing of the things He taught and you never will! You and I are worlds apart. Don’t talk to me about my own faith!” She stormed out of the kitchen.

The two kitchen girls were near the door, trying to listen to the conversation at hand. They at once tried to appear busy with other tasks when Flavia stormed out and headed down the passage to her room. Valerus followed a few seconds later and regarded them for an instant before going after Flavia again.

Her door shut heavily. He went over and tried it. It was barred. With what? Slaves could not bar their doors; there was nothing in there to bar it with. She had to have pushed her bed frame up against it.

He tapped it instead. “Flavia, open the door.”

It was a gentle voice but with the tone of command. He bit his lip in an effort to control himself, holding back the tears that were rising. In a small strange way, he wanted to break in and take her in his arms, but then in another he wanted to leave her be, even only for a while so that he could cry.

He tapped on the door again, and when he spoke his voice was crested with the crack of tears. “Flavia, please. I didn’t want to see you getting hurt. Please, Flavia?”

There was silence. The man held his breath to hear whether she had heard him, but the silence reassured him of nothing. He was almost certain he heard her crying.

There was a thud in the house followed by distant chatter. Valerus jumped away from the door and ran back toward the entrance. Then he heard his own intake of breath when Pedius’s voice broke from the atrium.

Chapter 23

Valerus didn't know how to behave or what to say to the family's return. His mind was so filled with Flavia and yesterday's incident that he was hardly aware of his mother and sister embracing him. Gaius greeted him shortly, noticing his uneasiness but choosing wisely not to say anything.

Valerus stayed around them as they spoke of their trip, repeating that it had been terribly crowded and, in fact, that was the reason they returned earlier than anticipated. Valerus listened, but as a deaf man would. He kept glancing in the direction of the slaves' quarters, wondering if Flavia was going to come out or if her fear of him was holding her back.

Finally the family members went their separate ways. Valerus did not move. He watched Gaius from across the room. The young man shrugged in his direction and then made a small movement with his hand, inviting Valerus to follow him.

He did. Gaius went directly to his room and held the door open for him without a word. Once they were both inside, Gaius shut the door and looked his way. "Something went wrong, Valerus?" he asked with his eyebrows raised.

"Master Gaius," Valerus spoke with the tone of a desperate man. "Tonight you must teach me to write poetry."

Pedius was in the kitchen checking up on the slaves and then toured the house to be sure all commands had been carried out to his satisfaction. After a late lunch, he reclined himself in the garden beside his wife.

"It's good to be back," Rectina announced.

"The wine was exquisite, but I agree." Pedius wrapped his arm gently around her. "The people make you want to flee."

Galen walked into the garden, went up before the two of them, and bowed shortly. "Master Salvius is here to see you, master."

"Salvius?" Pedius smirked. "I have no intent to see him."

"He says it is urgent."

Pedius waved at him. "Tell him that I will see him in the morning. We are tired from our trip."

Galen appeared obviously uneasy. Salvius was a hard man who did not take kindly to slaves; in fact, he had heard stories of how Salvius treated them. He felt uneasy to have to repeat what Pedius had said—especially after the man had been so persistent.

"He says it is *very* urgent, master."

Pedius sat up a bit. "I have no ambition to see his crude filthy face at this time! Tell him I have just returned from a trip and will see him first thing in the morning."

Galen bowed to him, trembling. "He mentioned that he will bring the city guard down on the house if you refuse, master."

Pedius's face went crimson. "What? What right does he have?"

"He says he has every right, master."

Rectina and Pedius shared a puzzled glance before he got up, straightening his toga as he did. "Very well," he said. "I will see him in my tablinium. Send him in."

❧

Salvius was a crude-looking man. He was quite obviously not rich; even his toga was made of a heavy-set wool. His face was unshaven and untrimmed. Along his left cheek, he carried a scar from a childhood street fight. It was a symbol to the rest of society as to where he had grown up and how.

But Pedius was a gentleman to his guests, despite his dislike of them. He greeted Salvius kindly when entering and indicated to the empty chair opposite.

"You have caught me at an awkward time, Salvius." He shook his head as they were both seated.

"My matter is very urgent, Pedius." Even his voice was hard, deep, and broken. There was wine on his breath.

Pedius clenched his hands on the table in front of him. "What can I do for you?"

Salvius appeared surprised by the question, but then his surprise was replaced by rage. "By Vulcan! I expect to be paid for my loss! You're not getting away with it!"

Pedius shook his head, leaned over the table and, using the same threatening tone, asked, "Are you drunk, Salvius?"

This only angered him more. The man's hands opened and he thumped them on the table. "I have accepted your proposal for our slaves to share fishing grounds, and I am grateful for all the help you have offered me over the years, but I will not stand for this! Satron was an obedient, well-respected servant. I paid a good sum for him! Do you think that your killing will just go unregarded?"

Now Pedius frowned. "What? Satron has been killed? When? Where?"

"Last night down by the fishing grounds. How could you not know that? Even the guard was involved. It took them the whole day to finally tell me who was responsible."

"I am afraid you are mistaken." Pedius shook his head. "I have been away in Baiae over the past two days with my family. I only returned earlier this morning. Only my son was here, and he would never venture into that district."

Salvius sat back, calmed by his statement but suddenly very bewildered. "The guard told me it was you." He said to him a little more uncertainly. "They interrogated several slaves, mine as well as two of yours. They definitely directed me to this house."

"I am sorry, Salvius, but I will need solid evidence that anyone from the household was involved before I can act upon this. Of course I would pay any losses and damage if the evidence shows it was one of my workers."

Salvius got to his feet, knocking the chair down behind him. "All right. I will bring the slaves in who have been questioned. Will tomorrow morning do? In the Quarta?"

Pedius nodded. "Yes, let us settle this. I cannot believe that anyone in this household would wreck property in this manner."

⁂

It was late; Marcus was checking on his guards before returning to the watch-house and the villa appeared quiet. Two lamps were still lit though. One was in Flavia's room, where the woman was sitting on the bed she had moved back to its proper place. Alia was sitting on the bed opposite, combing out her hair. "So what happened?" she asked.

"Nothing," Flavia replied flatly.

"We could all see something had gone wrong. You were in tears and Valerus sought you out like a hound."

Flavia looked the other way. The memory of the killing, of the severed head, haunted her; it had brought nightmares. She could not look at him; when she did, all she saw was yesterday's incident repeating itself again and again. She wanted to forgive him and tell him how much she loved him despite his violent action. Yet something held her back and she couldn't do it. She tried to analyze what it was but could not think clearly on the matter. She would have to give it a few days.

"Did he force you down? I warned you that sooner or later …"

"It does not matter what happened!" she snapped and jumped to her feet. "What do you care anyway? To you it's never been important. To your lot it's always been about the pleasing of the man and nothing more!"

She stormed off, muttering angrily under her breath as she walked to the atrium. Marcus was by the terrace that opened to the sea, having a soft conversation with one of the guards. He saw Flavia coming toward him. He was distressed by the woman's expression and even more worried when he noticed the tears in her eyes.

"Flavia." He turned to her as he waved at the guard to resume his duties. "What's wrong?"

Marcus was not a married man; he had been at a stage, but the woman wanted another and had left him terribly lonely. It was not so much the failed marriage that had broken him but his dream for having children. Flavia for some reason had partly filled that hole, thus he was taken by her pain and felt the need to comfort her.

Flavia sucked in air, trying to get a grip on herself. He carefully took her by the shoulder and pulled her through the open door so that they stood in the cool air of the ocean. "Just breathe, Flavia." He put an arm around her. "Take it easy."

"I want to see Gaius." She sobbed softly.

Marcus sucked on his teeth and shook his head. "Master Gaius gave me specific orders not to disturb him tonight … not for any reason."

It was as if his words pulled the last bit of air from the woman's lungs. She leaned into the captain of guard and took him around the waist, his *lorica* cold on her hands. Her grip was weak; she had no more strength from the hurt. She had not eaten since she watched Valerus decapitate a man; in fact, it was not only her loss of appetite that she had lost, but in the core of her being she knew she had lost Valerus and thus her reason to live. She remembered what Gaius had said to her regarding a man born blind and a man blinded and now understood the parable in horrific detail.

Maybe it would have been better if none of it had ever happened, if Valerus had never confessed his feelings to her.

She thought about this for a few seconds as Marcus held her in a comforting manner. Her brow creased when she realized that she disagreed with that thought. Despite what had happened the previous day, her time with Valerus had been worthwhile, all of it. She had really loved him then and nothing she had given into was regretted. And then she felt, though still scarred and bleeding, that she did still love him.

❧

The second lamplight filled the library where Gaius paced the floor with his hands clasped behind his back. At the table was Valerus, sitting with a papyrus sheet in front of him, an inkwell and a reed pen clasped in his hand. He was writing slowly but with determination. Every now and again he would stop to examine his work.

"Master Gaius," Valerus shook his head without even looking up, "this does not sound right."

The younger man came up behind him to read over his shoulder. He slowly began to shake his head and point down to the paper, careful not to touch the fresh ink. "You can't write that!" he snapped kindly. "I know you see it as a compliment, but there is a time and place for everything."

"And paper is not the place to do that?"

Gaius went to the empty chair across the room and sat down.

"Keep it for the bedroom, Valerus. You want to charm her. That you do with natural elements of beauty which relate to her. Not with," he waved his hand, "physical, bodily aspects."

Valerus picked up the sheet and scanned it. "But this first passage is all right then, isn't it?" he asked, pointing to the paragraph with his reed pen.

"Valerus." Gaius reached under the small bust, which was being used as a paperweight, and removed a blank sheet. "A woman is very different from a man. What you are writing is more what *you* want to hear from *her*." He walked across the room and handed it to him. "If you want to learn poetry, you want to get into the feminine mind and see exactly what she wants to hear and put it down on paper for her. You can't rely on your own thoughts and fantasies when doing this."

Valerus stared at the blank sheet in front of him and then up at Gaius who had taken his written work and was neatly folding it up.

"Become the woman, Valerus." Gaius shook his head without meeting his stare. "Women are beautiful creatures and they know it. Thus don't spare detail on describing something to them that they already know. Dig into their soul and surprise them with a beauty that they were never even aware of."

Valerus had difficulty in grasping this concept. He was learning a new form of thought—a pattern that he was completely unfamiliar with. How could he reach into Flavia's head and know what she wanted to hear? He was not a magician or a soothsayer. How could Gaius expect him to do it?

Gaius was suddenly beside him, one hand on the man's shoulder and the other leaning on the edge of the table. "Listen to me, Valerus." His voice appeared softer and more patient by his ear. "What is it about this woman that you love? Surely her physical state is a part of it, but it can't be all of it. What made you fall in love with her? What is it about her that makes you want her more than anyone else?"

Valerus smiled when he heard him ask this. "Her smile," he said softly. "The way she's passionate about what she believes and acts on what she knows to be right. The way she makes me feel alive. She's so different from all the others, slaves and non-slaves alike. She's alive! She's vibrant! She's . . ." He shook his head, trying to find the correct word. "She's a goddess!"

Gaius was nodding slowly. "Right," he said after a while and pointed to the blank sheet. "Put *that* on paper."

Chapter 24

June 23

Salvius came in the midmorning accompanied by two of his slaves, one of whom was the repairer himself. His master had draped him in a clean tunic for the occasion and the second servant was helping him walk.

Pedius looked at the slave from the tip of his nose as they walked into the tablinium and then at Salvius. There was a clear dislike to the man; Pedius was not a man to be seen dining with his slaves or visiting the areas considered theirs, but he had a considerable amount of respect for them. Slaves of a household represented the house; it was an unspoken law. Seeing the repairer, with his crooked back and rotting teeth, said something plain about Salvius.

They were seated rather than reclined for this meeting. The slaves sat at the feet of their superiors while two members of the city guard took position by the open doors. Marcus stepped in to bear witness to the proceeding. This incident was being held out of court, an action not often taken. Murder was a serious crime and assault, but both Pedius and Salvius had agreed to settle this between themselves. The one found guilty would have to pay the losses or for the time of the other. The victim of the act would be in the position to decide how the guilty ought to be treated to satisfy him.

After a short while Procimus and Moe were brought into the room and sat at Pedius's feet. It was obvious to anyone that they were a little nervous, unsettled.

"Let us get this underway," Pedius announced and opened his hand to Salvius. "Please state your accusation."

The man got to his feet. "Two days ago, in the later evening, Gacius came to me in a state, saying that Satron had been killed—decapitated—on my own property." He turned to indicate the guards by the door. "These two men were the first on the scene and bore witness to the kill. They can also claim, with full honesty, after a twelve-hour investigation, that it was the property of Pedius that caused this violation."

The guards nodded their heads when the stares turned to them. One of the men presented a scroll on which was written the entire report. Pedius took it from him and unrolled it across the table. There was a long silence as he read through it quickly.

"Right," he said finally and rolled the paper up again. "I have no doubt that this is an original script." He passed it back to them. "But I need to know who it was."

"My suspicion—as well as the guard—falls on them." Salvius pointed to the two fishermen sitting on the floor. "They of course deny it, but they were on the beaches at the time the guard arrived."

Pedius turned to his two slaves. He said nothing to them but merely raised an eyebrow.

Both men shuffled uneasily. They were not in the position to say anything really. They were innocent; Flavia had been involved and their master's son had performed the act. This truth was going to cause some violent reaction. They were, after all, only slaves and they knew that their word meant nothing. The testimonies of slaves meant nothing, nor were they permitted in court. They were but property, and Pedius would much sooner give them up as the guilty pair than to shame the family name.

"Well?" Pedius finally asked. "What do you know of this?"

"Was not us, master." Procimus shook his head. "I know that Moe here has already been charged with theft, but neither of us are murderers."

"You were on my ground when the guard arrived," Salvius announced slowly but very clearly.

"This is true, but so were many others. We simply flocked with the rest to see what the fuss was about."

There was a second's silence out of respect before Salvius opened his hand to Gacius, offering him a moment to speak. "It was not them. It was a young couple; a man and a woman."

"Now there are two involved!" Pedius roared and looked directly at Salvius. "Your story appears to change suddenly."

"Two were there," Gacius told him quickly, "but it was the young man who used my very own sword to cut off Satron's head!"

"What provoked this?" Pedius looked at the repairer who had not moved or said a word from his place near his master's feet. He appeared to be muttering under his breath.

"Not a damn thing!" Salvius snapped. "It was my property; both the people as well as the ground of which it happened! It does not matter what—if anything—provoked it!"

"What's all this?"

All the heads turned to the doorway where Valerus stood. In his hands he carried a rolled-up scroll. He had gotten up early to catch Flavia before her chores and was lured by the arguing voices to his father's study.

At once Gacius jumped to his feet, pointing a trembling finger at him. Valerus recognized him as well as the repairer too late before he realized what was going on.

"That's him!" Gacius announced loudly. "That's the man. Not a doubt about it!"

Pedius was on his feet just as fast, prepared to protect the family honor as far as he could. "Out of the question! That is my son and I resent the allegation!"

Silence fell like a thunderclap. Valerus stared at the gathered company, noticing how every eye was on him. Procimus and Moe appeared the most uncomfortable; dimming their stares and trying desperately to find something with which to occupy their minds.

Valerus himself hung his head, unable to protest or apologize. What could he say to any of them? It was an accident? A misunderstanding? None of that would be acceptable, he knew. The best he could do for himself, for Flavia, as well as for the family name was to accept it as it came to him.

Pedius's mouth gaped open a few times before he shook his head. "By Jupiter," he said finally, "it can't be true ..."

Valerus detached himself from the wall and entered the room.

"What were you doing in that part of town, Valerus?" Pedius asked softly.

Valerus did not answer; he could not without giving Flavia away. But then his silence was not necessary either. His father nodded. "You were there with the slave girl, weren't you?"

"She is not responsible for anything," he said, still with his head dimmed. "She had nothing to do with this."

"How can you say that?" Gacius was on his feet again. "She provoked the argument!"

"No! I did!" Valerus shouted, desperate to be heard above Flavia's accusation. "Besides, your men were carrying weapons which they used on the both of us."

"If this was an act of self-defense," Pedius said, "then there can be no accusation on your part, Salvius."

"This was on my property! My servants have as much right

to protect it as I do! Their clubs are for disciplinary purposes and chasing off trespassers." He pointed to Valerus. "Your son was the one who drew the sword that did not even belong to him."

Pedius was still staring at his son, unable to believe it. Valerus looked his way again and said, clearly and slowly for everyone to hear, "Flavia had some free time and I asked her to show me around. She is entirely innocent to this affair."

"Well then, let us rise to the next subject." Salvius raised his hand. "And that will be the question as to who has been feeding my slave." His hand came down on the repairer's shoulder, who winced. "I don't feed him that stuff."

You don't feed him anything, Valerus thought bitterly.

Pedius looked at Valerus again. "Have you been meddling with slaves, son?"

Valerus hesitated, which he felt a fool for doing. He should have confessed it, thus saving Flavia any trouble as well as himself a lot of grief, but he hesitated. Pedius spun to Marcus who was standing by the door. "Marcus! Get the slave girl, Flavia, in here this instant!"

The captain left on command. Valerus felt a hot flash run through him suddenly. The morning was not meant to go this way. In his hand he felt the paper on which was written his poem . . . and cursed himself. He should have found Flavia and have her read it. He should never have interfered with his father's business.

"If that girl has been using my stock to feed your slave, it's going to be the worst for her!" Pedius spat in Salvius's direction but threw an angry look at his son.

When Flavia entered, escorted by Marcus, Valerus looked her way and immediately saw the expression that fell over her. The betrayal—he had given her away. Following her shocked gaze, he then saw the tears come to her eyes. He shook his head slowly, hoping that it would be enough to make her realize that he had not given her away—on the contrary.

"Have you been feeding this man, woman?" Pedius demanded to know immediately, not prepared to waste any more time.

Lie, woman, lie, Valerus repeated in his mind. *Deny it all.* But then there was the dull ache in his stomach as he knew she would never do that. She was a Christian and he had heard her preach to him about the solemn oath she was dedicated to, which was not to tell any wicked lies. And it would indeed be wicked if she denied it. Pedius was furious and prepared to blame anyone to put an end to the matter.

Valerus watched as Flavia looked at the repairer, who was staring at his own toes, then looked back at her master and then Valerus; her gaze was now saddened by the thought of his betrayal. He knew that she was going to stand her ground and take full responsibility. That was what she preached.

Valerus felt his blood run cold when she nodded boldly and spoke in a clear voice, saying, "Occasionally I did master, but only with that which would not be missed in the house."

Valerus shut his eyes, well aware that his father could do anything with her, including having her killed. For a second, he pictured Flavia crucified as her Lord had been, but he erased this as quickly as he could, unable to bear it.

Her added comment to the answer had no effect. Pedius shook his head, disgusted and completely at a loss of words for a few seconds. A fisherman slave who stole the occasional fish could easily be pardoned, but a thief in his own home was a different matter entirely. He looked at Marcus who was still beside her.

"Off with her, Captain," he said to him. "I cannot have a thief in the house. Be so good as to keep her in your garrison until I decide what to do with her."

"It was just the scraps!" Valerus shouted as Marcus took her by the arm.

"And you knew of this, Valerus?"

The young man ignored the question and pointed to the repairer. "Look at him, Father! What loss did you take after all? Some of it was even expired! Insects had to be sifted from the grain!"

Flavia frowned, realizing the situation was not as she had assumed it to be.

"She has not done anything!" Valerus continued. "I am to be blamed for this matter entirely! Leave Flavia out of my matters! I am guilty of what you accuse me of!" Valerus opened his hand to Salvius. "What will your penalty be?"

"Valerus!" Pedius bellowed, unable to restrain himself. "Shut up! You are in enough trouble as it is!"

Valerus said nothing, knowing that it would make things far worse if he did. Instead he watched, speechless, as Marcus led Flavia away. He noticed that there was some care and compassion in his grip on her. For a second, she caught his gaze over her shoulder before disappearing. He fought the urge to go after her and turned back to his father, who had now turned to Salvius.

"It is truly a disgrace for me to discover that my household has dishonored you, Salvius." He shook his head. Then he opened his hand to him. "I am guilty of what you accused me of. I am prepared to pay for the damage and abide to the laws. What will be your request? Let us settle this now, here, out of court."

Salvius looked at Valerus and then back at his slaves. "I will ask three hundred denarii for my loss and as for him," he pointed to Valerus, "seven lashes will meet my satisfaction."

For a moment Valerus could not believe it; he did not think that his father would allow it. Then Pedius nodded and gestured to him. "Let it be done. I am pleased that this has been settled."

Valerus stared at his father, his mind still stuttering with incomprehension.

"The amount will be paid within the week," Pedius continued as he got to his feet. Salvius and his slaves followed. "Rely on it."

Salvius nodded and took Pedius by the shoulder in good gesture. "All is in order, then."

Pedius turned to the guards still stationed by the doors. "It's all settled," he told them. "Please escort the boy to the back terrace. Salvius will follow shortly."

Flavia followed Marcus on her own once they met the street. The captain let her go but made sure she followed alongside him. Flavia felt the ache in her stomach, the sick rise which she could relate to the time when she was sold. It was a terribly tight grip in her gut, and there was a bitter taste of bile rising in her mouth.

"What will happen to me?" she asked Marcus, her voice trembling a little.

He shook his head. "I don't know. It is the master's decision alone."

"Will I be pardoned?"

"Valerus might convince him."

She realized that Valerus was her last hope, but, despite what he said in her defense, she did not know if he would be prepared to go to those lengths—not after what she had said to him.

She remembered the way he stood up for her when the accusations began, and she wanted to believe that he would convince his father. But what if not? What would happen to her? Sold? Killed? It was not impossible. After all, a master could do whatever he or she wanted with property. It was not that he was losing any money from her death. She had been but a gift.

Suddenly she was angry. Valerus should never have gifted her to his father; he should have kept her for himself since the beginning. If that had been the case, would she have fallen in love with him, and him with her? She ran through all the events that led to this moment and realized how everything had fit together to come to this instant right here.

Unconsciously she took Marcus by the arm, seeking silent support. The only regret she had now was that she could not tell Valerus that she still loved him.

Valerus was very much in the same line of thought as the guards marched him to the back terrace. Though disputes were often dealt with out of court, the punishments were preferred to be held in a more public area. This way brutality among citizens was observed, recorded, and controlled. His father was fortunately not prepared to expose his son to this, at least not in public. Humiliation, Pedius thought, would have taught him a good lesson, but he was well aware what it could do to reputation.

Valerus was thinking of Flavia when he entered the small terrace. It was empty and their footsteps echoed across the flagstones. He had hardly ever been there; it was for the discipline of slaves.

The two guards led him across the ground to the farther reaches where the whiping post had been permanently erected. There were two other cruel instruments of torture used for slave punishment and discipline, which were, for now, disregarded. An unattended furnace, brandishing hot iron rods, was erected in the far corner.

Valerus said nothing nor did he move as the guards began to strip him of his toga and chiton. They were neatly folded and set on the bench nearby. The rolled scroll was placed on top of them.

Salvius arrived, carrying a parchment which he passed to the nearest guard who quickly scanned through it and nodded to his accomplice. Then they bound Valerus's wrists to the post, but they did not bind weights to his feet as they did to the slaves to avoid them thrashing about. Valerus watched from the corner of his eye as one of the guards picked up the whip from its hook. It was the simple singular whip used for beatings of discipline by the law and masters of the house. Momentarily Valerus felt like a slave: bound to the commands and decisions of his father.

"Would Master Salvius like to administrate the strokes?" the soldier asked.

To Valerus's surprise, the man shook his head. "No. The son of an accomplice? It would not be right. I will only bear witness to say that it has been done to my satisfaction."

One of the guards came around to Valerus, offering him a little piece of wood. Valerus took it between his teeth as intended. "Bite down hard," he suggested kindly.

Valerus did not need to be told. The fear was beginning to cause the impatience for them to begin. He could nearly feel the pain searing into his back before the first stroke even came down, and when it did it was worse than what he had expected. The second and third lashes threw him forward across the post, biting down so hard on the wood that he thought his jaw would crack. For a second he wondered how Flavia had managed such pain, but his guilt was quickly conquered by the next lash that cut him skin deep.

He lost the piece of wood by the fifth strike, and the men present were decent enough to halt the procedure to offer it to him again.

Valerus had little strength left in his jaw by the sixth whip and heard the wood piece roll across the floor. It was nearly over, he thought, but he was frightfully aware how time slowed when you were expecting something you so much dreaded. Only this morning he planned to give Flavia a love poem he had written and to beg forgiveness. Now he wondered if he would ever get the chance to, or if she would ever get to read it.

He cried out on the last stroke; the whip burned into his raw skin. He had lost count by the fourth and was nearly convinced that they had gone over the limit when one guard came to untie a wrist.

Both men supported him when he was freed. The whipping had left him disorientated, dizzy, and completely depleted of any strength.

The guards carefully led him to the stone bench that was set across the opposite wall and had him sit down. He winced as he tried to adjust his position. His clothes were brought to him before the guards returned to their duties. Salvius watched the young man from his place for a few seconds before following after them.

Valerus sat alone, trying desperately to get his breath back. There was a pulsating heat accompanied by a burning pain radiating down his back. He thought he could feel the run of blood, but he knew that it had not come to that.

Slowly he reached for his chiton. His hands were trembling. In a horrible moment he thought of Flavia—where she was and what was going to happen to her. He had been so focused on his own pain that he had not stopped to think about Flavia's fear.

He could not let his father sell her … he could not. He would have to convince him to pardon her or he would have to make an offer before his father made his decision.

Would his father listen after all this?

Valerus gripped the sides of the bench as he calculated his finances. He had six hundred denarii and a few sestertii more if he included his savings for what he had earned for the theater. A dancing girl of Flavia's stature was worth at least two thousand denarii, if not more. He was barely a quarter there. But then, after all this, perhaps his father would let her go for less.

With a sigh that nearly resembled defeat—nearly—Valerus rubbed his face. His mind had hit a wall, and he had run out of ideas as well as plans. He wanted Flavia, but there was nothing he could do in the short time he had left.

Chapter 25

Valerus woke up at dusk, unaware at which point he had actually drifted off. Momentarily he had completely forgotten about the whipping he had experienced, but the recollection of it returned ten-fold when he shifted his position. He winced as he sat up, slowly pulling his legs off the edge of the bed.

His chiton had been folded on the end of the bed, beside a clean toga. Valerus looked down and saw that he was only in his underwear. Just as well. Anything pressing against his back was unthinkable right now. How had Flavia managed it?

He went to his dresser and removed a smaller toga his mother had kept from childhood and wrapped it around his waist. He stopped and thought about what he was doing: Flavia had worn her tunica directly after her whipping. How could he not? Besides, did he want people to see what had happened?

Then again, in this household, everyone knew by now.

He got dressed in his tunic, wincing as it came down his back. Then, slowly and taking great care in the way it fell, he draped himself in his toga.

As he was about to leave the room, he saw on his table the poem he had written. Flavia's name had been neatly written at the top.

Carefully, as if frightened he might break it, he picked it up and read it. After a few seconds he felt the sting of tears and his vision ran blurry. He wanted her to have it more than anything. The day had not gone the way he had planned.

This caused fear. His father could have had him killed, but instead he had received a whipping and nothing more. There was no telling what would happen to Flavia. For the moment she was sitting in a condemned cell. Valerus knew nothing regarding the prisons built for slaves, and he wondered if she was forced to share a cell. He cringed as his imagination took dreadful control for a few seconds, but he pushed the images from his head.

Marcus was still a powerful asset, he realized. He might be able to pass the poem to Flavia. No matter what was in stored for either of them, Valerus knew that Flavia *had* to read it.

He left his room, trying his utmost not to show any discomfort or pain, and he walked to the atrium when he heard the murmur of voices. A guard was pacing the aisle and nodded his way. Valerus took his arm and passed the scroll to him. "This must be delivered to the slave girl that was arrested earlier today."

The guard looked from it to him. "It will have to be read before," he told him.

The young man exhaled slowly, completely put off by the idea of someone else reading a poem he intended for Flavia. He reached to take the scroll back from him before choosing against it. He preferred someone else reading it than Flavia never getting the opportunity.

"Please deliver it to Marcus, then," he said, finding it the better option. "He is to give it to her."

The guard nodded. "Very well, Master Valerus. I will have it delivered to him at once."

Valerus watched him leave before stepping into the *cenatio.* The family was reclined in a household meeting. He heard his sister's voice clearly as he neared: "… worth a lot. I think our better option would be to sell her."

Valerus stepped into the room, ending the conversation and getting all heads turned to him. His mother was up the next instant and beside him. "Are you all right, love?" she asked in a concerned tone.

Valerus threw his father a quick glance and then nodded to her. "No problem." But for the moment he felt so very different toward his family—his father especially. *Hate* was a strong word, but it was reaching for that. Valerus knew that he had to watch his step. He had gotten into his father's black book once too often in the last few weeks.

"We were just deciding Flavia's fate," Pedius said to him and gestured to the empty couch. "Join us."

Valerus sat down but did not recline himself; the pain did not permit it. He glanced around the room momentarily. "Where is Gaius?"

"Not here!" Pedius snapped impatiently. "This is family business, and I am prepared to hear the views of the family members."

"I say sell her," Anneria announced to them, repeating herself loudly. "I mean, what would we gain from her death? Nothing. She is a dancing girl trained in Hispania and I am sure that we could get a good sum for her."

"But who would buy a thief?" Her father shrugged. "And she has been whipped." Now he looked at Valerus. "And that puts a bad mark on the domus."

Valerus had never had more remorse than at that moment. He ought never to have done the things he did; he should never have branded her. This came as a shock; he suddenly remembered one of the stories Flavia had told him regarding Christ saying to do unto others what you wanted others to do unto you. This came as a frightful realization: he was going through with his father what she had gone through with him. But he deserved it. This brought him some sense of acceptance, but the guilt remained when he realized that Flavia was involved despite his revelation.

"Perhaps, but Anneria is correct; we could at least cover some of our loss in selling her."

"What loss?" Valerus nearly shouted. "They were scraps; things you never knew were missing even till now! She was helping someone! What could you possibly find wrong in that?"

"It's the principle of the thing!" Pedius snapped. "She was a thief in my house!"

Valerus sat back without another word, throwing his father a look that could have killed.

"I refuse to sell a slave from this household below two thousand denarii. I refuse a coin less!" Pedius shook his head. "That's quality! That says something about this house as well as all of us: We do not harbor worthless servants."

Rectina was beginning to see her husband's point. "And who, may I ask, will pay that amount for a thief?" she asked with a nod of her head.

"I would."

All heads turned to Valerus; he was not even aware that he had said anything. His mind was simply working in one realm and his mouth in another.

"With what money?" Pedius asked bitterly. "You already owe me three hundred denarii for Salvius's loss."

Valerus, aware now that he had pulled himself into a corner, knew he had to go with the currents. It was his only chance to ever see Flavia again. He gathered up his strength and looked at every face. "I will get it." He nodded. "Give me a few months, and I will have the money."

Pedius adjusted his weight impatiently. "I don't want her in this house again, Valerus! She is a thief and I don't know what stops me from having her killed. Everyone here appears to forget that I could get just as good a price for her if I sell her to the arena."

Valerus could not bear the thought, so he said quickly, "I will pay you three thousand denarii!" It was a stupid offer, and he knew it the moment he said it. He would never manage that kind of money even in a year, but he was desperate to say something—anything—to keep his father from making brutal decisions.

"Where are you going to get that kind of money, Velli?" Anneria was also sitting up now.

"I have plans."

"Well, they had better be good." Pedius shrugged, taken by the offer through sheer greed rather than rational thought. "You have a week ... after that I will do what I feel is best for this household."

"A week!" Valerus was on his feet suddenly. "That's impossible! I could never get twelve thousand sestertii in a week!"

"Neither can you in a year."

"Pedius, please." Rectina shook her head. "Give the boy a chance. He's in love." It was the first time that Valerus saw any compassion coming from her side regarding the situation. He did not, in fact, realize that they knew of the situation, but it had to be fairly obvious now. Obviously the family had been discussing the events and situation for longer than he had thought.

Pedius looked from her to his son and then to his daughter. Even she had a compassionate expression on her face.

He sighed and nodded, giving in to the majority vote. "Very well. I will let her go for twelve hundred denarii. You have one month."

Valerus wanted to protest again, feeling that he needed at the very least three months for any chance to accumulate that amount of money, but he saw in his father's expression that he was not in a position to negotiate any further.

There was, however, one more point he had to bring up. "Can

Flavia come home?" he asked. He had to. He knew he would not sleep at night if she was kept in a prison cell.

Pedius was shaking his head before he had even finished asking the question. "I don't want a thief in this house, Valerus."

"I will keep her elsewhere. I just don't want her sitting in a cell."

The two women in the room were taken by his concern and looked at Pedius, both pleading that Valerus's wish be granted.

Pedius was a man of the house, but he had always respected his wife and daughter, more so than Valerus, strangely. Perhaps it was because Valerus was more a stranger than a family member. But he gave in to the wishes of the women he loved so dearly. "Very well," he agreed, but with obvious reluctance. "I will speak to Marcus tonight and you can get her. But I don't want to see her here. Is this understood?"

Valerus nodded desperately. "Perfectly."

⁂

They were all gone, Flavia thought as she bit her nails, all those days with Valerus: playing in the fountain and walking the city together. They were nothing but memories now, clear memories. She remembered their first kiss followed by the look in his eyes that first evening she removed her clothes for him. She was forced to smile when remembering his unique smell as well as the feel of his hands on her.

She could not believe she had suspected him of giving her away, after everything they had shared, while he was actually only trying to save her.

She felt a heavy weight around her neck and touched the green pendant he had given her. She had nearly forgotten about it and she clenched at it, remembering the day he had first given it to her and she had accepted it with her forgiveness.

She wished she could get a chance to ask for his.

She was roused from her thoughts and memories by approaching footfalls. She got up and went up against the bars just as Marcus entered the holding. He smiled at her.

"Are you being treated well, Flavia?"

She nodded. There had been fresh straw in her cell. The men on duty were well mannered, despite her being a slave. She was a beautiful one at that, but Marcus had given strict orders.

Marcus smiled; he tapped the scroll on his palm before passing it through the bars to her.

"What's this?" she asked as she took it.

"Poetry … from Valerus."

She was surprised.

"I regret to say I was compelled to read it. Orders, you understand?"

"Thank you, Marcus."

The captain left her as she turned back and settled on the straw. She unrolled the scroll and laid it down, gently flattening it out. There was no name other than hers, but there was no need for it. Valerus had a beautiful handwriting and the words could only have come from him.

What you have done to me …
Allowing me to touch you as Venus did the time we first kissed
The smell of spring beyond Her date when we came together
What you changed in me since that first night …

What you have done to me …
The sweet taste has turned bitter since you turned away
And your glare tore me in two;
What you have made a blind man see …

So force me to die since you force me to be without you.
Love dictates to me as I write and Cupid shows me the way,
but may I die if God should wish me to go on without you.

She was crying by the second verse, her hand over her mouth as she tried to muffle her sobbing. She was becoming increasingly aware that it was likely the last she would ever hear from him. So much she wanted to reply, but she could not write poetry, nor did she have any writing material.

The events of the last few days drained through the psyche and she realized that it was in fact Valerus's killing profession that first led him to Neapolis where he had purchased her. If he had not been trained as a gladiator, he would never have suffered his injury thus would never have returned to the south. From this thought she wondered what life would have been like if he had never bought her from Cephys those months ago. Despite her fear and regret during those days that followed, this moment she knew it had been the luckiest day of her life, no matter what happened in the days to come.

She read it again, cutting her reading short when her tears blurred the writing. She buried her face in her hands. "Valerus!" she cried, "I'm so sorry!"

"How are you ever going to get that amount of money in four weeks?" Lucius demanded as he escorted his companion to the prison cells. It was already dark and Valerus was eager to get Flavia out of there as soon as he could.

"I will make plans," Valerus told him.

"You are insane! Are you going to rob a bank? Rob a temple?"

"Of course not! I'm not a thief."

"Well, you had better be thinking of becoming one."

Suddenly Valerus was on him, grabbing him by the tunic and pushing him back until he was up against the wall. "What would you have me do?" he hissed, his face only an inch from his. "See her sold off? Watch her being mauled by wild boars? Is that what you would have done, *friend*? If so, then I suppose I am insane, because I refuse it! *I refuse it*!"

Lucius had never seen this obsession and determination in his companion; in his eyes there was a flash of desperation that bordered on insanity. It was clear to him now that Valerus would, very probably, rob a bank if it came to it. He was prepared to kill …

Valerus pointed in the direction of the prisons. "Flavia is sitting in a cell!" His voice had lowered from a hiss to a soft growl. "She thinks I gave her away! I will not have her die thinking that. I will do what it takes—*everything it takes, do you hear me*—not to have that happen!"

Lucius caught his breath and nodded slowly. "Right," he said. "But I need to ask how you are going to come up with twelve hundred denarii before the given date."

"I have about six hundred denarii in my savings. I require six more."

"It's a lot of money, Valerus, to accumulate in four weeks. More than a legionnaire's monthly income."

Valerus released him and backed up a step. "I'll think of something." His voice was a little uncertain but defiantly with ambition. "Mark my words … I will."

Flavia was getting cold, despite it being full summer. The stone walls were radiating the cold, washing it down in the little cell where she sat. Marcus had been very kind to her; he had given her a cell of her own and had promised her some warm stew he himself was going to prepare.

For the moment, things were tolerable and she wished it could stay like this. She did not want to face tomorrow or the memories that sat in wait for a second when her mind would wander.

She had lost everything—everything! She had a good home—decent at least. She was helping people and she had actually felt, for a while, that she was making some kind of difference. Most importantly she had Valerus. She loved him and she knew she always would, despite what he had done.

Now everything was fading. She knew that everyone—Alia, Cotti, Luci, and all the others—were just memories, like those of her mother and siblings. And Valerus was going to be an ache in her heart till the day she died.

There was the ring of keys on her cell door followed by Marcus's voice. "Good news," he said. "Valerus is here to pick you up. It's all been arranged."

Flavia could not believe it as she got up from her place. The captain was standing in the doorway, his figure silhouetted by the lamp burning in the room behind him.

And Valerus was there. She did not expect to see any of his class in the prison for slaves, but there he was like a light unto her world.

Yet she could not move; she stood staring at his figure, wondering how she could approach him after everything she had said. His figure shifted slightly as he reached out his hand. "Come, Flavia," he said softly.

She was aware of nothing else around her as she stepped forward and had him take her hand. He smiled at her and took her into his arms gently as he kissed her. She forgot the argument of the previous day entirely under his touch; even Valerus showed nothing in relation to the quarrel. He winced softly when she grabbed onto his chiton desperately and started to cry. She could relate the feeling to the day Melani had saved her from the arena. That moment when there was nothing left—nothing at all—a little light was lit in the dark and she could once again see a future.

"Valerus!" she sobbed but could say nothing more under the strain of her emotions and relief.

He kissed her head. "Come on. Lucius is waiting. Let's leave this place." He nodded to Marcus, who merely smiled at them. Then Valerus led her from the prison, clenching her close to him.

*

A single lamp was burning in Lucius's small apartment where he sat opposite the young couple, sharing some bread bought earlier that morning. Valerus sat close to Flavia, his arm across her shoulders as he watched her eat. For a while Lucius also watched before getting up to prepare some bedding for them.

When they were alone, Valerus turned to Flavia. "Still hungry?" he asked her. She had confessed to her appetite when he had picked her up and he wanted to be sure that the little he and Lucius had to offer was enough.

She nodded. "This was far more than I needed." She smiled and then gently grasped him around the neck. He saw the tears in her eyes. "You saved my life today, Valerus. I'll never forget that."

"It's because of me this happened."

"No. You would never have gone down to the docks if it hadn't been for me."

He was about to remind her that it was he who had asked her to take him, but she put a finger to his lips and shook her head again. "You saved my life, Valerus. Let's leave it at that."

Carefully he took her face in his hands, feeling the softness of her skin as if for the first time. He came forward to kiss her but instead pressed his brow against hers. "You are my life, Flavia." His voice cracked. "I realized that today." It was true; the short snap of reality when he thought he was going to lose her had been a slap to his consciousness, and he never wanted to experience it again.

Yet at this moment he felt a strange and completely pointless sense of peace. He had no reason to feel comfortable with the growing situation; he knew what his chances were of actually gaining the money he needed in the short period of time, but, now that he was with her and they were no longer separated by stone walls or individual views, he felt that everything was going to work itself out. He had not left her and could not believe that the gods would offer the opportunities without the chances of achieving them.

A master could have his slaves quartered, burnt, flogged, or even thrown to the arena for disobedience and disloyalty. Flavia did not know what Pedius had first planned to do with her, nor did Valerus tell her anything, but he was grateful that he had walked in on the conversation when he had.

"Bed is made." Lucius came in from the bedroom. "I just covered one of the couches with some blankets and added an extra pillow. I hope it will do."

"Better than straw on cold floors." Flavia grinned.

Lucius returned it and picked up his cloak.

Valerus frowned. "Are you going out? It's late."

"Nightlife in Herculaneum runs late." Lucius winked at him, threw his cloak over his shoulders, and left.

The moment he was gone, Valerus turned to Flavia, who had tears in her eyes.

Valerus knew that she was never going to be allowed to set foot in the domus again and thus didn't know how he was ever going to keep her … he could not even afford her. He was not prepared to flee with her, not yet. The consequences for a runaway slave were harsh and Valerus knew he would have no chance if she was ever caught. For the moment there was still opportunity, and he had to play by the rules. He wished that he could just take her as much as she wanted to give herself to him. Between the two of them, money was not needed at all.

"Right now?" He took her hand and kissed her palm. "I have you. I simply have to make sure it stays this way."

Very slowly, Flavia began to shake her head. "How?" Her voice came out small and terribly fragile. Valerus felt that if he breathed too hard he would break it.

Carefully he took her face into his hands. His look became hard and he said, in a voice of authority that could not be doubted, "I will do whatever I need to do."

But what? What could possibly render him twelve hundred denarii in four weeks? The theater was not going to help him. What he needed was a miracle.

Chapter 26

June 26

The emperor was dead. The news reached Herculaneum that early morning and spread like a wild fire. Valerus was startled awake by the sound of chatter below Lucius's window. Apparently Vespasian had been ill for nearly two weeks and finally passed away in the later afternoon three days earlier.

This caused interest for several reasons. First was the fact that Valerus knew it was expected of the lanista to plan some spectacle in memory of the emperor and he would be far more lenient to his fighting program. Maybe he would get to fight in Pompeii, though this he doubted with his injury. Cornelius would keep him in the lower populated areas.

Valerus could not believe his luck; he only had a little over three weeks left and this had truly been God sent. Valerus felt guilty that he was thinking such selfish thoughts at a time when his emperor had passed on, but he could not help himself. He felt a sudden urgency to claim ownership over Flavia's name.

This brought Valerus to think of new things. The theater was not what he needed to raise the money for Flavia's value, nor could any work other than that which was in great demand by the open public.

However, there was also another concern regarding Vespasian's death; that was the thought of his successor, who would no doubt be his son Titus. However, Vespasian had been so much more lenient toward other religious sects, Christianity especially, after Nero's insane rule so many years back. Would Titus be the same? Was Flavia in any more danger now than she was yesterday?

He wasted no time, and by the afternoon he was gone.

Valerus leaned his weight against the outside wall of the small arena. The Herculaneum amphitheater was situated to the northeast, a fair distance from the actor's theater so that the cheer of battle would not interfere with the laughter of a crowd watching a comedy. It was a small structure, the outer perimeter mostly of wood. Valerus recalled his many training hours in the confines of its barracks.

There was a show in process of drawing to an end; he could hear quite distinctly that there were animals involved, people too. Though there was a Roman part of him that was terribly curious and yearning to watch from the crowd, two things held him back forcefully. One was the fact that he could not afford it—under no circumstances could he give expenses to luxury. And secondly, more than anything, he knew Flavia did not approve, and in some small unexplained way neither did he. Maybe he was also becoming a Christian; perhaps it was contagious and Flavia had infected him.

He could not help but smile at this thought.

People were beginning to mill out from their seats. Some began coming past him as they headed back into the city. Valerus waited, removing his knife to clean his fingernails. Cornelius always followed after the crowd, and that would still be some time. The theater had been packed, it appeared, for sport as well as for entertainment.

As the crowd lessened, Valerus became more alert, watching the people passing him until a white chiton and wool toga draped over a familiar shape stepped into the street.

At once the young man went after him, speeding up to walk beside him.

"Well, well, well, Valerus," Cornelius said without even looking his way, "I have not seen you around for weeks."

"I was busy," Valerus replied in the same hastened tone. He caught his breath and came straight to the point. "You must get me into a fight."

Cornelius stopped and stared at him, to be sure that he was serious. He was; no one could mistake the expression on his face. "What? You want to fight?"

"Definitely."

"With that leg?" Cornelius pointed to it briefly. "Are you mad? You will be killed in the first round."

"No, I won't," Valerus snapped. "I need to fight; I need the money. You have to get me into the arena again."

Cornelius sighed and shook his head. "Your worth with a sword does not match up to the time people want to see you standing. I am sorry, Valerus, but in the situation I can't do much."

"You are arranging a spectacle in honor of the emperor," Valerus said as he began to move on his way. Valerus jumped up and blocked his path. "I am desperate! I'll fight anyone."

"Anyone? Even a retiarius?"

"Just make it fair."

The lanista could not reject that. Of course slaves had no choice in who they fought; whether it be women, thieves, or professional soldiers, but a free man prepared to fight any opponent was definitely something in demand. He hesitated slightly before saying, "When last were you in the practice ring?" His tone had changed entirely.

Valerus's smile came from the depths of relief. "Not since the accident. But I have been practicing on the sly."

Cornelius considered.

"You want a spectacle, I am another gladius in the arena."

The old man sighed. "Very well, Valerus. I want you to join my gladiators in the practice ring first thing in the morning. You know the rules."

He did; once a man had made the oath to die by the sword, life was no longer the same. He was entitled to stay at the school, eat the given rations, and practice daily. He only hoped that his knee would keep up with training.

Chapter 27

June 30

Three days had gone by and nothing had changed other than Valerus's mood. Flavia felt useless and very much a burden when Valerus announced that he had found a good-paying job. What worried her, however, was that he did not want to tell her what it was. At first she thought it ought to be a surprise as he did wink and grin at her, but soon it became apparent that he *really* did not want her to know.

She saw little of him. He left in the early mornings and did not return until after sunset. And then, by the fourth day, he did not return at all, or the day to follow. Lucius returned from his rehearsal at the theater later than usual and saw her silhouette against the darkening sky where she stood by the window. The room was dark; the lamp remained unlit and there was an unsettling mood in the air.

"Flavia?" He carefully set his bag down on the table beside the empty lamp. "What is it?"

"He has not come back." She did not look at him, but he could hear the tears in her voice. His hands came up gently to clasp her shoulders. "I have not heard anything of him."

"I'm sure he is all right, Flavia." He tried to reassure her. "He knows how to look after himself."

"Did he tell you anything?"

"Nothing." He shook his head. "But I am sure if he had any trouble we would know. Besides, maybe he went home the last couple of nights."

She turned to look at him. Even in the darkness the fear glittered in her eyes. "He would have told me."

"I am certain he is all right."

July 1

Dawn broke; it was warm with a gentle wind coming in off the sea. Valerus walked through the gloom to the bars of the barricade. It was customary to be held in the gladiator school when you were fighting, to ensure good meals, early sleep, and a lot of practice. He had retaken his oath of *enduring to be burned, to be bound, to be beaten, and to be killed by the sword*, but it had not felt the same as the first time he had made it. He knew he was, once again, a slave to the world of entertainment. This time he only hoped that he would get out of it alive rather than dead, as had been his intent when having taken the vow the first time.

Valerus had lost the routine of it, though. Knowing that Flavia was just a short way off made staying locked up torturous. Cornelius's gladiator school had strict rules and the young man was in no position to protest or negotiate. Already he was receiving better food than the slave ration, and that was something to count as a bonus.

With his arm above his head, he leaned against the bars and let out a long sigh. He had not told Flavia about any of this and only hoped that she would not get wind of it. Not only did he want to keep her from worrying but also to protect her image of him. During the training he realized that the excitement he had felt in the past during battle was not the same. The fun was out of it; he no longer felt alive. Now he did it simply because he wanted Flavia, more than anything—even his life.

And the training was going better than Cornelius had expected, but worse than Valerus had hoped. His leg was causing him agony, even now hours after the last fight he could feel it throb around the knee. He felt it tremble the more weight he tried to put on it, and it was beginning to show. Some of his opponents had come across this and were already using it to their advantage during training, attacking on his weak side where he had trouble turning.

This concerned him to a point; the governor as well as Cornelius had the greatest vote in the arena for who died and who not. Of course accidents happened at times and no one could pass vote. However, gladiators cost money; they needed to be fed, trained, and looked after. A weak gladiator was a waste of money and time and could give a bad reputation to the host of the games.

Cornelius was not up for it. For this reason he kept a close eye on the training of all his fighters, Valerus especially. After the first few days, he was impressed by the young man's stamina and skill with a weapon, even after a year of injury. Now he had pushed Valerus up the ladder and into the arena for the next games. The pay was good; nearly a hundred denarii … if he won. But even if he did not, Valerus knew ways of making sure that he would get something out of it; the crowd donations were all his at least.

He gripped at the bars above him and bowed his head. Three more weeks and who knew where he was going to be? He had gotten out from having to fight animals—Flavia had done something to his psyche regarding the killing of beasts—but now he was up against tridents, shields, and nets. Valerus's successful fighting skill had always been in the aid of his sword and shield; he was a myrmillo fighter. Now, with his wound, he could not carry the weight of a shield in his left hand, so Cornelius had assigned him to fight as a *dimacheri,* a gladiator who fought with a sword in each hand.

Him with two swords. Valerus shook his head. Training was hard and he dedicated himself to it fully. There was nothing else he could do.

"Valerus?"

His head shot up to the familiar voice, and in the dim light he saw young Gaius. He was walking along the roadside and saw him behind the bars of the school.

Gaius was cloaked in a red toga while Valerus wore nothing but the simple brown wool tunic, fastened around the waist with a wide leather girdle.

The younger man walked up to the enclosure, looking Valerus up and down as he neared. "What are you doing?"

"Training," Valerus replied flatly. He felt strangely humiliated and ashamed to have taken up the profession he had now come to hate.

Again Gaius studied him from toe to head. "Why? Are you fighting again?"

"In memory of the emperor." Valerus threw him a look which told clearly that it was not his reason. Before Gaius could comment, Valerus sighed and asked, "What are you doing out so early?"

"I like the early mornings. It gives me time to contemplate."

"On what?"

"Life."

Valerus chuckled softly but said nothing.

"You seem to be doing the same thing." Gaius smiled for the first time and then added, "Does Flavia know about this?"

"No." He shook his head and kicked at a lonely pebble. He looked up at Gaius. "Don't say anything to her, or my parents."

"Is this about getting the money for Flavia? I heard about your offer, and I admire your determination. I can help you with …"

"I don't need your help." Valerus shook his head. "I have it all sorted out. I can't lose."

Gaius raised his eyebrows. "Oh? Really? You *can't* lose?"

"No, I can't."

"I hope you are not preparing to break any rules?"

Valerus laughed.

"When are you fighting?"

"In a week and again on the Ides. I have three fights before my father's deadline. If all goes as planned, I should have earned enough, along with my savings, to get Flavia under my name."

Gaius gently grabbed Valerus's hand through the bars. "I will cheer for you, Valerus."

There was a silent moment when the two men smiled kindly at one another before Valerus pleaded again. "Please don't say anything. I don't want Flavia to know."

"Would not dream of it. Besides, Cornelius's gladiators seldom meet a death." Once more he clasped Valerus's hand before turning to leave. He stopped and looked back at him. "I nearly forgot. What did Flavia think of your poetry?"

The grin that crossed Valerus's face told the young man everything, but he still paid full attention when he replied, "She adored it like a flower does the first light of morning after a winter's night."

"Remember those words, Valerus." Gaius nodded. "Before the fight begins, remember those words you just told me."

July 8

The day of the fight came quickly. Valerus discovered that he was terribly anxious—even frightened—as he sat in the tiny room that led to the fighting arena. Three other gladiators were in the room with him, preparing themselves as the seats were being filled. Many spectators came to look at them before going to place their bets. Valerus too observed each of them as well as their weapons, wondering who he would have to be fighting. The shields were heavy enough to break a man's skull, not to mention the iron fists and clubs. There was a full-length sword and a trident present.

Valerus himself was given a breastplate and his matching pair of swords. He got up and weighed them in his hands. It was just then that one of Cornelius's slaves entered carrying a bucket of oil for each gladiator to rub on himself.

Valerus felt reluctant and he cupped his hand and rubbed the oil across his bare arms, making them gleam impressively. Not all gladiators were inclined to doing so, but Valerus believed in the power of an image. It was, in fact, the way the oil made his form stand out that got him the many women he had had.

That thought made him feel ill. None of that had ever been real, he knew now.

He stopped the routine procedure and cleaned his hands properly before fastening the girdle over his tunic, a hole tighter than usual. He redoubled the lace of his sandals and then rubbed his hands through a packet of flour until his hands were properly dried.

The crowd was getting impatient; their calls and demands were echoing through the hallway and into the chambers of Cornelius's gladiator school. None of the gladiators present were new to the procedure and, like him, prepared themselves in the way that was expected.

Valerus discovered he was shaking with apprehension when the gladiators were prepared. Some were separated and taken to the northern entrance around the arena. Valerus was left with the retiarius, who was standing erect against the opposite wall, holding his trident in one hand and the net flung casually over his shoulder. There was some relief knowing that he would not have to fight him today.

They did not exchange a word. Valerus could not pick up the gladiator's apprehension, or any emotion for that matter. His face was covered with a visor, hiding anything that his eyes could ever hope to tell. Valerus wondered whether the man was feeling the same fear he was. Probably not. Fear was so far away after having fought many battles; Valerus could not recall ever being this frightened since his first few times in the arena. There had been some apprehension in Rome once, but that had been more to the fact that he knew the emperor himself would be watching.

Now it was Flavia; he suddenly had a reason to live. Dying in front of hundreds of spectators hardly seemed worthwhile anymore.

He heard Cornelius's voice, from the arena, announcing the arrival of the governor and other nobles. This was the start of it all. Two gladiators were going to be up against wild beasts, but only after Valerus and another had completed their own fighting, which Valerus knew he had to win. If he lost, there would only be the donations from the crowd and no more chance of fighting in Herculaneum.

He smiled to himself when seeing Flavia's face in front of him and reassured himself that that love was going to push him through. In a month from now, he was going to look back on this day and see it as a wonderful triumph.

She adored it like a flower does the first light of morning after a winter's night.

The words drew him up from his seat, clenching the two swords so strongly that his knuckles went white. He was suddenly ready to fight for her; he was prepared to do whatever it took if it meant being with her again. Kill? If it came to it, he would.

Lucius heard the cheering. Gladiator games were like any obsessive sport that was to the liking of all ages. Gladiators were cheered for, desired by women, and the slaves among the gladiators had a chance of gaining their freedom and getting rich.

The young man had a frightening thought when he heard the cheering and the cries of mercy. He stopped by one of the pillars near the arena stadium and watched a white handkerchief, caught by the breeze, tumble from the arena walls and land delicately near his feet. He wondered who was fighting; he had lost track of the entertainment events beyond the acting theater and was curious to hear what the row was about. Gladiators from Rome were popular but rare in these parts, but there were battles that even he was careful not to miss.

As the people began to leave, Lucius listened to their conversations, and their talk caught his attention. His imagination began to take better shape and his fear turned to anger. Was this what Valerus had taken up?

He snuck into the holdings as the crowd lessened and followed the muttering of cheerful voices. In the arena, a surgeon was attending to a myrmillo who was left bleeding in the sand.

It was not Valerus, he realized on closer observation, nor was it anyone he knew. It did not have him doubt his assumptions, though. As he continued, Valerus's voice became perceptible and, as he turned the corner, he saw his companion sitting on a small wooden bench. There was blood along his right arm and a second surgeon was carefully examining his left knee. Cornelius was standing by the main doorway.

" … handle the retiarius?" Lucius caught the middle of Valerus's conversation with the lanista.

"Your fight went better than I expected. I want you to fight the fisherman next. By your skill today, you have convinced me it will be a challenge and entertaining."

"I don't know if I am confident enough to …"

"You will be fighting as a myrmillo next, Valerus. Fish and fisherman or nothing."

"Lucius!" Valerus noticed him suddenly.

Cornelius looked around. "This place is not open to the public!" he snapped angrily. "Leave before I call the guard."

Lucius looked at Valerus quickly and left, throwing a quick glace of disapproval over his shoulder before he disappeared.

Valerus sighed and shook his head, noticing the pain for the first time pulsating from his knee. He should have seen this coming; he should have known that somehow Flavia would get an idea of the whole affair.

And Flavia? What would her image of him be when she knew? Would all this turn out to have been in vain? He loved her so much that the mere thought that fighting may turn her away repulsed him. He was close to laying down his weapons right there. But then what? He only had two weeks left and there was no other profession that would render to him the amount he needed.

He was still unsure as to how he was going to gain the money he needed; he had no idea how, but he knew he would.

He dreamt of her that afternoon as he lay on the small bunk in his cell. Several cells lined the corridor, the higher class and free fighters had curtains to pull across the bars for their privacy. By nightfall he took a bucket bath and washed the sand of the arena from his hair. He had barely put on a fresh tunic and was resettling on the bunk when someone tapped on the curtain. Cornelius's hand came through the bars and lifted the cloth to look his gladiator in the eye. "Up for a visit, Valerus?" he asked coldly, obviously disapproving of the idea but knowing it was a man's right to enjoy himself after a successful fight.

"Lucius?" Valerus asked as he propped himself up on one elbow. "The man from earlier today?"

The old trainer smiled; it was one of the few times Valerus ever saw it. He nodded and said, "And a fine young woman."

Valerus jumped from his place as the curtain fell back. There was the thud of the bolts falling back. For a second the young man could make out Flavia's silhouette through the curtain, and his heart pounded like a child's did when seeing the apple of his eye.

But this was far more real, he felt. It had been days since he had last seen her and the thought that she was right there both excited and frightened him. He did not understand this, but then felt that he didn't need to. It was real and very pleasant.

Lucius must have taken her shopping or brought her something from the theater. She was wearing a beautiful green stola decorated with a palla, a veil-like toga that she used as a hood along with jewelry. Her hair was fastened above her head and braids framed her face. For a second it did not look like her at all, but her soft gray eyes could not have belonged to anyone else.

Valerus did not grab her as he so much wanted to, nor did he embrace her. Strangely he felt that he had no right. It was as if she were a goddess and he only a mortal man. So instead he stood in his place as he tried to catch his own breath. He was not certain of Flavia's reason for coming here; it could have been to start an argument, protest, or, even worse, say good-bye. The few seconds that the two of them locked gazes felt like minutes passing by, Valerus feeling himself sinking with a weight at his feet.

Then she smiled. The relief was so intense that he nearly sagged to his knees in front of her, but stubborn pride kept him upright. He weakly returned her smile and then opened himself to her.

She crumbled against him and reached around to hold him. For a second Valerus looked up at Lucius who merely winked and left the two of them.

"You should have told me," Flavia whispered. Her voice was muffled against the fabric of his tunic, but he did not need to hear her. He knew what she was thinking and what she felt; he was feeling and thinking the same. How could he have thought she was *not* going to find out?

She stepped back and looked at the man from head to toe. He saw her notice the bad bruising on his inner elbow and the cut down his arm. She shook her head. "I don't want you to die for me, Valerus."

"I'm not planning to die, Flavia." He laughed shortly. "I'll fight for you, yes."

"Kill?"

His smile faded in his sigh. "No one was killed in the last game. I told you that training gladiators costs money—a lot of it. People don't easily pound denarii into the arena sands."

"But if you lost a fight, they could make the decision to, couldn't they?"

Valerus shut his eyes for a second and then nodded.

"Especially with you already being experienced," she continued, running one hand down his strong arm, "Cornelius won't lose much."

"Flavia, please stop." He took her face in both his hands. "Two more fights, that's all, and I should have the amount my father wants."

"*If* you win."

"Even if I don't, I get a small sum, not to mention the usual donations from the crowd. Cornelius and I go back a long way. This last display was no challenge for me. Two more fights, Flavia, and in a couple of weeks you will be mine and I yours. No more master or servant. It will be … Flavia, why are you crying?"

"What did I do to deserve someone like you?" She sobbed. "I am but a slave and yet you are prepared to fight and risk death for me. Why?"

"I love you; nothing has ever been simpler." He ran his hand through her hair. "And you know that you deserve every bit of happiness that the gods may offer."

He came forward and kissed her. It was a soft but passionate kiss, pulling her to him so that they were up against each other. He tasted her tears, but that only made him more desperate to have her.

Their faces were barely an inch apart. Valerus could feel her breath on his face. He fought to restrain himself; he dared not kiss her again, knowing that he would not be able to stop himself from proceeding further if he did. He trembled as he took her hands in his and kissed each of her fingers in turn. He kept his eyes shut, relying on other senses to take in her presence: her smell, the feel of her hands, and the sound of her breathing. He had never been so aware of anything—anyone—in his entire life.

Chapter 28

July 13

Lucius shook his head. "Flavia," he said, "I don't think this is wise."

They were standing at the entrance of the arena where a couple of hundred people had paid for their seats and were now piling in to see the fight.

Flavia frowned at him. "You don't? I want to see him, Lucius. I can't stay hidden from the man he is."

"But you were so against him killing."

"I still am, but how could I ever change him. He is not going to step out of it now, is he? He is who he is and he is doing this despite his conscious telling him otherwise." The incident of the decapitation still lingered in the far reaches of her mind, the blood especially, but it was dreamlike now after all the incidents that had followed.

"Flavia, are you aware that he could be killed? You may have to watch him die?"

She thought about this for a moment; Lucius saw the tears welling in her eyes before she blinked them away. "If he is going to die," she said, "at the very least he will know that I was there."

Most had gathered around the barred holding to view the gladiators and some placed their bets on those that appeared to have potential.

Lucius led Flavia past the mass to the nearest enclosure. Valerus was behind the bars and at once walked up to her. He was dressed in a loose-fitting wool toga fastened in the middle by a wide leather girdle. Along with this he wore a small breastplate and a bracer across each of his wrists.

He took her hands through the bars and kissed them. Flavia looked him up and down. He was wearing all his armor, including the bracers, but there was no visor on his head and no weapon on his belt. He looked so different; his hair had been tied back in a short, tight ponytail, an appearance she had never seen of him. It made him look strangely attractive; it felt as if she was falling in love with him all over again.

"Don't die," she said slowly.

Valerus chuckled and kissed the top of her hand again. "I don't intend to, Flavia."

She had to peer over his shoulder to his opponent; she could not stop herself. In the corner was a large man sitting on a plank bench. He was wearing nothing but a short undergarment and metal galerus on the left arm, but he had a build on him that was bound to bring Valerus some challenge. It reminded her of the repairer, only healthier, thus probably from a Germanian heritage.

She looked back and gave Valerus a worried frown. A horn was blown from the arena, making her jump. Valerus reached out and gently touched her cheek. "Go on, take your seat."

Carefully he leaned forward as she did. Both of them felt the coldness of the bars on their cheeks before their lips came together and they kissed. This brought a friendly laugh and applause from the surrounding crowd. When they parted, they stayed against each other, heads against the bars and sharing breath between each other.

Valerus only opened his eyes a slit to look down at her. "Don't worry about me," he whispered reassuringly, "I can't lose."

Another horn was blown. This time Flavia took a step back. "I love you." He did not hear her say it, but everything about her told him those three words—her posture as well as the look on her face.

As she moved away, Lucius materialized in her place and quickly grasped his shoulder. "Good luck, old friend." And then he too was gone in the crowd after Flavia.

Flavia had not been among the crowd of a fighting arena audience since the death of her mother, and even though that was more than eleven years ago, the memory of it was still all too familiar. But the crowd had not been as large as this; that arena had been small and cheap.

People shoved past, many being apologetic to the fact she was a woman—and a fine-looking woman as well. The clothes Lucius had given her were a fine example of a middle-class woman whose parents, at least, appeared to have done well in their lives.

Flavia was a little taken by the mass of the entire affair. Usually she was strong—her childhood had forced her to be, and she could manage an audience of hungry lustful men—but this was very different, leaving her a little bewildered. People were excited and hungry but not at all focused on her. Instead they were making for their seats, trying to catch a glimpse of the arena sands over the heads of others.

Lucius led her to the open seats where they took their places. Flavia looked out over the fighting ground below them. The wall lining it was at least three meters in height and the sand was a pale brown, unlike anything found in the area. She had been told that the sand had some absorption quality, to taking in the blood of the dead. At this memory she was certain she saw the stains of past battles marking the earth.

Not a track could be seen at this distance. Flavia wondered how many people had been killed on that sand who did not even want to fight, who had been—just like her—forced into an occupation that was so unlike them.

A gladiator stepped out. It was a Numidian beneath a silver visor and no armor across his chest at all. He carried a small shield strapped to one shoulder and a long sword in his right hand. Behind him was the retiarius Flavia had seen earlier sharing the small enclosure with Valerus. The net was flung across his shoulder and the trident he carried like a spear. White dust lined his hands where he had rubbed them in flour.

The shock hit her when she saw Valerus. There was no way to identify him from the distance other than the posture he held and the way he moved. He was wearing his visor now, but she knew it was him. In one hand he carried a long sword and in the other a large oblong shield. His walk was determined and confident. Behind him were a meridiani and *samnite*. They marched across the arena sand in single file, presenting their arms to the viewing public. The crowd concentrated on the gladiators, taking interest in their weapons and movement to decide on who their bets would be placed.

Once they had walked the arena length they disappeared into their holdings again, all but the Numidian. He crossed the sand to stand before the magistrate's benches and saluted his superior.

Lucius raised a hand to his brow and caught his breath. "Oh," he muttered to himself when remembering what was on the program.

A large boar was chased into the arena, stopping a few strides from its escape to grunt at the onlookers and sniff the air. Flavia held her breath, sitting erect as she watched the brutal fight that followed. The boar was not keen to fight at first and tried to escape, squealing as it ran along the walls. The crowd found it amusing, laughing when whip carriers had to be brought in to taunt it.

Lucius risked a glance in Flavia's direction, noticing that she had hardly moved. Her expression was like a stone bust: pale and horrified as she watched. After the boar finally decided to fight it was slain rather quickly. It would have been over for the boar faster if the gladiator had not dragged out the procedure so much, but the crowd demanded a show. Lucius noticed a perfect teardrop trickle down the side of Flavia's face. The paleness of her skin was obvious now; slowly Lucius reached out to take her hand in support.

She did not move as she watched the boar being dragged across the arena floor with a hook pierced through the chest, a streak of blood following behind it. A man appeared from the holdings to rub some sand across the blood stains, covering the brutality.

There was a short interlude when people left their seats momentarily to place their bets while in the arena a series of mock battles was taking place with wooden swords. Valerus was not among them. It did remind her of the theater, but only slightly. The killing of the boar haunted her. First her mother had been killed by a boar and now they had killed a boar for the same entertainment value. She threw a disgusted glance at Lucius, wondering how he could ever have grown up with the sport, but he was trying desperately not to meet her gaze.

As the spectators were returning to their seats, the arena emptied out. The fighters left one by one, the last one staggering slightly.

A silence fell. Flavia glanced at the people beside her; everyone was transfixed to the fighting ground below when the retiarius fighter appeared from the barriers, walking to the arena center. Behind him was the samnite.

Her heart jumped to her throat when Valerus entered the fighting ground from the opposite end, followed closely by the meridiani. The four gladiators met in the arena center, the retiarius standing to attention with his trident beside him held like a spear. His net was flung over his shoulder with his hand buried beneath the folds.

The four men greeted each other with a stiff nod and then turned to the governor who was personally attending the fight. Simultaneously the fighters raised their right hands and saluted their superior spectator.

Flavia was surprised from where she watched under the velarium; it was not the usual salute of "those about to die salute you," as she had heard people talk about. She decided to ask Lucius about this.

"That's only for the criminals," he told her from the corner of his mouth. "Criminals die in the arena, not the properly trained."

She felt the bile rise in her throat when the men turned to face each other again. The roar of the crowd had lowered to a hush. A gladiator guard came from the chambers to place the two men apart, paying good attention to the position of the sun before stepping back and disappearing in the barriers again. It could be seen now that the four gladiators were set in pairs and were merely fighting one opponent.

What if he was killed? What if she had to watch him die? It would be reliving the death of her mother.

A cheer rose when Valerus brought his gladius around and was blocked off by the metal trident. People in the front row, obviously younger men, jumped to their feet with arms in the air, forcing Flavia too to rise up and see over their heads. Soon the entire audience was on their feet, cheering at the fight taking place below them, two pairs engaged in their fight.

The cheer fell on deaf ears; Valerus heard nothing and could not turn his focus to anything other than the armed man in front of him, not even the reality that Flavia was watching from the stands or the referee that was following their every move. The retiarius also carried a dagger, and Valerus tried to keep this in his view as he fought off the trident and dodged the netting.

Retiariuses were far more agile than most people would think because they carried two weapons as well as a net. For one, he could use different approaches from different sides at the same time while Valerus had a sword and a shield; their weight was giving him trouble on his leg. His opponent would make the gesture of throwing out his net and as Valerus tempted to dodge the action, the man would come around with his dagger trying to cut him in the hip.

Nearly two weeks of training and a strict diet were proving some worth, but not in comparison to someone who had had that schedule for months, perhaps even years. The past memory of fighting as a myrmillo flooded back as it had in the previous fight, and Valerus parried the attacker, never giving into his urge to dodge a gesture other than when it really proved a threat.

If he would only toss the net, Valerus thought desperately. It was that waiting that got to him. As long as he had it, he was vulnerable. Being caught under it usually meant you had lost the fight, and Valerus knew now more than ever before that he could not afford to lose. If it was thrown at him and he managed to turn from it, he had a short window where his opponent would be caught off guard as he tried to recollect his weapon.

There was a change in the cheers from the crowd and it was only then that he noticed in the corner of his eye that the second pair had finished, the meridiani having brought down the samnite. The cheering changed to *"Habet hoc habet!"* rocking the foundations of the arena, which Valerus felt under his feet. But he could not let off his guard for a second.

The net was tossed falsely but convincingly. Valerus momentarily dodged before spinning around to parry the trident that came for his neck. The sword was locked in the spikes and in a flash ripped from his hand.

He heard the cheering go up again. Now he had only a shield with which to fight an opponent who had three weapons. The other did not, however, have the armor Valerus did, which brought the odds to equal once again.

There was a mock toss with the net and the young man retreated as the trident came forth, cutting him across the left knee as he jumped aside, turning the fall to a neat roll as the mesh was flung at his head and missed.

He tried to get up and stumbled. He cursed aloud when his weak knee gave out on him on his second attempt.

The retiarius rushed to him to take advantage and hesitated. He was not too certain if it was a ploy or an actual injury. Instead he jumped to recover his net.

Valerus felt the panic rise as the heat ran from his knee up his spine. He felt the numbness that had first been the reason he was released from his fighting oath. He tried bringing up his right foot, but his weight on the left refused to be carried and he fell over yet again.

This was no ploy. The retiarius circled cautiously, dragging the net behind for the show of it, and gripped his dagger in the hand. Valerus saw him come; it was as if he was watching from a distance.

Then the earth shook. It started as a vibration that first hushed the crowd and then increased to bring forth screaming. The retiarius dropped his dagger and tried for a second to support himself on his trident before falling over himself, the earth rippling under him. Valerus felt the ground rise and fall and heard the faint distant rumble that appeared to come from all around him—even beneath him. The people of Herculaneum knew earthquakes. They happened every few weeks, though seldom as violent as the quake seventeen years earlier, which had brought down the roof of Pompeii's great basilica. It had been the topic of conversation for months. Since then they were but a mild nuisance.

He took advantage and let the quake roll him over to his back, from where he managed to get the right leg up. He was on his feet again when the earth resettled after only a few seconds of tremor.

Valerus lunged at the retiarius as he got up again, swinging his shield low. The edge caught the man just above the knee, but his trident was in the way to offer Valerus a clean blow.

The attack was effective though, as it took the gladiator down again, blood coursing from his leg. Valerus charged at him, kicking the trident from his hand and flinging aside the net that lay beside him. He retrieved his sword, triumphantly brought it to the throat of his opponent, and glanced up at the crowd.

The audience watched without a sound. It had been a turn of events due to an unforeseen quake, and no one was certain how to respond to it. The cheering began from the men who had bet under Valerus's name, shouting *"Lugula! Lugula!"*

This demand for a kill brought up the protest of those who lost the bet due to the event, and they jumped from seats screaming *"Mitte!"* and waving their handkerchiefs.

Valerus saw the fight commencing in the audience and looked to the governor for guidance. He too was watching the crowd before finally turning his thumb down.

Valerus obeyed, dropping his sword and stepping back. This brought both cheers and angry roars from the onlookers. The young man glanced around him, suddenly remembering who was watching from the crowd. There was no way he could see her in the uproar, but the mere fact that he knew she was there forced him to smile.

He was one step closer …

Chapter 29

July 18

The training became more difficult and strenuous. Over the days before the next game, Valerus worked in getting some weight back on his left leg without any improvement.

One evening, however, Valerus was struck by more disturbing news. His fight was going to change in opponent. The fight which he had planned to take place against the retiarius was now going to be against a *secutar*; a heavily armored gladiator with sword and dagger. Cornelius planned to make it something spectacular and a little more of a challenge. He was preparing now to have eight gladiators in the arena combating wild beasts before putting Valerus up against a secutar followed by a retiarius combating the winner. It would be a spectacle in honor of the late emperor.

Valerus sat alone in his cell that night, rubbing his knee unconsciously. He was not prepared for the change. He needed at least a week to work back his strength and try to get past the pain. He did not have a week; he only had four days. The last two battles had rendered him two hundred denarii, a hundred less than he had hoped for.

The last fight had done something serious to his old injury. The pain that continually pulsated now ran up his entire leg, reaching his inner thighs. That night he was plagued by terrible cramps and he groaned as he tried uselessly to find some position where the pain was less potent. By dawn he was tired, wary, and in no state to fight. The pain left him sick and unable to eat his necessary ration before the training began. He was down within five minutes, retreating to the benches and throwing up repeatedly. By midday the pain had worked up to his lower back, and there was a numbness coming to his left foot.

By that evening, the night before the fight, the pain was affecting his neck and shoulders. He cried softly into his pillow. It was not necessarily the pain that brought the tears, but instead the growing realization that he was not going to win; in fact, it dawned on him that he was going to die … and die without Flavia. No lanista wanted the reputation of putting up with a cripple gladiator, and death in the arena was going to be his only escape.

Valerus found himself counting his breaths, suddenly so focused on his life that he thought nothing about the fight to take place the next day. He regretted having taken the oath and having left Flavia. He should have stolen her—eloped with her. There were so many places he could have taken her for safekeeping that were away from the cities as well as the cruel fate his father had in store for her.

He sat up and frowned into the darkness. His fate may well be decided, but he realized that Flavia still had a chance.

July 20

It was a massive crowd that gathered for the spectacle in regards to the Herculaneum population. Flavia, feeling a little more comfortable in the crowd, was led to the seats with Lucius holding her hand.

Unlike the previous fight, there was not a single seat open and the audience was cramped alongside one another. As Lucius carefully set her down, Gaius appeared alongside him, gently grasping his arm. "Lucius, are you?" he asked and then nodded kindly to Flavia.

"I am," Lucius said, looking at where the young man holding him and then up again. "Gaius, isn't it? Pliny's nephew?"

"The very same." He pulled Lucius from his place, giving Flavia a charming yet apologetic smile. "Master Valerus is asking for you." This was said in a whisper which Lucius just managed to hear above the din. "He says to meet him down in his cell. It has been arranged that the guard will let you pass."

The man frowned at him but decided not to question it. Instead he opened his hand to his own seat beside Flavia. "Please," he said to him. "Until I return."

"I will be delighted." Gaius nodded, threw his toga over his arm, and sat down next to her as Lucius made his way through the mass of people.

"I thought you had left for Rome along with your uncle," Flavia said to him.

"My uncle was close to the emperor, not me. I will be leaving for home and meeting him there in a week or so."

She nodded. "What does Valerus want?"

The crowd lessened farther down the steps until Lucius could hear the murmur of the audience from above. His footsteps sounded so much louder in the silence after the noise of above, and the sound of it brought a guard down on him.

"I am here to see the gladiator Valerus."

"The dimacheri? Ah, you must be Master Lucius."

The guard led him down the passage way to the gladiator cells where each man was preparing for the fight. Valerus was still sitting naked on his tiny bunk. His fighting tunic was sleeveless and spread out beside him as were his bracers and girdle. His two swords were leaning against the wall opposite him along with a bucket of oil. Everything appeared disregarded.

"What's all this?" Lucius asked as he stepped into the cell. The guard left them to their private discussion. "Are you not fighting?"

"I most certainly am." Valerus did not look up at him. "But I have to ask you a favor."

Lucius waited expectantly, but, when nothing more was said, he took a step forward and asked, "Yes?"

Now Valerus looked up at him. His eyes were unusually glassy. "I am not going to make this fight, Lucius. My whole body is in a spasm of pain; I can hardly hold the sword in my left hand." He clenched it a few times and winced.

"What?"

"I want you to get Flavia out of the stands. I don't want her to watch it. I have arranged that you are my benefactor; Cornelius owes me about four hundred denarii, no matter what happens to me in this fight, along with all the crowd's donations. I want you to take that money and promise me that you will look after Flavia."

"Stop!" Lucius snapped angrily. "You can't die, Valerus! Nor can I take in Flavia. You love her! She loves you; all she talks about is you. If you die today, you will kill her!"

"I don't want her to die," Valerus said softly. "If I concede now, I lose everything and she will fall back into the hands of my father. I can't have that. I told you that I am prepared to die for her."

"Valerus, listen to yourself." Lucius collapsed on the bunk beside him. "You did all this to be with her and now you are talking about dying. That means you will never be with her."

The man swallowed. "But she will be safe," he said slowly,

concentrating on every word. “Please, Lucius. I don’t want her to see me die.”

“Who says you are going to die? Cornelius is lenient.”

“Not to a cripple. The last fight hurt me, Lucius, and hurt me badly. I don’t know what it did to me, but I know it will mean my death in the arena today; neither the governor, Cornelius, nor the spectators are going to have any pity for a cripple. Habet hoc habet,” he muttered and shook his head. “I’ve had it.”

Lucius got up slowly, not taking his eyes off his companion. Valerus felt ashamed to have to give his companion such a task and hated even more when he tried to picture the look coming from Flavia’s eyes; it cracked his heart.

“Please, Lucius.” Valerus grasped his hand suddenly. “Will you do this for me?”

The man wanted to protest but could not. This was a terrible dilemma Valerus was going through and he had nothing more to do than ensure Flavia’s safety. Valerus was relieved when Lucius slowly nodded in acceptance.

Valerus blinked away his tears and nodded. “Thank you.” He then pointed to all his clothes and equipment. “Will you help me get dressed?”

Lucius did so, but reluctantly. He felt sick in the stomach to see his friend so fragile; Valerus could barely lift his arms to get into his tunic. Lucius’s thoughts kept turning to Flavia and how he was going to get her out of the stands without her realizing what was happening. She was sharp, especially with Valerus at stake, and he could not stand the thought of seeing it dawn on the woman’s face.

He fastened his companion’s sandals and then Valerus turned to the bed and took his girdle. “Could you pass me my swords?” he asked without turning around. He heard Lucius pick up the scabbards, one ringing as the hilt hit the iron bar of his cell. He was just fastening the girdle when a terrible sharp pain hit him on the back of the head. The blow drew blood and he felt the pain and heard the ring in his head as he collapsed against his bunk. He managed a quick upward glance in time to see Lucius brandishing the hilt of his weapon for another blow. When it came down, Valerus slumped across the floor, a thin stream of blood trickling on the ground

"Sorry, Valerus," Lucius muttered as he tossed the sword on the bunk, "but I won't have you and Flavia die on the same day."

❋

Flavia was getting anxious despite Gaius's presence. Usually the young man had a calming effect over her, but not this time. Her gaze was dimmed to her feet as the cheering rose yet again during the slaying of the animals. Gaius watched on, entertained but not throwing off his dignity by raving and cheering about it. Every now and again, without any real reason, he glanced at Flavia, noticing that she was trembling slightly. After a while he allowed his hand to fall on hers. It was cold.

A boar screamed from below.

Gaius noticed her expression. "Barbaric, isn't it?"

She nodded. "How is your uncle taking to Vespasian's death?" she asked him without looking up. The scream of the animal died away, to her relief. "I heard that the two of them were very close."

"He has returned to Rome to pay his respects." Gaius did not look around from the arena. "He will return to Misenum afterward."

For the first time, Flavia looked up at him and he to her. He smiled. "Do not be troubled by things beyond your control. Valerus is very determined."

"I know." She built up the courage and looked upon the killing ground. Most of the animals had been slain: five boars, a hyena, and two young lionesses. A third lion was trotting alongside the wall of the arena, terrified and trying to jump the wall as the gladiators came for it. Flavia looked away again when they stabbed it in the hip.

There was a second cheer that lifted when the last animal was brought down. Slaves and workers rushed in to remove the bodies, dragging them back into the chambers while others smeared the blood stains with dry sand.

"What did Valerus want with Lucius?"

"I am not in the position to say. He merely asked for Lucius. Little was said to me."

The arena was cleared completely. Flavia watched and listened to the cheering turn to excited murmuring before the gladiators stepped in. It was a sacutor followed by … Valerus?

She shook her head. It was his clothes, his armor, and a sword in each hand, but the way he moved was wrong. At first she thought it was because of his wounded knee, but then noticed he was walking quite soundly on it. His build was wrong as well; instead of the strong, muscular upper body, this one appeared finer and slender. The way he walked, following after the sacutor for the crowd to see, was so wrong. He walked as if he was trained to and the natural air was broken by the excitement of the crowd.

Valerus was frightened?

It then dawned on her; the man was walking as one would in the theater when rehearsing a play. That was not Valerus. Could it be Lucius who had taken the man's clothes and was now parading his weapons and the skills for fighting which Flavia knew he did not have? No, he wouldn't!

Her hand came to her mouth, wondering what had caused Valerus to make such a dreadful decision. He was not in the arena; instead he was replaced by a man who was quite obviously frightened. How could Valerus have let this take place?

"Flavia?" Gaius's hand fell gently on her shoulder. "What is it?"

She did not speak; she could not; she was not entirely certain, but the gladiator was so unlike Valerus. The sham fighters drifted in with their wooden swords as the two gladiators disappeared off the grounds. People got up from their places to place their bets and Flavia, frightened and confused, began to cry.

"Flavia, what is it?"

"That is not Valerus!" She sobbed. "That man is frightened! Can't you see it?"

Gaius shook his head, not certain as to whether he could believe her. The mock battle commenced below, but the young man was too disturbed by the woman's words to look on. By the time the gladiators returned to the arena, Flavia was desperately trying to think of something to do. She tried to convince Gaius to let her go down to the holdings, but he refused, saying it was strictly prohibited to the public.

When fighting started, Flavia began to cry, but watched on with horrified fascination. Could it be Lucius? He had known theater and he had learnt the ways of the sword at least for the stage, but ... could he win a trained gladiator?

Valerus's training for the actors was proving some worth. Lucius was handling his weapons well enough for him to pass off as a gladiator, but he was moving too well. Flavia looked up at the benches and noticed Cornelius watching on; obviously he too had noticed something strange in the arena below.

What would happen if he were caught? Surely the penalty would be high.

The sacutor was a professional, though, and his attacks were quicker than the actor could keep up with. The actor did not know the real procedure of fighting or the rules that Valerus had studied for the past seven years. Then again, there was no need to. Within three minutes the sacutor's hilt came up and hit Lucius across the jaw, throwing him back into the sand. His opponent stepped forward and set his foot over the young actor's wrist and held the sword at his throat. He glanced up to his superior for the procedure to follow.

The crowd had not been impressed by the fight; it was over so quickly that it could hardly be called a proper battle. There was no respect for a gladiator who could not fight; he was useless in the art of entertainment, time as well as money.

"Lugula! Lugula!" the chants began to rise up. *"Kill him! Kill him!"*

Lucius, trapped under the weight of his opponent, raised his hand in fearful supplication, begging mercy from the onlookers.

Flavia looked around desperately, not knowing what she could do to save the young man's life. Her knuckles had turned white as she clenched them. Lucius or not, she could not let him die. Beside her Gaius looked down in horror, jaw dropped open. "Gaius!" She wept loudly over the rising chorus. "Please, do something!"

The young man moved as if it was an internal reaction to her words. He suddenly got up from his place and stood on his seat. Several heads turned to him as he removed a small white handkerchief from his belt and let it go as the breeze picked up. It tumbled over the heads of the onlookers until it gently descended to the arena, falling but a few feet from where the gladiator stood over his victory.

This action caused an effect. Several women, above the roar of the crowd commanding a kill, released their handkerchiefs and threw them toward the fighting men. Within a few moments white specks decorated the arena floor. Flavia, desperate to join the movement but not having a handkerchief, pulled the green veil from over her head, stood up, and let it catch the wind. The people around her went quiet as she let it go, watching it dance softly through the air and down to the killing ground. It was purely by chance that it came to rest across Lucius's feet.

The silence lifted; one by one people stopped their cheering and waited the decision. It was a silence from eternity. The wind whipped up the sand.

The governor himself had come to watch the spectacle and appeared moved by the thrown veil. He got to his feet, looked upon the fallen gladiator and the victor, and gave the thumbs down.

The crowd went wild as the sacutor threw his sword aside and stepped back. Lucius pulled himself up to his elbows, wheezing beneath his visor. He noticed the green veil that had come to rest over his sandals and was forced to look up and across the crowd.

⁂

Valerus woke up to the sound of cheering. He was naked and lying on his side on the cold floor as if someone had tossed him there. His head was throbbing painfully and he slowly raised his hand to where Lucius had hit him. Momentarily he had no idea where he was; the world spun around him and the cheering above was more the sound of an approaching wave.

He felt the blood against the side of his head and suddenly everything came back to him. He heard the cheering and recognized the confines of his cell.

The fight! He had missed the fight!

He jumped to his feet, reeled back as the blood drained from his head, and collapsed on his bunk. Somewhere a door was opened, as the cheering was suddenly louder than before. Footsteps rang down the corridor when the cell door was opened and the curtains ripped aside.

Valerus saw his armor and weapons walk toward him. The visor came off quickly to reveal Lucius's face. "Valerus, quickly! Get dressed!" He began to strip off his armor and clothes and passed them to his companion.

"What have you done?" Valerus asked, bewildered and taking his tunic as if in a dream.

"Get dressed! Quick! Before anyone sees us."

"You took my place?" Valerus winced suddenly when he tried to lift his arm. At once Lucius came forth to help him get into his clothes and armor.

"Are you a fool, Lucius?" Valerus asked dreamily as the man fastened the buckles of his breastplate. "You can't fight. You could have been killed."

"I wasn't." Lucius, finished in having returned Valerus's clothes, hurriedly began to dress into his own. "And in turn, I saved something far more important than myself."

Footsteps entered the holdings and both men looked at each other. Quickly Lucius handed Valerus his visor and set him back to sit on the bed. "You fought poorly," he whispered hurriedly. "You were down within a few minutes when the sacutor hit you with his shield. You ought to have been put to death but the governor was moved by the veil tossed into the arena by some mysterious woman."

Valerus had to smile at this. "She did that?"

Cornelius entered the chamber at that moment, looking upon the stranger and then at Valerus with a small glint of satisfaction. "I did not think you were going to make it, Valerus." The trainer shook his head. "Your training went so poorly yesterday that I thought you had had it."

"I am determined, master." Valerus nodded and raised his hand slowly to the side of his head. It was damp and sticky.

"That was a bad blow you took, but I am impressed. Despite your weakness, there is a woman who appeared much moved by your determination."

"So I know."

Cornelius looked at Lucius and pointed to the cell gate. "You, leave here. Citizens are not welcomed down here."

Lucius left without a word and the older man sat down beside Valerus, looking at the wall opposite. "Your movements were ...

different from the norm." He looked at him. "What have you to say about this?"

"It's my injury," Valerus confessed quickly and convincingly. "It's been plaguing me since the last fight. I have trouble moving."

"So I noticed."

Valerus wondered if he knew; his questioning appeared so direct that it was as if he was trying to get a confession out of him. He would not do it though. Not only would the penalty be harsh, but he was certain he would lose all his winnings. He shook his head. "I can't fight anymore, Cornelius."

The lanista nodded slowly. "Burned, bound, beaten, and killed by the sword. You have taken this oath."

"Twice."

"It was the emperor who released you with your life the first time. He can do as he pleases. I, on the other hand, must obey the law. You have taken the oath to die by the sword, and it must be done."

"Release me, Cornelius. I can't fight; the disgust of the audience will only be repeated if you put me in the arena again. No one will bet on me and I will only cost you."

"You are already costing me. Four hundred denarii, as was our bargain for the winnings."

"I *need* that money," Valerus begged.

The trainer smiled suddenly; it was unexpected. "It's the woman who tossed the veil, no doubt."

The young man laughed, despite the pain and the headache. "It's always about a woman, isn't it?"

Cornelius also laughed now, bringing his hand down on Valerus's back so hard he was nearly thrown forward. "What foolish things men do for love," he announced loudly and got to his feet. "I have been well convinced. I will have my surgeons look at your injury tonight to help you deal with your pain. By dawn tomorrow I will make sure that you are released and paid in full."

Valerus had never felt so grateful; he felt the tears come to his eyes as he nodded to the old man. "It was an honor working for you, Cornelius. I am blessed to have done it twice."

It was early evening. Pedius was at his table in the library, settling some accounts. Usually it was the position of the wife to settle the business, but the man was looking for something to occupy his mind.

His daughter marched in and laid her hands on the table. "You won't believe what Velli's been up to," she told her father with a disgusted tone.

"I pray you will tell me." He could not help but smile.

"He's back in the arena." Pedius looked up at her. "At least he was today in memory of our emperor."

The man caught his breath and looked down at his documents again. "If your mother hears that, she will give Valerus the slave without a second thought."

"Mother knows nothing. I can't bring myself to tell her."

"Thank you."

"Do you think it right? I mean, he isn't the fighter he was, not with his injury and all."

"Let him do as he pleases." Pedius fished out another document from under the papers. "In a few days the slave girl will be sold off in any case and it will be the end of it."

"And if Valerus comes up with the agreed amount?"

"Then she will be his problem as far as I am concerned."

Anneria sat down in the open chair opposite and rested her chin in her hands. "Salvius called on you earlier when you were resting."

"The old bore. What does he want now?"

"He says he has more information regarding the incident."

Impatiently Pedius dropped his papers to the table and looked her way. "Did he not get paid in full?" he asked angrily. "He obviously thought of another way to get a few denarii out of me."

"Well, he said he would come by sometime tomorrow, so be warned."

With a smile he reached over the table and gently touched his daughter's cheek.

Chapter 30

July 21

Valerus sat by the table in Lucius's small room, counting the coins on the table. On the couch behind him, Flavia was leaning over his shoulder with her arms around his waist while Lucius sat opposite, counting after his companion to be certain the amount was correct. Outside the city was coming alive with the arrival of dawn. None of the three had slept that night. It was a time for them to celebrate the victory; the worst was over.

"Four hundred and thirty two," Valerus announced, and Lucius confirmed it with a nod. "The crowd was very generous." He cupped his hands and pulled the stack of coins into its pouch.

"That's a lot of money you have there, Valerus." Lucius shook his head. "More than a praetorian's annual wage. I hope it will be enough."

"My father said twelve hundred. With my savings, along with Gaius's little offer to help, I have enough, in the nick of time too."

"It was not worth risking your life though," Flavia whispered over his shoulder and looked at Lucius. "Nor yours. It was brave what you did, but foolish."

"Water under the bridge." Lucius got up from his place and turned to the window to draw open the curtains. "We both came out of it unscathed."

"Speak for yourself," Valerus snapped and brought his hand to the side of his head.

Flavia chuckled and kissed his cheek. "How's the leg?"

"Still painful," he told her, "but at least it's only in my leg now. I don't know what those doctors do, but it works."

"Don't forget to take the tea they prepared for you," Lucius reminded.

"I'll get it." Flavia got up off the couch and made for the small kitchen.

Lucius smiled at Valerus, who returned it. "Flavia is right. You were foolish to have done what you did. Brave, but a fool."

Lucius sat down opposite him. "I would rather die than to have to tell Flavia you are dead. The shock would kill her. I can't face that. It was more an act of a coward than bravery."

"Still, you took a great risk, all for the sake of us. For that I am indebted to you."

"I wish you only the best with her."

Flavia entered the room and passed Valerus a mug of lukewarm tea. It had a strong odor but had proved earlier to be very effective against the pain he was experiencing.

She sat down beside him and he put her arm around her. None of them said a word as the city noises flooded in. Valerus's thoughts were focused on one thing only: Flavia was his. He had the money and today he would pay his father to the last As; the theater still owed him a few sestertii and Gaius was prepared to help with any loose ends. All Valerus had to do was hand it over to his father. The world was certainly changing for the better.

❧

Valerus left for the theater to see Aurleus in the later morning, leaving Lucius and Flavia reclined by the table and playing dice games to help the time go by. They spoke little but laughed a lot, tossing the little bone cubes and keeping score on a tablet. They were not aware of the strange approaching noise until it drowned out the hypnotic murmur from outside. They then heard the bottom door being opened and several feet hurrying up the steps toward them.

There was no knock or formal introduction. Five watchmen barged into the apartment, throwing open the door so violently that one of the hinges broke. Marcus was at the head of the group.

Both Flavia and Lucius were on their feet, staring in confused terror at the armed men. Flavia was the first to recover and shook her head in their direction. "Marcus? What's all this?"

The captain's face was twisted, dreading what was to come. "I am sorry, Flavia, but you are to come with us directly."

Lucius stepped in front of the woman protectively. "You have no authority. Flavia is Valerus's property."

There was a hopeful glint in Marcus's eyes as he looked from him to her. "Is this true?"

"Valerus has the money," Flavia said, taking note of her own voice trembling. "He only needs to pay Pedius."

The captain of guard sagged in disappointment. Sadly he shook his head. "Then you are still Pedius's property, and he has ordered your arrest immediately. Please don't resist; this is above me."

"What?" Lucius shouted. "For what? On what grounds?"

Marcus made a gesture over his shoulder and the four guards came forth. They pushed Lucius aside and took Flavia by the arms. Lucius simply watched, horrified, as the guards produced a pair of shackles and clipped them over Flavia's wrists. She gasped as their coldness enclosed her. Her fear had not yet come through; it was happening so fast that she did not have any time to think or analyze the happenings.

Lucius, however, broke from the trance faster than she did. "No!" she heard him shout before he jumped forward, grabbing one of the guards by the arm and twisting it back. "You have no right! Let her go!"

Marcus sighed and stepped up to him. "Let him go, Master Lucius. This is above me as well as you. You can't fight this."

"On what grounds?" he demanded to know. The men were pushing Flavia out the door already.

"You will have to take it up with Master Pedius. I am only obeying orders."

The guard Lucius was trying to hold down suddenly broke free, turned, and threw a blow at the young man's head. Flavia called his name when he stumbled back against the open window. Flavia began to fight as they led her down the stairs, pulling and thrashing without any plan for what she would do if it was effective. Two men now took her by the arms, forcing her along the passageway, through the perfume stall, and out into the street. People watched from their places, especially drawn when Flavia let out a short scream of alarm. The fear was creeping in finally, and she knew that whatever charges had been placed against her, four guards to make the arrest meant it carried the penalty of death.

"Flavia!"

It drew her attention; Valerus's voice always did. She looked around and saw him on the street corner, staring with his mouth dropped open.

"Valerus!" Her scream was cracked with tears. "Valerus! *Please*! Don't let them take me!"

The young man started to run, but Flavia saw him stumble as she was led into the next street and out of sight.

Valerus cursed, tried to get up again, and collapsed, this time rolling over as he clenched at his knee and gritted his teeth. Once more he tried to get up, but his leg shot out from under him and he fell again.

Flavia heard him let out an agonized scream followed by the call of her name through the thickening crowd.

⁂

It was a quiet afternoon at the villa; Pedius was reading in the library. Rectina had brought him a cup of tea, which was steaming at his elbow, when Valerus bombarded through the door. He marched up to his father's desk and slammed his hands on the table. "What have you done?"

Pedius merely looked up at his son; there was no reassurance in his stare. "What I had to," he said levelly and turned back to his work.

Valerus, enraged by his behavior, snatched the papers he was reading and flung them across the room. "*What have you done*? We had an agreement! I still had two days! You can't change what was agreed on."

"But you did not tell me the whole story, Valerus." He too got to his feet. "One thing that I care about more than the happiness of those I love is the reputation of this household in view of society and the emperor. Vespasian was lenient to the growing Christian sect, but I don't know what Titus's views are going to be on those who harbor them."

Valerus's jaw snapped shut and he took a small step back.

Pedius walked around the table. "Salvius came to see me earlier this morning," he told his son compassionately. "He told me a few more things regarding Flavia's friendship with his slave. Were you at all aware that she was part of the faith?"

Valerus did not reply; there was nothing he could say. His father had caught up to him. Now, finally, the worst had happened, and it all felt like a strange unbelievable dream.

Pedius studied his son's expression and sighed. He turned back to his place on the opposite end and rubbed his brow. "Of course you did," he muttered as if to himself and resettled in his chair. "Keeping secrets appears to be your second nature."

"And what is my first?" he asked bitterly.

"Shaming the family."

Valerus felt the acid rise in his throat. Never in his life did he want to strike someone as he did his father that day. At his side he clenched his fists a few times to try to repress his rage.

Shaming the family? What about them shaming me in my choice of who I love? The anger, the deceit of his own family, made him want to kill again.

But this rage was momentary, as other thoughts—far more serious—replaced them. "And what is going to happen to her now?" he asked, ice hanging from his words.

"I will send word of her arrest. She will be sent to Rome for interrogation and probably her execution. It would appear that the emperor is not putting up with the rising faith. I don't want to be accused of harboring a fugitive."

"Will she be entitled to a lawyer?" Valerus asked suddenly, as the image of Gaius came to his mind. That may be the best chance for Flavia at the moment. Pliny's nephew may well be …

Will you listen to yourself, Valerus? You cannot let her go to Rome; the moment she is away from you anything can happen to her. You can't take any chance with Flavia's life, and letting her go could mean anything, lawyer or none.

"For a slave?" Pedius shook his head disapprovingly. "*I* am not even prepared to stand for her."

Valerus turned to the door, feeling broken. He had lost. Never in his life had he felt so helpless. This was actually the end of the road; there was nowhere he could go from here and there was nothing he could do without breaking the law.

His expression changed as he looked back to his father who had resumed his work. Valerus stared as his mind went further than before. His father's first threat had caused him to take the leap to an opportunity that nearly got him killed. This was a second moment to make a decision that would ensure Flavia's survival as well as his future. Breaking the law? He had been prepared to die for her only a couple of days ago.

"You are restricted to the grounds," Pedius said suddenly, pulling a block of papyrus papers toward him. "Your movement will be confined to the villa until I decide what punishment you deserve."

Valerus hadn't heard him. He instead looked from one corner of the room to the other as different options began to flit through his thoughts. They were not rational, and that caused him some hesitation.

For the first time, Valerus looked his way, his words suddenly reaching his psyche. "Are you putting me under house arrest?"

"I will be informing the guard, so you are as of sundown."

The young man's jaw dropped open. "What? You can't cage me in like some wild animal!"

"I can do whatever I want with you!" Pedius jumped up, raising his voice above Valerus's angry tone. "I am head of this household. I can have you killed if I wished! Keep that in mind. You have caused enough harm to the reputation of this family and I will have to make a pledge to have it stop *here*!" He thumped his fist on the table.

Valerus had never seen his father in such a rage. Keeping a low tone now would do far better than trying to fight his father's wrath.

"What is *reputation*, Father?" Valerus's voice had lowered to a calm state that nearly bordered on concerned. "A community's opinion of an individual of a group of people. Tell me, Father, why is the opinion of others so much more valuable than the happiness of an individual?"

"Leave the fancy quotes to Master Pliny." Pedius shook his head and lowered into his seat. "Get down to the kitchen and tell the cooks that you will be joining us for cena tonight."

Valerus watched, his mouth failing to keep up with his thoughts. He let the ideas travel through before focusing on one, and it was in this thought that he left the library and headed to the kitchen.

⁂

Flavia was locked in the lower cells of the prison built for slaves. Some had been locked away for long, even years, awaiting trial from their masters and word from Rome.

The young woman sat alone in a corner, feeling the cold damp rise up from the flagstones under her. Two guards were in the next room rolling dice; she could hear the faint tinkling sound as they rolled across the wooden table.

She had not seen Marcus since the arrest and kept wondering for what she had been arrested. Pedius had to have reason; despite his previous brawls with her and his son, Flavia knew that he was a man of honor and a law-abiding citizen. There *had* to be a reason.

Night crept in and the sound of the city outside dissipated until it was nothing more than a few occasional men and horses walking the road. Marcus came to the garrison an hour after dark; he spoke briefly to his men before stepping out from the shadows and into Flavia's view.

The young woman jumped to her feet and went to take his large cold hands through the bars.

"Flavia." He smiled and touched her cheek for a second. "What have you gotten yourself into?"

"Marcus, what have I done?"

"It's what you are. Master Pedius discovered that you are part of the new sect."

For a second Flavia felt faint, but she brushed it away. There was no point in fearing the worst anymore, so panic was of no help; she was prepared to take responsibility for herself. She had known the danger she was in since the day Melani had first warned her, and she had known, in her heart, that one day she would have to walk in her Lord's footsteps.

"What is going to happen to me?" she asked softly, fighting the tears that so desperately wanted to come.

"You will probably be taken to Rome for interrogation. It will be their decision as to what the penalty will be."

The first tear came through that moment. The fear of her own fate was suddenly lost in the flood of emotion at the thought of Valerus. She felt forced to ask, "Will I see Valerus again before I leave?"

Marcus drew back his hands and clenched at the cell bars. So much he wanted to reassure her, but he was in a debate as to whether false hope would be any better than no hope. He decided therefore to stick to the truth and what he knew from previous victims under the rule of Vespasian. "I don't know." It was obvious that he was struggling to speak as much as she was. "Pedius has put him under house arrest. He is not allowed to leave the premises."

"He was so close to paying!" she cried. "Gaius offered that which he didn't have! If only he had paid a few hours earlier." Flavia felt the collapse of the foundation of everything she had built over the years. Not even three months ago would she have protested to her own death or asked to be pardoned. Now, however, after having met Valerus and realizing that there was indeed more to the world than cruelty and blood sport, she wanted to beg for mercy. Life was suddenly worth living.

"I don't want to die, Marcus." She wept. "Not without seeing him again. I love him."

"Deny it," he tried to convince her. "Deny everything you believe ..."

"I cannot do that! It would be worse than denying that I loved Valerus. Oh, God! I wish I could see him again!"

The captain reached through the gaps and took her cheek in his hand. "You are a brave woman, Flavia. Only the gods can place in a woman so much love. It is indeed a privilege to know you."

Valerus paced his bedroom floor with his hands clasped behind his back. His thoughts were bound to Flavia and his inability to save her. To whom had his father sent the message? The senate? The emperor himself? Or was it simply the provincial governor?

If a messenger was sent to Rome, it gave him a window of a couple of weeks to …

He smashed his fist in his bed; there was nothing he could do. This was unfortunately above him. He cursed himself for not having asked his father for Flavia long before any of this had happened. The thought of Flavia in a prison cell awaiting execution … He thought her thoughts and felt the terrible fear come over him. For a few seconds he felt himself in Flavia's place before turning to his own ordeal, and that was to wait for her to die—which was nearly as bad.

A life without Flavia? It was an unbearable thought. He looked over his bed and thought of how little he deserved after the life he had led and then turned to the care and dedication Flavia had showed to a simple slave.

He collapsed on the bed and held his head in his hands.

Flavia! How could he have let it happen? He had fought in the arena and Lucius had risked his life to help him and Flavia. Now all that had been worthless; why had he done any of it?

You fool! You love her, that's why you did it … and you will do it all over again if it could set it right.

Chapter 31

July 27

Valerus did not know how he got by the days that followed, especially when he reminded himself of Flavia's situation and that he could not see her. He walked the villa from room to room, and despite avoiding his father at all costs, he was well aware that he was being watched. Every move he made was being done under supervision.

After his father had left the library, Valerus took station there, reading random texts of Philodemus, the Epicurean philosopher. He would have read anything to help pass the time and keep his thoughts distracted.

Gaius appeared in the doorway and offered him a sad smile when he looked up. Valerus could not return the gesture; he had never felt less like it. He returned to his reading without a word, but thinking bitterly how the young man's efforts had all been in vain. Nothing had ever been simpler than love? It was ridiculous. Having killed man and beast in the arena had been simple; it was straight forward with rules to follow and a referee to judge the rights and wrongs. Love had none of that, and that made it far more complicated than he could ever have imagined.

"I'm sorry about what happened," Valerus heard the young man say.

He still didn't look up, as he was now fighting back the tears that were accumulating.

"Did you know she was part of the new superstition?"

This angered him. Firstly, what did it matter if he did? And secondly, *superstition?* At least she lived up to the loving teachings of her God, while he as a Roman citizen had only worshiped bloodshed for the better part of his life. "So?" he said softly in the hopes that he would not hear it.

"It is frowned upon, Valerus."

"And for that she might be condemned?" Now he looked up at him. Gaius saw the glint of rage and aversion in his eyes, but there was very obviously also sadness and a great deal of regret. "What did she do *wrong*, Gaius? She did nothing more than help someone less than her. She helped and served unconditionally while I indulged myself in orgies and trained in the art of killing! I'm the one who ought to be condemned."

Gaius said nothing and stepped into the library, pulled a chair across the room and took station opposite him, resting his chin in his hand. Valerus regarded him with a strange fascination, wondering what was rolling in his thoughts at that moment. *He's such an intelligent young man,* he thought, *perhaps even more so than his uncle.* Pliny the Elder seemed to pass his time reading while young Gaius simply observed the world.

"What are you going to do?" Gaius asked suddenly.

Valerus shook his head, turning down to the scroll again, but he could not read any of it. His mind took control and the Greek letters blurred in the bubble of his thoughts. He was thinking of everything from begging his father to show mercy to the option of taking his own life. He could not stand the thought of Flavia being put to death and him lingering on without her. It was unbearable.

"You can't let her go to Rome."

"Over my dead body!" Valerus leaned toward him and spat the words, using more vigor than he had ever in his life. "I will be imprisoned, beaten, tortured, and thrown to the lions before that happened!"

For the first time Gaius smiled, liking the tone of his voice and the ambition therein. He did not speak right away, allowing the emotion to sink into Valerus's heart. Valerus felt the rage drop to the pit of his stomach, melting in the things he had experienced of the last several weeks. His eyes became glassy. Now Gaius spoke.

"Will you take me to this man who Flavia helped so kindly?"

Valerus was shaking his head before he had even finished. "I can't leave the villa, Gaius. I am a prisoner, at least for now."

"I am sure with me as an escort you father will permit it."

Valerus did not register his words; his mind was filled with Flavia and the painful hurt as he realized again and again that everything happening to her was because of him … *everything.* Gaius watched, studying the man's labored breathing and how he began to tremble wretchedly. Finally he looked up as red-hot tears finally rose in his eyes. He was beyond anger; it had been spent. All that replaced it was a bleeding heart and a future that looked so worthless that death was being viewed as an improvement.

"What do you want your future to be, Valerus?" Gaius asked him suddenly.

"With her!" Valerus's voice cracked under the strain.

"A home together? A family? Children?"

Valerus wheezed under the thought of what he had lost. Tears boiled out of him as he tried, unable, to gather the words in his mouth. Finally he gave up and simply looked at the young man opposite him. "I just want to be with her!" he managed to mutter in a single breath.

Gaius got up from his seat. "Come, Valerus. Take me to the docks."

❧

It was so strange to walk the slave's route by himself. Every step Valerus took reminded him of Flavia and the last day they had walked there together. Everything was so familiar and yet felt to Valerus to come from a dream.

The repairer's quarters were the same; even the old sheet hanging from the entrance. Valerus held it aside and bid Gaius to enter, who was grasping one end of his toga in his hand. Both men looked around in the gloom when the drape fell shut again. In the next room was the sound of a chisel hitting a wooden board.

They followed the sound and found the repairer sitting over his work, carving a beam. He looked up at the familiar face and the stranger and fear struck him back. He inched away, raising his hand in supplication. "No more," he begged. "Please, no more people. Stop here."

"We are not here to hurt you," Gaius told him. Valerus had never heard the young man speak with a domineering voice, but this was without a doubt the voice of command—master to slave.

The repairer inched back, shaking his head as he did.

Valerus came forward. "It's over. Nothing more can happen to you. You didn't do anything wrong."

The repairer sat up and looked from Valerus to Pliny and back again. His eyes watered slightly as he shook his head again. "Where she? Your young lady?"

Valerus turned his focus to the sting in his eyes and moistened his lips.

Gaius stepped forward. "She's not here at the moment."

"What you want then?"

Valerus shook his head. "Nothing." He sighed, looked at the small dead fire in the sand nearby and then the battered pot that hung from its nail. He then reached in under his toga and looked back at the slave. "I brought you something." He removed a small bag of grain and a handful of plantain. "This could help you with some of your pain." He shrugged. "Don't know how well, but it's something."

For the first time the slave smiled, exposing his rotting teeth. "They help." He nodded. "Previous master gave to me also." He carefully reached over to take it. Valerus thought of how much he resembled a stray dog reaching for a chunk of meat; frightened, cautious, and wary, knowing that at any moment the giver could turn out to be violent and cruel.

He took it and sat back again, weighing the grain in his hand. "This is a good meal," he announced and smiled at them again. "Will join?"

Valerus looked at Gaius, suddenly hopeful. For a few seconds he really wanted to until he analyzed the thought, wondering why. He wanted to serve this man as he had seen Flavia serve him. It was strange; he had never felt guilty about leaving a slave to his work; it was what they were there for.

"Unfortunately not." Gaius nodded, his voice softer than before. "Valerus is officially under my charge and I can't keep him out too long. But I do have a few questions to ask you."

Valerus frowned. *Questions? What questions?*

"What exactly did Flavia preach to you?"

The repairer and Valerus locked gazes; for a few seconds their thoughts turned to other things. Valerus especially was concerned about where this conversation was heading. Why would Gaius be interested …?

By the gods! He was a lawyer, was he not? Was he an interrogator? Was he in correspondence with the senate?

They were frightening thoughts, but Valerus could not believe that after everything Gaius had said and done that he was going to put both Flavia and him at even greater risk. In fact, as the thought turned in his head, he realized it was more likely that Gaius was more concerned about looking for something to help them with.

"He knows." The repairer pointed to Valerus. "He was with."

The young man turned to look at Valerus, hardly believing it. "Is this true?" he asked. "You too were preached of the Christ?"

"So?" Valerus shook his head angrily. "Nothing wrong with listening, Gaius! Besides, nothing against the emperor! Christians just want to help others."

"Don't be too sure." Gaius narrowed his eyes. "Flavia is a good exception, I can imagine, but no cult or religion is perfect."

It was a reaction and comment Valerus had not seen coming. Not only was this man defending the growing Christian society but was also, in a small way, degrading his own. "What?"

"There is no belief system that could work on the mass population of a growing world, Valerus. We have many gods, including one of love, and yet there are many things I frown upon. I share the views of our emperor that the Christian faith is a growing nuisance in our society, but what right have I to condemn someone like Flavia? This is why our emperor has allowed the practice of other customs in occupied lands. No one can ever—or will ever—find one form of religion that will work for everyone. We all find our cornerstones and build up from there."

Valerus shook his head. "So … Christianity for you is …?"

"Interesting." Gaius smiled. "There is always something to learn from every belief form. Put it all together and you may find a simple truth. And is that not what we all strive for, Valerus? Simplicity?"

❧

Flavia remembered a time when things were simple; even two weeks ago had been simple. At least then there was a future ... a horizon. Now there was nothing more than a bleak desert that shimmed with mirages and uncertainly.

She had opened Valerus's poem on the straw and stared, not reading, but merely looking at his writing technique, feeling his presence through the written words and wondering if she would ever see him in the flesh again. It had been a week since she had last seen or heard of him. Marcus often shared information with her regarding Pedius's decisions and Valerus's position but told her that the young man had little opportunity to pass on any news personally. He was under tight watch and was only allowed to leave the premises with a trustworthy escort. In a very strict manner, Valerus was just as confined as she was.

Both imprisoned separately. It was so hard for her to remember a time when she had no worries about tomorrow, knowing that he was going to be there. Now she felt how much of her fear and doubts could be lessened if she could simply feel his hands again.

She was not crying anymore, she was beyond that. Fear, rage, and heartbreak had turned her emotions around so much that she no longer knew how she was supposed to react. One thing she knew was that she loved Valerus, a man so unlike her, and that she was prepared to take that confirmation to the grave; it would be where faith led her.

Chapter 32

August 3

"Just let me see her! No harm can come if we are separated by bars!"

"Out of the question!" Pedius bellowed; his voice could be heard all through the villa. "I will not have you meddling with that part of society! That is the rule of this domus!"

"You are *not* my father!" Valerus paced the *triclinium* floor, circling Pedius as he would an opponent in the arena. "No father would deny what his son desires! *You are not my father!*"

The argument was bringing in a crowd; already Cotti, Luci, and Helen had been drawn from their evening tasks and were now watching from the potted fern as the two continued to argue. Behind them they heard more feet approaching at a hurried pace. It was getting very heated; Valerus had been trapped in the house for nearly two weeks without seeing or hearing from Flavia. His soul felt chained and he could take no more of it.

"Raise your voice like that one more time and it will be the absolute worst for you!" Pedius began to move closer to him, his fists clenched as if he was preparing to strike. "Do it once more!"

"Both of you! Stop this!" Rectina was standing in the doorway that led to the passage of the atrium. Both men turned to the commanding tone of her voice. She shook her head madly as she walked first to Valerus and put her arm across his shoulder. "Stop this," she said to him and then looked at her husband. "The pair of you. Your voices can be heard into the garden. It's only a blessing that we are alone. It would have been humiliating …"

"Gaius is studying in the peristyle," Valerus snapped and turned to his father. "He will have a lot to tell his uncle when he follows him."

"Shut up!" Pedius roared. "You have no authority to speak to me like that."

"But why can't I see her, Father?" His voice had come down a little, but only a little. "Why? You know that it may be for the last time."

Rectina opened her mouth to speak when her husband cut her off. "You don't know that!" He shook his head. "I don't know that. The decision is above us. This is *not* your last chance!"

"It is!" Rectina said quickly to fit it in above their voices.

Valerus spun around, staring at her with a fearful look, one she had not seen on him since he was a child of five. Avoiding his gaze, she walked toward her husband and passed him a scroll of paper. "Word has come," she told him and then looked back at her son. "I am sorry, Valerus."

Valerus felt the breath being drawn out of him as his father unrolled the paper and quickly read through it. Slowly he began to nod, as though satisfied. Valerus felt it hours before he suddenly said in a clear calm voice, "It appears that Flavia is to be sent to Rome. Interrogation, no doubt."

Both parents noticed how their son trembled across the room. They heard departing footsteps as the three slaves, who had also heard the news, hurried to pass it on. Valerus fought all his thoughts as they tried to get through his mouth at the same time, bombarding him with accusations, curses, and even pleas. His stare caught his father and then the tears came; his eyes glistened over before a tear cut a groove in the dirt of his cheek.

Silence fell like a thunderclap from the heavens; parent and son stared. Pedius felt, for a second, a great pity and regret on the senate's decision and wondered if he had perhaps stepped over the line. He did not let the sympathy take over and so shook his head and straightened his toga. Valerus was all ears as he simply said, "I will arrange an escort for you to go see her in the morning. Flavia will leave day after next." With that offer, he walked from the room, leaving Valerus and Rectina alone together.

The woman turned to her son and saw him sink to his knees, his eyes looking through the walls, through the situation and through his life. Everything was suddenly empty to him.

"Valerus." There was a crack in her voice as she walked to him. Weakly the young man raised his hand, beckoning her to stop. He was wheezing. He could not believe that it had actually happened. All his hopes, and his efforts had been in vain. His life was empty again … there was nothing left.

"You know it's for the best." Even though she said it, she knew it was not true.

Valerus brought his hands over his head, caught his breath, and suddenly screamed. No man had so openly expressed his emotion in the family; this was a first and it was terribly shocking.

"No!" Valerus dragged the word through his gasping breath. "No! By all the gods, please! *No!*"

Rectina didn't know what to do; how she hated seeing her own son experiencing such anguish, and yet there was nothing she could do to relieve the pain. She so much wanted to go up to him but he refused, falling back on her approach and raising his hands to cast her off. "No!" he sobbed again before pulling himself to his feet.

"No! Flavia! No!" He turned from the room and knocked a vase from its stand. He would have punched holes in the wall had he been strong enough, but instead he bruised his knuckles until they bled.

August 4

Flavia did not hear the news until Valerus came to see her the next morning. It was the first time in nearly two weeks that she got a glimpse of him, but his attitude toward her was distant and somewhat cold. Marcus led him into her cell, and although she wanted to embrace him, she could feel this was not the time. His stare went right through her and it was obvious that words were hanging on the tip of his tongue.

"What is it?" she asked, catching herself taking a step away from him. "What's wrong?"

Valerus could not bring himself to say it and stuttered in his effort. That moment Flavia knew that she was going to have to face a life without him, that there was no telling what she would have to live through over the few weeks that probably remained of her life. Finally, when the struggle became too great, he walked over and took her into his arms, pressing her to him so hard that it hurt. Flavia clenched to him, feeling the need for it. She did not need to say anything, but it was perfectly clear why he had come.

He had come to say good-bye.

The hurt cut her like a knife; no pain had ever been more real. She dug her face in his toga, catching the unique scent that could only be his, and she started crying when she thought about it being the last time she did. She could not stand the thought and so said, without having much control of her own voice, "Please don't leave me."

"I don't want to!" he said with his cheek pressed to her hair. "Believe me … *I don't want to!*"

Flavia felt the strength drain from her when she discovered that this was going to be the last time they would ever get to see each other. It did not feel real—more like a nightmare from which she could not wake up.

"I love you, Flavia!" His voice trembled. "Don't ever forget that."

She could not return his words; she was sobbing now, unable to hold herself back anymore.

"I will try to live with the discipline you've shown me," he said.

"Master Valerus!" A guard was standing a short way away.

Valerus did not look around but merely stepped back to look at Flavia's red wet face. "I wrote to you," he said softly, "saying that I would die if the gods should wish me to go on without you." He pressed his brow against hers. "I am dead, Flavia!" He wept. "I can't live with the memory of this moment."

Now she stepped back, catching her breath in short fast gasps. She took his hands into hers and kissed them. "Strength." It was all she could say before the tears took control again.

When he left later he screamed a curse that could even be heard from the villa.

Four of the slaves were discussing Flavia and the recent events around the table that night, sharing some bread and honey. Alia was the only one not eating; instead she hung her head sadly over the woodwork.

"I never knew a man could love a woman so much," she cracked sadly. "I really had no idea."

Ursalus, who was sitting beside her, kindly took her around the shoulders.

"Poor girl." Helen shook her head. "Christian or not, it's not fair to separate the two like that. What a terrible outcome for such a happy story."

"Bribing the guards wouldn't work?" Alia asked them.

"Not with it involving the senate," Helen replied. "This is too big to come down to one guard."

"Quiet!" Cotti hissed when they suddenly noticed a figure pass by the door. None had the time to see who it was. They were all quiet to listen; there were footfalls despite it being terribly late for everyone to be up. Gaius often went walking in the evening and the early morning, but this was well out of his hours.

The footfalls were getting closer until the figure reemerged in the kitchen's lamplight. On closer observation they recognized Valerus, his eyes red and swollen as he looked upon the company.

All four slaves got up and greeted him respectfully. He approached them, not interested in formality. He walked right up to Cotti.

"How do you get out of here?" he asked her suddenly and softy.

She was taken back; Valerus had never spoken to her so directly or with such urgency in his voice. She looked at him and shook her head, bewildered. "Master?"

"All slaves find ways of sneaking out of the villa from time to time. Flavia managed it and I know you have also in the past to see your lover. A watchman now stands at the door and another walking the grounds. How do you avoid them?"

Cotti looked at the other girls for assistance, but they all looked away, not wanting to be involved. Cotti turned back to her master and saw the desperation in his eyes. Slowly she nodded, thinking about what he could do for Flavia if he got the chance. "Do you go to the back terrace, master?" she asked.

Valerus said nothing but simply waited for her to continue.

"Good footholds in the wooden beams; going out from the inside is much easier than coming in from the outside."

Valerus smiled. "I won't be coming back in."

⁂

Nightlife in Herculaneum was busy not so much in the streets as in the taverns. There was the occasional brawl in which the night watchmen were quick to interfere, but, other than that, the goings-on were well mannered and kept to a balanced mood of enjoyment, song, and wine.

Marcus sat alone at the table nearest the hearth in a little tavern of the lower city. A few oil lamps were burning from the roof, illuminating the smoke. Across the room a group of young men were rolling dice, drinking wine straight from the jug, and passing each other small coins. In the center of the room, sitting with his back to him, was a lonely man covered in robe and hood. He was taking as much interest in observing the wine in his goblet as drinking it.

The captain's mind was far from merrymaking. Flavia had been special to him; she was not like other slaves of the household and, if she had belonged to him, Christian or not, he would not have kicked her off so suddenly. It was indeed unfair; in fact, he was beginning to question his own religion when he thought about the things he had done. What had Flavia done? What had she ever practiced that could be observed as a threat or meant she needed interrogation?

His thoughts then turned to Valerus, wondering how he was handling the situation. Not too well from Flavia's reaction. Without a doubt he knew that the young man was scheming something; it was not his style to sit back and surrender—a gladiator never did. In this respect, he and Flavia had a lot in common.

He took a short sip and, when he opened his eyes, he noticed that a figure had slipped in across from him. A brown hood was drawn back to his neck and a familiar face smiled his direction.

"Master Valerus! How did you get here?"

"The villa is big; my father cannot know where I am all the time."

"Well, don't stick around too long," Marcus warned. "When he realizes you've gone, I will be after you."

The young man chuckled. "Listen to me, Marcus. I need to know a few small details regarding Flavia's transfer to Rome."

"What do you need to know?"

"When is she leaving? By what road and how many escorts?"

The relief that came across the man's face was obvious. "They will leave in the early morning, soon after sunrise, out the east way by chariot with one driver and a guard."

"That's it? I was expecting it to be a lot more."

"She's only one woman. They are not expecting much resistance."

Valerus smiled and leaned back a bit. "From Flavia, I would agree."

It was Marcus's turn to laugh. "I take it they are not expecting *you*."

Valerus leaned closer and lowered his voice. "There is but one thing I must ask of you ..."

Chapter 33

August 6

Those few hours before dawn were when it was most quiet. It was too early for the birds and it was an end to the sound of crickets and night owls. Herculaneum was dormant. The only small activity was around the guardhouse where the soldiers were gathering at the end of their patrols. Soon the day watch would be brought in and they would be entitled to a few hours of sleep. Some had skipped off early while others dozed alongside the walls with their swords across their laps.

A figure looked around the corner where the street turned from the building. Valerus kept his eyes half-shut so that they would not reflect in the torches. He watched unobserved for a while; two men were chatting by the open entrance and were roused by the sound of approaching hoof beats across the flagstones.

Marcus rode up at a steady trot and dismounted before the animal had even stopped. He passed the reins to another soldier. Without a word, he disappeared into the building.

Valerus leaned back again. "Right. He's here. All we can do now is wait."

Lucius was sitting with his back against the wall of an insula, rubbing his hands anxiously. It was not a cold night at all, but the mere thought of their fate if they got caught brought him a chill.

Valerus looked around again. "There are a lot of them," he muttered to himself. "I was expecting half of that at the very most."

"We may both end up in Rome to face trial." Lucius shook his head.

There was a brief silence before Valerus caught his breath. "There she is." His voice was suddenly hoarse.

Lucius got up to look over his companion's shoulder. Flavia was standing in the halo of the pilot lamp that was hanging above the door. Marcus had removed her shackles and now stood behind her with a strong hand on her shoulder. Her face was pale and her expression swept with far more regret than fear. Her stola had been removed and was now replaced by the usual slave's tunic. It appeared so plain on her in comparison to her beauty.

Valerus shivered, suddenly feeling cold; it was like a snap of death when he saw her, feeling the empty hole inside him filling with concrete. He wanted to kill every man who touched her.

There was a distant sound that caused both men to look around. More hoof beats, this time by four horses and the rattle of chariot wheels. Up the road a small lantern was approaching, rocking gently from where it hung above the wheel.

"That's it. The chariot. Marcus did well in arranging them to leave in the dark." Valerus looked at Lucius over his shoulder. His companion had already gone; he barely made out his shadow disappearing along the wall. Valerus sighed and turned back. He could trust Lucius to put his part into play; he had more confidence in his friend than in himself. He had to play his part and he was alone in it. If anything went wrong …

When the attention of the guards was drawn to the approaching chariot, he took the chance to cross the open road and go into the shadows beyond where he disappeared.

Whatever happened next, he knew it would have to be worth it. Flavia was everything to him, and if he was condemned to the arena as a criminal, at least he would know that he had done everything in his power to ensure her safety.

The chariot was the large four-man chariot pulled by four horses, prepared to take Flavia and her two escorts to Rome for interrogation and probably her execution. The driver was armed with a dagger and began tending to the horses, checking their buckles and traces for the journey ahead.

Valerus observed closely as a guard came from the garrison and saluted Marcus before taking Flavia by the shoulder and stepping up on the chariot. He pushed her to stand on the front beside the driver who had returned and was now adjusting the reins.

Flavia turned to have her back to the horses and folded her hands in front of her. For a second, she glanced in the direction of Marcus who merely smiled kindly and stepped back. The guard took station in front of her, his hand resting casually on the hilt of his sword.

The fidgeting horses were set into motion, rocking all three back for a second. The driver brought up the reins to get the proper feel of them before setting them into a trot.

The sound of the horses' hooves on the flagstones was approaching. Valerus sat with his back against an empty barrel, trying to calm the racing of his heart. In the arena he could be killed, but there were strict rules and it was equal, fair play. Here Valerus realized that the odds were very much against him. If he missed the chariot, or if the horses were set into a canter before leaving the city, he would miss his only chance.

He rubbed his knee slowly. "Don't give me any trouble now," he whispered. "You can cripple me for life, but only after today."

The sound was so close now that they could not have been more than a few yards away; the light of the lantern was beginning to illuminate the dark corner where he hid. The first sign of dawn was stretching behind Vesuvius.

The chariot rattled by. Valerus let it trot past for a few paces before swinging himself out after it. Flavia saw him an instant before he grabbed the chariot railing, which was the moment the escorting guard swung around with his dagger.

Valerus fell across the chariot's floor feet first. His intention was to scythe the legs out from under the guard, but the measured area was only enough to throw him off balance momentarily.

The guard fell against Flavia who threw up her arms and pushed him away. He stumbled forward a couple of paces, tripped over Valerus still outstretched, and fell hard onto the flagstones behind and below.

The driver was in a panicked state, wondering whether to whip the horses into full gallop or to pull them to a stop. The guard was down but not unconscious. In the light Valerus could see him getting to his feet and heard him screaming for the guard.

Hoping that the sudden jolt would throw him off, the driver snapped the whip over the horses' heads. Valerus was suddenly at his side, grabbing the leather reins from his hand. "Stop the horses!" he hissed and heaved.

The animals threw up their heads, shrieking from the sudden yank. Their forelegs shot out, bring them to a stop on their haunches, so violent that all three passengers toppled against the front railing.

The driver made an attempt to escape, but Valerus was up in an instant and his elbow caught him straight on his jaw, throwing him back so that he rolled off the chariot.

The young man looked down at Flavia as he took up the reins again. She was staring with round-eyed disbelief at the sudden change of events. He whipped the horses into a canter from a standstill, throwing her a quick glance, but did not say a word, nor did he smile. It was too early for that.

There was a burst of power; he felt the strength as they pulled away, momentarily being yanked into a world of speed and freedom. The wind rushed past, whipping hair across their faces.

They were outside the city when it was becoming obvious that people were coming after them. Behind them against the black walls was the shimmering of lights. Valerus knew that a four-horse chariot could never outrun one horse and rider at a full gallop. Horses strapped so close together were naturally off balance and jittery.

At the second milestone he pulled them off the road, having them settle abruptly in a cloud of dust. In the direction of the town were the shouts of alarm and more lights appearing.

Valerus jumped off the chariot and pulled Flavia up behind him. A small dense cluster of trees grew along the mountain foot where a figure on horseback appeared. Not a word was exchanged when Flavia recognized Lucius on a bay horse. The animal was nervous, pacing to one side as the couple approached hurriedly.

"Take her north across the mountain," Valerus told him.

Flavia spun around to look at him, grabbing him by the hand. "What about you?" she asked desperately.

"I will follow. I need to take the pursuers the other way for a few mille passuums first."

She made a small weak sound as she fell against him, taking him by the neck and pressing her brow against his. He held her, but only for a few seconds, feeling her body up against his and allowing her strength to rebuild his own. He then turned to Lucius mounted on his horse. "Come down the east side." He helped Flavia up on the horse's back behind Lucius. The horse shifted its weight uneasily. The woman took Lucius around the waist.

"I'll see you in Pompeii, friend." He smiled.

Lucius nodded his direction and turned the horse northward to the woods again where they both disappeared.

Valerus, suddenly captivated by the disrupted silence, ran back to the chariot. The horses were unusually calm and one had taken the opportunity to graze the roadside. The young man snapped the whip over their ears, bringing all their heads up sharply, and kicked up the earth when it was snapped again. Behind him the lights were approaching; obviously it took some time for the watchmen to bridle their horses, but they were on the way now and catching up.

The young man leaned across the railing and cut off the lantern; it shattered across the flagstones, flickering a moment before being swallowed by the darkness.

They would first be drawn to where the light had been, Valerus thought, and there would be no indication that he had stopped, but they were going to follow the road, for a chariot of this kind would not do well on bad ground. It was not intended to go off road; it was intended to get to Rome, which meant paved roads all the way.

The first horseman was catching up with two more trailing close behind it. They were not carrying any lamps and the sound of their galloping horses was drowned by the rattling of the chariot's wheels. They were on Valerus by surprise. He loosed the lash again, letting it snap above the horses' ears just once without touching them. The first horseman galloped up alongside him while the next began to overtake. The young man, whip still in hand, lashed at the rider who shrieked and fell back. The second rider up ahead was reaching across, trying to grab at the bridle of the outer horse.

Valerus decided to give him a helping hand. He leaned across the chariot bar and snapped the tracers that bound the animal to the axel. The horse's hind quarters skated out of line, throwing the rider ahead of him off balance for a second, but its bridle was still attached to the horse beside it. Valerus momentarily pondered his next move. He lashed the whip once more to keep the horses in speed, then jumped the chariot railing to stand on the yoke pole. He cursed when the pain ran up his leg suddenly. The two horses on either side of him tried to turn their heads his way, but the reins forbade it.

Still supporting himself on the rail, he took a small step forward, knowing full well what a messy death it would be if he were to fall among the galloping hooves of four horses followed by the wheels of a heavy chariot. He reeled when the guard ahead managed to grab the bridle and yanked at it. The chariot swayed; the half-freed horse began to pull out its hind quarters so that it nearly ran perpendicular to the others.

The speed was coming down and the two other riders caught up. One of the inner horses tried to kick at Valerus when his hand came down on its rump. Gathering his strength and ignoring the pain, Valerus swung his leg over the nearest horse's back, drew his knife and began to hack at the strap that bound the horse from bit to bit.

When it tore loose, the horse sped ahead of the others, its rump hitting the horse and rider so hard that both tumbled across the flagstones. Valerus felt the thump as a wheel went over either man or horse; he could not tell.

He was now on the back of the outer horse tied to the yoke pole. He leaned across the animal's neck to unclip the strap that bound it to the pole when a whip seared into his back. With a grunt he looked over his shoulder. A guard was keeping steady pace beside him. In his hand he was carrying a whip, spinning it at his horse's flank for a second strike.

Valerus turned back and fiddled the strap until it came loose on its own accord and slipped from the bit's ring. He then turned hurriedly, feeling another lash as he removed the chain lock at the horse's flank.

He was free. The chariot, now being pulled by two horses on the right of the yoke pole, skidded across the flagstones and overturned within a few meters. For a yard or two the panicked horses dragged it before being forced to a standstill.

Valerus hauled back on the reins and passed behind the whip bearer. When the guard looked around wildly, he saw the young man come around with the scabbard of his sword. He tried to turn his head away but there was still a ring when it hit him across his helmet.

The horse was empty the next instant.

There was one more, though, and by the quick glimpse he was heavily armed. There was a bow slung across his back. In the distance even more were underway, these with lights flickering his direction.

He pulled the horse off the road and spurred it in the ribs, cutting away a few more of the traces.

Now it was a matter of speed. If he could outrun a fully armed guard, he would make it around the mountain to Pompeii before the late morning. For the moment, however, he could not afford making any indication as to where he intended to go. Flavia was safe as long as he did not lead the watchmen to her.

The bow carrier was falling behind as Valerus's horse found its speed, but more were catching up, obviously with fitter animals. He was still making headway though. If he could make it to the woods before the first light, he was certain to lose them.

Something hit him on the back of the head; it was terribly sharp and caused him to fall over across the animal's neck. The horse's gait diminished to a trot, bringing Valerus to a terrible state of uneasiness, feeling himself being thrown across its back. His hand went up to his head as he tried desperately to kick the horse onward.

Two riders suddenly sped past him, one whipping his horse across the rump as he did. The creature reared and sped off only to stop sharp on its haunches when another rider cut it short. The horse turned, unaware of its rider slipping from its back, and trotted off with its tail extended, snorting alarmingly.

Valerus picked himself off the ground, head spinning. Again he lifted his hand to the sharp pain and this time felt his hair soaked in a warm sticky substance. He looked down at his palm; in the dim light of the incoming dawn he noticed the red tinge.

A sling master had been an excellent shot.

He looked up to where two horsemen stood nearby. He felt the panic rise and threw himself over to see three more approaching from the roadway, and they were all armed. He pulled his weight up on his elbows when one dismounted and walked to him. He was wearing a brass lorica and breeches, the clear indication of a soldier. There was a sword tied to his belt. He appeared more annoyed than angry.

"You're in trouble now," he said levelly, his breath wavering a little. He looked up to the other watchmen. "Return him to the garrison. We will question him there."

Chapter 34

Lucius knocked on the door. The sun was well in the sky and there was no fear of waking anyone up. The house was very much in the center of the city, a fine one which stood on the street corner. Flavia looked across the road where people were going about their daily business. Flowers were growing on the hedge of a private home, decorating the open flagstones with a rainbow of colors. It made her smile. After the last twenty-four hours, she was discovering that there was indeed beauty left in the world.

The door was opened by a male slave. At once the slave stepped aside and gestured their entry. They did so, entering through the door and into the passageway. For a second, Flavia admired the mosaic dog on the floor along with the depiction of animals framed by borders before they entered the atrium. Potted ferns lined the far wall, which opened to the peristyle beyond.

The atrium ground was heavily decorated with even more mosaic panels of elaborate patterns. In the center of the atrium was a fountain; beside it, a large black dog dozed, not having heard their arrival, and along the walls and pillars potted ferns flourished. It was a strange setting; the house had no openings or rooms to the east and west of it, but instead ran north to south like a large corridor. Flavia could see more rooms opening beyond the atrium. There was the sound of children laughing and playing up ahead.

Lucius and Flavia were momentarily left alone to admire the décor before a middle-aged man appeared from the rooms up ahead, his slave following in his wake. He was dark-featured, his eyes large, and he wore the clothes of wealth. Flavia looked down at herself, at the tunica that had been forced to replace the stola Lucius had bought her, and then at Lucius, who was just as casually dressed with his inner legs messed with horse hair.

"Can it be real?" The man opened his arms. "Lucius? By all the gods, it's has been years."

Lucius caught his arm kindly and the two men greeted each other as old friends. Flavia was a little baffled, not knowing the history that was being portrayed.

"How many years?" The man took a step back and looked Lucius up and down. "You must have been twelve when I last saw you."

"Too long, old friend."

Then the houseman turned to Flavia, for a moment regarding her dress coat suspiciously before smiling to the young man. "And who is this lovely young lady? Your wife?"

"Unfortunately not." Lucius laughed. "This is Flavia, who I have brought from Herculaneum. Flavia, this is an old friend of the family, Paquius Proculus."

Flavia smiled at him but said nothing.

"Proculus," Lucius's tone was lower set now, "we need to speak. Please, this is an urgent and private matter."

"But of course." Proculus opened his hand toward the peristyle. "Come. Cena will be along shortly. Please join us."

⁂

Valerus sat alone in an unguarded cell. He was stripped of his toga and left only with his tunic and girdle; all possessions and weapons were taken off him. He had his back against the wall with his knees brought up to have his elbows rest upon them. His head was in his hands. The events had taken a turn for the worst; he was taken and now kept in the slaves' prison until some explanation could be found regarding his behavior. Marcus had sent a messenger to the villa to report the incident to Pedius, who he hoped would not press charges. It was against regulation to keep a Roman citizen in the slaves' holdings. If Pedius could arrive and present his son's identification papers, Valerus would at least be kept under house arrest until trial.

And there was going to be a trial, Valerus knew. He had listened to the conversation of the guards and heard that one man had been killed; the wheel of the chariot had broken his back and killed him in the moment. This qualified Valerus to be charged with murder, though he could plead it was an accident. He could possibly get away with that, but there was no way he could justify the fact that he had stolen property belonging to his father.

His leg ached terribly. His actions and daring attempt on the chariot had left the old wound throbbing. He winced as he stretched it out in front of him and carefully massaged the knee. He had asked the gods to cripple him only *after* Flavia was safe, and now that request was growing heavy on his mind.

Valerus lifted his head when the door was unlocked and opened. Two men came to pick him up off the floor and escort him into the main office. Marcus was standing at his desk with several more watchmen lining the wall. At the head was his father. For a second, father and son caught each other's eye before Pedius looked at Marcus questioningly. "What is this man accused of?" he asked coldly.

The captain hated to have to say it, but this was the stage where he could no longer act upon favor. "Three accusations of theft," he began slowly. "A chariot, a horse, and a slave. Also murder, attempted murder, and speeding on a public road."

He looked at his son; the glare in his eyes shimmered with fury and Valerus knew he was not going to get any help or sympathy from him. Pedius shook his head, turned back to Marcus, and pointed a trembling finger in Valerus's direction. "I don't know this man!" he snapped, but his voice was kept under tight control. Both Marcus and Valerus stiffened when he said it. "I've never seen him before in my life. Probably some runaway slave! You have wasted my time!" He stormed from the room with Marcus going after him hurriedly.

Valerus, still between the two guards, could not believe what he had just heard. He felt the red heat drown him as the feeling of faint overcame the sheer horror of the situation.

Pedius walked a short distance and then stopped on the street side to catch his breath, which was coming in fast and sharp. Marcus caught up with him. "Master," he shook his head, "you cannot identify your own son?"

The man had his eyes closed and face turned to the sky. It was obvious that the shock of seeing Valerus between two guards and hearing his crimes had been a step beyond that which he could handle. Slowly he looked around to the captain. "What about the slave girl?" he asked him.

Marcus shook his head. "Gone. We are trying to pick up some trail, but it's possible Valerus had a horse waiting for her."

"You ought to speak to Lucius. I would not be surprised if he has a hand in it."

"Master Lucius left for Octavianum to visit his mother two days ago, right after Flavia's arrest. He is beyond suspicion."

Pedius rubbed his brow, shutting his eyes again for a second. "Get me that slave," he muttered and continued on his way.

Marcus shook his head and went after him again. "What about your son, then?" he asked desperately.

"Obviously he knows her whereabouts!" The man spun around to face him, stopping him dead in his tracks. "Get it out of him. I want that slave back in Herculaneum by the end of the week, do you hear me? As for *that* man," he gestured his head to the watch house, "treat him as you would a runaway! Brand his forehead for all I care! Just get me the information I want."

When he got back to the villa, spitting and muttering under his breath, he was greeted by his wife. Rectina fell against him desperately. "What happened?" she asked. "Was it Valerus?"

Pedius considered for a moment what to tell her before voting on the family reputation and the avoidance of devastating his wife further. "No." He shook his head. "Just a runaway of mistaken identity."

Rectina sagged with relief. "Thank goodness. I got such a fright when the message first arrived."

Pedius left her in the garden and entered the library. For a while he scavenged through the shelves, tossing parchments and papyrus scrolls as he desperately searched for the family documents. He found them on a small shelf behind the table, bounded in a leather folder. Sheer rage boiled out of him as he flipped through the contents. Most of it was family history: forefathers, grandparents, and their marriages. Valerus's documents of his birth and citizenship were clipped between his and Anneria's, and just the sight of his name brought a hiss from his teeth. He tore the pages out and ripped them apart, kicking the pieces across the floor like a spoilt child.

He could not control or withstand the rage and humiliation that boiled out of him. There was also hurt, shame, and a terrible sense of loss. Mostly there was guilt; he had looked directly at his own son and refused to see him. He condemned him to the punishment of a runaway slave, and though at that moment he had felt his son well deserved it, now the effects of the decision were beginning to show.

In his fit of emotion, he smashed a small bust against the wall, shouting incoherent curses to every god he could name.

It was only then, as the rage subsided slightly, that he noticed young Gaius standing by the door side, watching without a word or even a look of distaste. Pedius, humiliated yet again by having given into his rage, straightened his toga and turned to pick up the fallen parchments and scrolls. He began to straighten the shelves himself without the help of a slave; it was obvious he was seeking some form of distraction.

"My pardon, Master Pedius." Gaius lowered his head when the man looked his way again. "But I feel I have overstayed my welcome. I will be leaving today."

Without a word more he left the master to try to relieve that which plagued him.

Proculus looked across to where Flavia was reclined among his family members as Lucius finished explaining the story of the last couple of months. Nothing was said about Flavia's Christian background and for this reason she said nothing and allowed Lucius to tell them the incidents over the last forty-eight hours as he saw it.

She knew what Proculus's view was of her: she was a slave who did not deserve the respect of a nobleman. But also there was reason for respect when hearing all the stories of Valerus's daring ways to claim ownership. In the end, stealing had been the only option left available. Proculus had to admire Valerus's determination.

Proculus's wife, Asilia, was moved by the story and inquired about Flavia's childhood and saw well to her courage.

The family of Paquius Proculus was a large one but still young. They had three children, the oldest being six and the others five and four. Flavia complimented the woman for looking so good after three pregnancies. The children were playing between the pillars, running into the house and around the garden *piscina* as the four adults spoke and discussed matters in the peristyle.

It was a beautiful day to be out, Flavia noted. Not a cloud lined the sky and only a light occasional breeze stirred the trees. It was reaching for midday.

There was a crash from inside the house, followed by the dissolve of the children's laughter. "Oi!" Proculus got to his feet and made his way in. "Enough! What was that?"

After he had gone, Asilia smiled at Flavia. "We will help you," she agreed even before her husband had. "Someone of such a story deserves all the help the gods can offer."

"I am very grateful," Flavia said honestly. It was true. Since her arrest she had thought the world dark again. There was a dawn on the horizon now and she felt things were going to come right. All that she lacked was Valerus's company.

"What about you, Lucius?" She suddenly looked up at him.

"I will have to leave as soon as Valerus arrives. I am to take the road out to Octavianum to visit my mother. It was what Valerus informed the captain in Herculaneum to avoid any loose ends. There will be an investigation, I am sure."

"If you are frightened, you could leave now," Asilia reassured him. "We will not mention a word and Flavia will be safe with us until Valerus comes. I guarantee you."

Lucius looked at the young woman and could not bring himself to leave. There was still an undying concern on her part that Valerus would not turn up, and he could not leave Flavia with that uncertainty.

"I would prefer staying a while longer," he told her and reached for his goblet of wine. "If it's all the same to you?"

⁂

Valerus did not come by that afternoon and, when the sun touched the ocean, Flavia became terribly anxious. Something had gone wrong. The fact that there was no way of discovering what, or in any means fixing it, gnawed at her heart. Lucius especially kept her from leaving, announcing that the streets were dangerous after dark.

She paced the atrium around the *impluvium* dozens of times before Asilia came to try to comfort her. She was not successful, nor was Proculus in his efforts. The couple was reassuring and took the moment to direct her to her room, which was on the left of the peristyle and consisted of a small bed, a small bronze basin, and a table holding a bust. She smiled and looked their way. Proculus and Lucius were soon hushed out of the room while Asilia settled on the chair by the table, trying to breech a friendly conversation with the young woman.

"Do not be troubled," she tried to reassure her, "I am sure he will be along the moment he can."

"But why can't he?" Flavia was looking out the window, hoping to see something that may indicate Valerus's presence. "It's unsettling. He ought to have been here by now."

"How is Valerus doing?" she asked with a smile. "It's been years since I last saw him."

"You two knew each other?" Flavia now turned around, interested.

The woman blushed and nodded. "Oh, yes." She smiled. "We've had a few encounters at the Lupanar."

"When was this?" Flavia asked as she sat down on her bed.

"About six, maybe seven years ago, just when he started training in Pompeii. We met often after hours."

"But you were married then, were you not?"

"No." She shook her head. "I was living with Proculus, but I couldn't resist the son of Pedius, the thracian."

Flavia lost her smile, suddenly feeling a little threatened by the woman. "How often did the two of you meet?" she asked suspiciously.

Asilia thought for a few seconds before replying. "About four times, perhaps five. Someone wrote a crude comment on the Lupanar one day that shook us off from each other. A few months later Proculus proposed. Oh, well." She shrugged. "Fond memories."

They were not fond at all, to Flavia's opinion. She looked Asilia from head to toe, from the red curls in her hair to the pearls on her sandals. She was beautiful in a way, but then she recalled that beauty had nothing to do with it. At that time, Valerus took other things into consideration.

It took her back to places she no longer wanted to be: the art of erotic dance and its true purpose. She shook her head in an effort to dislodge the memories.

"But you are a fine woman, and I am pleased Valerus has found someone to love." Asilia suddenly reached over to touch her knee. Obviously she had noticed her expression and was trying to set it right. "You are beautiful despite being a slave. We will take good care of you, and that is a promise."

Flavia was forced to smile, blinking back the tears as she took the woman by the hand. "Thank you," she whispered. She had never meant the words more than when she said them that day.

Chapter 35

Valerus was escorted into a small chamber, smaller even than the cell he had been in. Two small stools were set in the center under a lamp hanging from the roof. Valerus did not like the effect its light made on the room. It was eerie and cold.

He was urged onto the seat and left alone. After a while he stretched out his left leg with a wince. The terrible numbing pain was moving up his leg again from his knee. Bending it felt like a terrible effort that was not worth the try. They had bound him, but not in shackles. Instead they had used rope and fastened his wrists up behind his back so that his fingertips reached for his elbows.

He lowered his head in the flickering glow. Night had fallen, and there was no telling what was happening in Pompeii. Valerus could only hope that Proculus remembered him through his father and offered Flavia refuge. He was convinced that Flavia would be safe there, but Valerus was acutely aware that he knew Proculus's wife … very well. This caused a little apprehension. He did not know what type of man Proculus was; Asilia had seldom mentioned him during their little encounters. But Lucius was there, and that was a comfort at least to a point.

He had not slept for nearly forty-eight hours, but Flavia still dominated most of his thoughts and on her subject he could think clearly. He wondered if she was safe and especially what she was thinking. He hoped that his absence was not going to cause too much alarm. He hated the thought that she may try to return to Herculaneum to find him. With her ambition and courage, it was very likely.

A man entered the room; Valerus looked up and identified him as a provincial soldier. He wore breeches tied with a string and wore a red toga. He also wore a bronze *cuirass,* presenting his rank as well as his importance.

There was a knife at his belt.

He sat down across from the young man and rested his hands on his knees. "Right," he said in a slow and heavy set voice, "I am here to formally interrogate you."

"Formally?" Valerus asked. "What would be informal?"

The large man raised his fist. "You would not have any teeth left."

Valerus caught his breath. "Right." And then he turned his head the other way.

"I have been told that you have killed a guard in an effort to try to steal property belonging to Pedius Cascus. Do you deny this?"

"I didn't try to steal property! I succeeded!" Valerus felt insulted by his poor choice of words. "The death was an accident and there are many who can vouch for that."

"Fine. Then we can move directly to the next subject. Where is it?"

"*It*?" This was a hiss that slithered from between his teeth.

"The slave girl." The soldier sighed. "She was last seen mounting a chariot with a driver and escort, who is here, by the way, so don't try and deny it."

"I was not going to."

"Excellent. You commandeered this chariot, throwing off both driver and escort. By the time the men caught up with you, the girl was gone. Please care to fill in the blank."

"I have no intention to."

"I feel it appropriate to say that I have authority to hurt you."

"You have no right! I am not a slave or a simple peasant who you can question as you please!"

"Apparently no one knows who you are. Not even Pedius could identify you and there are no identification papers. The captain here appears to know who you are, but he has no authority. My orders come from Rome and I have full authority to question criminals in the art of theft and murder." The soldier leaned back a bit, fiddled at the side of his belt, and removed a small sharp knife. Valerus's eyes fixed upon it but he fought himself not to express so much as a twitch of apprehension.

"This knife is made specifically for men of my profession." He held the blade in the palms of his hand under the light for Valerus to get a good look. "It serves many purposes. It's beautiful, so I don't like to use it often. As the captain here refuses the practice of the usual *informal* forms of interrogation, I will be forced to use more … civilized methods. Do you know what this knife is used for?"

Valerus did not want to answer him but did not want to appear ignorant either. So he said, "It's not used on the battlefield, I know."

The legionnaire smiled and nodded slowly. "More so for after the battle."

Valerus swallowed; this was a situation he had never even imagined himself in. He was completely at the mercy of one man. It was a small room and no one was present. There was no one who was going to come for him and giving up Flavia was most certainly out of the question.

It dawned on him then that he was not going to see the woman again, no matter what happened. If he told them, she would be caught without him even getting close. If he lied or refused to comply, he could die in the cell that very night or be brought to Rome to face trial. In neither of those scenarios was there any way of being with Flavia again.

He sat up, straightening his back so that he could look the guard levelly in the eye. His expression was stoic, but his heart pounded with the fear of the immediate future along with the disappointment that he was alone again.

"Let us keep this clean," the soldier said. "You have stolen property and hid it where?"

Lying could cause more problems, Valerus realized. He knew he was going to be sent to trial and he preferred not to have lying on the record along with murder and theft. For this reason he remained quiet, not prepared to say a word.

His eyes were fixed on the knife. It was a fine piece of workmanship with a bronze handle and a long, thin blade, but there was ugliness to it; it was like looking at the curve of Flavia's back with a whip streak running across it.

Carefully the man flipped it into the air and caught it by the handle as it came down. "Well?"

His gaze turned back on him, and in the instant his eyes were drawn from the knife it came down, hilt first to smash against his wounded knee. Valerus had never felt anything like it; the pain even drew on his strength to scream. He tried to shift his position, nearly falling from his seat as he gasped and turned in an effort to conceal the anguish the man had caused.

"I thought the scar looked as if it could still cause some discomfort." The soldier played with the knife between his fingers. "Either you are ex-military or a former gladiator. Either way, I am not impressed by your ability by the look of that scar."

Valerus was still fighting the burning sting that was running up his leg and hardly heard a word the man said, including when he repeated his question regarding Flavia's whereabouts.

The interrogator's next gesture brought Valerus to a scream as the knife cut him across the scar, there where the gladiator had wounded him a few weeks before. The tenderness of the wound increased the pain. He felt the sting of tears come to his eyes when he looked up again. Other than a short gasp that followed, he refused to utter a word.

"All right." The man got up from his place. Valerus watched in silent apprehension as the soldier removed his toga and hung it on a nail before removing the bracer on his right wrist. "Perhaps I will have to amputate your leg a piece at a time," he said as he slipped his fingers through a brass knuckle, "but let's first see what I can get out of you."

"Stay where you are!"

Valerus looked up and the soldier around to the voice. A figure was standing in the doorway, cloaked and hooded with his face in shadow. In his hands he was carrying a small single-shot crossbow, which he waved in the direction of the guard. "Back off, if you please, soldier."

The man froze where he was, keeping his eyes fixed on the stranger's weapon, then backed away from Valerus's side. The figure entered, walking sidelong against the wall until he was up by the young man. Valerus watched his movement, trying to identify his posture, but nothing gave any indication as to who he was; even his voice was muffled as if he had strung a cloth across his mouth.

The strange arrival checked his bonds a second before coming up again and moving back to the wall. "Cut him loose," he demanded of the soldier.

The interrogator complied without a word, using his knife to remove the ropes. The weapon carrier looked on and waved him off again when Valerus was freed.

"Can you walk?" the man asked Valerus with concern.

Valerus tried; he pulled himself up slowly and stood on his good leg. Blood was trickling down his calf. He carefully set it down, winced, but managed to put some weight on it.

The hooded figure turned to the soldier. "On your knees! Face the wall!" He walked up behind the man and threw out his crossbow. It struck him on the back of his head. He crumbled neatly at his feet.

"Come on!" He waved to Valerus, gently taking the young man's arm and setting it across his shoulder.

"Who are you?"

Another figure suddenly appeared in the doorway; this one he recognized as Marcus. The captain waved to them urgently and gestured back into the main chamber. "Master Gaius! You had better hurry. The men I sent off are about to return."

"Come, Valerus. Not a moment to waste."

Now Valerus could place the voice of Pliny's nephew; it was muffled under his scarf, but it was definitely his. The boy led him out into the street; it was well past sunset already and Venus was resting softly beside a crescent moon. Two horses were tied to their posts at the entrance. Marcus hurriedly passed Valerus a small leather pouch which jingled as he took it from him. Not a word was said as he quickly fastened it to his girdle.

"Can you ride, Master Valerus?"

"What? Of course I can!"

"Excellent! Up you get." He gave the man a leg up before taking the reins of his own horse.

"Don't forget about me," Marcus said, stepping up to Gaius.

The young man turned around violently, striking the captain across the face before jumping on the back of his horse. Marcus lay where he had fallen, a deep red bruise on the side of his head.

"No loose ends," he said to Valerus with a smile as he dug into his saddlebag and produced a fine toga. He passed it to Valerus. "It's all been arranged."

❧

There was a nippy breeze coming off the coast that night, which was unusual. The two men had legged it out of the city and were now following the *cardo* leading to Pompeii. Once well out of the city, they slowed to a trot and then a walk. Gaius had cast back his hood and removed the scarf that he had used to muffle his voice. His toga was visible beneath his cloak and Valerus could recognize the *clavi* of his status.

Valerus's hand rested upon his knee in the effort to gently ease the bleeding, which had lessened when they had first escaped the city. His firm hold on it was still a desperate action to try to keep the pain to a minimum as he had often done, which was proving impossible. The entire leg pulsated and there was a burning rash that extended to the center of his back.

"You all right, Valerus?" Gaius asked him, concerned.

"I hope so."

"Marcus came to tell me about the situation; he appeared desperate to ensure that nothing happened to you. Poor soul; he didn't know where else to turn. Your father had gone completely over his head and is unapproachable on the subject."

"Why do all this?" Valerus shook his head without looking at him. It was a profound question at the moment: Why? Gaius was a lawyer and a fine young man with a lot of potential, yet he risked it all for a small, unimportant reason. Valerus could not help but wonder if it was all sincere.

"I have already told you, Valerus: I like a happy ending to a good story."

"You are risking a lot for that."

"Not really. I left for home this morning, according to Pedius as well as the rest of the soldiers stationed here. What happened tonight was simply a loose knot."

"They could trace this to you."

"Nonsense. I am a lawyer; I have been trained in the art of speaking. I can talk my way out of anything. Besides, no one will suspect me. I am not the sort to help fugitives and runaways."

"And Marcus?"

"He told me everything: your little plan that went wrong despite him agreeing and making sure that Flavia left before sunrise. Well done on her escape, by the way. It was most exciting to hear the story."

"I ought to tell you in greater detail then." Valerus smiled for the first time.

"You should!" Gaius laughed. "I may write about it one day; what men do for love."

"Marcus helped you into my cell tonight?"

"I could not have done it without him; he made them believe you confessed to Flavia's location, thus sending most of his men out to investigate. It gave me a small window."

"I hope they don't find that he was involved."

"With that blow I threw him?" Gaius asked. "Definitely not. That's too convincing, I think."

The crescent moon was nearing the horizon. Venus was slowly being erased by the shadow of the earth.

"Did Marcus return the money to you, Valerus?" Gaius asked suddenly.

Valerus desperately tapped his hips, momentarily forgetting that the captain had passed it on to him. He sighed when hearing the jingle. "That he did."

"Excellent! It will be more than enough to keep you and Flavia comfortable while that leg of yours heals properly. At least give it a month. It will even cover the cost of the surgeon should you require it."

The roads were dormant; not a soul stirred. After the moon had set, the horizon became a perfectly detailed line against the night sky; Vesuvius itself stuck up from the earth like a blocked archway to the northeast.

All was quiet.

They walked past the Pompeian tombs lining the Herculaneum road and stopped a fair distance from the gates. Gaius pulled his hood back over his head. "This is where we part ways, Valerus. I need to be off. I do not wish to be seen."

"Of course." The man leaned across the neck of his horse and grasped Gaius's arm. "I cannot thank you enough for what you have done for us."

"All for a happy ending."

"I think you ought to take the horse with you."

"Can you walk?"

"I will manage. I don't want to draw attention."

"Slip into the shadows," Gaius advised with a smile.

Valerus winced as he slid from the horse's back and stood crooked on his good leg.

"I advise you to have a doctor look at that leg of yours. Get a good rest before you attempt to take on any more chariot acrobatics."

He chuckled. "I will do as you recommend." He passed him the reins of his horse.

As Gaius took it, his face suddenly went soft, almost as if saddened by having to leave him at the gates of Pompeii. "Farewell, Valerus. I hope to see the two of you again."

Valerus watched him leave, waiting until his dim figure was swallowed by the shadows of the tombs. Once the sound of the horses had completely disappeared, he turned to the city.

It all came back to him. He staggered along the main road for a fair distance before taking the second intersection northward, stopping on occasion to rest the throb that was lifting again. Memories began to flood back to the time he was last here, remembering his training and the successful fights as well as all the women. Here, he had had many. They were fond memories in a very strange way, yet at the same time he felt terribly guilty. How could a man like him—after everything he did—still deserve a woman like Flavia?

It's going to be strange to see Asilia again, he thought. The last time he had was up by the Lupanar, where he had had a few drinks and was enjoying the woman's company … probably a little too much. It may even be a little awkward.

A dog suddenly jumped up against a gate in aggression, snapping its huge jaws between the wooden beams of the small fence. Valerus jumped; the silence had been so tranquil a few seconds before. The sound had snapped his senses completely.

The house of Paquius Proculus was where he remembered it to be: on the street corner two blocks west from the tailor. Asilia had brought him there the first night they had met in the tavern and shared an evening of sex and wine. It was only afterward that he discovered it belonged to the man she lived with. That had been a shock, he remembered. After that, it was only by the Lupanar where they met.

It was late. Should he tap on the door? He glanced around him. He could not stay in the street for the rest of the night. Besides, it could not be past midnight yet.

He then noticed a light filtering out from under the door. He raised his knuckles and tapped gently. There was some distant muffled mutter before the door was opened by a slave who bowed at the presence of his toga and gestured him in.

The decoration of the house had changed, he noticed. The potted ferns had not lined the atrium then as they did now, nor had there been a black lining painted at the foot of the wall. He noticed the furniture as well as a doll that lay disregarded on the floor beside the water feature.

This was a reassuring reminder; he had forgotten that she was a mother. It made him feel a little more comfortable.

"Valerus Cascus!" Asilia suddenly filtered in from the master bedroom. Behind her, her husband followed in her wake. "How wonderful to see you again!"

Valerus did not find it appropriate to embrace her, at least not in the presence of her husband. She was still beautiful: the red locks curling alongside her face and the high set cheeks. He recalled at that moment that it had been her deep green eyes that first attracted him to her.

He greeted the two of them with a brief bow.

"You have missed Lucius by several hours," Proculus announced. "We were getting worried."

"I have been through worse." His hand went down to try to massage his knee. It was an automatic reaction when it pained, and the moment he did, Asilia noticed the dry trickle of blood from the wound.

"What happened?" She immediately took the opportunity to go to him, taking him gently by the arm for support. "Austs!" she called to her slave. "Bring some hot water and bandages."

"Where is Flavia?" Valerus had to ask it.

"She retired only a short while ago. But please, let us first tend to your leg."

He allowed two slaves to tend to his knee, cleaning the wound before bandaging it. He declined a meal and preferred to retire, with the reason that he had not slept for nearly two days.

The room he was led to was dark and quiet. Only when he held his breath did he pick up the soft breathing of a sleeping woman.

He removed his toga and girdle before bending down to remove his sandals. Then he walked to the bedside. How much he wanted to wake Flavia for her to see him! He watched her sleep for a while as he had previously done before removing his tunic and slipping in beside her. She merely stirred and he was asleep before he even got to put his arm around her.

Chapter 36

August 7

Valerus woke up on his own, to his disappointment. The sun was set low, filtering through the window, and by the light it was either early morning or the later afternoon.

He sat up, letting the sheets brush down his chest, and suddenly felt how every part of his body ached. Worst of all were his legs, the left one especially. He winced as he brought up a hand to rub his shoulder.

Some birds chatted from the trees in the peristyle outside the door. By the simple feel in the air, he concluded that it was in the afternoon and that he had slept all day, and he had slept like the dead: not a single dream or twitch from the outside world, not even Flavia when she had left had drawn him from his sleep.

He threw his legs over the edge of his bed quickly so as not to feel the pain that came with it. He blinked in the suddenly bright light. He took a quick cold bath from the water pan, hoping the cold would help soothe some of the muscles that ached so much. Slowly, clenching his teeth against the stiffness and pain, he went to pick up his clothes and discovered that someone had neatly folded them on the table on the other side of the room. He smiled to himself as he walked up to them and ran his hands through the fabric. Only Flavia would have thought that far without acting as if it was a command.

After getting dressed, he stepped out directly into the garden where he saw Flavia and Asilia reclined opposite each other. *It's so strange to see them together,* he thought. Two lovers: one of the past who had been no more than a game and the present one who was real and tangible. The feeling was rather odd and there was some guilt when Flavia saw him over the redhead's shoulder.

He had expected her to jump and run to him, but instead she got up from the couch, standing in his way like a small shy girl with her hands crossed in front of her. Asilia noticed her gesture and looked back, also getting up when seeing him.

Valerus was not certain who to greet first; the woman he loved or the woman who had saved and sheltered her.

His decision was made by Flavia's smile and he went forward like a desperate man to embrace her. He put his arms around her with a strength she had never felt before. His wet hair dripped over her as he felt her bury her face in his shoulder, recognizing her smell along with the smoothness of her skin. In an odd way it was difficult to believe that they were finally together again. The last two days had felt much longer, and Valerus was certain he had aged more in them than in his whole life so far.

Valerus leaned back to look at her, gently brushing some tears from her eyes before embracing her again.

Valerus was given an early meal to rejuvenate, sharing a little of the occurrence since they had parted in Herculaneum. Austs the slave was once again cleaning the wound of his leg and re-bandaging it, stating that it should have gotten stitches, and Valerus now needed a good rest to allow it to heal.

He decided to do just that. Valerus and Flavia reclined together on the couch while Asilia saw to the children. The sun had set and there was a fiery red lining the western horizon. Neither spoke; there was no need to for the time. They were together again and they were both marveling in the moment.

As the darkness fell and lamps were lit, they heard Proculus return. The dog, which had been dozing under their couch, sprung up to greet his master when he stepped into the peristyle. At once the couple got up to greet him.

There was coldness in the air; even Flavia could feel it. Valerus did not know what—if anything—Asilia had said to him regarding their earlier years, but Proculus was a modest man who welcomed him with good gesture and regards. Still, Valerus could feel his discomfort in the presence of his wife.

Afterward he joined his wife in the atrium. Neither Valerus nor Flavia listened to their conversation as Valerus leaned in carefully and kissed Flavia on the shoulder. She giggled when his tongue ran across her neck to her ear.

"So what happens now?" she asked him.

"Exactly what I'm doing." He sighed and kissed her neck.

"It's safe to stay here? After they tried to interrogate you like a common criminal?"

He sat up a little and moistened his lips. "No, it's not safe here ... at least not for very long. I would like a week for my leg to come right and then we ought to leave for Ostia."

"Where are we going?"

Valerus shrugged. "Away. Ravenna. Verona. Does it matter? We shouldn't stay in one place for too long."

"Won't a week be?"

He put his arm around her, coaxing her to settle against him again. "I would not worry. As far as the guards are concerned, we tried to escape northward, so that is where they will search. They will go after Lucius especially, but from him they will find nothing."

She had to agree with him; he had thought of the little details to give them a small window to rest and recuperate; not that she needed it as much as he did.

"Will you dance for me tonight, Flavia?" he suddenly asked softly in her ear.

"I was planning to," she said with a mischievous smile. They looked at each other and suddenly Flavia's expression became a little more serious. She turned over a bit and cupped his cheek in her hand. "You saved my life, Valerus. You were nearly killed for it."

His face gave on the same expression as he too took her face in his hands. "I will die for you, Flavia, if it comes to that."

"I don't want you to die for me. I'd rather die with you than me having to continue alone." She suddenly produced a scroll from under her. Valerus at once recognized the paper on which he had written his poem to her weeks before.

"I want to hear you read it to me." She handed it to him.

Reaching over her shoulder, he took the scroll and unwound it. It had been through a lot and the ink was smeared in places. It had also been trampled at some point, but to the both of them it was something that brought the two of them together.

He read it to her as the evening fell to a darker shadow and then to the night that reigned. In the lamplight, he read it again and again, more as an oath to her than anything else.

And then she danced for him. In the flickering lamplight, he watched her find a flowing beat which could be heard only between the two of them, her arms moving up and along her body like waves rolled across the sea. Valerus watched without much expression other than a small faint smile, loving the sight of her.

She did not end or break the rhythm of her dance as she led him to their room, moving with every step as if she was under the control of an eternal chant. He was so into the moment that he was not even aware of his trouble walking as Flavia led him to the bed and set him down on its edge. He watched her dance from his sitting position, holding himself up by his hands.

Then, still in that graceful movement and without a single word being exchanged, she removed her tunica as well as what undergarments she had. He grinned for the first time as she came forth and straddled him, running her hands and then arms across his shoulders.

At this moment he participated, unable to resist. He brought up his arms and wrapped them around her, keeping himself up by using her as leverage. They kissed before Flavia got off his toga and then his tunic. The feeling of skin against skin was so remarkable to her as well as to him that they both pressed against each other until their strength failed to get them any closer.

Flavia reached down below his subligaria and the young man caught his breath. Strangely that didn't seem as important as this moment now, but he could not bring himself to stop her. She wrapped her legs around his waist as they came together and in that instant Valerus felt something he never had before; a true union. Suddenly the pleasure and the orgasm no longer mattered; it was this moment, here as they sat combined together, that was magic. He opened his eyes to look at her, wondering if she experienced the same thing.

Her eyes were closed and she moved only slightly to his rhythm. Then she looked down at him, noticing the awe and revelation in his stare. He reached up, very slowly, and ran his hand along the curve of her back until it reached the silk of her hair.

Their gazes locked, the motion stopped, and the physical pleasure became a background. The two of them were momentarily looking into each other's soul, knowing everything about the other and feeling far more than their physical bodies were capable of.

Valerus lowered his gaze and then, with both hands up against her back, pressed his face into her neck and began to cry. "Flavia!"

She felt his tears on her shoulder and shared the emotion rising up to greet her. "I love you, Valerus," he heard her mutter while he cried.

Together, wrapped around each other's arms and legs, they spent a long time merely experiencing the true form of humanism.

Flavia woke up during the night; Valerus was moving around beside her, reaching down to his knee every now and again. Finally she turned over to light a lamp. As she did, he sat up and pulled the blanket off him.

"Valerus? Are you all right?"

In the faint glow of the light they both looked down at the wound on the young man's leg. She caught her breath. "That does not look good."

It didn't. The knee had gone red and it was terribly swollen. Valerus was rubbing it gently but Flavia noticed him wince every now and again.

"Valerus? Is it painful?"

"Terribly." He caught his breath and turned his leg off the bedside. "Must have hurt it earlier when we were …"

Flavia crawled forward and looked over his shoulder. "Maybe you ought to have someone look at it."

"I did!" he snapped at her.

It had been months since his injury had caused him this much distress. He could not afford it; they could not stay in Pompeii for too long. He looked at the woman whose gaze was hard set on him; he saw the uncertainty in her eyes and realized that every day they stayed in one place the more he was putting her at risk. He could not allow it.

He reached over and took the lamp from her. “Don’t worry.” He forced a smile. “It’s not too bad. I had Austs look at it earlier.”

“What did he say?”

It needed proper attention; it needed stitches, it needed to be looked at by someone trained in the field. He did not tell her this though. Instead he turned around over his shoulder and gently touched her cheek. “It’s nothing.” He set the lamp down and blew out the flame. Then he put his arm around her and pulled her down on the pillows with him. “Let’s go back to sleep.”

He did not say anything more to her, but as she snuggled up against him and he rested his arm across her hip, he felt the numb throbbing from his left leg, reaching for his lower back. It was hot and so terribly painful that he had to fight back the tears welling up. Flavia was asleep in a few minutes and her breathing was deep and steady, but he could think of nothing but the pain and the risks he was putting her through.

Chapter 37

August 13

Three days passed in which Valerus tried to recover, but despite the rest and the hours of leisure, the leg was not getting any better. Flavia was getting concerned when he openly began to complain about the pain. At times when she saw the wound, she became increasingly worried. It was not healing. His interrogator had cut him across the knee over the old scar, and the skin around it was now getting to look dark and dangerous. Proculus ordered his slaves to tend to it on the fourth day, which brought several gasps.

By the end of the week on the Ides, the fever hit. Flavia got up that morning and let him sleep, but as she lifted the sheet over his shoulders she felt how warm he was. He did not even stir to her touch when she began to feel him all over. He was burning hot.

She hurried out to find the family reclined and enjoying breakfast in the peristyle; the children were playing around the garden while the slaves served their masters. She bowed to them out of habit and desperation when they saw her coming.

"Valerus is not well," she informed them worriedly. "He has picked up a fever."

Asilia looked at Proculus. The man sat up a bit. "Did he wake up yet?"

She shook her head. "You remember how early he retired last night? He has not been up since. He did not even respond to me."

"This is getting serious." Asilia turned to her husband. "No wound should take that long to recover. I think we ought to take him to the surgeon."

Proculus shook his head. "That's too much of a risk. He is a fugitive, remember, and so is Flavia. We cannot risk both of them."

"I would take the risk." Flavia went up to the couple and sat down at the foot of their couches. "I will do it, as long as it means Valerus is going to be all right."

"We can take Flavia to the outer villa," Asilia proposed suddenly. "We can tell them that she is a new slave for the vineyards. No questions will be asked then. She can stay and work there while Valerus is taken care of."

"You are not going to separate us?" Flavia appeared horrified by the thought.

"You are of no help here, Flavia," Proculus informed her. "At least there you will be safe until Valerus's recovery."

She was shaking her head. "I won't leave him."

Asilia reached out and took her hand. "Flavia, it's safer that way, please. The surgeons are not always reliable and could easily sell the two of you for a few denarii. It will be safer for you to be elsewhere."

Flavia's thoughts took over for a few seconds, wondering whether begging would be a better way to go about it. But then Asilia did have a point; it was dangerous to be seen anywhere in the city, with Valerus especially. Pompeii was not far from Herculaneum and a search was bound to be put out here.

She looked at the couple and realized what was actually bothering her; she did not want Asilia to be alone with Valerus or give her the opportunity to be. The stories Asilia had told Flavia in good nature had disturbed her since they were spoken. But then, looking at the way she held her youngest son to her breast and remembering their loyalty till now, she knew that they were far more to be trusted than what she had given them credit for.

She nodded slowly. "Where is this villa?"

⁂

Valerus woke up when an unfamiliar hard hand was laid on his shoulder. He opened his eyes and blinked in the sharp light. "It's late," he muttered, aware that he had no control over the manner in which he formed the words; he mumbled more than spoke and felt terribly weak all over as he tried to sit up.

Proculus helped him by taking him gently by the arm. He winced when his body shifted position. Without a word, Proculus folded back the sheet to look at his wound; dark colors had begun to invade what had once been pale and tanned. Streaks followed up his veins, which had reached for the surface of his skin.

Proculus shook his head. "Come, Valerus." He carefully pulled his feet off the bed. "We must have that wound properly tended."

Valerus glanced around the room for the first time, aware suddenly that Flavia was not present. "Where's Flavia?"

"We are taking her somewhere safe," Proculus announced as he offered him a chiton and brought forth a folded toga. "You are in danger and we need to get professional help."

"I can't leave the house," he murmured as Proculus fastened his sandals. "I can't go anywhere without Flavia."

"I can't ask for a house call, Valerus; that could point a finger directly at me. I will tell the medical profession that I found you in a bad state just outside the city. That way my wife and I will be safe as will Flavia."

"What about me?"

Proculus looked up at him. He could not answer; there was nothing to say. He looked back down and finished fastening the sandals before coming up and helping him into his chiton and toga.

"I'm not leaving Flavia!" he exclaimed weakly, but he was ignored.

"You are, unfortunately, not in a position to decide."

⁂

It was a beautiful piece of land where the villa was set a short way northwest from the city. Asilia took Flavia there personally while Proculus looked to Valerus. Flowers bordered the outside wall and several slaves were at work pruning the bushes and picking flowers. It was luxurious. It was high set, making the most of the view to the south and west. On entering, they approached the peristyle, walking along the ambulatory and into the main atrium opposite. Flavia noticed two men reclining in the peristyle when they passed; they were dressed like slaves, but surely it was not allowed for them to lounge around like that? Not for country slaves at least.

The man who greeted them was large—not overweight but of large build. His shoulders were squarely set even under his tunic; he wore a plain gray toga, announcing that he was not a slave but not as highly stationed as Asilia or her husband. Flavia understood the setup well; her moving life between Gaul and Italy had taught her that rich familias who owned land often lived in a nearby city while the farmland was kept under work and guarded by a steward. As long as their commands were clear, stewards had no right to go against the wishes of those who paid them. Stewards were not slaves but had taken up the role as an easy occupation.

This man had the typical features of one, Flavia noticed: the stern look and the air of importance that was not actually his. He smiled at her but she did not return it. She did not like the look in his eyes; it was one she had seen too often in her past.

"Jurgen," Asilia greeted him. He nodded in response. "This is Flavia. She will be staying here and helping around the villa for a few days."

"What will you have her do?"

Asilia shrugged. "Let her help in the kitchen. Take her to the vineyards. I am sure she will enjoy getting out a bit."

"Definitely!" Flavia smiled for the first time. She had been locked in for so long that being outside in the fresh air was going to be a delightful change.

Asilia's look became stern suddenly as she looked the steward in the eye. "Proculus's command; she is to be treated well. None of those rumors we have previously heard."

"They are only rumors, my lady." Jurgen shook his head.

"And give her her own room. Proculus will be around in a day or so to make sure all is in order."

The large man looked Flavia up and down then at the mistress. "Is she a slave?" He had to ask as he judged which of the two empty rooms he would give to her.

For a second Asilia hesitated before shaking her head, and despite that she confirmed it, Flavia knew that second was all it took for Jurgen to know. His stare stayed fixed on hers and Asilia broke the tension by taking Flavia gently by the hand. "Come, Flavia," she said with a smile, "let me take you on a tour."

Flavia would have gone anywhere to get away from the steward; his stare was hard and too much like those she remembered. Luckily he was working for someone and had to obey commands.

Asilia took Flavia for a walk through the villa, showing her the peristyle from the ambulatory, and then moved to the kitchens, which were open and in view of the garden.

There were many small bedrooms and two main tricliniums,

each with four reclining couches lined along the walls. Flavia caught a glimpse of Jurgen's bedroom, which was open to the atrium farther in the house. Life here was lived in luxury despite it being country work. As Asilia took her outside, following the paved path farther out, the slaves' quarters became apparent. Some of the more valuable slaves were given rooms in the house while the others, forced into harder labor as punishment, were set to live in wooden shacks that lined the outer wall of the villa; others were even forced to sleep in prison cells. Tunics were hanging along lines and several of the open doorways revealed blankets on the ground beside dead hearths.

Country slaves had difficult times and hard work to complete, which was why it was considered a punishment to be sent to work in the country. Most of it was done in the summer sun and in the heat with flies and sweat. Most were men; women were seldom capable of keeping to the master's schedule after a few weeks, and even the men who Flavia saw were struggling.

They were working the vineyard, turning soil, running in manure, and working irrigation from the Sarnus River, which ran south of Pompeii. She saw that some had been branded on the forehead: runaway slaves who had been caught. Some were stripped to their waists and she was certain that she saw whip streaks along some of their backs. For a second, Flavia thought she too would have to endure it if she were caught, but she was not a runaway slave; she was a condemned Christian. Worse things were in store for her.

"It's a beautiful view from here." Asilia turned her from her thoughts.

It was true. Mount Vesuvius stuck up from the green horizon ahead, darkened where trees had been planted, everything from oranges to olives. Flowers were still blooming in clusters all the way to the mountain foot, filling the world in a bright array of colors.

"I would love to help in the vineyards!" Flavia exclaimed as she looked around at the bountiful world. "It's been so long."

"You are welcome to. There is a lot of work needing to be done. Jurgen will show you to the storage rooms where the baskets are kept as well as the tools and manure. We will certainly be grateful for the extra hand."

"Anything." Flavia shook her head. "After what you have done for me and Valerus."

"Old friends." Asilia laughed. "The Cascus family helped Proculus for many years when he was first getting started in the business."

"You are the one who provides the Cascuses with the wine."

"We have so many samples in our cellars."

The name turned Flavia's attention to other matters. "Do you think Valerus is going to be all right?"

"Of course! He has fought in the arena; I am sure he has survived a cut in the leg before. He just needs the proper treatment."

"How long do you think it will take?"

"I would give it at least a week. I will do my best to keep you informed of his condition, but you must be patient."

Flavia nodded. Patience was something she had always been good at; a slave had to be.

Lucius was considering when it would be appropriate to return to Herculaneum. He felt at peace to be away from the chaos that he and Valerus had caused, but there was also a bit of unrest knowing that his actions may well cause suspicion.

His fear of this soon attracted the happening. Someone knocked on the insula door of the house of his mother in Octavianum one late afternoon. When he answered it, he was confronted by a soldier who wore a bronze lorica and a ring of office bearing the seal. The colored ribbon across his chest announced he was a soldier. There was a military sword on his belt.

Lucius swallowed to conceal the anxiety that for a second had jumped from his control. The soldier had to have noticed as he kindly said, “Don’t be alarmed. I am only here to inquire about a few recent incidents.”

The young man stepped aside. “Of course,” he said as he gestured the soldier in. “Please.”

A woman appeared from the next room, elderly and with black but graying hair. She looked at the soldier worriedly and then at her son. Respectfully the man introduced himself, placing his hand on his chest as he did. “I am Floronius, privileged soldier of the seventh legion from Rome.”

“What’s happening? Lucius? Why is he here?”

“Please do not be alarmed, madam.”

“It’s nothing, Mother. Please …” He shook his head in her direction.

She became tightlipped and decided to let her son deal with the matter. She returned to the next room, letting the drape fall behind her.

Lucius turned to the soldier and opened his hand to an empty couch where Floronius reclined himself. Lucius lay down opposite him. “How can I help you, soldier?”

“My men and I are investigating a number of accusations taking place. Roman officials have arrived only a few days ago from Rome and have met some … complications in association to our tasks.”

“What was their task?”

“To see that a Christian prisoner arrived safely in the mother city.”

Lucius was aware that Floronius was watching his reaction carefully so he did his best not to give anything away. He merely shook his head. “And? What happened?”

The man waved his hand as if it was unimportant. This was a surprise to him and he wondered what he was plotting. Finally, when he spoke again, Lucius felt himself being pushed into a corner. "Do you enjoy a good gladiator spectacle?" he asked suddenly.

Lucius recovered and grasped his composure in a second. "Occasionally." He nodded.

"Do you attend often?" Floronius asked, and then he added faster than Lucius could reply, "I try to get out to as many as possible. I am a gambling man and I have won some small fortunes in the past. The games in Herculaneum in memory of the emperor have been quite spectacular from what I've heard."

"I think it's still going on, branching into Pompeii."

"I believe so." He nodded. His smile was beginning to worry Lucius; it was one that said he knew everything but was giving him a chance to confess to save them all a lot of time and trouble. The problem was that Lucius was not sure that he knew.

"I am here to make a few inquires." The smile suddenly disappeared and he turned his stare to the ceiling for a few seconds before back at him. "There has been a terrible incident only a few weeks ago that cost many people a lot of money."

"I will help where I can, of course."

"Do you fight, Master Lucius?"

"I am an actor." He smiled. "So I suppose I do in a way, if the script reads it."

"In one specific fight, which it is known that you attended, the gladiator, Valerus Claudius Cascus, was brought down by the sacutor. Do you remember this fight?"

"Most certainly," Lucius replied and then caught himself. *Idiot! You didn't! You were not in the stands! Don't tell him you were in the stands with Flavia while it was Gaius! Tell him you were down in the holds waiting for Valerus to finish. He knows, you fool. He's trying to catch you!*

"I was down in the holds during its duration," he added quickly. "Valerus told me he was certain not to win and he wanted my help if anything were to happen."

Floronius was giving him that same unsettling smile. "You gave up your seat for a friend …"

"Young Gaius," Lucius told him, but he felt a lump come to his throat. *He knows!*

"A lot of money was lost by very wealthy men," the soldier continued. "Some people suspect that it was not Valerus in the arena. I am making inquiries to ensure that we don't see another riot as we did in Pompeii."

Lucius put on a genuine frown of concern. "Who was it then?"

"You don't know?"

"Of course I don't! Are you accusing me of having taken his place?"

"You just confessed to having been down in the holds. Surely you must have seen who was coming in and going out."

Lucius stuttered, suddenly feeling trapped. He thought quickly of his options and saw a small escape route. "It was Valerus," he announced. "I helped him get dressed and it was he who left the cell."

Floronius sat up, pulling his pallium out from behind him, and rested his hands over a knee. "I will have to ask you to accompany me back to Herculaneum. The lanista Cornelius is also being questioned as are several comrades regarding the situation."

"What about the Christian prisoner?"

"There are others looking into that," the man confirmed. "I have reason to believe that the incidents are interlinked. Friends: they will do a lot to help each other. Even break the law."

Chapter 38

August 18

Valerus woke up to a spinning world. He felt drugged; he probably had been. Turning his head slightly, he saw the braziers burning along the walls; by the light they gave off and the darkness that cloaked him, he knew it had to be late night, perhaps reaching for early dawn. He felt terribly weak, disoriented, and nauseous. He had a stabbing headache and, as he reached up to it, realized that he was tied down.

A little alarmed, he tried to look down at himself. He was fastened to a medical board; he had seen these several times during his profession as a gladiator and had only once been strapped to one. Qualified doctors used the available anesthetics but others relied on tying down their patients to avoid thrashing. This was one of them. Leather straps bound him to the board, two across the lower leg and one a short way above the knee. A cross buckle was fastened over his chest and three more along his arms. The small padded blinders on either side of his head kept him from seeing or moving his head much. The board was shaped to fit a human body and it was fit with hinges so that the different limbs could be lifted or lowered at will, depending on the procedure necessary. Currently his left leg was lowered, his heel nearly touching the floor. He was covered with a thin blanket but could feel that his injured leg was exposed.

He had no recollection of coming here. There had been nightmares of pain, blood, and being forced to walk when he couldn't, but those were vague and somewhat unreal. He could feel the cold sweat of fever and suddenly became aware of the pain. It was focused on the wound in his leg, but it was definitely throbbing all the way up to his groin as well as down to the heel of his left foot.

For a long time he tried not to focus on it and tried to distract himself with other thoughts, like those of Flavia and where she was, but even the woman he loved and cared for was distant in the rising pain. He did not know how long he was biting down on his teeth before someone finally came into the room, carrying a small lamp in the palm of his hand.

"Ah, good," the strange voice said to him. "You are awake." The lamp was set down on the table by the wall and Valerus could hear the newcomer washing his hands in some unseen bowl of water. "You need feeding. It's been two days."

Valerus blinked in the light. "How long have I been here?"

"Reaching for five days. You had a good meal day before last and you need to keep up your strength."

"What happened?"

"Bad case of blood poisoning." The man was now walking around to the wounded leg. Valerus winced when his leg was lifted slightly. There was a click of a hinge as the board was brought up a short way and locked into position. He felt him wipe the blood from his calf and then knee.

"How bad?" Valerus asked as he tried to see the extent of the injury.

"You've woken up, so obviously not as bad as I thought. The

surgeon was right; you are a young, strong man prepared to fight. You are on a strict, heavy treatment of plantain."

"You have bled the wound?"

"For a good amount of time, and I hope it will be enough." He lifted a bandage that Valerus was not even aware was on him. "Looks very good. I am impressed. How are you feeling at the moment?"

"Feverish," he said and swallowed. "Drowsy."

"It's to be expected with the blood loss you have endured. It's important for you to keep up your strength. I brought you something to eat."

"Anything I take in now is going to come up again." Valerus confessed.

"You must eat." The man began to unbuckle the straps of Valerus's arms as well as those two that crossed his chest. Then he removed the blinders on either side of his head and smiled over him. "Would you like me to raise the back? Or do you have the strength to sit up yourself?"

Valerus considered it for a few seconds, and although pride wanted to refuse the help, he realized that he was far too weak to do anything else.

As he was helped up, Valerus saw that the man was young and obviously an apprentice to a far more experienced surgeon.

"I'm Celadus," he said as he suddenly locked the hinges and kindly laid a hand on Valerus's shoulder. "I'm really impressed by you." He passed Valerus a steaming mug.

Valerus smelled the contents and thought it resembled chicken soup. The mere smell of it made him nauseous. He looked over it to Celadus and was about to introduce himself by his name, remembered the risk, and went by his second name instead. "Claudius," he said flatly.

Celadus did not appear to be listening in any case as he went to clean his hands yet a second time.

“Will it still need bleeding?” Valerus asked cautiously.

“We will have to see. At the moment I don’t think so, but we will have to keep an eye on you for a few days more before making any decisions.”

“Who brought me here?” He decided not to mention any names and instead let the question be answered by another.

“I don’t know,” the young man answered. “I only returned from Nola day before last.”

Feeling the dizziness grasp hold of him suddenly, Valerus leaned back against the wooden board behind him and sighed, resting the mug between his legs. “What time is it?”

“I would predict in the late decima of the morning.” He turned to wash Valerus’s wound carefully, using a new cloth with every swipe and stopping on occasions to wash his hands.

Valerus shut his eyes and tried to hold down the nausea. His thoughts turned to Flavia; they were also realizing his luck. He had made it through severe blood poisoning and he had friends who he could trust. Finally he opened his eyes to the apprentice and asked, “How long before I will be allowed to leave?”

“The surgeon will be coming later this morning to stitch it up. We had to cut it open a good deal to clean. After that, a day or two under treatment and observation, and you ought to be released.”

Flavia was getting terribly uncomfortable working at the villa. Jurgen had entrusted Flavia with Dasilus, an old man with a white beard and short gray hair, to supervise the young woman as well as most of the slaves working outside. He showed her where the storeroom was for the baskets and gardening tools and where the grapes were to be stored and trodden. At the sight of the other slaves, Flavia did feel comforted, knowing she was back in the company familiar to her. There was an inner connection to all slaves and they always got along; Flavia especially was one to always merge into the groups of the outcast and the downtrodden. She thought of her friendships back in Herculaneum: Cotti, Helen, and all the others. She wondered if Luci ever got to speak to Gaius as she so much wanted to. Flavia wished she had had a chance to see them one last time, even if only to say farewell.

Most of the slaves under Proculus were male, which explained the setup of the working area. The vineyard was part of a shareholders organization. Wealthy men who could not afford a good piece of land by themselves worked together to purchase land from the governor and now shared the bountiful fruits among them. The largest shareholder in the business was Vetti, who also lived in an exquisite villa in Pompeii. He had more than forty slaves working in the fields and ten or so more at the villa. Proculus was only a minor player in the huge financial circle that took place on the harvest grounds.

The vineyard itself stretched to the base of Mount Vesuvius, in such fertile soil that grapes grew large and plentiful. The sorting area and storeroom were on the opposite side from the villa, so Flavia moved from her quarters in the villa to join the other slaves in the wooden structures lining the vineyard. She did this also to get away from Jurgen; his company was terribly unsettling. Flavia had the feeling of being stalked by him when she began to see him in the vineyard where he usually never ventured. Some slaves commented on his presence and others warned Flavia of his violent streak. He had taken part in beating disobedient slaves and often deprived others of food. Luckily he could not go too far over the extreme otherwise his superiors would see the effects on their servants.

Flavia was relieved to have left the villa to stay with the slaves; it had been a good choice. Socres, one of the older slaves under the hand of Vetti, was viewed as the “leader” of the work force, inspiring and encouraging slaves who felt to be on their last legs. He had, in his younger years, been a runaway, and now carried the brand of "FUG" on his forehead. *Fugitivus*: it was a lifelong reminder that once he had tried to resist being a slave only to be caught and scarred for life. Two of his fingers had been deliberately crushed as a punishment and still today they were flat and blackened.

But his heart was good; the incident had made him compassionate to the youngsters and stoic to the harshness they were often exposed to. Under his wing, he had Labu, a young Numidian boy who had arrived from North Africa only a couple of months earlier. Jurgen had already beaten him into submission and now Socres was trying to rebuild some of his esteem.

Flavia shared his hut with the boy, feeling most comforted and safe in his presence. She returned to a simple life of cooking over a fire and sharing flatbread with some wine. Every couple of days in the later afternoon a messenger often arrived to give news of Valerus and the happenings around the city. It was rumored that guards had entered the city from Herculaneum and had made same inquiries before leaving again. Valerus's condition appeared to be improving and it was only time now that would bring him back to her.

She read his poem in the evenings by firelight and felt the pendant hang from her neck as she fell asleep. Life suddenly felt simple again.

August 20

Dark clouds loomed over the city of Pompeii with the promise of rain that morning. Flavia and Socres were up the minute they saw the clouds. Working in the heat of the summer was something any of the slaves would have tried to avoid. The darker clouds and cool breeze made a refreshing change as they stepped out of the shack.

Flavia wore the tunica she had washed the day before; it was still a bit damp, but she forced herself to wear it since she had nothing else. She thought of the beautiful green stola Lucius had bought her, but strangely there was no regret that upon her arrest it was replaced with the basic clothing. She had always felt better in what was familiar to her. The tunica of a slave was all she had known other than the erotic clothes of the dance.

When they got to the vineyard to join the others, Dasilius was there supervising … so was Jurgen. He smiled when he saw Flavia, who merely dimmed her stare and concentrated on other things.

Most slaves were working on the ground, turning the soil and adding manure. Flavia decided immediately to help with the work while Socres turned to his other duties. She took Labu with her, keeping him as far from Jurgen as possible. She helped turn manure into the ground; the fresh smell of wet earth was empowered by the compost; the overcast sky made it cool and pleasant.

Labu was sitting in front of her when he glanced up over her shoulder and gasped. The second it took for Flavia to register his action was the time it took for him to get up and bolt.

"Coward!" A voice laughed behind her.

She looked around and saw Jurgen come her way, his walk determined. Her first reaction was to glance around to see if there was anyone in the vicinity and then the fear dawned when she saw she was a good distance from the other workers.

She was not going to let her fear of this man make the decision of her coming actions. She stood up and turned around to face him. After all, Asilia told him she had to be treated properly. What could he do?

He was so large and strongly built but not in the same way Valerus was. Valerus was well built and well developed while Jurgen appeared over-exercised and bulky. He was a lot taller than Valerus, with broad shoulders and a thick short neck. Flavia knew how easy it would be for him if he tried to dominate her in any way.

"Finally I catch you alone." He smiled and stopped a few feet from her. It was too close for her liking and she took a small step back. He chuckled. "Are you afraid of me?"

Flavia shook her head. "No, but I don't like being near you."

"Why?"

"You ought to inquire the gods as to why." She was shaking her head.

"Is there a man that you love?"

"What business is that of yours?"

"Well, where is he then?"

"Give him time."

Now he stepped forward. Flavia considered retreating but instead stood her ground, not ready to show him her vulnerability. He came right up to her and placed his hand on her shoulder. She twitched slightly under his touch; it was so cold and heavy that it felt to be pushing her down.

"But until he comes you are under my charge." It was obvious how his gaze went down to the dim lining of her breasts beneath her tunica. She hated it; most men had a tendency to do that, only Jurgen was one of those who did it very obviously, enjoying the change in her expression when she noticed.

She stepped back, jerking her shoulder away from under his hand. "Don't touch me," she sneered, reaching down and picking up her basket. As she walked off, she heard him chuckling.

"What will you do?"

❧

The rain hit in the later afternoon. It drizzled through Pompeii as it emptied, people jumping the flagstones across the street and rushing for home. A young couple, giggling under the shower, chased one another in play.

Valerus watched them from the street corner where he stood, leaning the better part of his weight on the crutch placed under his arm. He smiled and turned skyward, letting their laughter dissipate in the rising rustle of rain. The outdoors was such a good change from the small room he had been confined to for the last eight days. The pain was still evident but he could already put a little weight down on it. At least he did not have a fever anymore.

The entire affair had cost him forty-eight denarii, not including his meals, and just over a week of his life and escape. He had hoped to be as far as Ostia by now.

It could not be helped; it had to come to a procedure that could lead to a healing and it could only get better from here. He knew he was going to see Flavia again and that thought lightened his guilty burden considerably.

He knocked on the door of Proculus and shivered slightly as he waited for a response. It was not a slave who answered the door but Asilia herself. Her face brightened when recognizing him. He had not shaved at all in the days he was treated, so a fine short beard had begun to sprout along his jaw.

She pulled him in with a chuckle. "Get out of those soaked clothes while I get you a blanket," she said and hurried off.

He removed his toga and held it in his hands, watching one of the children who had come in from the tablinium and now stood against the open doorway facing him.

Not a word was exchanged when Asilia returned with a thick wool blanket, which she gently placed over his shoulders. "How are you feeling?" she asked as she took the wet tunic from his hands.

"Better." He smiled for the first time. There was a chuckle as the child ran off. "I feel a little drugged being on my feet again, but I'm told it will pass."

"Can you walk?" she asked, looking at his crutch.

He nodded, carefully leaned his crutch against the wall, and turned to her with a proud smile. “The crutch makes it easier, but I can put weight on it, better than I could before, actually.” He carefully leaned his weight forward a little to show her.

She nodded, impressed. “Would you like something to eat?”

“Where is Flavia?”

They had both spoken simultaneously and Valerus had to repeat himself to get an answer.

“Up at the villa,” she told him. “We were afraid that the surgeons may come here with inquiries.”

“You did the right thing. She is well?”

“Proculus has gone up there for a meeting with the other shareholders only an hour ago. We have been keeping a kind eye on her.”

Valerus sighed, relieved. He looked around the atrium. “You are alone?”

“Most of the slaves are given time off the week after the Ides,” she informed him, kindly leading him into the triclinium. “The cook is here though, and you have not answered my question regarding a meal.”

“I am really anxious to find Flavia.”

“You’re not hungry?”

Valerus did not like her persistence; it made him uncomfortable. He was in the house of one of his previous lovers, and alone. It gave him a strange sensation. He shook his head. “Please, Asilia,” he said to her, pulling out of her grip. “I want to get to Flavia first. Then we can discuss a meal.”

He saw the look come over her face, the disappointment and the indecisiveness. It only confirmed his uneasiness and he took opportunity of the silence to slip out quickly.

She stopped him, gently grasping him by the shoulder. “Please wait, Valerus. There is something I must tell you.”

“No.” He shook his head. “None of this, Asilia. What we had was a long time ago, it was a game. It was not real. Besides, you are a married woman now.”

She was shaking her head while he spoke. "No, Valerus, it has nothing to do with that! I love Proculus and I would never dream of being unfaithful to him."

"What?" He couldn't believe her; it contradicted her actions now as well as those from years back. "You didn't keep to that when we were at the Lupanar."

"I was young and foolish! You have no idea how often I regret what I did. I never told Proculus; I never had the heart to see the pain it might cause. After we were married I actually wrote on the wall of Primus stating that I would never want to sell my husband! Not for all the gold in the world!"

Now Valerus frowned, realizing that she was telling the truth. The tone of her voice was urgent and desperate, but not for sexual tendencies. He realized that there was something far more important on her mind. "What is it then?"

She had gone quiet, moving slowly to take his hand into hers. When she finally looked up, he saw tears in her eyes. "Come with me," she whispered.

She led him through the atrium to the small bedroom on the right of the door. Two of the older boys were stationed in their room, the six-year-old playing on the mosaic floor while the five-year-old slept soundlessly.

Valerus stared at them. For a moment, the boy looked up from what he was doing before going on as if they were not there. The young man looked at the woman beside him, who was smiling at her two boys.

"What is it, Asilia?" he asked in an effort to try to read her expression.

"You remember those passionate meetings we had," she asked him with a smile, and before he could answer she nodded in the direction of the six-year-old. "He's yours."

Valerus looked at the boy sitting on the floor, playing with small blocks of marble and then back at the woman beside him, his mouth hanging open. He could not believe it; he did not want to believe it. Did he have a son? Was he actually a father without having known?

"Proculus and I were married when I gave birth to him," she said without looking his way. "Proculus asked no questions; we had made love several times over the past months before our wedding. He suspects nothing, nor have I told him anything." Now she looked at him. "I just thought you ought to know."

The young man looked back. The child was regarding him curiously now. For the first time, Valerus noticed how much the child resembled him: the thick hair and the sharp nose was definitely not from either Asilia or her husband. His skin was also slightly darker than that of his siblings.

Slowly he dimmed his stare from the boy and stepped back, shaking a little. "I did not see this coming." He shook his head, struggling for breath. "This is not happening." He did not say this in a way that he hated the thought or that he was completely disgusted by it, but he was suddenly viewing his future with Flavia very differently, wondering how this was going to influence things.

"Valerus, please," Asilia grabbed his arm. "I don't expect anything from you. I have everything I need and Proculus is a good husband. I just thought you ought to know."

Valerus stared at the boy again, catching his breath and turning back to the atrium. Rain was coming in through the *compluvium*, sprinkling over him as he took a few steps around the impluvium. He ran a shaking hand through his hair.

Him? A father? What did that mean about Flavia? Should he tell her?

What a damn fool he had been in his younger years. It was all well to view himself as a thracian, a fine gladiator, and count his success by the women he had had, but now the realization and the reality of it was slammed into his face, threatening to destroy everything that was now far more important than the game.

Asilia watched from the doorway, concerned by his reaction. She bit her lip and then asked with concern, "Was I wrong to tell you?"

The man stared at her, unable to say all the things that raced through his head. Instead he dropped the blanket from his shoulders and limped forward to take the wet toga from Asilia's hands.

"Where is this villa?" he asked flatly.

Her face fell and she said softy, "Northwest from here. You can take the Herculaneum road; there is a turnoff to your left after the tombs."

Draping his toga over himself, Valerus then took the crutch from its place by the wall and disappeared into the wet street. The woman stared unmoving at the open doorway and the rain still drizzling among the insulas. Then she turned back to watching her sons. A sad smile fell across her face when the six-year-old looked her way.

Chapter 39

His mind had never worked so much regarding an individual subject. A father! He could not believe it. How would that affect the future? How would Flavia take the news? Would he tell her? Did he have to? Did any of this actually change anything?

All he knew now was that he had to see Flavia; he knew that the sight of her would bring everything into perspective again. For the moment, he felt a little lost and he was certain that Flavia would ground him again.

He was also feeling guilty, not just because he had gotten Asilia pregnant, but also by the way he had left Asilia standing there after she had told him. She had said that she did not expect anything from him. Was that true? Did she only want him to know?

Valerus did not feel that he needed to acquire permission to enter the villa. He did however avoid the sound of voices coming from the cenatio, as he recalled Asilia telling him that there was a meeting in there.

He stepped out again and walked the perimeter of the villa, cursing a little as the cold water stung the fresh wound on his leg. Through the thin veil of mist, he noticed the small shacks belonging to the slaves. There were over a dozen of them, some with smoke coming from the windows.

It was his better option and he made his way toward them, desperate to get away from the thoughts and images that plagued him.

His thoughts controlled his motion and he opened one of the doors at random just as a master would. Three middle-aged men looked up from their blankets where they were reclined, sharing a small meal that stewed over their fire. Their stare broke the trance and slapped Valerus back into reality.

"Sorry," it was the first time he had apologized to a group of slaves for having intruded. "I am looking for Flavia. I have reason to believe she is working on the premises."

One of the men got up from his place. He was naked and quickly wrapped a small towel around his waist. Without a word he waved in Valerus's direction, beckoning him to follow as he left through the door past him.

Valerus followed, his mind drifting again. They could not have gone more than thirty paces before the slave pointed to the next shack and bowed. Valerus only nodded and watched him leave. Turning back to the door, he took a deep breath, putting the current events at rest for the time being and opening the door.

He had to smile when he saw her. She was sitting opposite the entrance on a blanket, turned to the fire. The men looked his way before she followed their gaze. For a second, the world held its breath before she jumped to her feet. "Valerus!" she wept, all her emotion bursting when she saw him.

They embraced, throwing their arms around one another. She pressed against him while he buried his face in her neck. His concerns of earlier faded, but only slightly. For the moment it was Flavia; they were together again, and his greatest concern now was keeping it like that.

Chapter 40

August 21

Valerus woke up slowly and smiled sleepily when he felt Flavia pressed up against him. They were still in the small shack, sharing the tiny room with Socres, an Arabic man Flavia introduced as Marabl, and the young Numidian boy, Labu. Together they had shared a good meal and a bit of wine. Valerus had never been more grateful for the hospitality.

It was so good to be back with her again; it fulfilled him and made him complete. He was well aware that they had to leave the city and find haven elsewhere, but for now they were together and that urgency had diminished. He gently kissed her head, feeling the short ends of his beard catch her hair. The doctors and their apprentices had cleaned him well but neglected to shave him. For the moment, he was prepared to accept it, depending how Flavia took it.

A numbing throb returned to his lower knee and he was suddenly reminded of yesterday's discovery: he was a father. In a strange way, he felt terribly responsible and felt compelled to help with the child's upbringing, but Asilia had strictly told him that nothing was expected. She did not want Proculus to know. What then could he do? What exactly was expected of him?

Perhaps nothing, like she said, but that felt unnatural and against his principles. And Flavia? Should he tell her? He could not see her being too upset. He had been young and foolish at the time with a good reputation and usually a good dose of wine. Would she get angry? Would she leave him?

He shook his head. No, she would not do that, but she was likely to put his life into full perspective again.

Flavia stirred under his arm and turned over, catching his face through half-closed eyes. She smiled sleepily. The light of dawn had barely touched the horizon and the slaves still had a half hour to sleep. Valerus looked up across the dead fire at the other sleeping men and the boy. How he wished they were not here for at least this time.

Gently he came over the woman and kissed her lightly on the mouth, then moved to her cheek before running his tongue up to her ear. She chuckled and turned away, which led him to do the same to the other ear.

"Valerus, stop!" she said playfully, getting her hands in between them and carefully pushing him away. "There is a time and place for everything."

He bit his lip, fighting the urges that were coming through strongly. In the past, he would not have bothered to hold back. Now he was disciplined. He rolled over with a sigh and pressed himself against her, resting his arm across her hip. "I love you, Valerus," she whispered in his ear.

He let her words sink in; it brought forth that same feeling he had had the first time she had said it to him. It reached into him and warmed him from the inside. He never thought a few words could make him feel that way. He smiled and touched her cheek. "I love you too, Flavia. More than the world itself." He saw by her expression that his words had the same effect on her.

"Let's go out," he pleaded. "I'm not going to sleep again and neither are you. Take me around the vineyards, Christian."

There was no way that she could refuse a man who asked it so kindly. She nodded, turned over, and reached for her clean tunica.

Some dark clouds had moved in again, though not the heavy ones of yesterday. A cool wind caught their hair when the couple stepped out into the dim gloom of a coming dawn.

"It's cold," she whispered as her long loose hair whipped against her shoulders. She raised her arms to fasten her hair in a bundle with a leather strap and at once Valerus took it to do it for her. "Maybe we should stay here," she wondered out loud as he fastened the knots and looked up at the dark clouds above them.

"Perfect weather for a walk." Valerus grinned. Two days ago the heat had been unbearable, but now it was cool and promising some relief from the sun. Besides, a brief walk was bound to warm them up quickly.

The vineyard was quiet and deserted. It was strange for Flavia to see it like this after the busy days she had spent there.

They took the path that lined the vineyard rows and picked one at random to walk up.

Valerus sound it strange; as if he was wasting his time. Flavia was beside him, holding his hand at her side, and said nothing. He knew that she had noticed his limp; it was more distinct than before but far easier to manage.

Valerus was reminded of the walk they had taken together on the beach the night they had made love; this was a lot like that, as was Flavia's expression. Only this time he knew that he could make the offer.

The many rows of grapevines and the cool air made them feel like children again, and in a mischievous, innocent manner he knew Flavia was not going to let him have her as easily as then.

He watched her from the corner of his eye and bit his lip when she looked his way. He took the opportunity and stopped abruptly, took the woman by the hips, and leaned in closer to kiss her. To his complete surprise, she jumped out from his hands. He did not comment but walked forward. He found her behavior even more encouraging. When he took her by the shoulders, she ducked out from under him and ran up the line. She looked over her shoulder and noticed that he had not moved but was only watching her with his head slightly craned. She remembered his bad leg and stopped, silently encouraging him to come after her.

He did, but at a slower pace, wishing that he could run after her as she wanted him to. Then, when he was only a few steps away, he leapt, grabbing her by the upper arms and pulling her to him. He kissed her without uttering a single word. She tried to pull away again, but this time he was expecting it and held onto her.

"What are you doing?" he asked, chuckling softly.

"Being silly."

"Well, you'd better stop, slave, or I might just have to discipline you."

"Then you will have to catch me." She pulled free and ran, taking advantage of a bare hedge and slipping into the next row. Valerus followed at a leisurely stroll, watching on with a smile as she scampered and darted to the left into yet another row.

"You can't run forever!" he called to her then ducked down behind the vines. Slowly, making as little noise as he could, he followed the row to where she had disappeared into the hedge.

She must have gotten impatient, he thought with a smile, as he heard her shuffling only a few feet away.

"Valerus?" she called when she thought it was getting to be a bit long.

He was not responding but instead crept closer until he could make out her face between the leaves.

"Valerus?" Her smile had faded into a worried look. He watched her get to her feet and glance around. The vineyard was frightfully quiet with nothing more than the wind rustling the leaves. "Valerus!" She called again.

The air felt heavy. Valerus had to suppress his laughter when she turned in circles, looking over the many rows of grapevines.

Suddenly, without warning, he jumped at her from behind the thick brush. She screamed as she was thrown back onto the soft earth, but the scream ended in embarrassment when she saw Valerus lying over her, laughing as he held down her arms.

"When you can't run," he told her, "there are better ways of moving about."

Flavia covered her eyes with her hand and laughed until the tears came. The smile on her face was unmistakable. For a moment, they stared before he kissed her gently and brought one hand to her hip.

He moved aside to kiss her cheek and then her neck. She had a unique taste, sweet nearly. He came up again and carefully ran his lips across her eyes. Flavia put her arms around him, relying on her other senses to feel him press against her. There was a magic when they were this close together; it was as if he was complete; the presence of her was like fulfilling something he had not thought at the time was missing.

He was kissing her neck now, moving down to her throat. Carefully he pulled the top of her tunica down across her arm to kiss her upper breast. He then looked up. His desire to make love to her was gone and was replaced with full satisfaction in this moment. He ran his fingers through her hair and then down along her arms. The moment was perfect. He remembered reading the papyrus from the library of the philosopher Philodemus who stated that the criterion of a good life was pleasure. Valerus had never been one to believe such things, but it was this moment that Valerus saw a simple truth in that statement, just as Gaius said one should. This moment was a godly one, and nothing could be grander or bring more pleasure to any man.

He rolled over and lay beside her, listening to her heavy breathing. She turned her head to look his way and a silence followed. The two listened to the wind, the soft whistle through the poles, and the first distant rumble of threatening rain. There was a faint glow to the east.

Both their moods changed when he gently kissed her again. "I know you went through a lot while you were a slave and I the arrogant boy," he said softly in a quick pause, "but I am so grateful that it was you who I purchased coming from Rome."

A mischievous smile crossed her face as she sat up a bit, propping herself up on her elbows. "Do you remember what you first wanted from me?" she asked. It was not an accusation or a guilty reminder, but instead a teasing play of words.

"I got it," he said as he grinned and kissed her before she could comment. "I have it right now. In fact, you taught me to perfect it. Your perfect world."

"I did not need to go across the ocean to find it, though." She took his face in her hands and brought her lips to his. Then she pulled him so to be up against him and encouraged him to lay his weight over her again. He did so, suddenly feeling the rebirth of his passion as well as his urges. He recalled Gaius's question regarding his future with Flavia: a family … children.

This reminded him of what Asilia had told him. He stopped the motion and pulled away from her slightly. The guilt was getting to him again and he felt he had to say something to relieve the pressure.

Flavia was regarding him questioningly, wondering what had changed his mood so suddenly. "Flavia," he said slowly, still considering turning the subject elsewhere. He decided to get through the moment. "There is something I feel you need to know. I discovered it only yesterday but I don't want to keep it from you."

She frowned but the conversation ended there by a loud call from across the vineyard.

From the direction of the villa was Jurgen, obviously having spotted the lovers across the wine rows. He was making his way toward them briskly. Valerus saw the threat of his motion and jumped to his feet, keeping Flavia behind him protectively.

"What's all this?" Jurgen demanded as he approached. "Who are you?"

"I'm with Flavia," Valerus announced, looking the man head to toe. He was huge; Valerus knew that he would not stand a chance if he chose to fight. He would have made a brilliant gladiator and a terrible opponent. Valerus wondered why he had never gone into the profession. A coward perhaps?

Jurgen looked on disapprovingly, obviously wondering what Flavia saw in a man who he could so easily bring down if he chose to. For a moment he wanted to, even if only to prove some unspoken point. He reframed himself, though, knowing he had to act under orders.

"Ah, yes." He nodded to Flavia. "The mistress told me that a young man would be around to pick you up. But as long as you are here, there is work to be done."

"We'll get some buckets," Flavia told him and reached for Valerus's arm. Despite Jurgen's size and obvious strength, she felt safe with Valerus. Also she liked to see the look on the steward's face when he realized that he could not go against the commands of his peers.

Jurgen watched the couple leave toward the villa and grunted under his breath. He was not used to being defeated in any field. Strange how such small things made him feel so incompetent.

Flavia glanced over her shoulder once before she leaned to Valerus. "We must leave," she whispered to him.

"Let's give it a day or two," he whispered back. "If we run out so suddenly, people will ask questions." He looked back. Jurgen had disappeared. "Him especially. We must cover our tracks, Flavia. We can do that by not being in too much of a hurry. Besides," he said as he kissed her hair, "no one suspects us of being this close to Herculaneum."

❦

In Herculaneum, Marcus sat at his table rubbing his hands nervously. He did not like the ranks from Rome; they behaved as if they owned the better part of the world, including his watch house.

And what they did was not interrogate, he thought. They merely worked on a person until they got what they wanted to hear, no matter whether it was true or not. Technically they had no right, but, under the command of the senate, they believed themselves to have every right and were not confined by any rules.

He glanced up when the cell door opened. Floronius stepped from the darkness, an associate passing him a clean cloth without exchanging a word. Marcus then noticed how he began rubbing the red tinge from his hands.

By Vulcan! What has the man done?

"Well, that's over," Floronius said as he smiled kindly at the gathered party. "He's confessed."

Of course he would after that! For a moment Marcus feared something had been said against him, but then he recalled that Lucius did not know of his involvement … to a point. "Anything serious?" he asked.

"Far more than we thought!" The soldier tossed the cloth aside. "Theft and attempted murder, even the fight was a setup!" He nodded to a small group of assembled men. "You five with me. We will be heading for Pompeii directly." He turned to Marcus, who had known better and was now on his feet to attention. "I trust you will put Master Lucius in his own cell. He could use a few hours to sleep it off."

Marcus nodded stiffly and cursed aloud after the men had gone.

Chapter 41

August 22

The couple worked the vineyard together, enjoying the shared labor. Valerus had never been among slaves as he was the next day and he had never thought of enjoying it. His wound had given him a handicap and he was permitted to rest more than the others. Flavia often joined him in the shade of a tree but Jurgen made sure that their time together was as limited as possible. It was this effect that caused Valerus and Flavia to seriously discuss their departure that day, and through the course of the early afternoon they agreed to leave during the night.

For this reason Valerus wanted to leave the vineyard in the later afternoon to see Proculus and Asilia; he felt they at least needed to know and be thanked for their help. He understood why Asilia had agreed to help; she felt it her duty to tell Valerus the truth while the young man felt it his own duty to leave in better face regarding the issue he had with his son. Surely he couldn't just leave without seeing the boy at least once. Again there was the twist of guilt at the thought of leaving the two of them, perhaps forever.

He felt he could do with a good wash as well as a shave first.

Pompeii had a small *thermae* for bathing; he had used it often in the past. It was the only bath that still functioned after the earthquake seventeen years earlier. Restoration of the central baths was underway, but he wondered when they would be open for public use. But the forum bath was luxurious, despite it being small. He touched the pouch at his belt and remembered the amount he had won in the games those weeks back. Thus he considered offering Flavia to join him as the baths did, after all, have a women's entrance.

She was turning the soil; her hands were black from the rich earth and sweat was sitting on her brow. He said nothing when she looked up at him but merely offered her his hand. She smiled when he pulled her up. "Want to join me for a bath?" he asked her without really expecting an answer.

She grinned. "With you?"

He looked her up and down, seeing how her clothes had been dirtied over the days. She had a spare tunica which she went to get before he took her by the hand and led her by the main road into the city.

Valerus wore a basic tunic with a wide girdle along with the toga Gaius had given him; he appeared like the common lower class, and with a beard he doubted that anyone would recognize him if he merely walked along the sidewalk with the rest of the community. Flavia too blended in; her hair was tied above her head which gave her a completely different appearance.

He escorted her to the women's entrance of the baths; it was the first time he ever did. During his stay in Pompeii, bathing was a daily occurrence, but he never approached the women's entrance on the left corner other than in some of his fantasies.

Some women were chatting near the entrance, one with a towel over her shoulder. Valerus stopped near to them and took both of Flavia's hands. "Don't leave without me," he told her firmly. "Wait inside until I call for you."

She nodded and smiled when he passed her a few coins. "Don't forget to tip."

Once she had gone inside, Valerus decided to take the road down to the main forum. It had been so long since he had last been in Pompeii that he wanted to see the city again.

It was alive and bustling with life, far more than Herculaneum ever did. The streets were broader and chariot ruts were engraved in the main streets. On reaching the forum, he was reminded of his earlier years. It was far more crowded than he remembered; people concluded business, visited temples, and sold their goods here. To the west was a dais, which was occupied by a speaker addressing the crowd with news and political speeches. Valerus stopped dead. The orator was addressing the problem of runaway slaves and the rewards for their return. One was from Herculaneum.

Valerus merged into the crowd and got a little closer to hear.

It was not Flavia, to his relief, but he stayed a while longer to make sure that nothing was said in regards to the incident. But it appeared that he had arrived late; the talks were drawing to an end and the speaker turned to Pompeian politics.

Valerus put his mind at rest, deciding to innocently ask some citizens at the thermae. Returning to the baths, he felt his leg beginning to ache, and he cursed the fact that he had left his crutch behind.

He paid the usual entry fee of a quarter as when the slave by the door shook his head. "No water, master," he announced. "You can use the water there is, but there is nothing coming from the system."

Valerus frowned at this. "What? No water?"

"We can't work it out, master." The slave shook his head. "So the wells and irrigations have also gone dry. We are terribly sorry for the inconvenience."

"You still have warm water, do you?"

"Yes, master."

"For the women also?"

"They still have the hot baths, as I am told."

"I could use a good cleaning and a shave. If you could get someone to oblige?"

"Certainly." The slave bowed and felt to follow up on his request.

Valerus got undressed in the *apodyterium*. Only one other man was in the room with him, but several tunics and togas were hanging from the wooden rails and iron hooks that lined the walls.

He did not want to leave Flavia alone for too long and thus turned to the hot baths directly. Several men were in the process of cleaning with what water remained. Valerus waited for his turn and then joined the people at the basin, washing himself of the day he had spent working in the dirt of the vineyard.

He thought about soaking himself in the bathtub at the end of the room, but wondered if it would be good for the wound, still fresh and stitched on his knee.

Deciding that it was better not to, he entered the warm bathing area and took a seat along the wall. More men were here, sitting back with their eyes closed while slaves massaged or shaved them. Most appeared to be waiting for the water to return. Strangely, Valerus had an uneasy feeling that it was not going to be for a while still.

He let a man shave him as people came and left across the room between the changing room and hot baths. Somewhere in the distance was the echo of sportsmen in the gymnasium.

Next to Valerus was a man of fine build, probably with a gladiator or military background. He had been cleaned and shaved and was now merely enjoying the quiet moment. He appeared strangely familiar, but Valerus could not place him. Instead he decided to follow his example and shut his eyes while he was being shaved.

The slave had barely done his cheeks and was moving to the

tricky part under his nose when the peace was shattered when a voice rang out louder than it should have: “Floronius! The gods have a sense of humor. I thought it had to be you!”

Valerus opened his eyes a fraction to see the speaker. It was a large, tall man, bulky with a strange accent on his tongue. It was Jurgen, and it took all his effort not to react to the twist that came to his gut.

The man beside him got up and greeted him with a short manly embrace. “It’s been years, Jurgen!” Floronius laughed. “How have you been?”

“Very well. I was out in the forum when I heard the news. When did you arrive?”

“Late last night. Been waiting for the blasted water to return so I can wash.”

“Wells have gone dry on all the farmlands around the mountain. Started last night. Luckily I had six women to take my mind off of it.”

“Six?”

Floronius grinned. “Too few for such a stallion.”

There was a brief chuckle before Jurgen turned his attention back to the water problem. “Herculaneum gone dry also?”

“Believe so.” Floronius lay back again and sighed. “I ought to be back in Rome by the end of next week. I have every reason to believe that the slave is here.”

Valerus did not move or open his eyes, but he concentrated on their conversation above the other chatter.

“I think I have some information for you,” Jurgen said, “regarding the slave girl mentioned. Does she have a lover?”

“We first suspected it was the man we brought in from Octavianum, but apparently he has confessed that it was Pedius’s own son.”

Valerus felt the breath being drawn out of him. They were discussing him and Flavia. He gently and slowly beckoned the slave to stop, leaving some hair across his chin and beneath his nose. He was frightened that after the shave he would be recognized, yet Jurgen did not know him as clean-shaven. There were pluses on both ends.

And it was that moment that he remembered where he had seen the soldier Floronius; he had been his interrogator back in Herculaneum, the one who had caused him the injury that cost him nearly two weeks of his life and his escape.

And the man they brought from Octavianum? Could it be Lucius? Would he confess to anything?

This thought made him sit up a bit.

What have they done?

"There is a woman who has been put under my care. Her young lover met her yesterday."

"Will you take me to her?"

"First I want to discuss the reward offered as well as the possibility of remaining anonymous."

The soldier caught his breath and removed the towel from around his waist to dry his underarms. He tossed it across the bench near to where Valerus sat and nodded to his companion. "Let me get dressed and we can discuss it further over a drink."

"I know a wonderful *caupona* not far from here."

Valerus waited until both men had left before reaching for his towel and dabbing his cheek, deciding to leave the few short hairs to be shaved later.

Men were not allowed in the women's section of the baths, but waiting for a slave to call Flavia out was not an option. Valerus barged into the changing room where several young women screamed at him. He glanced across at the faces before darting to the next room.

Flavia was seated on a marble bench in the warm bathing area when he found her wearing a towel across her waist. More women shouted at him and tried to cover themselves as he grabbed Flavia by the wrist.

"We must leave!" he told her urgently. "Now! We can't wait!"

He pulled her back into the changing room where she got dressed hurriedly. A slave girl was approaching angrily. "Don't worry; we are leaving!" He pushed her aside and made for the door. He looked around for any soldiers or guards.

Flavia had never known Valerus like this. He was frightened obviously. He stood by the door, keeping watch for a second before pushing her into the street ahead of him, looking back over his shoulder in case of any pursuers.

"What's happening?" she demanded to know.

He did not answer. His only thought was to get Flavia out of the city and away from the potential danger. They first took the road out to the villa before thinking better of it and turned to join the Decumanus Superior road, which led to Nola.

Soldiers were along that road; Valerus was not sure whether they were looking for them or the other slaves who had been announced as having fled their masters. He turned back to the city, going with the flow of the crowd back toward the baths.

Pompeii homed and fed over twenty thousand citizens, nearly double that of Herculaneum. Thus it was easier to merge into the crowd. The forum was the ideal place; more than a thousand people walked the square, going about their business and following up on political issues.

"Valerus, please tell me! What happened?"

He pulled her into a second street where a cart was in the process of collecting urine jugs from the roadside. Behind it was a patrol and he pulled her back into the forum.

He didn't know where to go. He had to get her out of the city.

He decided then to leave by the marine road, but, as he pulled her after him, she jerked free. "Valerus, stop! Tell me what happened!"

People milled past, unconcerned by their affairs. Valerus reached out and took her by the hand. "I think they managed to break Lucius," he told her hurriedly.

Flavia's mouth gaped open.

"I overheard two men at the thermae discussing it. They are after us. They know we are here."

"Who are *they*? Officials from Rome? Or Herculaneum's guard under your father's command?"

"Does it matter? They are after us. We must leave the city." *Damn Asilia!* He thought as they passed the basilica. The couple had helped them considerably; they would not have made it without them, but going to their home now was out of the question. No doubt names were going to be passed and he could not put Proculus in such a situation … or his son.

This brought a twist of guilt so hard that he stopped in his tracks. Flavia nearly cannoned into him. For a second he considered returning to Asilia to apologize for his reaction, but he could not put Flavia through that.

"What is it?" she asked when he did not move.

He had to go back. Valerus felt the tug from the inside. He had left Asilia so coldly the last time they had seen each other. It felt as if he was not prepared to accept what she had told him. The least he could do was to appreciate her honesty and to show acknowledgment that the boy was his.

But Flavia? He could not leave her here or take the risk of pulling her along.

Forget Asilia and the child! You did not know of him until yesterday afternoon! What difference will it make?

Right! He let that statement propel him forward, pulling Flavia with him.

More guards were stationed at the marine gate. Valerus cursed to himself. He ought to have left the city the moment he had been released from surgery. Going to the baths had merely given them time to position the guards.

The other gates were also going to be under observation. It was then that he realized they should have left by the Vesuvius road through the vineyards and orchards. But that would bring them too close to the villa … and Jurgen. The man was obviously the sort to give them up for the small reward that may be offered.

They had to hide, at least for a day until the heat died down. But they could not be anywhere near the vineyards or Proculus's home. Once Jurgen confessed the story, there would be soldiers swarming those areas.

But how fast could they be there? Already there were men positioned at the gates, obviously since the soldiers had first arrived and there was no telling when they would be at the vineyards. Maybe they were already there.

Four provincial soldiers suddenly appeared in the street ahead, coming their way. Valerus pushed Flavia into the nearest open doorway, pushing her back until the men had passed.

A small family of two parents and three children looked at them fearfully. Flavia merely smiled their way before following Valerus out again.

They retreated to the main street and into the forum, where they were certain the crowd would help hide them. Most were gathered around the *suggestum* and upon the temple steps, so the couple made toward them and merged in.

Without knowing why, Valerus looked around at Vesuvius towering above them, the hillside looking peaceful through the heat of the sun, with bright green grass growing to the very top. It drew him suddenly and he clenched at Flavia when another fear, from an unknown source, took hold of him. He took her around the shoulder and moved with the crowd into the Temple of Jupiter.

⁂

Rectina could not take it anymore; it had been over two weeks. The silence of the villa was just too much for her. There was the sound of trickling water from the fountains as well as Anneria in conversation with a companion, but the domus lacked one sound in particular, and that was the sound of Valerus's voice. She had first tried to distract herself with her own duties—working the house accounts and supervising the domestic workers—but, after so many days, she could take it no more.

Her husband was reclined in the peristyle, enjoying a late cup of wine and catching up with some reading. Through the open way was a clear and calm ocean. She marched up to him, prepared to announce her thoughts and opinions as openly as she dared.

"Where is Valerus?" she first demanded to know.

He looked up at her and carefully set the goblet down on the table beside him. She waited for a short time before it became obvious that he was not going to answer her. She sat down at the end of the couch, gently pushing his feet aside to make room for herself.

Pedius stared at her for a few seconds from the corners of his eyes. He had not told her about their son's act of theft and law breaking; he could not bring himself to. According to her point of view, he had run away when Flavia was taken to Rome. She was likely under the impression that he had taken his own life. However, the fact that her husband was taking it so well led her to believe that he was keeping something from her.

She was now determined to find out what it was.

"Where is our son, Pedius?" she asked softly.

He sighed and looked down at his notes.

"Why won't you tell me? He is my boy! I have a right to know."

"No son of mine would do the things he does." The man sat up a bit.

"He's in love; religion was not going to stand in his way."

"Apparently nothing will! He appears to do whatever he wants! What is it?"

This question was directed to Galen who was standing at the peristyle entrance. He bowed respectfully to the two of them. "There is a man here to see you, Master Pedius," he said to him. "He says he was once a servant of yours."

Pedius threw a quick glance at his wife and then beckoned Galen to bring him forth, merely to change the subject his wife was trying to bring up.

In walked a man dressed in the lower class of a freedman. Across his shoulder he carried a small knapsack. He was strongly built but not large and had light golden hair falling to his shoulders. Pedius sat up on his approach, trying to place those fine features. He remembered that face but it was more rugged and with a beard.

"Afternoon, master." The man bowed.

Pedius smiled, recognizing him from the voice. He sat up completely. "Harolde! Well, who would have thought? Free?"

The man chuckled and nodded. "Since last week," he announced proudly. "My master released me from his services."

"Congratulations!" Pedius said. "It must all be new for you."

"Still getting accustomed to wearing a toga." The freeman chuckled.

It was good to see an old slave return. Even though he had previously been disobedient in the house, obviously his new master in Surrentum had been pleased with his loyalty and services to free him after only a few months.

"Wine?" Pedius felt inclined to offer. Harolde was, after all, no longer a slave.

"No, thank you. I am heading for Baiae."

"What can we do for you, Harolde?" Rectina smiled kindly.

Slowly the man went down on his knees, dropping his sack in front of him and removing a small pouch that jingled. "My lord," he spoke slowly. There was a hint of a fearful tremble on his voice. "I have come to ask you humbly for Cotti, the slave who works with the washing. She is still here, is she?"

This brought Pedius back to the reason why he had sold Harolde those months back; Harolde had gotten Pedius's slave girl pregnant and Pedius was not prepared to stand for it. Out of respect of him being a freedman, he did not comment but only nodded in response.

"How is she?" Harolde asked, concerned by Pedius's sudden change of attitude.

"She is well."

Another silence followed in which Harolde emptied his pouch into the palm of his hand. It was not much, merely eight hundred sestertii. He moistened his lips and held it out toward Pedius, who regarded it from the tip of his nose.

"I know it's not much." He shook his head. His voice trembled. "It's all my savings along with what my last master gifted me with. Please accept it in exchange for the woman I love so dearly."

Pedius did not know why he was hesitating. The amount he was offering for a good female slave was considered an insult. Cotti was worth at least triple the amount, yet he could not come to refuse the offer. He felt for a second as if it was Valerus kneeling in front of him, begging for the woman he loved, and he felt this was his chance to right all his wrongs. He turned to his wife for support from the feminine side.

The woman was only looking on, from Harolde to her husband and back again.

Finally Pedius called across the garden to Galen, who came

hurriedly to his side. "Call for Cotti," he commanded him, and then he looked back at the freedman who appeared to be holding his breath. He gave in and nodded with a growing smile. "She's yours," he announced. Harolde jumped to his feet but was silenced before he could speak. "She has duties to complete and will be available by the end of the week. You can pick her up then."

The man appeared to fight the joy that was bubbling up. He fell again to his knees and crawled up to his previous master, placing the money in his hand and clenching it shut. "Thank you, Master Pedius! How the gods will reward you for your kind gesture."

Cotti came into view then. In her arms she was still carrying the dirty laundry, preparing to take it to the cleaners. When she saw her lover and father of the child, she dropped the basket and ran to him.

Pedius and Rectina watched the reunion of the two and the expression on her face when Harolde announced that he was free and had just bought her. Gently he placed his hand on her rounded stomach.

Pedius looked at his wife; he could see the tears in her eyes. He had helped change the lives of two people, and ironically it had not been the life of his own son.

"Bring Valerus home, Pedius," the woman pleaded softly. "If it's an issue of honor, take it up with Mars! Give him the slave girl, just bring back our boy."

Chapter 42

Night blanketed the city and a beautiful moon was rising to the east, giving them light for the evening ahead. Valerus and Flavia stayed in the crowd surrounding the temple for as long as they could before turning into the smaller streets where dogs barked at them from poorly constructed wooden fences between the streets.

Where to go?

He looked at Flavia who merely smiled. As long as they were together, there was some strength left that kept them both going.

They came across a line of small shops and insulas. It was quiet with only a few people ambling around a fresco. There was the sound of singing from a merry tavern nearby. Fresh bread smelt good. They found a bakery nearby where the open bread ovens were lit only some steps from the grinding mills. A few wooden benches had been placed in the vicinity.

"Come on," Valerus said as he took Flavia's hand. "Let's have something to eat."

Fresh bread was a treat to most slaves, who usually were given the leftovers and crusts. Valerus enjoyed the meal they shared under the Pompeian sky that evening, watching Flavia opposite him. She was worried but was trying to hide it from him. He smiled at this, realizing that he too was frightened and yet not about the soldiers after them.

He looked up. Over the buildings he could barely make out the black hulk of the mountain. It loomed and it was unsettling. He could not explain it. He analyzed it for a while, trying to figure it out. It was a strange twist in his gut, like what he would get if he was being stalked from behind. Yet it was not for the reasons he thought. The soldiers who were after them and the fact they were imprisoned in the city did not match to the feeling; it almost appeared to be a background to it.

He must have been thinking for quite some time because, when he looked up, Flavia was staring at him. She had finished her slice while he had only nibbled on the edges of his.

"Where are you, Valerus?" she asked with a sweet smile.

He returned it and shook his head. "We must find a place to hide for the night," he said without answering her. "The steward I am sure has caused a stir. We only need to lie low for a day or so until they give up the search. We must make them believe we have already left the city."

"We cannot go near Proculus," Flavia said as if reminding him. "We cannot get them more involved."

Valerus caught his breath. That was still something he needed to do—go and see Asilia and acknowledge that he had a son. He had to do it; it was a risk to have to go back there as it was a risk to leave Flavia on her own, but seeing Asilia again one last time was necessary.

A hand dropped on the bench between them. The baker stood over them. "Payment still outstanding," he announced. "We are closing for the evening."

"Of course." Valerus pulled the pouch from his girdle. "How much?"

"Two as."

The young man passed the coins to him and refastened the pouch. The baker looked from him to Flavia. He had been in the business for many years and had learnt to read the expressions of many customers. This couple appeared terribly lost and confused. "First time in Pompeii?" he asked out of curiosity.

Valerus opened his mouth to reply truthfully about his years of training and traveling, but then remembered himself and simply nodded instead.

The man looked at them again and asked, his tone softer now, "You two have a place to go?"

"Not really." Valerus smiled and looked up at him.

"There are a few good inns …"

"No. We can't go to an inn." Valerus shook his head.

Dawn befell the man's face as he suddenly understood. He nodded. "Is there a reason you don't want to be seen by, say, a passing patrol?"

Valerus caught Flavia's gaze and saw the uncertainty within them. He moistened his lips and looked up at the baker. "Do you have any wine?"

"You will have to go to the tavern for that. There is one farther east, but I would rather keep my wits if I were you. There are many provincial soldiers about and the exits are being guarded. I'd watch my back."

He left the couple to digest his words. Flavia was the first one to turn from the bakery back to Valerus. "He's right." She shook her head. "What are we going to do? Staying here is just a danger." She clasped his hand. "I was nearly taken from you once. I don't want it to happen again."

Valerus got up from his place and followed after the baker to the small fresco where he was talking to a fine redhead woman—his wife perhaps. They were in the process of locking up for the night. A young male slave was set to guard the grounds for the evening.

"Excuse me," Valerus said as he leaned over the wooden board that was being used as a counter. "Would you have lodging for us for the night?" He remembered the money he had earned and added, "You will be paid well."

The couple glanced at one another and then to him. "We do not hide fugitives." The baker shook his head. His wife said nothing; it was not her place to.

"If you could be so kind as to hear our story, I am sure you would take some pity on us."

That seemed to hit the right note, for the wife especially. It brought a smile to her face and she caught his eye with a tinkle.

"Please," Valerus continued, trying now to break the baker. "It has been a terribly hard month." He momentarily gestured to his leg and then at Flavia watching from her seat, "As for her … we're both a little run down."

"You know that there is a price on your head."

"How much?"

"Four hundred denarii. And that's only for information."

Valerus took a small step back. "I spent a few years here." He tried a different approach. "I trained and fought in this very theater six years ago. It was my home for a long time."

"You were a gladiator?"

"Seven years."

"And now you are a fugitive with a woman? What did you do?"

Valerus looked at Flavia again over his shoulder. The light from the brazier caught her profile perfectly while the moonlight illuminated her in a soft glow. He had to smile at the image; it was among the most beautiful he had ever seen.

He looked back at the baker and his wife. "I fell in love."

"But we are not hiding them!" Socres raised his hand in a plea of mercy. The soldier still had his fist raised over him. The slaves had been gathered in the villa atrium and were now being interrogated by Floronius and his band of five soldiers. One of the younger male slaves had already been beaten severely and Socres had also taken a few blows.

"They are not at the villa or the surrounding vineyards." Floronius was leaning against the wall, playing with a knife between his fingers. "They could not have left without you seeing them."

"I told you that I did!" Socres said urgently. "Valerus invited Flavia into town and they left together. That's all we know! Please stop hurting the boy."

The soldier waved to his associate who stepped away from the slave now prostrated on the floor. "We are offering four hundred denarii as a reward. As you are slaves, money really means nothing to you, but I am sure we can come to some agreement."

"We know nothing, master. We have told you everything there is to say."

Jurgen was suddenly present in the entranceway, his large arms folded across his chest. "You can't trust a slave, Floronius!" He smirked. "They are all liars. They are not even human."

The legionnaire went to him, taking Jurgen gently by the arm and leading him out. Once outside they turned to each other. "You want your reward; you had better make a plan on finding them," Floronius said to him.

"I think you want the reward as much as I do."

"Only if she's as good looking as you say she is. For the moment I am under command of Rome and her senate. Christianity is to be brought to heel. Once we find them we can delay their order for a couple of days only."

Jurgen laughed loudly. "A couple of days will be more than enough!"

"We haven't gotten either of them yet. Proculus claims not to have known of the situation, so they are, technically," he spat on the floor, "innocent."

"They could be anywhere in the city," Jurgen said to him. "But they must be in the city. They could not have left with the guards stationed at every gate. We merely have to find them."

"That will be your job as of now," Floronius told him. "You find them and I make the arrest. From there we can discuss sharing the woman between us."

Chapter 43

Valerus stared at the small fire burning in its hearth. A baker was only expected to have an indoor oven. Flavia was asleep beside him, her head carefully resting on his thigh. His hand gently caressed her head.

"Some bread with *garum?*" The baker stepped in, holding a plate in his one hand and a bowl in the other. "My wife makes the best sauce in the city."

"You are too kind, Terentius." Valerus smiled as he took it and set it on the small table nearby.

"My wife is soft for a love story." The baker reclined himself on the couch near him, also looking into the oven's fire; its flame was deep red and glowing.

Valerus stared, transfixed at the flickering light, considering his best options for the moment. There was a strange urgency to get out of the city and it was more urgent than the fact that they were being stalked. This feeling was hesitated by one thought alone, and he knew he would have to deal with it before doing anything, including informing the woman who slept beside him.

"I need to go out, Terentius," he said softly, hoping that Flavia was asleep and not listening with one ear. "There is something I need to do."

"It's dangerous out there, Valerus. If you get caught, I could also get dragged into it."

"I know, but this is something that I have to do. Will you keep her safe while I am away?"

Terentius caught his breath. "I won't go announcing that she is here," he replied honestly. "But if she is found here, I will deny everything you have told me."

"I understand." Valerus carefully moved out from underneath Flavia and placed a pillow where his leg had been. Then he got up and fastened his girdle. "I won't be gone long."

Pompeii was one of those cities in which you never forgot your way around after having spent a couple of months there. Valerus kept to the back streets; those narrow and leading past insulas as well as small taverns and other businesses. He came in the back way from the usual route to Proculus's home and there was, as he suspected, a guard walking along the Decumanus Superior.

Valerus stepped back into the shadow, hiding himself as the man swept past. Then, taking the risk of the open advantage, he went forth to the front entrance.

It was barred. It was also then when he realized how late it was; there was no lamp lit inside and no glow seeping in under the doorway.

He retreated and took refuge behind an old barrel when the guard returned, and, as he passed, Valerus became aware of another sound: a drunken giggle and dragging footsteps coming his way. He risked a glance up and saw a familiar figure. He could not place him until he was caught by the guard's lantern.

It was Austs returning from the tavern; obviously his master had given him the evening off and he took opportunity to intoxicate himself. Valerus watched him amble past. He was not too drunk as he recognized the house and managed to tap gently under the circumstances.

A light approached and the door was open by a younger slave carrying a lamp in the palm of his hand. Valerus sped up and entered along with him, radiating a sense that he was expected to be there. It was this air of importance that did not cause any alarm from either slave, who merely looked at him questioningly.

The lamp carrier raised the light a little then smiled. "Master Valerus." He nodded. "Good to see you again. Asilia has been asking about you."

Austs only chuckled and staggered to his quarters without a word.

"I need to speak with the mistress, please," Valerus begged of him. "It's urgent."

He waited in the atrium, every now and again glancing up at the two small rooms on either side of the entrance he had come in from. Within them was the definite presence of children sleeping soundlessly.

There was the patter of feet and a lamp light became increasingly sharp when the curtain was drawn away, separating the master bedroom from the atrium. Asilia came in carrying a second lamp, looked at him, and waved the slave off.

"You should not be here, Valerus," she told him.

Valerus was quick to get straight to the point. He walked up to her and took her hands into his. "I'm sorry!" he whispered. "It's not that I'm ashamed or upset about the boy. I was just not expecting it."

"Valerus, please." She raised her hand to his mouth. "It's over; it's been over for six years. It has nothing to do with you anymore. I just felt you ought to know."

The young man shook his head and dimmed his stare. "I feel responsible." His voice was hoarse.

"You are." Asilia chuckled softly. "Those were passionate meetings we had; you drove me on as much as I did you. But that's over now. It was years ago."

"I know." He looked at her again. "It just reminds me of how irresponsible I was; a mere boy who did not think further than his own pleasure."

"Is this what this is about? You feel guilty of your own actions? Please, Valerus, you don't need to do anything. Caphisus is well looked after and loved by both me and Proculus. There is nothing expected of you."

He smiled. "Caphisus … that's a nice name." He bit his lip, running the event over in his head. There was nothing he could do; in fact, doing anything now could very well break up the family. After all the help they had given and the risks they had put themselves through, Valerus could not stand the thought of being responsible for that.

"Can I see him?" he asked her.

She led him into the small room; Caphisus was sharing a room with the middle son; his bed was small and placed against the farthest wall. It was a warm night so he wore no blanket and lay open in a night shirt.

Asilia watched as the young man stepped in and knelt by the child's bedside. Carefully so not to wake him, Valerus laid his hand on the boy's head and then his chest to feel the gentle beat of his heart and the breath he drew in.

"How old is he now?" Valerus asked her softly.

"He will be six next month."

He stared a while longer still. It was a strange and unfamiliar concept to grasp: he was a father. He felt a little disappointed when reminding himself that it was not a child that came from Flavia.

Maybe, one day …

He got up and turned to Asilia, who was standing patiently in the doorway bearing the light. She was smiling at him as he walked up, took the lamp from her, and blew out the tiny flame. Then, hidden by the dark, he took her on either side of the face and kissed her gently. Him not seeing her helped to overcome the guilt of before, perhaps the dark shadowed a few more things than just what the eye could see; perhaps even the further reaches of his soul, which he still could not bring himself to look at.

Her taste was so different from Flavia's. Though he was well aware that he did not love this woman, he did not feel guilty in kissing her. He felt like the boy he had been those years ago, but with far more control.

She did not resist him and also took him by the shoulders. It felt good to feel her young lover up against her again, even if only for a few seconds.

He drew away and licked her taste from his lips. "I am honored to have shared those evenings with you," he said honesty, feeling that it would make everything so much easier if he accepted it. "They will remain fond memories."

"You did it very well." The woman chuckled. "Valerus ... the young thracian."

Valerus did not know what those last words did to him, as his mind was in a different place altogether when he stepped through the front door and into the street. He was smiling oddly, strangely proud to have a son he could call his own. The guilt had been well diminished and was replaced by a sense of pride and appreciation. He suddenly felt no fear or reluctance to tell Flavia; in fact, he wanted her to know simply so that she knew who he was as a man.

It was only when he saw the flickering shadows up ahead from a nearing lantern that he remembered the current situation and jumped back behind a wall. A man whistled and Valerus knew he had been seen.

And he could not run; the leg would not support his full weight. Instead he took to the low wall and used it to pull himself up onto the rooftops.

How different it all looked from above. Most insulas were built on the same height, making his passage easy as he walked the tiles as well as thatched roofs. He glanced over his shoulder; it was dark without any lights coming in pursuit. There were, however, halos growing from the streets around the area of Proculus's home, convincing the young man that they were well aware of his presence … but surely they could not have gotten a good look at him.

Some of the homes had built gutters along the end of their roofs; some of the poorer owners had even built theirs with wood, at the very least diverting the rain water from their front doors. These gutters were not sturdy enough to hold a man's weight and Valerus avoided them, keeping to the tiles and stone linings instead.

After several yards he crouched down and listened. A dog was barking nearby but other than that it was quiet. The glow of lanterns had diminished and the city appeared quiet again. It was wrong. Valerus did not trust this silence. This silence was more the sound of an indrawn breath.

Nothing. In the far distance he made out the sound of chatter and perhaps even laughter. He got up and continued on his way, planning to find the staircase that led to the second story of an insula and to climb down from there.

The thatch was slippery so he tried to keep to the tiles, which were not much better other than the fact that they were not tilted as sharply. And some of the tiles were loose; he slipped on one which made him stumble, but the sound was muffled by the wind coming in from the sea.

There was a strange—almost sulfurous—smell to it.

Someone was coming up the road; Valerus noticed the light flickering along the walls below. He crouched down again, stretching his wounded leg downward and knocking off a loose tile. At once he dove and tried to grab it before it reached the gutter, but missed. It slid along the tilt and missed the gutter by the way wall and fell over.

He held his breath. The second of silence felt longer than it could have been before the sound of it smashing on the sidewalk below rang in the silence of the later evening that left a ring in his ears.

"On the roofs!"

Valerus felt the blood drain from his head, leaving him feeling faint. He had thought momentarily that they were not after him. How cruel the events had suddenly turned.

He could not stay on the rooftops; any man who saw him up here would know exactly where he had gone. Thus he jumped to the nearest staircase below, misjudged the distance, and collapsed. Valerus was certain he had broken his leg; the pain was so dominant that for a few seconds he could think of nothing else. However, he was still able to get up and, by placing a minimum amount of weight on it, he made for the street below him.

There was a lot of activity going on but not by as many people as he had thought. He could hear the calls and talking of men, but there could not have been more than five. Still, five men could easily block off a crossroad as well as a turning. It was a potentially dangerous situation that he could not allow himself to get caught in.

His mind went to Flavia and the memories he held of her. No! He could not get caught; there was something too precious in his freedom, which he could not stand losing.

People were coming up the street now and Valerus, knowing that he could never outrun a soldier, crept into a small street between the insulas. Before they had even passed him a voice from a window above called, "He's here! Under my window!"

Cursing, Valerus stepped out directly into the light of a flaming torch. The men had not expected him there and Valerus took advantage of their surprise by punching the first one across the jaw, knocking him out with a single blow. This gave the second man enough time to draw his sword but little time for anything else. It was allowed for a gladiator to disarm an opponent but not to pick up his weapon. Here, however, there were no referees and thus no rules to which Valerus was bound. Having learnt this in training, Valerus grabbed the man's wrist and twisted it back to offer him safe passage to the man's flank. Once on his side, he threw out his right leg and tripped him over his ankle. Due to the angle of his wrist and weapon, he was forced to release the sword and the hilt fell perfectly in Valerus's hand as he stumbled back. He knocked the man out with a strong blow against the head.

He spun around to yet another call coming from the other direction. Across the flagstones was the approaching light from the next street. For a second, Valerus glanced up at his traitor before making for the other way, turning the corner just as more men entered the street from the other end.

He sunk against the wall, hiding between a market stall and some urine jugs. The men came past—three of them—as Valerus held his breath. If they saw him here, there would be no escape. They were all well armed. Their movement was hasty and focused on ahead; not one of them saw him.

Softly, Valerus exhaled and pulled himself out of the shadows. He looked both ways before crossing the street and heading back to the baker's.

He had not gone ten paces when he stopped and looked over his shoulder. The silence that reigned after the commotion of earlier was unnatural; Valerus did not take to it kindly. It was the same feeling he got when he was fighting in the arena and an opponent was coming up from behind; he knew his opponent was there through some internal instinct.

He could not see anyone, but he was not prepared to take the risk in rejoining Flavia just yet. For this reason he took a road leading south and then turned east at the next junction. He increased his pace, but not so much that it would arouse suspicion.

He walked for a long time, turning corners and returning to previous streets. After some time he was certain that the pursuers had given up, but he refused to take any chances. As he wandered, he came across another narrow street, which held a young passionate couple and a third man writing on the walls. In his hand he held a small jar of paint.

Valerus merely glanced at the couple in their embrace before joining the vandal. He stood beside him and read the crude message he was painting on the wall.

Valerus smiled to himself, thinking how much he wanted to express the same hatred and defiance to his father. After all, if it had not been for Pedius, Flavia would have been his a long time ago. They would not be fugitives, exiles in Pompeii with the provincial soldiers after them.

"This some tavern?" he asked the man.

"No." He was too engrossed in his message to look Valerus's way. "House of Iucundus."

"You two had a … disagreement?"

The man smirked but said nothing more. Instead, without a word, the graffiti artist handed him the small jar of paint. Valerus could not tell its color—either a deep red or black. Whatever color, he felt inclined to write his own thoughts on the wall. Whether his father ever got to read it or not was irrelevant; it would make him feel a lot better.

He took the jar and used his fingers to write on the wall, letting his very anger and feeling of betrayal drive him to write what he so much wanted to tell his father. He wrote:

Whoever loves, let him flourish. Let him perish who knows not love.
Let him perish twice over whoever forbids love.

"Nice," the man beside him said with a nod as Valerus stepped back to view his artwork. "Something standing between you and your woman?"

Valerus replied with the same smirk the man had given him and tried to hand him back the jar of paint. The man refused it. "Keep it." He shook his head. "I'm done for the night." He then reached for a small shoulder bag that was on the stones nearby and flung it across his back.

Valerus watched him go and turned to the young couple who was giggling from the shadows. He left them to their privacy, set the paint by the corner wall, and decided to slowly wander back to the baker's. Any pursuers by now would have given up the chase or lost him in the maze of streets.

It was a lonely walk back as his mind went to the inscription he had put on the wall. He very much wanted his father to read it, but he had not signed his name and refused to do so. His father had, quite literally, forbidden him to love Flavia, and this realization angered him. What right did he have to make such decisions? He was not Jupiter, or Minerva, and certainly not Venus. He had no right! No right at all to dictate who he loved and who not.

When he reached the home of Terentius, no lamps burned. The door had been left unbarred, which he thought very decent of the couple as he slipped inside. Flavia was still asleep by the fire as he had left her with a pillow set beneath her head. He smiled sleepily, aware then of how tired he was. He turned to shut the door when it suddenly flew open, its edge slamming him in the face and drawing blood from his nose. Flavia was startled awake by the sound and was sitting up when four armed men barged into the room, pushing Valerus back until he was pressed to the wall. Two men held him there while another came for the woman.

Flavia turned to run, but the man was too quick and caught her by the wrist, yanking her back to him. She screamed before biting him in the wrist. He groaned and struck her across the face.

"Flavia!" Valerus called to her, but he was also silenced by a blow.

"Silence! Both of you!" Floronius stepped into the room. His hand was resting casually on the hilt of his sword. "Following you is difficult." His words were directed to Valerus. "But I have the best under my command." He looked at Flavia, who was weakly struggling in a soldier's arms. It was obvious that she could not escape, but she was going to make a point that she was not surrendering her freedom.

A lamp was lit and Terentius was in the room the next instant, looking upon the happenings with surprise and horror. Floronius and he locked gazes. "Harboring fugitives?" he asked with his eyebrows raised.

"He knows nothing!" Valerus snapped. "Never told him a damn thing!"

Terentius blinked and hesitated for a second before saying. "I know nothing of fugitives."

Floronius glared at him a second before walking up to Flavia. His icy stare turned warm on his approach and he smiled when he was standing in front of her. She tried to pull her wrist free to push him away, but the men were too strong for her.

Floronius lifted his hand and ran his fingers down her face. Jurgen was correct to have labeled her a beauty; the gray eyes and the light hair were a pleasant change from the women he had had in the past; as she was a Christian, it was a pleasant change.

Valerus watched on as the man stood up against her, feeling the fury and terror beginning to take control. He felt the fearful questioning of what he would do if the man tried to take it any further. There was nothing he could do, but he knew he would not be able to stand back and watch.

"Get away from her!" Valerus snapped angrily.

Floronius kept his hand on the woman's cheek and slowly turned Valerus's way. The smile he threw the young man was terribly cruel and unsettling. Luckily it was short-lasting before he looked at Terentius. "I have some questions for you," he said and then turned to his company. "Lock them up." He waved them off. "Separately."

Chapter 44

August 23

Valerus had thought they would be taken to Herculaneum. Instead they were taken along the Herculaneum road and turned off it even before reaching the main villa. Both he and Flavia were taken to another building whose outer entrance had rows of pillars to the east and west. The entrance itself was guarded by two men at the iron gate, which led directly into the atrium. Valerus took note of the position before they were ushered inside and down the steps into the cellars. These were the sleeping quarters of the lowliest of slaves as well as runaways. Chains were set against the walls over sleeping mats and old blankets. Some slaves were present, chained by the ankles, and did not even move on their passing. Others were absent, obviously having been put to work in the early hours as punishment by cruel masters.

Valerus was pushed up against a wall and two iron shackles clasped him around the wrists. Two more were clamped over his ankles and he was forced to sit as the chain between them did not permit him to stand at full height. The shackles on his wrists were connected to the wall, making him a complete prisoner.

Opposite him, Flavia was also forced down, but she was shackled only on the ankles, which lined with the wall.

The guards left them and the two locked gazes. They were out of reaching distance, which only cut deeper into Valerus's guilt; he could not even hold her. Slowly he shook his head. "I'm sorry," he whispered.

"This was not your fault, Valerus," Flavia tried to convince him.

"We should have fled the city the moment I was released from surgery. I should not have come home tonight … Why did I wait? I am so sorry."

Flavia reached her hand out to him, inching across the floor as far as she could go. Valerus simply watched her; he was not worthy enough to touch her. He had done this to her … It had been his injury, his delay, and his fault that they were here.

Flavia stopped when she had reached her maximum distance. He looked from her open palm to the look in her eyes and then down to her feet. Again he was shaking his head.

"Valerus!" He looked up when she called to him. Her hand was still outstretched and tears were building in her eyes. "Please, Valerus …"

Moving slowly, he came forward as far as his shackles permitted and reached out. He could not touch her … not even close. They locked gazes and he felt the first tears run down his cheeks.

He had failed her. All his efforts, all his hopes had been in preparation for something that he could not change. How cruel the gods were to have gotten them both so far only to get caught.

She, however, put on a brave smile; it had a rainbow effect on his tears. Valerus was the first to lower his hand and she followed after him. He did not look at her; he couldn't. Instead he shut his eyes and took a few deep slow breaths before looking up. "Whatever happens, Flavia," he said to her, "*No matter what happens*, if anything is asked, I too am a Christian."

Flavia was taken aback. "What?"

"I'm going with you, no matter to where. If you are going to be condemned as a Christian then so am I. You must promise me that you will tell them that."

"I will not tell them what is not true!"

"You must do this!"

"I won't!" Flavia was crying now. "I am not going to pull you into my death, Valerus. You are nearly there already because of me. No! You must take the chance with your life."

"What is life without you?"

She couldn't answer him; his tears and emotion had saddened her considerably, swallowing her breath and removing her voice. She shook her head before burying her face in her hands. The young man caught his breath, wanting now more than ever before to hold her, feel her against him at least one last time. Perhaps the last chance had passed and this was the closest he would ever get to her.

They were left alone for a long time, probably all morning. Nothing much was said and both Flavia and Valerus were in their own thoughts. Flavia for one was concerned as to why they had not been brought to Herculaneum; surely they were wanted there. But this … she looked up and around. This was a villa, a private home of a slave dealer. Why had they been brought here? If they were going to be sent to Rome, surely someone had to have come for them by now.

Flavia watched the man opposite for a long time, aware how his concerns bordered beyond their future. By noon, however, he began to doze and settled back against the wall to sleep. The young woman smiled. When last had she watched him sleep? Weeks ago when they had been reunited in Pompeii. She realized then that he had not slept for two days, and again it had been because of her. How did she deserve a man like him? He had sacrificed family, reputation, and life to try to save her. Flavia's only disappointment was that it had been for nothing, and that he would have to go on living knowing that he had failed in his efforts. Her death was inevitable, she knew. A runaway Christian slave had but one future. Valerus, however, still had a chance and Flavia's fear was that he would not want to take it. One question did cross her mind though, and that was where Valerus had been last night. It was a question she was meaning to ask, but the timing was so wrong. What did it matter at the moment in any case?

She watched him all through his sleep. He was sitting up against the wall with his shackled wrists at his sides. His head hung slightly over his left shoulder and his wounded leg was bent at an awkward angle due to the chains holding him back.

He was beautiful when he slept; the shade of a beard and that dark hair of his framing his face. His breathing was shallow and every now and again she was sure he was dreaming as his eyes would gently flicker.

Someone was coming down the stairs. Flavia turned from Valerus to the doorway while the young man was jerked from his sleep, the sound carried well.

Floronius stepped into their view. He was in casual civvies of a tunic, toga, and laced sandals. He smiled Flavia's way before Valerus made an attempt to jump to his feet, only to be yanked down again by the weight and tension of his chains. He groaned.

"Easy." Floronius nearly laughed. "Bad leg you have there."

Valerus cursed and came up on one knee, leaning back against the wall. "Why are we here? Keeping us chained up like common slaves!"

"You are common slaves! Runaways! And we have ways of dealing with them."

"We?"

It was like a staged play; on cue, Jurgen stepped into the room. Flavia was the first to catch his gaze and she trembled when he threw her that smile that spoke a thousand words. She shrunk back, but that did not stop him. He walked up and squatted beside her. "You really have an enduring spirit, don't you?" He placed his hand on her cheek.

She smirked and knocked him away. "I should have known you would give up lives for a few denarii!" she hissed.

Jurgen laughed. "That, yes," he agreed, "but also a lot more." He got up to undo his girdle. From across the room Valerus felt the blood drain from his head, leaving him dizzy but completely aware of the situation. He was suddenly focused on the large man before looking over to Floronius, who seemed to notice his dawning realization. He shrugged his way. "Sorry that you will have to watch this, Valerus." He could not help but smile. "But there is not much privacy with all the slaves around."

Again Valerus made an attempt to jump up, only this time the chains pulled him down with a cry of pain. Flavia had her back pressed up against the wall, also having realized what was in the making. Jurgen had now removed his girdle as well as his cloak. He was preparing to remove his tunic when Floronius threw a hand down on his shoulder. "I'm first."

"We had an agreement," Jurgen sneered.

"Yes, if you brought us the girl. But you were worthless in the arrest."

Jurgen was in no position to argue with a person of higher rank; he had taken orders all his life and saw no reason to resist authority from Rome. He stepped aside and let the man past him.

Valerus felt himself tremble as Floronius removed his toga. He noticed the look on Flavia's face, that same look of fear she had given him the first night he had tried to have his way with her. But even that had been different. Valerus was not going to deny that he had slept with many women—including slaves who had not been keen but were in no position to argue. He did not, however, chain them up and physically force them … and never would he with their lovers present.

"No!" he shouted, yanking at his shackles. He could not sit and watch it. He refused. He would not allow these men to touch her in any way.

"Sit back, Valerus." Floronius was still on his knees unbuckling his girdle. "You can't break chains." He then leaned over to remove the shackles on Flavia's ankles and did not expect resistance from such a fine young woman. She let him remove the chains, but the moment a foot was free she lashed out, kicking him full in the face so hard that he flew back. For a second, Valerus had to smile, remembering the resistance she had shown him. However, the rage quickly returned when Floronius clouted her across the face. It fueled Flavia as she brought her arm around and slapped him against the ear.

He grabbed her wrists and forced her back. She kicked out, resisting in every possible way. At one moment her knee got him in the groin, but the force had not been enough to draw him back.

Valerus watched, transfixed and horrified as Floronius now prepared to remove his subligaria. He could not do it; this was a situation he knew he could not watch. He jumped up, letting the chains hold him back but not causing him to collapse. Jurgen looked his way when he screamed a cursed, and then stopped. His sudden silence even caused Floronius to look up at him momentarily.

Valerus shut his eyes and took a deep breath to compose himself. Outside his world he heard Flavia scream and his breathing turned to short sharp gasps. He called on the name on every god he knew, including Christ, before looking back to the happenings in front of him.

None of it was familiar anymore. The two men and Flavia were just figures, strangers in a red world. This was an anger that he had never given into, not even in the arena or in the face of death. The world had fallen away, as did he as a person, leaving behind red, raw rage.

He screamed and lunged forward. He was forced back by the shackles but there was the sound of a straining link. When he lunged again, the sound was more distinct; in fact, both Jurgen and Floronius looked his way, bewildered.

Once more Valerus took a breath before throwing himself at Floronius. This time the chains on his wrists snapped, tearing the link from the wall. The chain that bound his wrists to his ankles slipped though the broken lead.

He bombarded the man, throwing him off Flavia and hitting him so hard across the face that blood spurted from his mouth and nose simultaneously.

He had no thought of going to Flavia or seeing if she was all right. Now all that was there was the rage, the inner beast that had smelt blood in the air. He hit Floronius again, this time knocking him out before Jurgen came for him.

The man was huge, but Valerus's anger made him twice his size. He jumped to his feet, nearly stumbled due to his fastened ankles but recovered and threw a punch into the man's stomach, knocking the wind out of him. As Jurgen doubled over, Valerus brought him down with an upper cut, striking him so hard under the chin that he was certain he heard his own knuckles crack.

The man went down at his feet.

Valerus stared, feeling the fury of the moment draining out of him and leaving him completely spent of his energy. He slumped to the floor and looked down at his bloodied hands. For a moment he was blank and wondered how the blood had gotten onto them.

"Valerus?"

The voice brought him back to reality. He turned to look over his shoulder and saw Flavia sitting up, desperately trying to cover her breasts, which Floronius had torn her tunica from. Like a dream, he crawled up to her, reached out, and pulled her against him, feeling the tears of sheer exhaustion wet his face.

Flavia clenched his tunic, trembling and sobbing from the ordeal he had just saved her from.

Valerus moved his arms across her shoulder and heard a jingle. Looking down he saw the ends of the chains he had broken hanging from his wrists. It was like a dream. He did not know where the strength had come from or how he had managed it, but the sight of Floronius forcing himself over Flavia had been enough to make Valerus break iron chains and bring down a man nearly twice his size with his bare hands.

"Come, Flavia," he whispered when he got his breath back. The present situation was filtering back into his psyche quickly now. "Let's get out before they wake up. I don't think I'll have the strength to do that again."

She looked down at both men. Floronius was bleeding heavily from his nose. Blood was sprayed across the floor near her feet. "I don't think I want you to," she confessed with a soft smile.

Valerus got his ankles free before removing the broken chains from his wrists, again completely surprised by the fact he had broken through them.

Moving through the villa was easy enough; as long as the two of them walked with an air of importance and the fact that they were meant to be there, no questions were asked. On getting outside, however, things changed suddenly. No slaves were meant to be in the reception room. Immediately on their entry a young man jumped up from the place he was sitting by the wall. "Where did you come from?" he demanded to know, but Valerus moved quickly and bolted to the next room, hearing the calling rise up as he went.

Urgently, Valerus pulled Flavia after him, recognizing the main room that led out. Two more men were running toward them from the rows of pillars. They appeared to be slaves of the villa, but higher up the ladder, as they were shaved and wore clean tunics. They were not armed, which again confirmed this fact.

There was a moment of consideration to explain, but then, remembering what the men had tried to do, he decided to flee. It was not usual for slaves to escape from here, as was the reaction of the pursuers. Flavia could tell that they had no idea what to do if they caught up.

The roadway was the problem. Leading to Herculaneum were more provincial soldiers. On their presence Valerus and Flavia simultaneously turned back to Pompeii, merging in with the crowd of traders and merchants. The festival of Volcanalia provided some cover and people were coming in from the country. They had just passed the tombs and were about to enter the city when more provincial soldiers appeared ahead. Valerus pushed Flavia away from him. "Let's go around them separately," he whispered urgently. "Don't look up at them; just keep walking."

Flavia did not argue but dodged among people to the opposite side of the road, always keeping Valerus in sight as he did her. The soldiers passed between them, not once looking their way, and on entering the city Valerus and Flavia came together again.

"Quick! To the Sarno Gate!"

It was literally on the other end of the city, and going through the narrow streets of Pompeii in the busy hours of the day was a long walk. Valerus glanced up at the sun. It was just past noon.

They followed the Decumanus Superior road for several blocks before turning east down beside an unnamed fresco when more soldiers came into view. From the narrow street of insulas the couple turned up the road leading to Sarno.

They were going to make it; Valerus felt the relief bubbling up from him. That escape had been their last; from here on it was not going to be any more of this.

He had rejoiced too soon. A mounted soldier suddenly came into view before they could even turn into the nearest street. He could not tell if the man had seen them, but Valerus was not going to take the chance; obviously his father was still after him.

Grabbing the woman's hand, he ducked into the nearest street beside the armory and disappeared into the crowd with Flavia pulling in behind him.

Valerus knew one thing for certain: he was not going to see Flavia being taken through the same ordeal again … never again. Seeing what he had and trying to fight the images that still haunted his imagination was enough. What would he have done had the chains not broken under his rage?

He did not want to think that far, he couldn't bear to.

It was getting late, and it had been two days. Lucius had recovered after Floronius's interrogation and now sat in a small slave cell, boiling in his anger. He wanted to protest being kept in a slaves' prison, but then he was found guilty to have helped Valerus in theft and attempted murder. He had confessed. How then could he protest?

He rubbed his arms and winced at a scab on his elbow.

Surely there had to be a law against such brutality. He was, after all, a Roman citizen. He remembered that Floronius was under command of the Roman senate, and that was above even a wealthy citizen.

Lucius was not a man who had taken much interest in the laws of the empire or what was issued by the emperor. It was this ignorance of his own rights that kept him silent.

Marcus came and unbarred Lucius's cell door. The young man was on his feet in an instant. The captain smiled at him. Lucius's face was riddled with bruises and a scar was visible above the left eye.

"I hope this is not another *civilized* method of getting answers," Lucius sneered.

Marcus shook his head. "Pedius has dropped charges," he informed him, obviously pleased by the decision.

Lucius could hardly believe it. "I'm free to go?"

"Yes, but you are not to leave Herculaneum. Unfortunately the gladiator incident is not Pedius's business. There will still be inquiries regarding that, for you as well as Valerus."

"I have no intention of leaving the city," he said. Then he thought about it for a second before asking, "What about Flavia and Valerus? Has Pedius pardoned them as well?"

Marcus smiled and nodded. "We are heading out to Pompeii within the hour to give the command."

"You cannot command the legions from Rome."

"That's why we intend on finding the couple before they do."

Chapter 45

Night fell earlier than Valerus was used to; the world was suddenly dark. He held Flavia on his lap as they sat together in the dirt between two insulas, hidden by debris and empty jugs of clay. Neither could sleep, each kept awake by the breathing of the other. Valerus held the woman against him, frightened to let her go. The past twenty-four hours had come too close to tearing them apart and Valerus didn't want it to happen again … *ever.* It had been a brush too close with death.

Flavia changed her position slightly under his arms and he smiled weakly. He so much wanted to make love to her then; not for the physical pleasure of it, but more to be reminded of that pure union he had felt with her previously. After the way she had been treated earlier, he wanted to touch her gently again, to prove as much to her as to himself that he was not like them.

He caught his breath sharply when remembering the events and the imagination that still haunted him. Someone like Jurgen was not going to let him get away with it, and Valerus knew that the steward would join the hunt with Floronius as far as he could. And what would he do once he caught them? It was not so much himself he was afraid for, it was for Flavia. It was difficult enough just to allow his mind to picture what they wanted to do back at the villa. Now that fear felt terribly threatening.

He could not take the risk of trying to leave the city during daylight or early evening. Once they found a Roman legionnaire and a Pompeian steward unconscious and bleeding in the place two runaway slaves had been, the city would be swarming with guards and provincial soldiers. Already there were many more on the streets than was usual.

Valerus felt at his sides and cursed to himself, realizing he did not have a coin on him; he had left everything in the home of Terentius. At least with the baker, it would come to better use than in the hands of Floronius.

All that work, all that effort, and all that fighting ... for nothing. But he had Flavia and she had been worth it; she was worth all the money he had ever owned.

August 24

They fell asleep for a while and were startled awake by a brief tremor humming beneath the street. The sun had already risen over the rooftops and the world looked a little brighter for both of them. They had made it through the night without being pursued and without getting caught. It was a day closer to freedom.

Valerus looked around the corner; a small fresco was near to them and his hand automatically went to his empty girdle. He was hungry, so was Flavia. They had not eaten a thing for the last twenty-four hours.

He found himself in a position he had hoped never to be: poor, living on the street, and depending on others to ensure his survival. In a normal situation he would have found something to do to earn a little money, but as a fugitive he could not risk the exposure.

But the fact still lay that they had to eat something, anything. He looked around to Flavia who was trying to brush out her long hair with her fingers and then back at the fresco. An elderly woman was buying a fish fillet and a jar of garum.

He decided that it would be worth the chance; it was not as if they had much choice. "Come on, Flavia," he said without looking at her. "Let's get ourselves something to eat."

❧

Terentius was not at the bakery counter, but his wife was, which was actually a relief. The young couple watched the tiny bakery from a hiding place until Valerus carefully pushed Flavia back. "Let me go …" he began but Flavia cut him off by saying, "There are more women than men. You will draw attention. Let me go."

She dusted off her tunica and then walked out into the open. Valerus held his breath as he watched her. She walked with an air of importance like a slave running her duties for the master. She marched right up to the main counter where Terentius's wife recognized her immediately. "Flavia!" she exclaimed. "What a relief to see you … after what's been happening." She looked around for Valerus and when not seeing him looked back at her. "Where is your young lover?"

"He's all right." Flavia smiled then looked to the baking ovens. Fresh bread smelt so good.

"Something to eat?" The woman noticed her gaze. "You look hungry."

With a sigh, Flavia laid her hands on the wood. "I don't have a coin on me," she confessed sadly. "Everything was taken off of us last night."

"I never demanded a coin." She turned around, pulled a fresh loaf from the rack, and handed it to her. "Eat up. I want the two of you to make it out of here before the end of the day."

There was a sundial erected by the fresco. It was midmorning.

⁂

They ate in the lee of some building, tearing pieces off the loaf and sharing it between each other. It was not much of a meal, but it would keep them going for another day. Afterward they casually walked along the busy streets, first blending into the crowd of the forum before slipping down to the gladiator barracks to the Stabiaein Gate.

Soldiers were positioned there and at every other gate they tried to approach. There were also searchers in the streets, more than usual, and the couple kept out of their way as well as they could.

A rumble stretched out across the city followed by the tremor everyone had gotten so used to over the years. It was light; not a single scream rose from the city and not a toddler wailed. Yet this tremor was long lasting, it did not appear to want to end. Valerus took Flavia's hand and settled with her by an empty table in a crowded caupona to wait it out where people were complaining that their goblets inched across the table in the vibration.

Flavia didn't like it. She watched people come and go along with the occasional goblet that reached the table's edge before the owner could grab at it. The air was hot and heavy, even for the inside of a caupona. There was something wrong … very wrong.

Valerus appeared impatient. He was. The vibration was not meant to last this long—it never had. Like Flavia, he felt that this was bizarre and unnatural. If it were not for the guards sitting at every gate, he would have left without delay.

They left the inn when the owner began to make a scene at them sitting at his table without eating anything. The last thing they wanted was the provincial soldiers to be brought down on them.

Uneasy and frustrated, the two walked along the Cardo Maximus and then back toward the forum where they could rely on the crowd to hide them.

It was just past midday and the sun was hot. Not a soul looked their way as they went along their businesses.

A provincial soldier noticed them through the crowd; Valerus recognized him the moment their eyes met; he was one of the men who had brought him and Flavia to the villa the day before.

He yanked Flavia after him as he bolted, limping into the thicker crowd around the temple steps. Behind him an alarm was called and he cursed under his breath when two more soldiers appeared on the temple steps overhead.

He should not have fled; fleeing made him even more visible, but it was a reaction that owed nothing to thought.

Flavia saw three uniformed men trailing when she risked a glance around. The vibration had everyone on edge and many curses were raised as they pushed through the crowd and commencing business.

And then it stopped suddenly and a silence reigned. Flavia also halted and automatically looked toward Vesuvius; she could not tell why. Valerus was at her side. The crowd was standing still also, feeling the deep breath being taken by the atmosphere.

There was suddenly an explosion. Flavia had never heard a sound like it before. It was so loud that she—as well as several others—instinctively dropped to their knees with their hands over their heads. In the distance a child screamed. She lowered her arms when she felt Valerus come down beside her, taking her by the shoulders protectively, but did not get up. Instead she frantically looked around for the cause of the noise when it suddenly repeated, this time longer, as if it was drawn out.

People got up around her and began to mill around. Flavia followed their gazes but rooftops blocked her view.

But then what they were looking at was far higher than rooftops. She and Valerus saw a strange white cloud forming over Vesuvius like a young tree growing and spreading out its branches. Perhaps it was a cloud, but it appeared finer, like when the fog lifted from the sea.

Several people around her were pointing to it, trying to make their own interpretations of what could cause such an unusual phenomenon. The guards who had been pursuing them had also turned around to look. Valerus felt he had to take advantage of the distraction by scampering, but Flavia remained transfixed.

Valerus did not try to explain it, but he did accept immediately how it made him feel. The sense he had had of urgency was now suddenly even greater than before. He cursed the soldiers for keeping them imprisoned in the city. The feeling was unmistakable: they had to get away from here.

From far away, moving under the streets toward them, came a deep low hum.

The ground was still and the air around them seemed uncomfortably heavy and silent. No birds chirped and the whole city seemed to hold its breath. A dog howled somewhere, but the city was not used to this kind of silence, especially during the busy hours of the day.

The noise began with the deep hum of earlier and increased in volume until it became a deafening roar. The ground suddenly jolted away violently. Valerus fell back; Flavia screamed, so did most other woman and even several men. The ground rippled beneath their feet, swaying walls. In the distance she heard something collapse with the rumble.

The sound that followed was unlike anything she—or anyone—had ever heard; it was like a rushing river, only louder and spitting. Flavia threw her hands over her ears but still heard the noise in every detail. People around her were shouting and pointing skyward. Valerus looked up from where he lay, following their points.

The mountain was burning; it was gushing flame and smoke from its summit. The force of the explosion had thrown over toddlers and several small fresco awnings. Two horses, bridled but riderless, galloped past them and a moment later he heard the wail of a child who had been trampled. Nearby another horse was frantically trying to free itself from its harness while people broke into blind panic, screaming as they dashed for their homes and loved ones. In one short moment, the whole city had turned into chaos.

When Flavia saw the giant reddish-black cloud rising from the mountain, her face paled. She threw both hands over her mouth to stop herself from screaming. The ground once again returned to the earlier vibration, now created by the sheer force of the eruption, and the sun above her pounded down. She began to shake; the shock was too much, too unexpected.

Valerus went up to her and took her by the shoulders. The guards were nowhere to be seen, but suddenly Valerus felt an even greater threat.

Carefully he carried her to the nearest wall and sat her up against it, keeping the two of them out of the way of the crowds now running for every street that branched from the forum. She was catching her breath in quick short gasps, shaking when she looked back at the mountain.

The black cloud was rising even higher now, becoming lost behind the clouds. The darkness of it was red tinged near the base, blending into a darker maroon and then gray and black as it rose. Every now and again there was a sharp spark of light blasting from the mountain top.

Flavia had faith in her belief in the things Melani had taught her. She was certain she understood human nature which went from merciful to bloodthirsty. But, at this moment looking upon the strength of a mountain, even she no longer knew what to believe.

Chapter 46

Valerus nearly had to drag Flavia from the streets to one of the nearest insulas by the sit-in bakeries. The door was locked and no answer came from his desperate knock. So instead he used all the strength he had left to break it open. The house seemed to be abandoned; there was no life or movement inside except for that vibration in the floor under their feet. The owners had probably left the day the wells had dried up. He gently laid Flavia down on a carpet near the door. She was shaking uncontrollably, as if very cold. He took a tablecloth and covered her with it, hoping it would keep her warm. He looked out the window and noticed horses on the loose, running past in blind terror, some with riders on their backs and others empty. His heart raced; he didn't know what was happening, he could not understand it. The mountain had gone mad.

He wondered what had happened to the guards outside, but as he looked out onto the streets so many people were running toward the shelter of their homes that he was forced to believe that they too had fled.

"Valerus?" he heard Flavia call him in a harsh whisper, "Valerus ..."

He knelt beside her and raised her head a little. She was breathing quickly and irregularly and he saw the way she struggled to speak.

"What is it?" he asked, trying to sound calm.

"What's happening?" she gasped and held onto his arm, "What's happening?"

Valerus shook his head. He didn't know what or how to answer her. How could he if he didn't know himself? "I don't know," he whispered hoarsely.

Flavia heard the commotion outside and sat up. He took her hands in his and rubbed them.

"I'm cold," she whispered.

"Then keep yourself covered." He went behind her and covered her shoulders with the cloth again.

Another loud bang echoed in the room and the tremor that followed was more a monotonous hum, which did not cease or change its tone. Flavia's hands began to shake so much that Valerus had to clench them even tighter before they slipped away.

"Try to calm down, Flavia," he said gently but firmly. "It's going to be all right."

Flavia saw the corners of his mouth rise into a reassuring smile, so she tried her best to smile back, though not very successfully.

A shadow suddenly fell over them. Flavia gasped. The light shimmered for a second as if the sun tried to fight before drawing dark. Valerus got up and went to the door. The sun was blocked out by a thick, dark cloud. Curious, he stepped out and walked among the people who still ran about fearfully. He stood in the middle of the road, just staring up at the mountain and the sky above him. His heart raced like never before; he could feel it throbbing against his chest. The black cloud had expanded from high above the mountain and now moved to cover the city. It blocked out the sun entirely; there was not even a faint glow behind the darkness, the cloud was moving incredibly fast, faster than any usual cloud ever did. It loomed over him like the shadow of night after the sun had set.

And it was … raining?

Gray flakes had fallen on his shoulders and as he brushed them away, noticing how quickly they crumbled into nothing. With a frown he stretched out his open hand, palm up, and let the flakes trickle onto it followed by small pumice stones. They were weightless, but he felt that they were warm. When enough had accumulated, he clenched his hand into a fist and brought it to his nose. The smell of sulfur came to him; it permeated the surrounding air.

He put his hand over his mouth and nose and watched the ash fall more gently than raindrops.

The mountain began to roar again, making the earth tremble so violently that Valerus swayed across the flagstones while nearby runners stumbled. The amount of ash that accumulated on the fallen passersby was alarming. He returned to Flavia, coughing under his breath. He tried to rub his eyes clean, but the more he rubbed them the more they watered.

Flavia raised her head from where it rested and looked at him. He saw the way her eyes screamed for reassurance. He sat beside her and rubbed her shoulders again. He didn't know what to tell her to make her feel better. The world had gone mad, and everything was out of control, for him as much as for her. She had stopped shaking, but her skin was still cold and pale.

The sky was growing darker outside as the cloud kept moving farther and farther across the city, blocking out more of the sky as it went. Mount Vesuvius kept spurting flame and stone from its summit, and every time it paused a large earthquake followed along with more ash ejected into the air. The steam that was still building up turned the magma into froth, and this was also being emitted as pumice along with the ash, causing the air around it to become hotter and denser by the minute.

Valerus felt the urge to run, but Flavia was in shock, holding him back. She hardly moved, gasped for air, and spoke little. Whenever there was an earthquake, she would start shaking again and he couldn't move until she did.

He sat beside her, rubbing her shoulders, arms, and back, trying to keep her as warm as possible.

The shadow changed to darkness. Valerus watched the falling ash through the open door; it was as gentle as petals while the pumice fell like hail. The wind was from the northwest. Did that mean that none of this was happening at Herculaneum? Had Herculaneum's sky grown as dark as here? He thought of his parents, his sister, and Lucius, wondering how they were taking it.

Lucius ran to his insula where his helper, Protia, was standing outside the stall and staring up from the street toward the mountain. He came up to her and grabbed her by the shoulder, trying to support himself.

"The mountain's gone mad!" he announced as he stared.

"The gods are angry," the woman commented with unusual calmness.

The streets were crowded and many heads blocked their view, but they could see the giant black cloud and flames being thrown up from the top with incredible force. He felt the northwesterly wind brush his hair and saw the black cloud moving toward them. The sky above Herculaneum was becoming hazy and the air began to smell of sulfur. He noticed the blackness raining down in the southeast.

It was over Pompeii, he suddenly realized. He hoped that Valerus and Flavia had managed to leave.

Many citizens began to pack their bags and evacuate, but many more refused to leave the safety of their homes. Lucius didn't know what to do. He wanted to run, never mind leave, but the law of the senate, he could not break it. What about all that?

Many carts and chariots were packed along the road with the horses struggling to break loose. He listened to the echo of their neighing; dogs were howling.

He hoped Flavia was far from the mountain. He couldn't stand the thought of her being in any danger. Despite knowing that Valerus loved her and would take care of her, he remembered Floronius, his beating, and what he had confessed. If Pedius could get to them before the soldiers, he would offer Flavia and his son refuge. If he got to them too late …

Lucius saw some ash and pumice fall onto his sandals. He looked at it for a second before shaking it off. It was then that he heard hoof beats coming down the street. He looked up quickly and jumped aside as a crazed horse galloped past.

Lucius looked around him frantically and then at Protia. "Let's get things packed," he told her.

"You want to leave?" She followed after him. "But I thought you were not …"

He looked at her so sharply that she fell silent. "The mountain is making the decisions now."

"But they will know where you've gone."

"And where am I going?"

She did not answer him, as it was getting clear that he was not going to Octavianum and to his mother.

Lucius nodded her direction. "We are heading west. To Vulcan with the laws!"

From across the bay the phenomenon could also be seen, though with less fear. Young Gaius was sitting at his table in his bedroom upstairs, catching up with his studies that he had neglected for the last few days. He had an excellent view over the bay with Herculaneum visible on the far shore. For the moment, however, he was concentrateing on his documents, making notes of them as he went along.

Footsteps approached his door. He did not even look up when his mother looked into the room at him; he had learnt to recognize her pace over the years. "Gaius, are you seeing this?"

Now he looked at her. "What's that, Mother?"

She rolled her eyes and walked in, making for the window. "Come look at this."

Gaius got up and came around to look; his pace slowed when he noticed the black cloud over Vesuvius and stopped dead. The cloud itself was unusual in size and appearance; as it came from the summit, he best viewed it as an umbrella pine, branches splitting out from a long trunk. He could see, even from a distance, how the black was rising steadily up from the earth to behind the clouds. When he held his breath he was nearly certain he could hear a distant rumble.

He turned to his mother, who was still staring. "Has my uncle seen this?"

She could not break her gaze away but shook her head. "I'm just about to tell him."

Gaius took her by the arm. "Come ..."

Pliny was reclined in the peristyle; it was his routine to have a rest after the afternoon meal. A slave was in the process of filling his goblet of wine when Gaius and his mother entered from the ambulatory.

"Pliny!" the woman called, "have you seen this?" She pointed in the direction across the bay.

The elder only had to look up to see the strange shape over the rooftops. At once he pushed the documents he had been reading aside and rushed to the portico to get a better view. Around them people were also pointing in the way of Herculaneum. After staring awhile, he called for his shoes and then rushed to the upper floors to get a better view.

Gaius came up behind him, looked over the bay again, and shook his head. He had never seen anything like it. It was suddenly unclear where the smoke was rising from. He had been so sure at first sight that it was from Vesuvius, but now suddenly the darkness of falling clouds had blocked the better view. In some places, it actually appeared white, but dirty and blotchy.

"I've never seen anything like it!" Pliny announced to his nephew. He turned to a slave who was hovering near his shoulder. "How many boats standing?"

"Your galley and another ready for your command, master."

"Prepare them both. I will require the escort."

The slave bowed and left to abide to his request. Pliny smiled at his nephew. "This deserves an investigation." He smiled to him. "What say you, nephew? Up for a little adventure?"

Gaius looked back at the mountain and heard for a moment a distant roar. His uncle had studied many books and written even more of his own. Pliny enjoyed going out to places no one else had ventured. For this he had had great experiences even in his younger years as a soldier. This was the reason why Gaius was rather ashamed that he knew he was not like his uncle; in fact, in relation to his uncle he considered himself a coward.

Slowly he shook his head. "I would rather continue with my studies." His uncle had, after all, given him a lot of writing work to do.

Chapter 47

Flavia was talking with less difficulty after the first hour and the look in her eyes told Valerus that she was going to be all right, but she was still pale and cold to the touch. For this reason he did not mention the urgency he had to flee. She was thirsty, but there was no jar or water supply in any of the rooms. Most houses usually had some form of water storage, but, as the house had been abandoned for at least two days, there was nothing but furniture. He took the chance to rest his leg, which was aching terribly around the knee; he had strained it too much over the last couple of days.

The pumice and ash were increasing in the streets as another hour passed and were piling up in the corners. After a while the screaming seemed to ease slightly so Valerus stepped out to see if anything had changed since the last time he looked, but the only difference was that it was darker and …

… the ash was nearly fifteen inches in depth. He could not believe it.

He knelt down and felt it. It was warm, almost comfortably so. The pumice fell like light hail, harmlessly bouncing off him in small chunks. He took up a handful of it with the ash and smelt the sulfur burn the inside of his nose. He coughed a few short coughs and then rubbed his hands clean. The mountain hadn't stopped roaring and sending black smoke into the sky. The ground shifted slightly under his feet, humming to the roar of the mountain. It was loud but nearly hypnotic.

Instinctively the young man looked up at the sun to estimate what time of day it was, but it had been blackened out. He swallowed hard and looked all around him, realizing how itchy his throat was. He took a breath to cough, but, as he did so, particles of ash and pumice filled his lungs. The more he coughed, the less he could breathe. He put his tunic over his nose and mouth to protect himself and then realized how dangerous it was keeping Flavia here any longer.

"What is it?" Flavia asked when she saw him enter with his eyes watering uncontrollably.

"We have to get out of the city!" he gasped between breaths, "It's not safe here, Flavia, the ash is drowning the city! It's difficult to breathe out there!"

"But what about the soldiers? Valerus, they are watching the gates!"

"In this?" He looked at her. "I'm going to get a horse. They can't stop a frantic animal."

"I'm coming with you."

"No, you're not." He held her down as she tried to get up. "You're in shock!"

"Don't leave me!" Flavia protested, unwilling to be left behind.

Valerus smiled as he crouched down and touched her cheek softly. "I'll come back for you," he whispered. "Surely you know that by now." He kissed her gently before getting up, but as he turned to walk off she grasped his hand.

"Be careful," she whispered. She let her hand drop onto the tablecloth, which covered her chest and legs, but as she watched him leave and saw the way he covered his mouth and nose, she wondered if she should have let him go. She felt like getting up and running after him, but her legs didn't feel able to carry her weight. The roaring from outside made her shiver and she pulled the cover over her shoulders in her effort to ease her fear.

Valerus hurried down the street. He remembered stables in the south block near the home of Proculus. Automatically his hand went to his side and he cursed when he remembered that he did not have a coin on him. He hissed under his breath; he was not going to let that stop him from getting a horse.

As he moved through the smaller streets, he began wondering where everyone was. It all seemed deserted, but that quickly changed. When he reached the main street leading to Proculus's front door, he saw hundreds of people running in all directions, carrying furniture, household goods, and clothes. Toddlers needed to be carried through the accumulating ash; some lay limp in the arms of their parents. The screams echoed in his head; he covered his ears momentarily, hoping he would not have to remember it.

Looting had started earlier than Valerus had anticipated.

Then what of the horses? What if they had been stolen as well?

He ran down the street before the home of Proculus, starting to feel nervous that he had left Flavia alone. When he reached the stable yard, he noticed most of the doors open. He ran up to the nearest one. It was empty.

"No!" he shouted in fear and desperation as he ran to the next to see if any horse was still there. They had all been taken and the empty stalls stood open. Pumice was floating on the water of the troughs.

He felt on the inside of the wall for the bridles, but they also were gone. The blood rushed from his head: they had waited too long. He looked toward the blackened sky and covered his mouth and nose again. The ash and pumice were accumulating at an alarming rate; he had only been standing still for a few seconds and his shoulders were already being covered in the gray rain. He shook the pumice from his hair.

The mountain roared again, but the young man didn't move. He was wondering what he should do; he didn't want to accept that he had come all this way for no reason. He ran through his options only to realize he had none, except to escape the city on foot. He would have to carry Flavia if he had to. He had seen shock occur in opponents in the arena as well as criminals sentenced to death. He had experienced it himself during his first fight when a retiarius had cut him along the arm. Perhaps that was where his fear for the fishermen fighters was first born.

It was the same power that fueled him as in the villa the previous day, the power that made him break chains. He could not surrender to the terror; not with Flavia in her state. One of them needed to find an escape from the city before it was too late.

And time was, to Valerus's inner feeling, running faster that it usually did.

He put his hand against the wall as if hoping he would get some reassurance from it and looked around once more. To his sudden surprise there was a bay horse standing in its stall, watching him calmly and flicking its ears about. He couldn't believe he had missed it, but he quickly snapped out of his surprise and went up to it.

On his approach, though, the bay horse suddenly leapt at him, baring its teeth and hitting its front legs against the stable door. Valerus quickly backed off. It hadn't occurred to him why anyone hadn't taken such a fine animal, but clearly the horse was mad or simply petrified with the strange turn of events. The closer he got, the more aggressive the creature became. He put out his hand in the hope that the animal would smell it and become accustomed to his scent, but instead the horse threw its head high and whinnied fiercely; it didn't want humans near it. Valerus heard the way it pounded its hoof against the ground. He looked at the horse; it was really an impressive creature with its large head and a long black forelock falling over its eyes. He wanted to feel for a bridle but the animal kept snapping at his arm when he brought it forward. There was no way he was taking this horse; the animal had made it quite clear to him. The man gazed around for other locked doors, but they were all open with the promise of being empty.

The sound of looters worried him; Flavia was still alone. Maybe he could quickly try the other stables, but as he began to walk away he heard the horse behind him snorting. He turned to see the magnificent creature looking at him with his ears flicking back and forth nervously while it bobbed its head.

Did you see the fear in its eyes?

Valerus couldn't leave the creature. He felt it unfair that the horse was given no chance to flee. Man had locked it up, taken it away from its home.

He turned back and the animal quickly bared its teeth again. As unobtrusively as he could, he put out his hand to open the latch and the horse backed away into the shadows as he did, but then suddenly charged at him again. Valerus left his shirt over his mouth and nose as he crouched and tried to open the latch while staying as low as he could. He could see underneath how the door was being battered by the large hooves on the other side. The horse tried to snap at him again but Valerus was too low for it to reach him. He got the latch between his fingers and pulled back the lock. The horse charged it at such speed that Valerus didn't have a chance to jump clear. The stable door smashed open against the side of his head, knocking him flat into the ash and pumice.

He was knocked out for a while for when he opened his eyes a slit, ash was laid gently over him like a blanket and pumice stones lined his body. He raised the upper part of his body, coughing frantically, and lifted himself to his knees, covering his entire face with his tunic as the powder burned his eyes. Blood trickled from his eyebrow and the rough wooden door had scraped the skin off his right cheek. He felt the warm liquid run down the side of his face and brushed it away with his fingers, then looked down at the blood, estimating that he could not have been unconscious for more than a few minutes, despite the amount of ash.

He got up and steadied himself on the nearest wall.

Then a thought struck him: Proculus was bound to own horses, even if only up at the villa. But the villa was off bounds; he could not go anywhere near it. He was, however, only a block away from Proculus and Asilia.

He headed up the street when suddenly he stopped for no reason he could explain. His eyes turned to the exploding mountain up ahead as he heard a strange whistling in the air. He looked around, confused at where the sound was coming from, and then noticed something in the air in the direction of the mountain. He didn't know what it was but he instinctively threw himself to the ground, fearing falling rocks. The flying debris passed only a few feet over his head and smashed the flagstones a short distance ahead in a cloud of ash and pumice.

He looked out for more, but the world around him suddenly seemed a lot darker. There was no more sky, no more natural light except the occasional flash that Valerus could not pinpoint. Flames pierced the darkness like shooting stars; the red glow illuminated the dark summit of the mountain and even from here Valerus, through the heavy ash fall, could see the dark cloud rolling across the mountain top and along its sides.

The urgency returned as he pulled himself up and quickened his pace. The ash was falling heavily now, tinged red from the burning background. Valerus kept his hand over his mouth and nose, trying desperately not to cough too hard when the ash scratched the back of his throat. He saw some people coughing frantically as they went by, which only resulted in worse attacks.

Like heavy snow, Valerus thought as he moved through the crowd; *snow with hail.* It fell in some places in tight clusters. His eyes watered in the fumes that were carried with it.

In the distance, another piece of smoking debris smashed in the crowd; he heard the screaming that followed.

No guards were stationed outside the house and the street was filled with crazed and frightened people. He took the chance and hammered on the door.

The relief he felt when the door was opened was great, but not as great as the surprise when seeing that the man who had answered it was Jurgen. It only took an instant for the two of them to recognize each other and a second later Valerus turned to run … and stumbled.

Jurgen's speed did not compare to that of an injured man and he caught Valerus by his tunic, yanking him back and throwing him into the house across the mosaic floor. Valerus picked himself up onto his elbows and heard the door being shut behind him. He cursed when his wounded leg prevented him from getting up.

Jurgen gave him a hand, reaching down to take him from the back collar of his tunic and pulling him up as if he weighed nothing at all. Once on his feet, Valerus took the opportunity of surprise to spin around and hit the man across the jaw.

It had an effect. Jurgen let him go and stumbled back a pace. The few seconds it took Valerus to contemplate hitting him again or running were enough for the giant of a man to recover and hit Valerus so hard that he fell back into the atrium. Blood was seeping from his nose when he looked up at the advancing Jurgen. He was smiling and Valerus could see he was missing a tooth, probably since their escape from the villa the previous day. Jurgen was not going to show any mercy, he never would have in any case.

The young man tried to get to his feet, but again Jurgen picked him up. "Proculus put me in charge of his home," Jurgen announced cheerfully, his face an inch from his. "He told me to *deal* with trespassers." This time his punch was like the wrath of the gods, spinning Valerus a full turn before he landed hard on his chest.

He spat blood across the mosaic.

"That's it?" he heard Jurgen say from behind and above him. "That's how you put up a fight?"

Valerus felt himself trembling; he did not have the strength to fight this man, at least not this time. He wasn't sure what had fueled his strength and rage the previous time, probably the fear of watching Flavia being hurt, but that strength was absent here. He realized his weakness without a weapon in the face of a man of such size. There was no way he could win this.

He brought up enough courage to turn over and look up. Jurgen was standing at his feet, clenching his hands in a fist. When Valerus made no attempt to get up, he opened his arms to him. "That's it? That's all you have?"

Valerus looked at the blood on his hand and snorted. He looked up at Jurgen who appeared surprised at his submissive behavior. "I know when I've lost a fight," Valerus muttered as he pulled himself up along the nearest pillar.

Jurgen was a little puzzled; he was not used to opponents surrendering; usually they whimpered or fought back in mad rage. This man was doing neither.

From the awkwardness of the moment, he hit Valerus again—it was all he knew he could do. This time the blow came across the jaw, throwing the young man back again before he slumped to the floor.

Helen, Cotti, and Luci were following the mistress across the atrium and up into the library. The ground rumbled beneath them; several scrolls and documents had already toppled from their shelves. They were set to work recollecting all the scrolls and documents and packing them into cylinders and then crates. It was a lot of work to be done; the library was the keeper of a lot of records which the family had praised for years.

Rectina looked on the work before she too began to help in the safe packing of the information she found so valuable. Pedius had left only a day before and she was not surprised or worried that he had not yet returned. He had promised he would return with Valerus by the first *calends*, which was in little less than a week. For now she decided to make her presence as productive as possible.

Harolde joined the women and began to help with the packing; it was the most he could do to help the woman who would soon be his. As they slipped papyrus scrolls into cylinders and handed them over to Helen to be packed in the crates, the roar of the mountain suddenly shook the very foundation of the villa. Luci screamed briefly before it returned to the monotonous vibration.

Procimus came into the room carrying a lamp. It was not completely necessary, as the sky was still fairly clear to the west and north, but the black cloud was fighting to block out the light and they all knew it was only a matter of time before it did. Ash was falling outside, but only lightly without cause for alarm, and yet Rectina was desperate to get the library evacuated.

"How will all this ever be moved, mistress?" Helen asked as she sealed the first crate. "It will take many horses."

Rectina stopped what she was doing and took a step back to look upon their work so far. The slave girl was right; Alaine had gone down to the stable yards along with Moe, but what would three horses help? What if the animals were frightened and frantic? They had, after all, every right to be. The villa was set a good distance from the town, which meant a farther way to travel and less opportunity for help to be offered.

Then the answer came to her. She looked around to Procimus and spoke quickly. "I want you to send a message to Master Pliny in Misenum. Tell him we cannot evacuate the library by land. We need his help coming in from the sea. I am certain he will agree that some of the documents here are not worth putting to any risk."

Chapter 48

Flavia felt her heart thumping in her chest and was unable to bring it down. It exhausted and frightened her. It must have been hours since the eruption began, yet she still felt distressed and floating. Nothing around her felt real and the world appeared to have lost its color; it all felt like a dream to her. Her thumping heart was all that kept her in focus of what was happening outside.

Screams were still coming in from the streets, but there was no way Flavia could see much farther than the door frame. The inside of the room was shadowed black and cold while the door opened to another dim yet darker world beyond. Both were equally dark, but in different ways. Against the blackness, she could see the falling of ash and pumice.

There was another roar from the mountain.

Valerus ought to have been back by now. How long had it been? By the speed the darkness set in over the city, it was difficult for her to estimate how much time had passed since he had left, but whether it was less or more than a couple of hours, she felt the fear setting in.

She forced herself up, feeling how all the blood dropped from her head and nearly brought her to faint. She grabbed the edge of the nearest table and caught her breath. When she looked up again, the world appeared a little clearer.

She reached the door and watched, as if from a dream, people scampering through the pumice-covered street carrying what possessions they could. She could not believe how much had fallen; in the corners of the street and buildings it had already accumulated well past her knee.

She ought to stay; she knew that was the sensible thing to do, but to what end? There was no way they would find each other in the chaos that surrounded the city now and Flavia was sure that the guards manning the gates had fled in the panic.

She could not believe that she had just thought that. She could not leave, not without Valerus. But she could not sit here waiting for him either, it was just as dangerous as having to go out to look for him.

She took the tablecloth and wrapped it around her, using one corner as a hood and the other to hold against her mouth and nose; she saw that most people outside had done the same using blankets.

At least like this, she concluded, if she were to die, it would be in search of him.

Valerus opened his eyes and blinked in the gloom. It was dark, but a shadow danced against the wall from a flickering flame. He didn't have the courage to move just yet; the world was spinning under him and he felt the empty bile rise in his throat. His thoughts were a mess; he had visions and dreams of fire, boiling water, and the earthquake of seventeen years ago that shattered the better part of Pompeii.

He groaned, bringing both hands to his head, and tried to recollect his thoughts.

Slowly, frightened that Jurgen was in the vicinity, he moved his hands in under his head, making his movements as inconspicuous as possible.

Somewhere outside there was a scream from a man, which brought Valerus frightening thoughts.

Looters? What if they found Flavia alone in a deserted insula? They were capable of anything.

He turned over, felt the numbing throb of his head, and tried to pull himself up. It was then he noticed that his feet had been bound with a length of rope. With a curse more of frustration than surprise, he reached down to undo the poorly fastened knots when a large foot fell at his side. Valerus did not even need to look around to see who it was.

"There's nowhere for you to go, Valerus." Jurgen's voice sounded terribly cheerful in the face of Vesuvius's wrath.

The young man stopped his attempt and leaned back on his hands. He was about to comment on his statement when Jurgen continued by saying, "Floronius is on his way. He's better at getting answers than I am."

"Yes," Valerus nodded angrily, "I remember. And what, pray, do you have to ask me?"

"Where are you hiding the girl?"

"In that?" Valerus gestured his head toward the window where dark silhouettes were running past. "How could I even know?"

Jurgen came down on his legs beside Valerus; the young man could feel his breath in his ear. "We all want to leave here, and the only thing holding us back is that woman of yours. Cooperate, and we may all leave the city alive."

"And what will you do with her?" Valerus's tone had suddenly become sarcastic.

Jurgen reclined himself on the nearest couch without a word. He was smiling though, which was an answer in itself. Valerus nodded to himself and then looked around the house. "Where is the family?"

Jurgen was in the process of pouring himself a goblet of wine. "They left a while back to go to the temple to make a few offerings." He raised his goblet. "Wine?"

The young man could not believe it; he had never felt more like running than now; he had to get away from the city, and it was not so much to get away from the senate as it was to get away from the mountain. He doubted that the gods could offer any help.

A door shut from farther in the house and a figure approached. Jurgen looked up and then got to his feet as Floronius stepped into the lamplight. He was in the process of dusting ash from his clothes. The two men locked gazes; Valerus saw the bruise on his cheek and the spark in his eyes. He had seen it before. Some gladiators he fought had had that gleam in their eyes; it was the gleam of insanity, the one which refused defeat. Those opponents were often reckless and were disqualified before the second round. They broke the rules and Valerus had nearly been killed by them without judgment from the onlookers.

Floronius had suddenly become far more dangerous than he already was.

Flavia stumbled through the crowded pumice-covered streets, being shoved from both ways. She did not know Pompeii or where the stables had been built; her best definition of the town came from the homes of Proculus and Terentius. The villa where she had lived for a couple of weeks she knew, like Valerus, was off bounds. Also, she refused to leave the city without him.

She squinted ahead of her. It was terribly dark now. The ash was like a gray wall dropping ahead of her, the pumice coming down like heavy rain. The mountain roared over the city but there was nothing but a faint glow to the north. She was using the tablecloth as a hood and protection against the air. It stung, she noted for the first time suddenly. Looking down, she saw that the pumice now reached her thighs.

Behind her there was a whistle. She spun around when a rock projectile smashed through a roof a short way up the road, followed by frantic screaming. She tried to look skyward, but that was impossible with the falling ash. Her eyes were already watering.

A hand suddenly grabbed her by the arm. "Flavia?" a familiar voice asked desperately.

She blinked at the figure holding her. He too was using a large piece of cloth to try to protect himself from the falling debris. It took her a few seconds to recognize the figure shadowed in darkness by the hood.

It was Pedius and behind him was a larger figure.

She lashed out immediately, her knee striking him in the groin. He let her go with a wince and she fled, stumbling clumsily through the rising ash and pumice. She heard him call her name but did not respond; she was not going to be caught here away from Valerus; she refused it. Having been separated from him before was enough and she promised herself that it would not happen again—never again.

She nearly stumbled over a large soft object, and her imagination made her cringe. She regained her feet and ran. Another hand suddenly grabbed her, this time on her shoulder, and yanked her back into the arms of a man. She screamed and bit into his hand.

"Stop it, Flavia!" another familiar voice cried as she positioned to lash out with her leg. It was a voice she had not heard since Herculaneum. She looked up and recognized Marcus. He was pale even in the dark and it was clear that he had not shaved that morning. Pedius was joining up behind him as he pulled her into a quieter street.

Flavia shook her head desperately. "No, Marcus, please." She looked at Pedius when he looked her way. "Not now, please!"

"Where is Valerus?" Pedius demanded coldly. "Where is my son, woman?"

"I don't know!" she shouted to be heard above the roar. It sounded as if it was getting closer.

"You don't know?" Marcus frowned.

"He was looking for horses! He has not come back."

The two men looked at each other before Pedius gestured to Marcus. Flavia could not believe it when he released her. She soothed her arm and turned to Pedius. The questioning look in her gaze made Pedius catch his breath and say, "We are both looking for someone we love then. Where could he be? Let's find him so that we can go home."

Flavia's jaw dropped open. "What? You can't fight the word of the senate!"

"That's why we must find him before they do."

"They already have. We only escaped from them yesterday."

Pedius did not like to admit it, but he had some admiration toward the slave girl when he thought about their escape. There was a certain air about her that forced him to smile.

"Get down!" Marcus suddenly threw himself across the two of them. Flavia felt a swish of hot air come past her face and felt the flakes of stone cut her along the cheek as another rock hit the street beside them. If it had not been for Marcus, the debris would have hit her across the neck. The sound of it was muffled by the mountain that was roaring again to the north.

She was pulled from the ash and pumice, coughing frantically. Her cloth was wrapped across her neck, mouth, and nose, and when she looked up she saw it was Pedius who was helping her up.

"Where would Valerus go? Where *could* he go?"

"Why are you doing this?" she demanded of him. "You wanted to get rid of me! It's because of me that we are exiled here!"

"We want our son back!" Pedius snapped. "We want him back and we are prepared to give him anything!"

Her gaze went down to Pedius's girdle. He smiled and pulled his knife from its sheath just as Flavia took a small step back. She was so surprised when he passed it to her. "I am not going to hurt you, Flavia," he told her as she took it. "That is a promise."

⁂

Valerus coughed. The ash and pumice were getting into the house from the compluvium and covering the ground. He had been pressed to the floor and was kept there. Floronius's questioning was more brutal than it had been in Herculaneum. For one, he was using none other than his hands, and Valerus was one punch away from losing consciousness. For the moment, the soldier was postponing it, but he was keeping Valerus against the floor, each breath drawing in some of the ash into his system.

"Well, Valerus?" he asked softly.

The young man shifted his head enough to speak. There was blood on his teeth. "One more punch," he muttered, "and I won't even know who Flavia is anymore."

Floronius rolled his eyes. "I want to go home, Valerus," he muttered softly. "I feel an urgency to leave here, but I am under orders: I am to return with the Christian girl. You are simply a bonus."

"Then go look for her!" Valerus hissed and then winced when the soldier pulled his head up by his hair.

"As long as we are looking for her, your life will be made into a hell!"

"Floronius!" Jurgen called from the main atrium.

Floronius threw the young man down at his feet and walked across the tablinium to where Jurgen was standing near the open doorway. The ash was falling in a thick sheet, a lot of it spilling into the entrance passage. The pumice now reached nearly a meter in depth.

"Soon we're not going to be getting away from here!" Jurgen said to him.

"You can't see anything!" the man cursed.

Three figures appeared in front of them; they had not even seen them approach in the dark. Two men, and the third merged into the shadows.

Flavia caught her breath; thank God for the darkness. She had managed to recognize Jurgen and Floronius before they did her. She covered her face with her tunica to keep the ash from her breath and pulled the tablecloth over her head.

Floronius and Jurgen turned to the two men, studying them carefully so as to label them as Flavia's accomplices. "You are?" Jurgen demanded.

Pedius was concerned; he knew how politics worked and he knew the trouble he could have if there was any indication that he was going against the laws of Rome. He was also aware that Valerus would never return home if Flavia was captured. For the moment all he could do was play the game by the senate's laws, and the first was diplomacy.

Pedius invited himself in, brushing the ash from his toga and then removing the cloth from his mouth and nose. Floronius recognized Pedius Cascus of Herculaneum immediately. He stepped back respectfully and gestured him into the atrium.

Pedius did not wait for any invitation. He walked across the house to the light flickering near the end of the master bedroom. He stopped when he saw the figure prostrated on the floor in the middle of the room.

Valerus looked up; blood had dried beneath his nose, his cheek was raw, and there was a cut above his eye. Pedius had never seen his son in such a state—even during his occupation as a gladiator—and again he felt that same remorse when he realized that it had been his decision that caused his son to be like this.

The surprise of seeing his father forced Valerus into a sitting position and he felt how the blood drained from his head and blurred his vision momentarily when he did. Pedius seated himself on the couch beside him.

"Valerus," Pedius said as he shook his head slowly. There was compassion in his voice.

"Father," Valerus greeted him back, but the son refused to say anything more. After all, the father did not deserve to be spoken to.

With a sigh, as if reconsidering his actions one last time, Pedius picked up his toga and threw it across his shoulder. The young man did not look up at him; he did not feel his father had earned it.

Then, to his complete surprise, Pedius came down to his level, squatting down on his knees in front of him and resting his hand on his shoulder. Valerus was certain he saw a shimmer in his eyes.

"I'm sorry." Pedius's voice trembled when he said it.

Valerus stared, feeling himself slipping from reality a moment before the words drew him back again. "What?"

"I'm sorry," Pedius repeated. "I really am. We want you to come home."

"I'm not leaving without Flavia."

Momentarily Pedius looked over his shoulder to where Floronius was speaking to Marcus in the atrium. He looked back at Valerus. "She's yours."

Now Valerus's head shot up.

"She's yours." Pedius smiled at his expression. "It will take the senate some convincing, but I am, after all, an aristocrat."

Valerus shook his head; it could not be real. If it was, then it meant that everything was simple again. He could have Flavia? No more running? He could go home?

"I mean it," Pedius continued as the questions began to rotate. "Your mother and I have had enough of worrying about you, first as a gladiator and then as a fugitive. Come home. We'll give you whatever you want."

"I just want the woman I love, Father." Valerus felt tears come to his eyes. No moment, no desire, had ever been simpler. The relief he experienced was beyond anything he could have thought or imagined. It was the relief that brought tears to his eyes and erased all shame of revealing them.

He wept; the strain and resistance from the last few weeks drained out of him in racking sobs. Pedius came forth to take him in his arms when the distant hum suddenly became a loud torrent roar.

It happened so fast that even Valerus was uncertain of what actually happened. There was a crack and a loud roar unlike that which had come from the mountain. The flame beside them was blown out and ash suddenly filled the air they breathed.

From the atrium both men cried out, but they were cut off sharply.

Valerus felt the weight come over him and then darkness like he had never known it before.

Pliny was getting impatient. The earth was completely blackened to the east … and spreading. He was beginning to suspect that the cloud was going to reach them; people had begun to pack their belongings and flee northward.

"You think this wise?" the helmsman called down to him. He had already taken his position on the stern of the ship. It was one of the sailboats; the dozen or so oars were used mainly for the extra speed, but the wind was well in their favor.

Pliny looked up from the ramp; even from a distance his face was twisted with concern.

"Everyone is fleeing! Why hurry to the place from where everyone is hastily leaving?"

Pliny had a moment's flashback to his years in the military. He had lived and fought across the empire; northern Europe, the fields of Germania, and then south into the African province. His reputation and status lifted him quickly to a naval admiral and any time he was permitted to return to Rome he was at the side of Emperor Vespasian. His demise appointed Pliny as prefect of the Roman navy and now he had been settled for a rest in peaceful waters … and it was boring.

He looked back across the bay to the black cloud hugging the earth; it had swallowed the coastline of Herculaneum. On very clear nights he could make out the flicker of lamplights; this, however, was complete darkness. To the west the sun was setting, filtering light over the dark duvet to the east. For the first time he noticed flashes like those of a lightning storm. Unlike an approaching storm, though, these flashes illuminated nothing but the darkness of the clouds from which they came.

It was frightening; it was not natural. Some of the flashes were far lower than they ought to be yet never touching the ground. Once he looked at the helmsman and smirked. The man was a coward. To Pliny, despite the fear, the strange phenomenon deserved a closer inspection. He turned back to his ship. "Pull up the anchor!" he shouted and walked up the ramp.

"Uncle, wait!"

Two men were running his way through the mass of people who were waiting to be accommodated by boat to safer havens. On closer inspection, Pliny recognized his nephew with a second man whose dress coat of a plain tunic represented his social position. He was waving a scroll over his head.

Pliny went down to greet them.

Gaius was out of breath but opened his hand to Procimus. "A message has arrived from Herculaneum for you!"

The slave passed him the scroll and spoke as he did. "Mistress

Rectina is desperately asking for your help," Procimus told the man as he unrolled and briefly scanned through the message. "She is alone and terribly frightened. She wants to evacuate the library but cannot escape by land. She is asking for your assistance."

Pliny threw him a quick glance and looked up at the sails which had been released and now caught the northwesterly. His greatest reason for visiting Rectina regularly over the years had been for the library; it was a routine he hoped his nephew would one day continue.

"Of course. I will come at once." He gestured to Procimus to board the ship. "Come. We could use an extra pair of hands."

A little reluctantly, the slave did as he was told with Gaius following after him. Halfway across the ramp, he grabbed his uncle by the arm. "Uncle ..." He hesitated, feeling a little embarrassed. For a second he decided not to say anything, but then he thought of Valerus and he knew he would never forgive himself if he did not ask his uncle, "Will you bring back Luci?"

Pliny shook his head. "Luci?"

"Lucinda. She's a young woman working under Rectina. Please bring her back on your return."

The old man smiled and winked before touching his nephew on the chin with his fist.

Gaius stayed on the dock to watch his uncle set sail and cursed himself for not having admitted to it while he had been in Herculaneum. He had been drawn to the young woman, but the fact that she was a slave had kept him quiet.

It had not stopped Valerus, and Gaius knew that Valerus Cascus had taught him a greater lesson than any of his studies ever could.

He looked eastward and only hoped he still had a chance to apply his learning.

Chapter 49

Flavia had heard the crash above the roar of the mountain and the screams that followed. Pumice and ash dropped around her, but there was suddenly a cloud of it ejected, hanging in the air like a fog. She could not see through the darkness at what had actually happened, but her concern fell to the house itself.

All that ash and pumice … over a meter in depth in some places. How heavy did it become?

Forgetting the dangers of Jurgen and the senate, Flavia ran through the rising fall to the front door of Proculus's home. He had to be here; why else had Pedius gone inside?

The main boards of the ceiling had come down. The depth of mountain debris made it impossible to get through.

"Valerus!" she screamed into the darkness.

The darkness was unlike anything she had known. In usual darkness one could make out silhouettes, shapes, and movement. Here she could see nothing. The darkness swallowed everything and any sound was swallowed by the roar of the mountain and the falling ash.

She reached out and felt the wood of a board. She glanced up. The roof had completely caved in, spilling pumice into the main rooms. "Valerus!"

Despite the roar of the mountain and the screaming of fleeing residents, the world was suddenly quiet as she listened for the sound of his voice.

Nothing.

Flavia pulled herself up on a tilted beam. She coughed as the ash pulled up after her, following the motion of her body. She coughed again and pulled the tablecloth over her nose. She reached out her arm for the next beam and then her leg when she found it farther than expected.

Even in the atrium the ash was too deep to consider leaving the safety of the wood. But she saw a figure had pulled itself up a short way, enough to come clear from the debris. On closer inspection she recognized Marcus. At once she slid down the wood to reach him.

There was no reaction; his hand was cold when she touched it. Blood was smeared across the side of his face and blinded an eye. His other eye was slightly open, but there was no expression in it.

Flavia drew back her hand with a gasp, seeing then where a second beam had struck him on the back of the head as he had tried to crawl to safety; his neck was in an unusual angle.

She looked up into the darkness again. "Valerus!" she called. Her voice was lined with tears as she feared he had suffered the same.

Again the silence reigned in the falling ash. Her eyes had adjusted to the darkness best they could, but they brought nothing but vague shapes ahead of her.

"F … ! … ere!"

They were only sounds, but they were definitely from a human being. "Valerus!" she called again and forced herself forward over the beams and through the ash. "Valerus! Where are you?"

A hand suddenly reached out from under the wood and grabbed her by the ankle. She screamed as it pulled her off balance and she fell back, throwing her weight on the beam to keep her from falling into the accumulated pumice below her.

She glanced over her shoulder and saw Valerus, his head just visible above the debris. His hand was extended, desperately looking for something from where he could pull himself up and out.

At once Flavia spun around, lay over the beam, and reached to take his hand. When she pulled, she discovered that something was terribly wrong; Valerus was not that heavy. He merely moved an inch before something held him back. The young man took advantage of the short distance and shook ash from his hair and began to cough frantically.

Flavia could just reach his head from her position. She removed the cloth from her face, pulled up her tunica to replace it, and then reached down to tie it around Valerus's mouth and nose. His coughing seized slightly, but Flavia noted the ash and pumice he was buried in were rising.

Valerus tried to speak but coughed instead. Flavia took his hand again and heaved.

He did not move. It became obvious that he was trapped beneath the debris.

"Flavia!" His voice was broken and raw. He coughed again before he struggled to free his other arm. He did, and reached up to take Flavia's other hand.

She tried again to pull him free, heard Valerus gasp through some unknown pain, and then fall back into the ash.

"Valerus!" She let herself slip down the beam and risked going into the debris after him. Digging through the ash, she caught him by the shoulders and pulled him up as far as she could; there was definitely something holding him back.

He was coughing frantically now and Flavia desperately brushed the pumice from his face, hair, and shoulders and shook it from the cloth protecting him.

"The rope!" Valerus said urgently and tried to clear his lungs. "The beam caught the rope!"

Flavia brushed the ground with her feet, trying to feel which rope he was referring to. She did not find it.

Once more Valerus coughed before catching her gaze. A streak of lightning lined the clouds overhead, lighting her face for a second and drawing him away from the chaos of the moment. He looked up. The darkness was lit with lightning streaks, flashing within and above the clouds. He had never seen lightning this close to the ground.

He looked back at Flavia and saw the crazed panic in her stare. She was strained in her effort to keep his head above the ash and pumice, and he knew she could not hold him forever; the debris was coming down heavy and it was only a matter of time before they would both be buried.

He reached up to lift the cloth from his mouth.

"What are you doing?" Flavia demanded desperately.

"Flavia, listen to me," he cleared his throat before continuing. "You must get away from here! Take the road to Stabiae. Once you get there …"

"No, no, no, Valerus! I'm not leaving you here!"

"In Stabiae you must find a man named Pomponianus, a friend of Pliny the Elder. Remember? He was living with my parents for a short while after you arrived. I am sure he will help you to Misenum where Gaius …"

"Stop, Valerus!" Flavia screamed to be heard above the roar.

"You can't hold me forever, Flavia! If you stay here we are both going to die …"

"Then we will both die!" The first tears sprouted from her eyes. "But I am not leaving you here!"

"Don't let everything I did be in vain, Flavia." They locked gazes. When Valerus spoke again his voice was calmer and only a little saddened. "Everything I did was to free you; the fights in the arena, stealing you here! I did it all to save you."

"You did save me!"

"Don't die here, Flavia!" He shook his head. His voice now too was racked with tears. "Not after everything I did to keep you alive!"

Flavia started sobbing, burying her face against the beam beside her. "I'm not leaving you here!" she cried again. "Please don't make me leave you!"

"You can't move beams. And you can't hold me up forever."

The woman stared at him; his words had triggered a memory of only a few days ago. She could not move beams? Valerus had broken through chains to get to her.

She suddenly felt angry; why did God bring the two of them together if one of them was going to die? She would not have it, she could not have it. She cursed aloud, letting the sorrow surrender to the rage.

With a cry of rage she let him go. He fell back in the ash, a cloud rising in the shape of his body, yet the pumice was keeping him just above the debris. It was obvious now that he was at an awkward angle.

Flavia turned to the beam beside her, not even thinking of Valerus trapped and suffocating beneath her. All her strength and focus was on the beam in front of her and the absolute necessity of having it moved.

She thought of going on without Valerus, and it repulsed her. She could not have it … she refused.

She threw herself against the wood, gripping her hands under its weight. It did not move, but she would not accept that. She stopped to catch her breath and pushed. There was a slight shift that fueled her strength.

Then it lifted, barely an inch, but she threw it back a good way with a short cry. Her hands were bleeding when she stepped back and coughed, realizing that her tunica had slipped from her nose.

She pulled it up again when the reason for her strength suddenly returned. She spun around to Valerus who was already up and clearing his lungs with his hands over his mouth and nose. His hair was gray with the falling ash and so were his clothes.

Flavia fell against him, quickly refastening the cloth around his head again.

His eyes were watering as his coughing became even more frantic, but he had the strength to put his hand around Flavia's shoulder for her to guide him out. As she did, he suddenly remembered his father who had been right beside him.

He looked back urgently.

The darkness swallowed any figure there. Ash had fallen to cover the beams and the atrium floor. If Pedius had survived the collapse, he would have suffocated by now. Valerus remembered the last image he had of the falling beams; one had knocked his father back several feet. There was no way anyone could have survived a blow like that.

But he had to check. *How? In that?*

He looked from the darkness to Flavia, her face momentarily lit by a bizarre lightning streak overhead. The fear and urgency had returned to her expression. Valerus looked back once more, realizing that he had to pay attention to the living. Flavia was alive, and on that he needed to hold.

He swallowed as his stare pierced into the gloom. "I forgive you, Father," he muttered softly. "I'm sorry."

Flavia helped him over the beams and removed the rope that bound his ankles. The ends were ruffled where the beams had trapped them. Valerus resisted his urge to cough, knowing that it only made it worse and his eyes were watering so much that he had to trust Flavia completely as to where he put his feet.

The street was not much better. In a strange way the air was a little clearer, but the difficulty in breathing was much the same.

Valerus looked around him; the city was being lit by flashes of lightning and in the air were red streaks of falling debris.

Most people had taken refuge in their homes while others had made the decision to flee, carrying their belongings over their heads through the deepening ash and pumice. On the roofs people were trying to clear the accumulating weight.

Valerus was not going to take any more time looking for a horse; by now it was obvious that none were left in the city. Also there was a relief that Floronius would not be after them anymore.

Flavia took Valerus's hand and led him away from the mountain and toward the southeast wall. The young man pressed the cloth closer over his face, struggling to breathe through the itch of his throat, and by the next street she was forced to put his arm across her shoulder to support him.

A hand grabbed her on the upper arm and spun her about. Valerus stumbled from her side. The woman first feared he would be engulfed by the ash before she turned to her own danger.

Jurgen was standing over her, now grasping her by both wrists. The side of his head was bleeding, gleaming when the lightning flashed and his right hand was wet and sticky. Flavia kicked at him, but the pumice broke down her accuracy and she merely hit him in the calf.

"It's not going to be so easy!" Jurgen yelled at her, frustrated, hurt, and angry. Flavia had never seen the madness gleaming in a person's eyes since Seianus. Her old master used to get a mad sparkle in his eyes before he lost himself in rage. Flavia had learned from early in her life that any gleam like that was followed by a beating, perhaps even a life-threatening one.

Desperately she tried to pull away but he yanked her back to him.

"Jurgen! Stop!" Valerus pleaded when he saw Jurgen pull a knife.

The large man looked up at him; Valerus also saw the gleam of insanity. "You're next! Floronius may not be around to take you to Rome, but I am going to make certain that this Christian gets what's coming to her."

"There are more serious things at stake!" Valerus shouted. His gaze had now gone to Flavia's expression. "Look around you! How can you possibly think about that now?"

For a second Jurgen looked around before looking back at him. "You're right! Let's get it over with!" He brought his knife around to her throat. Flavia gasped, convinced that it was the last breath she would draw, but Valerus's reaction pulled her from Jurgen's attention.

"No! Stop! Wait! Please!" Valerus had his hands raised over his head and faced him squarely, showing his plea and vulnerability.

Jurgen looked up at him again.

"Don't … please." Valerus's voice was a lot more grounded this time. If he could just keep Jurgen's attention focused on him … "Anything else, just don't hurt her."

"She won't feel a damn thing!" Jurgen roared.

Valerus's gaze suddenly shot up over the man's shoulder. It was so sudden and focused that Jurgen knew it was not a trick. He risked a glance back and saw the flying debris growing in front of him from the mountain, dragging a burning tail behind it.

Jurgen threw the woman aside and followed after her onto the ground.

"Flavia!" Valerus had the time to shout her name before he too was forced to throw himself from the way of the debris' path.

The heat sizzled past him and he was on his feet the next moment, taking no notice of the screaming a short way up the street. He heard Flavia scream, and that was above all else.

"Flavia!" The ash had buried them but her scream drew him to where she was.

Jurgen was drowning her in the pumice, holding her down by the shoulders as the ash accumulated over her. He had pulled off the cloth that protected her and her coughing was cut off in her inability to draw air into her lungs.

Valerus felt that same anger come over him as he had a few days earlier, only this time he did not wait for it to accumulate and propel him. Instead he reacted in the moment, bombarding the man and throwing him aside. He felt the ash and pumice come over him, but the cloth Flavia had given him protected him to a point. Jurgen had none and was coughing as Valerus threw a blow across his face.

Flavia was slowly picking herself up, pulling her tunica back over her face as she coughed frantically. Through the fall of ash she saw the fight; Jurgen grabbed Valerus by his raised wrist and struck him.

Valerus disappeared in the debris.

Flavia was trembling. What could she do against a man of such size and strength? She watched, horrified as Jurgen turned to where Valerus had fallen and adjusted the position of the knife in his hand.

Knife! *She* had a knife!

She felt around desperately for what Pedius had given her and found it pierced through the rope she was using as a belt over her tunica. It was the first time she had held a weapon in her hands with the clear intention of using it. She knew she *had* to use it; she was not in a position to consider anything else. If Valerus died, then she knew she would also, either by Jurgen's hands or by heartbreak. She moved her fingers about and shut her eyes. "Forgive me, Lord!" She felt a tremor and let it throw her forward.

The knife Pedius had given her had been well sharpened and hardly met resistance when piercing Jurgen in the back. The large man jerked and attempted to turn around to her but she stabbed him again, this time so focused on Valerus's life that she was completely oblivious to what she was doing. She jumped back as the man fell before dropping the knife from her hand as if it had burnt her. For a second, she looked at Jurgen's body lined in pumice before jumping over him to Valerus.

He was conscious and accepted her hand to pull him up again. The cloth was still placed over his mouth and nose. For an instant they locked gazes before Valerus's went down to Jurgen who had nearly disappeared under the volcano's debris.

"I killed him." Valerus looked up at Flavia, her voice trembling. He saw tears glistening on her cheeks. "*I killed him!*"

"You saved my life, Flavia." He took her face in his hands. "Should I hate you for that?"

Flavia blinked, analyzing his words and hearing herself under them. They both offered each other a few seconds to realize what had happened and the necessity thereof before he took her by the arm and continued hurriedly toward the gate to Stabiae.

The blast was sudden; there was no rumble or roar from the mountain to announce it. The sound was much like a deep hollow pop that reached through the ears and into the brain of each person. There was no sound to anyone other than that explosion, which lingered longer than it should have.

Its force lifted Valerus off the ground and he felt Flavia's fingers slip from his hand. For a second there was an empty peace as he floated on air before he fell heavily into the ash, feeling that itchy, coughing sensation fill his lungs. He was up above the pumice as fast as he could manage, gasping for clean air. Instinctively he covered his mouth and nose again. The screams around him, which had been of fear, had now changed to those of pain and agony. He turned to look up the street, noticing the loud hum that dominated the better part of his hearing. The world sounded different, as if it was far off. He brought a hand to the side of his head, feeling the hot sting that came from his touch.

There were so many people and so much panic around him

that he wanted to look everywhere at once, but his head spun for a moment, blurring and distorting everything around him. He did noticed a dead—or unconscious—body hanging from the nearest rooftop that had not yet collapsed, then saw more people getting up from the ash and continue to run. He could not follow though. Instead he stumbled a few steps forward before grasping his head in both hands in the hopes it would clear his mind. He groaned; a sharp headache was picking up from the back of his skull. It felt as if he was bleeding from the inside.

Flavia? He glanced up through the falling pumice and shimmering world. Behind him Vesuvius roared again, but it sounded so far away this time across the humming in his head. He walked forward, dazed, as if he was scared of what he might find.

A man in blind panic suddenly ran into him, knocking Valerus to the ground. He was up again in time to see the man run off into the darkness. It was then that he saw Flavia, or rather the broken pattern in the ash and pumice stones as they lay before him on the road.

It was her, completely buried. She was lying on her stomach with her head down and was motionless when he dusted the debris from her face. Frightened that she might have broken something, he carefully picked her up from the rising pumice. A small trickle of blood was running down the side of her head. His world stopped momentarily and he felt the hot rush descend over him when he imagined the worst. The mountain had shrunk away as had the growing perils of Pompeii; that moment it was Flavia alone that filled the bleak spaces of his eternity. For this reason he felt his heart skip a few beats when her head suddenly jerked. She opened her eyes and gasped.

"By all the gods, Flavia," he whispered, "you frightened me!"

Flavia was stunned for a moment. She didn't remember who he was, or where she was, until she saw him smile at her; it brought it all back.

"Are you all right?" he cried. "Flavia, talk to me."

She wanted to answer him, she tried to answer him, but no

sound passed her lips no matter how hard she tried. She gasped again. Valerus recognized that same shock in her expression that he had seen earlier.

"You don't need to talk," he whispered when her eyes closed. Then he pressed her against him, hoping that it would be enough to keep her warm and that he would never have to feel the wind of eternity sweep over him as it just had.

He had to get to Stabiae, but, after a few steps carrying her weight, he cursed aloud and realized he could go no farther.

⁂

Pliny did not like the look of the horizon. For one, it was no longer there. The black cloud was moving in across the ground like a blanket. The roar was the only sound to be heard over the sea; it had even drowned the screaming, which was until only a short while back very distant. There was no sign of Herculaneum—not a light or a boat. It did not appear that any boats were making it off the coast.

It brought an ache to the pit of his stomach; it was the same ache he got when he knew he was going to lose a battle or an argument. It was the feeling of defeat.

There was an explosion from the mountain that made several men flinch.

"We ought to turn back," the helmsman called down to him. He was also watching the disappearing horizon with great concern. "We will never make it through that."

This brought Pliny a mixture of emotions. The helmsman was not only a coward, but also ignorant. Pliny refused to follow the command of such a man, but then he was considering the same thing. A rumble could be heard above the roar and pumice had begun to cover the boat's deck.

Pliny turned to the helmsman squarely. He was not wearing any part of his military outfit; the centurion garb was not meant to be worn in peacetime in home waters. He had, however, taken his silk toga with its fine border to remind those around him as to who he was and that his command was law.

But the horizon was unfriendly and the ash fall was becoming heavier, turning to pumice the closer they drew to the coast. The water was already covered in a gray blanket and navigation was going to be difficult once the darkness came through.

Pliny had sailed many waters and mastered many storms, but this was beyond him. He knew in his heart that he would not manage through such a dark place, but he did not want to give in to the command of a helmsman.

"Steer southeast," he commanded. "We will head for Stabiae."

Luci was by the docks with Helen and Moe. There was a crowd gathering on the beaches waiting escape by boat; it was too dark now to consider any other way. Most people were taking shelter in the boatyards, stables, and the slaves' shelters.

The girl tried to look over the water, which was nothing more than a thick moving mass of ash and pumice. No lights were ahead and the world appeared to end abruptly up to where the eye could see.

"He should have been in sight by now." Luci shook her head. Her voice trembled a little. Behind them the mountain roared viciously.

"Can he ever sail through this?" Helen asked as if to herself, still trying to see into the gloom.

"Maybe Procimus never even got to him."

"Surely you don't think …?

"If I had free choice," Moe grumbled, "I would have left a long time ago. Lucius did."

"He left?" Helen was not surprised to hear it, but her tone sounded as if she was.

"Everything's locked up. No answer at his door."

"But he was forbidden to leave Herculaneum."

"Who is going to stop him?" Luci asked them both. "Look at this!"

They did; the crowd was building up. It had to be over a hundred people now gathered, seeking refuge and shelter while awaiting the ships. There was a lot of screaming from the city; falling rocks and other debris were coming in, breaking through homes and killing people in the streets. This was another reason people felt a little more secure on the beaches. There was shelter which was situated along the ridges and protected by the city itself. Also the open ocean gave some sense of security.

Some provincial soldiers were trying to keep the panicked crowds under some control, directing them to empty chambers while they all awaited rescue. All attention was fixed to the ocean.

"We should tell the mistress." Helen shook her head. "It would be safer to wait on the beach."

"I will go," Moe volunteered. "Besides, I think it would be …"

His sentence was cut off abruptly by a short but monstrous sound from the mountain. Luci fell across the dock from the force of the shock while Helen stumbled, slipped on the wet surface, and dropped into the water where she disappeared in the gray sludge.

People were thrown from rooftops and others thrown to the ground. The roar then raged for a second before more debris began to fall.

Luci glanced up and momentarily saw a hand coming from the dock near to her, desperately trying to grasp at something. The explosion had left Luci's mind a mess; the screaming around her was muffled by the ringing in her ears. She stared … and it was only after the figure disappeared beneath the water and did not reemerge that she realized it had been Helen.

Chapter 50

The ash and pumice were getting deep; Valerus struggled to keep above the debris. He had cleaned out a good space and was sitting with his back against a wall, draped in the cloth Flavia had been using. The ash and pumice were falling at a slight angle from the northwest and he took opportunity to sit up against its flow. On his lap and holding her close to him, Flavia still lay unconscious. Every now and again he checked to see if she was breathing easily through all the coverings he had put over her face to protect her.

It was getting terribly hot; sweat had lined Valerus's face, which glittered and glowed in the flashes from the lightning. It was the first time he had ever witnessed a dry storm; the lightning streaks cracking overhead in the low pumice clouds and never appearing to reach the ground.

Worst of all, his leg ached. He cursed internally when feeling it throb under Flavia's weight. He could not carry the woman; he could not take her with him in his desire to flee. Thus he had chosen to stay with her until she regained consciousness or until they died together.

She was worrying him. Though it did not appear that she was

having difficulty breathing, her breath was still shallow and greatly spaced. This concerned him. Blood still caked the side of her face.

The jolt from the explosion had been violent, and the fact that she had regained consciousness told him that she was also suffering from shock … among other things. Because he could not know what the other things were, he was getting increasingly concerned.

There was a rumble and short tremor, bringing the young man's head skyward. It had to be past sundown, Valerus was certain, but there was no light; no glow to the west and no stars overhead. It was darker than any night could be.

The ash was muffling the noises of the city and, as it accumulated, silence reigned above the deep constant rumble. Behind him Vesuvius glowed red; the deep sound that spread from it set him nearly into a hypnotic state.

He pressed Flavia up closer against him, fearing the image of continuing without her.

❧

The wind was well in their favor and Pliny was able to get his ship into harbor without too much hassle. Dozens of people had gathered on the beaches, frightened and trying to keep clear of the rising ash fall. There was nothing much to see to the northwest other than the blackness welling up, but it drew attention for it was a blackness like never before, sweeping across the horizon like a wave. There was, however, a distant red glow, like fires in numerous places against the mountain. There was a lot of crying and screaming around Pliny as he made his way across familiar streets, followed by two of his fellow sailors. The rest had stayed on board to man the ship and to keep away the desperate, panicked crowds.

Pomponianus owned a luxurious villa on the nearest slopes overlooking the bay and was truly surprised when Pliny knocked on his door. "Pliny! I should have known you would grasp such an opportunity!" He pulled his old friend into the atrium and out of the pumice dropping heavily outside.

Pliny brushed some ash from his shoulders and cleared his throat. It was, he noticed, difficult to breathe outside. Inside, lit by braziers and lamps, the air was somewhat clearer. In the atrium, however, the air was thick and smudged, especially over the pond where ash rained from the compluvium. Pumice floated on the water surface. There was still a haze in the room, like smoke from a fire. Again Pliny coughed.

"We were bound for Herculaneum," Pliny told him, "but we could not make it through. The ocean is thickened out and the air is darker than any night."

"It's been going on for some time. It's so dark up near Pompeii we can only see the red glow of the mountain. We are still considering evacuating, but most of us are terribly frightened to leave the house."

Pliny looked up at the surrounding crowd; the household was a large one and several frightened children clung to the tunicas of their mothers. Pliny smiled at them in a reassuring manner and then said, "I think the worst is over. No need to be frightened, children."

He too was frightened, but would not reveal it. If he showed fear, he knew it would spread quickly around those close to him; it was a necessity of a naval officer. He looked back at Pomponianus. "Is cena being served?" he asked brightly, concealing his own fear by the tone of his voice. "A meal would be most welcomed."

Pomponianus was keen to depart from the area; the fact that Pliny had arrived by boat only urged him to want to leave as quickly as possible, but the admiral appeared so at ease that he did not feel it his place to lecture, command, or request.

Instead he had the slaves run his companion a bath with which to clean off the ash while they prepared a light dinner. Pomponianus stood in the courtyard as he looked over the rooftops to the blackened sky, which appeared to be bringing in a shadow. Even from here he could hear a rumbling.

Pliny joined him, wearing a casual chiton and rubbing his hair dry. The pumice and ash were a nuisance and he stepped under the ambulatory without uttering a word.

Pomponianus followed after him. Inside, a nervous family was settled on the reclining couches in the *coenaculum* awaiting the meal. Pliny joined them and smiled at the worried faces of children.

"Did you see the fires, Pliny?" Pomponianus asked him as he sat down opposite. "There are several, all in different places."

"Nothing to worry about," the elder said. "Bonfires left in the panic or empty houses caught alight. Rest easy." He reached over the table to grasp some nuts.

Pomponianus was concerned; he had, after all, a family to look after. The night had come so early and no normal night had ever been as dark as this. He looked at the faces of his children, his youngest son especially, who regarded him with round-eyed terror.

Few of them ate anything at all and merely watched impatiently as Pliny ate and very much enjoyed a fine meal.

In Herculaneum, panic was still lining the beaches; desperate crowds scanned the darkness of a thickening ocean for any rescue ship. Luci was lying on the dock, watching the thick waves batter violently on the logs and poles below her. Her gaze was empty; she was not expecting to see Helen again after she disappeared an hour ago, but she could not bring herself to let off her guard.

The thought that she was possibly still drowning plagued her.

A hand fell on her shoulder. "The mistress has arrived," Moe told her sympathetically.

Luci got up from her place and followed him back to the beach where Rectina was standing with her daughter Anneria. Alaine had come with her as had Cotti and Harolde. Luci could not believe how finely she had dressed: gold bracelets, stola, hairpieces, and even rings. Despite the panic and growing chaos, Rectina did not want her servants to forget who she was. Anneria was also wearing her finest stola and had clipped long blonde hairpieces into her own hair.

"No sign?" Rectina spoke loudly over the noises of the crowd.

"Nothing! Helen was flung over into the water a while ago … I don't think she will come up anymore."

"I meant any sign of Pliny?" Rectina asked.

Luci had to combat every part of herself not to burst into tears in the face of Rectina's lack of sympathy toward the dead. She shook her head. "No, my lady."

At that moment Alia and Ursalus approached them, wrapped in wool mantles to protect them from the pumice fall.

"Don't bring out the containers or the cylinders unless he comes into view," she told them, and then she turned to Harolde. "You and Moe can return and continue packing. Those containers which are filled can be brought down to the atrium." She turned back to the dancing girls. "You two will stay here with Anneria and myself." The last sentence had a definite tinge of fear to it.

"Where is Helen?" Ursalus inched to Luci's side.

Luci glanced back over the water, saying nothing. The ash still fell over the rising waves like a blanket over the water and the pumice stones drifted among it. Other than the ocean itself, there was no movement.

Then she turned to the west where the party had disappeared and her gaze fell on Vesuvius. She too noticed that its glow had extended along the outer ridges. The ash fall here was not as heavy and she could see more of what was happening. The mountain appeared to grow to a certain height, higher than the mountain ought to be in a red glow, but then appeared to fall back onto itself. It reminded her of the main fountain in the peristyle.

The air was getting heavy and terribly hot. She thought of Lucius and cursed that she did not have his freedom to flee.

Valerus could not believe that he had dozed, but the roar of the mountain had awakened him with a jolt. Concerned, he lifted the blanket without any thought and was suddenly swarmed by ash and pumice. He hurriedly threw the material aside, hoping it would wipe the debris clear; it was only then he discovered that he was nearly buried in it.

Fearful, he stood and picked Flavia up into his arms to rise above the settled ash and pumice.

The glow over the mountain appeared different now, Valerus noted. Earlier it was aglow only from the summit; now it appeared to be running down the edges of the mountain. He squinted; it was difficult to see across the debris that fell like snow.

The sound it was making was different also; it was the noise that had jolted him from the doze. The sound of the rumble was somewhat sharpened and perhaps even a little louder. There was still the occasional scream in the streets as stones were flung from the mountain over the city.

He looked down at Flavia in his arms. He could not believe it; she was awake. Her eyes were open and staring at him and the world dreamingly. Her expression appeared pale and distant.

"You all right, Flavia?"

She looked from the lightning above him to his concerned face. He was relieved when she managed to smile and then cough weakly.

He readjusted the cloth across her mouth and nose and then looked around him.

"I'm cold ..." she murmured weakly as he pressed her to him.

This was disturbing to hear; it was certainly not cold. Valerus was glistening with the perspiration from the rising temperature, and it was only after Flavia said this that he realized how hot it actually was. It was a heat beyond summer.

It was the shock—it had to be. Valerus refused to believe anything else.

Valerus could no longer take the accumulating pumice; it was reaching his chest height already. It was light and fairly easy to move through, but the strain was too much when he carried Flavia's weight. She had closed her eyes again and was not stirring in his arms, which made him even more desperate to leave. Yet he could not carry her weight, nor could he stay outside. He had to at least get indoors.

There were many silhouettes of people up on their roofs, trying to safeguard their homes by brushing off the accumulating pumice. An insula with a structural roof meant a safe haven; it also meant more people, and Valerus had been betrayed more than once over the last couple of weeks.

Yet, with all that had happened and all that was about to happen still, he could not believe that anyone could possibly be interested in earning a denarius in all of this. Yet Jurgen had been.

He coughed and tried to readjust the cloth that protected him before looking down at Flavia, checking to see if she was still well covered.

He could not afford keeping her outside. It was coming down even more thickly and the fact that she was cold in this heat had to signal the coming of a fever. He had to get her under shelter; the risk outside was getting too great.

Ash rained down on them, more so than ever before. He stepped back, pulling Flavia with him, and shook the debris from his hair.

"Sorry," a voice called down from above them. "Didn't see you through all this muck."

Valerus looked up. On the rooftop of the gladiators' barracks stood a man holding a large shaft in his hand, obviously clearing the roof of ash and pumice. He had a dark beard and against the red glow of the mountain he was a dark silhouette.

One thing that stood out, even in the darkness, was his smile.

Chapter 51

August 25

It was difficult for Valerus to sit still, even in the presence of a fire and a sleeping figure. From above them there was still the sound of Stephanus and Pedanius trying to save the roof of the gladiators' barracks. Opposite him was another gladiator who Valerus had never met. He had a bad scar on the side of his head and had been laid to sleep on a couch. His breathing appeared shallow to Valerus, much like Flavia's. Along with him also was a young woman, finely clothed and huddling near the flame. She held a small chest on her lap and every now and again threw Valerus a fearful look. Occasionally she did smile, but it was wracked in fear. Valerus could tell that she had been fleeing when the heavy pumice forced her to take shelter. Whenever she looked at Flavia there were tears in her eyes, and it became a growing realization that she too had lost someone in the last few hours.

Valerus did not speak, but he was grateful for the shelter offered by the gladiators. The barracks had, after all, been home to Valerus for two years when he was a young thracian gladiator.

Flavia was lying beside him with her head resting on his thigh, breathing deeply and far more difficultly than he was. He brushed his fingers gently through her hair. She did not stir.

"Is she your wife?" the woman asked, briefly pointing to Flavia.

Valerus looked at her for a long moment before slowly nodding. "I hope her to be." He smiled for the first time since they had taken shelter.

From outside another projectile hit a fleeing citizen. The screaming was not as clear as before; the ash muffled everything, including the roar of the mountain which was more a vibration felt than a sound heard.

He looked at Flavia again, wiping some ash from her cheek and then a few strands of hair from her eyes.

"What do you think of all this?" the woman asked him worriedly. "The Armageddon of the gods?"

Slowly and meaning every movement, he shook his head. What caused this? Not even he could guess. It was not even something from the world Flavia had created in her mind. He focused on the tremor that had become so a part of the moment; he felt it vibrate the inner core of his being and felt the urgency that it triggered.

He was not meant to be here—neither was Flavia. Why had the gods brought them together and then sent this danger upon them? It was this moment when Valerus thought for the first time that perhaps the gods had no control over anything; perhaps even the gods wished they did not have the power.

Outside there was a terrible collapse followed by more screaming, this time closer than before.

The heat was getting intense.

"I want to leave here."

Valerus looked at the woman the moment she said it and saw the weak smile pulling at the corners of her mouth. "I don't feel safe here. But I'm so frightened out there."

For a while they were both quiet, studying each other's faces until she saw what she was looking for in Valerus's expression; the same fear that reassured her that she was not alone.

"I would have left if I could manage Flavia's weight. I am not leaving without her."

"That's it." The two men who had been outside came into the barracks again. "I'm not bothering myself with the roof anymore." Both men removed the gladiator helmets they had been wearing to protect themselves and threw down their shovels. Valerus looked upon them as he would an opponent in the arena. They were clearly gladiators; their build promised it. The one named Pedanius went to kneel over his unconscious companion while the other took a respectful position opposite the woman and stoked the tiny fire.

"We have a small cart around the back …" he announced to Valerus, but he was cut off by Pedanius. "We are not leaving. We can't leave Crassus here nor can the woman make it through that rising debris. Besides, it would be better to stay here and wait it out. It can't go on forever."

"And what good is it without a horse?" Valerus added, realizing that it was a ridiculous question. A cart of any kind—horse or not—could be all the help he needed. They were three adults and they could get it along while it carried both women and another. He was suddenly aware that the cart was probably all he would need to leave the city.

Gently he brought his hand to cup Flavia's cold, pale cheek. Her skin was so soft; it made him smile. He leaned over and kissed her on the mouth softly. It reminded him of the times when she opened to him and he had made love to her. The magic of those moments suddenly pushed him to do whatever it took to get her and himself safely out of the city.

Obviously Stephanus was as keen to leave as Valerus was. Valerus had fought and nearly died for Flavia. In return she had saved his life and pulled him into her world. It was more than he could ever have asked for and he did not want the moments with her to turn into memories.

The cities around Vesuvius had lost order; panicked people sped through the streets and even with the rising pumice people were taking opportunity to loot and rob what they could. In urgent fear, there had been physical confrontations between criminals and those fleeing; some had ended with a knife and bodies were along the pavements quickly being buried by the fall. Following that were the projectiles coming from the mountain. Structures were giving way now from the continuous tremors. People were stumbling over the unseen rubble that littered the streets and there were panicked cries from children and parents who had lost one another in the chaos. Others had taken refuge in the basements of their homes, barricaded from the outside by the rising debris. Those who decided late to chance an escape found themselves trapped in their own homes and villas.

Darkness reigned. No night ever touched this form of darkness; there was little with which to judge distance and space other than the flash of lightning and the continuous red glow from the mountain. The smell was getting overwhelming, and along with the pumice fall it was not possible to step outside without any form of protection.

Valerus helped Stephanus strip cloth and tie pieces across the faces of those present. Pedanius refused angrily while the woman's own fear drew her away from the protection offered. He turned to Flavia. She was lying still by the hearth with her head turned in his direction but with eyes closed. Occasionally she coughed weakly but otherwise showed no indication that she was reaching consciousness.

Valerus crawled up to her on hands and knees. "Flavia?" He gently pulled her up to hold her against his chest. "We're leaving … we are finally leaving the city."

She did not open her eyes to his words, but there was a pang of relief when he saw the faint, weak smile she gave him. He held his breath, frightened that it may blow the smile from her face, then after a few seconds he leaned down and kissed her brow. "Come on." He carefully slipped his arms under her and, as he picked her up, he stumbled. Stephanus came to help him.

"There is still a lot of debris coming from the mountain," Valerus warned Stephanus. "Perhaps we ought to cover our heads with pillows." He looked to the bedding that had been piled in the room; several pillows lay in the bundle. He was prepared to do anything to ensure Flavia's safety, yet he had seen the rocks first hand and doubted it would be of any help if one hit them.

For this reason, he agreed when Stephanus pointed to the helmets that lined the wall. Together the two of them picked out those that fit them. Across the room, Pedanius grumbled angrily.

"You are actually going to leave?" he snapped. "It's madness! You saw what it's like out there."

"Precisely why we are leaving."

"It's death and you know it."

Valerus looked at Stephanus, who had the same expression on his face. If it was death, he was prepared to die running.

"My lady?" Stephanus opened his hand to the woman, his voice slightly muffled beneath the helmet. "Would you like to join us?"

She looked from him to Valerus and then to the unconscious gladiator on the couch. She turned back and shook her head. "I think I'll wait it out."

Valerus then carefully tied a pillow to Flavia's head, more for personal satisfaction than protection.

The mountain roared; the woman gave a short scream before

going silent from the looks of the men around her. Valerus was suddenly transfixed to the image. For an instant he saw Flavia in her place. He wished he could speak to Flavia and could know what she felt. He also desired so much to tell her his secrets, which he had so selfishly kept from her. His son. He wondered how far they had gotten. He wondered if he could have been of any help. *I ought to have been there,* he thought bitterly. *I ought to have taken some responsibility for the boy.*

Outside it was getting terribly hot; the heat hit Valerus as he stepped out into the pumice and broke into a sweat. To the north, the mountain roared, reaching into his bones.

He and Stephanus left, the cart was of no use for only the two of them. The healthy gladiator was carrying Flavia without any apparent effort. In a small way, it was humiliating for Valerus not being able to protect her as he wanted to. Instead he was carrying a short sword in his hand. It was a risk to expose an escape so openly in the panic-stricken city of Pompeii. His fear was that they may be approached by desperate people. The sword was the last resort. Yet outside the barracks was silence; the street appeared deserted and still. From somewhere up the Cardo Maximus were the distant screaming and the fall of order.

Valerus gave Flavia a long, loving look, thinking how strange it was to see her in the arms of another man. He then pulled the blanket over her head, protecting her from the fall of ash and pumice before looking northward up the street to the mountain. Valerus did not like the look of it; he hadn't since the start of the eruption. The glow was getting far more distinct along its slopes, especially on the west flank. This had him think suddenly of his mother … of home. He thought about his father lying dead under several feet of ash. Valerus realized then that even if he did manage to get away from this place, he would be running from it for the rest of life.

"Let's get away from here," Valerus murmured. It was going to take a lot of effort to move in the rising debris. In some places, it had reached over a meter in depth.

But it was better than staying in the city. Anything was better than staying in a place where he was certain to die within a few hours.

“I don’t think there is any ship coming, Mother.” Anneria shook her head, still looking along the blackened earth. “It’s been hours.”

The ash and pumice fall had taken a toll on the water and beach. People were taking refuge in stables, slaves’ quarters, and shipyards. The smell in the air stunk and people began to cover their noses as much for the stench as they did in protection against the ash.

People were coming in from the city constantly; some rumor had spread that a boat had arrived and many citizens clung to that belief. Moe had come with a few small cylinders and joined the crowd to gaze seaward. They informed the mistress that most of the documents and papyrus had been packed into boxes or left in their cabinets. Rectina suddenly appeared less concerned by it than she was before.

Some provincial soldiers were still trying to set order among frightened citizens, but the last blast had left bodies on the beach, which broke down people’s willingness to save anyone but themselves. Families were huddling in the crowded rooms which they were accommodating, including lovers and elderly couples. Rectina scanned through the crowd of frightened faces, drawn especially to the women who sat on their own. One young woman was pregnant, sitting in the corner and clenching her rounded stomach. She had tears down her cheeks, which glistened in the flash of the light. Beside her Luci was squatted, seeking some comfort by a mother figure.

Rectina did not know how to react or what to do that could

accompany the compassionate emotion she felt. She was not part of the class that looked out for strangers; she had never mingled with people below her family's status. Thus she behaved in the way she always had: she turned away and looked out across the sea again. There was nothing to see out there. The world was dark. Outside ash and pumice fell like heavy snow. Much of it was turning to slush on the edge of the water. Some of the docking ramps were already buried under the debris.

Her daughter was correct; no more ships were coming in now. She knew that Pliny, though a fine fleet admiral, could not navigate in this.

The rumble from the mountain suddenly changed in volume and was followed by a deeper tremor that rushed through the city. Harolde took Cotti into his arms just as they were swallowed by a red glow that brightened the world, flickered, and disappeared. Luci stumbled to a nearby family, hands clenched over her ears.

The rumble remained. Anneria screamed when another explosion erupted from the mountain, throwing her arms over her head as it rocked the walls. A nearby horse, still trapped in its stall, began to kick fiercely at its gate, shrieking when a second glow swallowed the city. Though dimmer and shorter lived, there was a greater sense of concern connected to it.

Rectina did not know how she knew it, or how anyone else could have felt the same she did, but suddenly panic hit. It was suddenly a clear reality that they were all going to die.

In the moment dozens of people got up and ran, not knowing to where, but it was an inner cry that they had to get away. They were running from their own fear, from the mountain, and from the increasing heat. There was a shriek when a boy's hair sizzled followed by several more shrieks. Rectina ran blindly, panic-stricken and suddenly cursing for not having done it before. Boiling tears squeezed out of her eyes as her world fell away and she saw it as for what it really was: nothing had ever been real … nothing. Slave? Master? What was the difference when the fear at this moment was so very much the same to them all? What had she been living for? What had she ever accomplished? It was not for this.

A soldier, dead from the earlier blast, blurred past in a heap of ash, which propelled Rectina for her last few steps. Harolde had pushed Cotti into the farther part of the chamber and knew—like all others—that it was the last moment he was going to have with her.

The air was pulled from the room, followed by a moment of peace and silence. Harolde took opportunity of the instant and kissed Cotti one last time, praying that it would last centuries.

Chapter 52

Pliny slept for longer than he had intended for when the urgent rapping came he noticed the pumice fall had nearly barred his door. One of Pomponianus's attendants appeared terribly apprehensive when he escorted Pliny into the main courtyard, which led into his room. The courtyard had filled with ash, debris, and pumice stones and the level had risen. Any longer and he would probably not have made it to the main atrium to meet the arrivals. The figure in the front removed the helmet he was wearing to reveal his features.

"Valerus Cascus!"

Valerus lurched into the house, pushing the attendant aside and pulling the cloth from over his mouth and nose. Sweat lined his face and his eyes were red, swollen, and watering terribly. He had trouble recognizing the old friend of the family and relied more on the sound of his voice.

He grasped the old man by the shoulders. "Master Pliny!" he gasped but said nothing more as he tried to clear his throat. Behind him Stephanus entered the atrium, still carrying the unconscious woman across arms.

"Where did you all come from?" Pliny asked them as Valerus tried to clear his throat. "Pompeii?"

"It's terrible," Valerus managed, eyes tearing. "I don't think we would have made it had we waited any longer." Then looked back across the lamplight to where debris was leaking in from the courtyard. It was at this moment that he, as well as Pliny, noticed for the first time that Pomponianus and the family were reclined there—they must have been up the entire night.

Pliny turned to them, looking around and then at Pomponianus. "How long have I been asleep?" he asked them a little anxiously.

"We will be reaching for dawn soon," he replied sheepishly. "If there still is one."

"I've been asleep most of the night?" Pliny was shocked by the facts. He spun around to Valerus who was standing by Flavia, gently with his hand laid on her brow. He nodded his way. "How bad is it?"

"The tremors are far more distinct in Pompeii," Stephanus answered. "So is the smell. A lot of people are trapped in the city and the heat is picking up."

"I meant for the young lady."

Valerus threw him a glance but said nothing. Instead he turned back to the danger regarding Vesuvius. "Stones are still coming in from the mountain. Some so large that both your hands can't cover them."

"Ah," Pliny said as he pointed briefly to the helmets tucked under their arms and the pillow that was still fastened to Flavia's head. "The pillow, yes?"

"These helmets saved our life more than once!" Stephanus announced.

"It's not safe out there, Master Pliny!" Valerus left Flavia's side to confront the old man again. "I am surprised that you got here, but more so that you have not left yet. If you had seen what we saw …"

❋

Valerus was given a guestroom where he could lay Flavia down while Pliny and his companions debated. Valerus adjusted a pillow under her head and then pulled in a stool to sit down at her side. He took her hand into his and held it desperately while staring into her pale sleeping expression. Her breathing was shallow and there appeared to be no change in her chances of waking up.

He leaned over her and listened to her breath—it gave him a strange sense of hope. Then, being so close to her, he put his arms around her, carefully drawing her to him. "Don't go anywhere," he whispered, pressing his brow against hers. "Don't make any decision now, please."

There was a soft murmur that passed from her lips and for a second he held his breath before realizing that it was not necessarily important. She had heard and acknowledged him, and that was all the hope he had wanted.

To the north, Vesuvius sent out another tremor that spread well past Stabiae.

⁂

The streets were becoming impassable; along with the accumulating ash and debris, remaining citizens in every town around Vesuvius were set in a blind panic that led them into buildings. Even looters had taken the decision to save themselves rather than try to gain riches from abandoned homes. In Herculaneum the city had fallen quiet, the silence only the dead could accomplish, but in Pompeii the noise had accumulated in the forum. Other streets were now deserted. Families had been separated and lost children had formed bands in their fear and attempt to escape the onslaught. Many were cowering under surviving roofs while others were trampled and suffocated in the streets while they sought out their parents. Others gathered in the crowd of the forum and on the temple steps, hoping for a familiar face. Some bands were luckier to have an older guardian to help guide them to empty homes or public buildings.

Slaves, who had taken the fearful decision of running from masters, were seeking shelter as well as refuge. Some had crowded into the public baths, cramming into the corners where the roofs were the steadiest. Most had stripped cloth from their tunics to protect their breathing while others were simply using their hands. Many were naked; having managed to free themselves from their shackles they had fled without clothing themselves. Those still trapped and chained in the homes of their masters merely sat, burying their faces in their knees to wait out the worst.

Proculus and Asilia, along with the children, had first left for the temple and had now flocked with the population into the forum. They had tried to head back to the house across the mad-stricken streets, but with the children it proved too dangerous. In his arms Proculus carried his middle son while Asilia had Caphisus on her arm, who could not manage the pumice anymore—hardly could she. The pumice was lying nearly as high as his head, and there was no telling what obstacles it was covering.

The mountain was still gushing to the north and the heat was getting unbearable. There was a terrible tremor that felt to be moving across the ground but had ended rather abruptly. It had been this surge that pushed Proculus and his family to chance an escape.

The tremors were picking up again and the red glow of the mountain was spreading well around the base. In the forum there were the cries of a fleeing city muffled by ash. People were everywhere but there was little to see other than gray rain against a blackened sky. The lightning had eased much over the last few hours and darkness now reigned as never before. Several people had taken to the temple, bearing offerings seeking forgiveness from Vulcan and Mars for whatever deed had led to the Armageddon.

It was at the base of the steps that Proculus stopped, not going farther. For a second he wondered why he hadn't considered heading north through Herculaneum and into the country he knew, but it was as if the roads that way were erased from time and memory.

There was another violent blast, snapping at the ears and throwing people to the ground. The screaming intensified before the rumble of another decaying rooftop broke through the noise.

Above them, the temple roof was giving way. Asilia turned and fled farther into the open forum as the first masonry cracked off and smashed the better part of the steps, which threw a pillar from its stand. Many made it to safer havens but a few cries were ended abruptly as the pillar collapsed, spewing ash into a cloud above it. She turned to watch the horror of the scene as the crowd tried to flee, realizing that her husband was not beside her, nor was their second child. Their oldest was at her side, clinging to her tunica.

"Paquius!"

And the heat—it couldn't be ignored anymore. It was getting too hot to breath. It was burning the lungs.

She covered his mouth and nose with her forearm and turned to the children.

"Cover yourselves!" she shouted, determined to protect them at all costs.

They all turned to the mountain as it boomed again. In the low light they could make out the dark clouds lining the mountainside.

Asilia adjusted Caphisus on her arm and glanced through the darkness for her husband. For the moment, it was the ash and pumice in the air that were causing the greatest difficulty in their escape and her greatest concern fell on the children with her. For this reason a shelter—even if only for an hour—felt the best course to take.

Valerus had not moved from his position beside Flavia nor had he turned his gaze. Her breathing appeared a little better now and some color was returning to her face. For the first time in hours he smiled, feeling a presence that was at least promising.

The blast struck through the open window, killing the tiny flame of the lamp and knocking Valerus from his seat.

Ash and pumice lined his body when he opened his eyes again, hearing, vaguely the distant patter of falling stones. Flavia was still where she was, moving slightly as if roused by the explosion. He crawled up to her on his knees and gently touched her brow. She was so cold.

Outside his room was a frantic discussion before one of the house slaves opened the door, carrying a flaming torch in his left hand. The warm gust of air danced shadows across the walls.

"We are leaving, Master Valerus," he announced.

At once the young man got up and gestured the slave forward. "Help me. I cannot carry her."

Without a word the slave handed Valerus the torch before carefully picking up the woman from the bed. Valerus followed closely as they crossed the courtyard, following the awning by the wall where the ash was not as thick. There were stones in the square, some still glowing.

Pliny was in the main atrium, coughing heavily under his breath. With him was Stephanus along with Pomponianus and his family. They had taken Flavia's example and were now in the process of tying pillows to the tops of their heads and those of the children. Valerus became aware of the screaming from the streets outside.

"My crew is aboard," Pliny told them. "They were commanded to clear the deck of debris. I did not, however, take into account the rocks."

Valerus noticed for the first time that he was speaking with difficulty, much like Flavia had the last time she had managed to talk. He could not recall ever hearing the rawness in Pliny's voice as it was this day and wondered whether he was suffering the same as Flavia was, though only mildly.

"No strays!" he continued, coughing terribly before pointing to the man who had come with Valerus. "You are welcomed, as is Valerus and his young lady, but no more. You let on one citizen and then you have a riot on your hands. I don't need anyone swamping my ship."

"But you came to rescue …" Stephanus began.

"It's panic!" Pliny roared and then coughed before continuing. "The moment I offer passage, hell will break loose. I will have to return with more ships. Until then the residents will have to wait."

"Perhaps the ships have already been swamped," Valerus murmured when acknowledging what he had said.

Pliny spun around to him. "I gave a command to my crew!" he snapped angrily, enraged by the fear finally setting in. "It was one I had to take!"

The explosion had roused most of the remaining citizens in Pompeii, so did the smell and the difficulty in breathing. Shelters brought no aid to the air they breathed and Asilia gulped in an effort to catch her breath. Every breath she took brought a weight to her lungs and increased the difficulty to try again.

She tried to smash in the door, blocked by the risen ash and pumice, desperate to get the two children in under a roof.

"What is it?" her son suddenly shouted beside her.

Asilia looked back down the street through the screaming. Toward the north something was moving down toward them and it was a wall; a growing moving gray cloud that was lit by a distant dawn.

It was her breath that gave out on her first. She fell against the door she had been trying to open, clenching Caphisus to her and watched the dawn set again as her vision failed. She saw once more the darkness racing quickly their way, faster than any man could run.

❧

On the shore of Stabiae, a crowd had gathered, many carrying baggage and personal belongings on their heads and shoulders. Mothers carried infants on their backs and men carryied children on their arms. They were swamping the docks, desperate to get on any available ship that was leaving the area. Pliny's crewmen had been forcefully instructed and three dead men lay by the foot of the ramp. Now people were keeping a distance but were still as desperate, crying curses at the helmsman.

Valerus followed like a shadow behind the slave carrying Flavia, every now and again looking over his shoulder to see the woman's sleeping expression. "We are leaving, Flavia," he muttered, forcing a smile even when he had none to spare. "We're going to make it."

As they reached the shore they were forced to push people aside. The people threw Valerus looks as he passed by, some even making gestures in his direction. He could handle the anger and hate they had toward him. It was the fear he could not stand. Some merely stared at him, many with tears in their eyes. Some were still children, standing deep in the pumice sludge that the ocean was bringing in.

There was suddenly commotion up ahead. Valerus tried to see over the heads ahead and only saw people spreading, moving away as if some beast had entered the crowd. As he drew nearer, he saw a figure that was seated on a sheet spread on the pumice mud.

It was Pliny who was resting his back against one of Pomponianus's tenants. Pliny was suddenly frightfully pale in the blackness that surrounded them.

At once the slave carrying Flavia passed the woman to Valerus and ran forward to be of assistance. Valerus watched them speak for a while before the slave sped off in the direction of the villa.

It was in this moment when his attention was drawn to Pliny when someone, drowning in fear, rage, and wine, grabbed Flavia by the hair on the top of her head and threw her from the man's arms. It was the same instinct that had nearly cost him Flavia's love in the past that propelled him again. He threw his weight aside, catching the aggressor in the face with his fist, throwing him back into the crowds. An angry roar rose when he cannoned into several men, spilling their belongings and loved ones into the sludge.

Valerus was kneeling in the mud over Flavia, pulling her head up to his knee when someone struck him on the side of the head with a brick. He fell away from her, for a second aware of nothing but the dull throb. Then he came up, spitting ash-mud and pulling himself up to his hands and knees.

The crowd was panicked and desperate and looking for any tool with which to relieve the tension. Several men took the opportunity and decided to join the fight, fortunately in Valerus's favor. As the fight commenced and was submerged into the crowd, the young man crawled up to Flavia again, picking her up as far as his strength could. He rubbed the mud from his eyes and then from her face. He felt the cold damp of the slush seep in through his tunic; he was nearly waist deep in it as he knelt beside her.

Then she woke up and looked at him. Valerus felt the relief and the peace when her eyes looked into his; it suddenly made the world such a better place and for a moment the chaos died away. He smiled and ran his fingertips along the side of her face, leaving long mud streaks where he had touched her.

“Valerus?” Her voice sounded so different, as if coming from elsewhere.

“I’m here.” He smiled, aware how his own voice cracked with tears. “I’m not leaving you.” He put his hand on her head.

“You didn’t tell me you had a son.”

Valerus frowned; it was an odd place to bring up the subject for one, and there was guilt along with her statement, but his greatest question was how she had known. He had not told her—he intended to—but with everything that had been happening it never seemed appropriate.

Neither did this. He stared at her, hoping she would say something more, but instead her eyes closed again.

“How do you know that?”

She did not react to his words.

“Flavia?” He gently shook her. “How do you know that?”

She smiled. “He’s here.” She opened her eyes again to look at him.

At once Valerus looked around. “Where?”

“Everywhere,” she whispered, but it had been the loudest and strongest thing she had ever said. It pulled Valerus from the screams, the crowd, and a burning mountain. Everything disappeared—everything other than the woman he held in his arms and the words she had just said.

He took her face in his hands, shaking only slightly from the sheer exhaustion of the last few hours. Tears were streaming from his eyes, leaving grooves in the dirt on his face.

“What do you mean by that?” he asked her, his voice now wracked in tears.

She tried to lift her hand; he helped her and pressed it to his cheek, feeling it go cold against his skin. Her touch was a reassurance that she forgave whatever actions he thought to have been wrong, that she did not dwell on the man he used to be or who he was this moment. Instead she was looking at the man he was going to become.

He stared into her eyes, seeing the world and every moment he had lived. He saw himself looking back for a few seconds before his reflection too began to fade.

"Flavia?"

A small spittle of blood had appeared in the corner of her mouth.

"No! No! No!" The words shook him wretchedly. "No, no, no … no …" His breath gave out on him that moment and he cried, taking in air with wracking sobs. He pulled the woman to his chest and tried to draw enough air to scream, but even that failed. He coughed, cursing internally and pressing her to him so tightly that it hurt. The slush from her tunica drew into his, pulling a shiver up his back.

Ahead of him Pomponianus, his family, and two slaves were trying to get Pliny to drink a cup of water to no avail. The old man had his mouth open, gaping at the people around him in sheer terror as to how his breath had so suddenly given out on him.

Still holding the woman to his chest, Valerus looked up behind him and saw frightened children looking on from behind their parents, nearly chest deep in the pumice mud, which was only accumulating. Where the fight had broken out to his left a body lay motionless, face down in the mire. A woman was crying hysterically over it. On his other side, Valerus saw the trampled remains of a dog that had been given no regard in the stampede.

The horror of it all made him cling to Flavia like a child would to a stuffed toy. He suddenly felt like a child himself, wishing at that moment that he could cry out and wake from the nightmare, that he could know that it was not real … that none of it had *ever* been real.

The air changed; breathing was no longer a difficulty but painful. There was a sulfurous smell that stung the eyes and burnt the throat. Without so much as slackening his grip on the woman, Valerus pulled his tunic up over his lower face. He glanced up and an enormous figure cut out the sky above the heads of people now fleeing past him. A black cloud was rising from the earth, moving up over the hills, and appeared to be growing in size as it rushed their way.

The world stopped that moment for Valerus. Feeling the weight of Flavia's lifeless body in his arms made him ready to die. He nodded into the direction of the growing surge of fumes in a welcoming acceptance of its wrath.

Ahead of him the smell appeared to rouse Pliny, who tried to get up with the support of two slaves. He stumbled forward with a few staggered steps before collapsing again.

The rumbling ended suddenly, bringing the screaming to an abrupt stop. Ahead, the surge drew up one last time and then appeared to shrink back as if the gods had commanded it, pulling the air with it. Valerus fell over, clenching Flavia tightly under him, trying to shield her body with his.

Still in a horrific trance and through the slush of running feet, Valerus watched Pliny die on that shore under the glow of Vesuvius.

Gaius had dropped the papers he had been working on and ran to the first room balcony where his mother was overseeing the disaster. The clouds that had once risen from the mountain were now lining it, spreading across the bay and moving toward them.

He grabbed the woman's arm. "Come, Mother! Run!"

All of his uncle's books as well as his studies were left on the study's table as the two fled the house, taking to the streets where several hundred more people were fleeing. Behind them the dark cloud moved in like a flood and the ash fall thickened suddenly. Grasping at his mother's hand and refusing to let go, Gaius pulled her after him. All the while she looked back toward the harbor, hoping to see some sign that Pliny had made it into dock.

Darkness enveloped them. Still running, propelled by panic, people stumbled and called desperately to one another. Several thousand had taken to the streets, many abandoning their belongings when the surge came their way.

Then it ended—so suddenly. The darkness pulled away like a dark cloud blown by the mountain winds, throwing the storm back across the countryside. Around them the screaming ceased slowly and was replaced by a silence that had never been heard in the city.

The bay was still enveloped, but even that appeared to be drawing away and above the gray cloud came the distinct view of a silver lining.

The sun emerged briefly, shadowed by blowing smoke.

Gaius glanced around him, still clenching his mother's hand as the world seemed to return after having changed so much. Ash lay in the streets like new fallen snow.

It roused the sensation of a passing storm.

Chapter 53

Valerus clenched desperately to Flavia, refusing to let her go. In front of him the slaves and tenants of Pomponianus had left Pliny's body on the shore and had left for the ship.

Valerus, knowing now that he had been abandoned and that Pliny's death had cost him his escape route, turned to the last bit of reassurance he had.

It was not the image of Flavia he had wanted, especially at such a time. Instead of that smile and powerful stare which he had been prepared to die for, she was now empty and without expression. Her eyes were slightly open, her head tilted so that her hair lay spread out in the slush beneath her. There was blood in the corner of her mouth.

"Why?" Valerus hadn't the strength or the breath to ask it any louder than a whisper. Tears boiled out of him, smudging the ash down his cheeks. With a shaking hand he removed the few hairs that stuck on her face as if it had been plastered there by honey.

A hand fell on his shoulder and yanked him away from her. "Master Valerus!" A man spoke urgently. "Let us leave quickly! The wind is in our favor."

Valerus groveled back to Flavia's body and retook her onto his lap, not having heard a thing the man had said. His life was now in front of him and it was dead; there was nothing left.

"Master Valerus! Come! We must focus on the living." This time the man's grip on his shoulder was doubled, pulling Valerus up and throwing him across the crowd. Valerus recognized his face: it was Procimus. For a second, questions were asked before he set them aside and tried to regain his balance. He slipped and stumbled through the mud. In front of him, the crowd closed in and Flavia disappeared from his view.

"Flavia!" Valerus screamed out of sheer determination, hoping in some strange way that his call would bring her back.

"Enough, Valerus!" Procimus roared.

Valerus hit him, or tried to at least, but his strength failed by sheer exhaustion. The tenant recovered from the weak blow and returned a punch, nearly triple the strength.

Waves suddenly touched Valerus's ankles and he noticed that he had missed the ramp by an inch and was stepping into the ash-thickened sea.

"I can't leave her!" he cried again and tried to break past him.

The man shoved him back until he was knee deep. "She's dead! Accept it!"

"No! No! I refuse!"

"All you'll achieve now is dying with her!"

"Let me!" The tears had come again.

The next punch that came threw him back another step; Valerus was certain he had lost a tooth. When he came around another blow caught him, this time having him collapse into the water.

It was the heat that woke him, the first time he had felt sunlight in more than a day. Valerus blinked in the glare penetrating him from the nearby window before he managed to focus and see the curtains blow in the wind. The light was faded though, as if blocked by a thin sheet of clouds, or smudged by ash. On turning his head, he discovered he was reclined on a couch in the main *biclinium* of a rich man's home. Across from him was a table drowned in scrolls, documents, and books followed by more reclining couches lining the wall opposite.

He sat up slowly, wincing when he felt a terrible burning sensation in his lungs and throat. Someone had covered him with a thin sheet and replaced his muddy ash-covered tunic with a fine chiton that appeared of Greek origin. He looked down at his hands, staring blankly at the cuts and bruises that lined them, wondering whether it had all been a dream.

Once more he looked around and felt the hope and peace fade away when he realized that Flavia was not present. He was alone.

With difficulty he pulled his feet off the couch and got up, feeling heavy under the weight of his own head. Slowly, dreamlike and clenching the sheet around him as a mean of security, he walked to the window, limping under his bad leg.

The bay lay ahead, stretching out to the foot of Vesuvius. A dark cloud still covered the main features of the mountain as well as the cities surrounding it, yet it was distant now, far away and unreal. He turned his head to look farther south. A lot of boats peppered the ocean, especially in the direction of Stabiae.

"Evening, Master Valerus."

The young man turned around to see young Gaius coming to join him by the window. He had a smile on his face that appeared a little sad. This brought Valerus recollection of Gaius's uncle's death on the shore of Stabiae, yet there was no compassion or pity; he had no more of it left, not even for himself.

For a long time the two of them watched the mountain without a word. Behind them a slave came to the room and began sweeping up the debris while outside the city continued. To the west the sun was setting over the day like any other.

Finally Gaius drew a deep breath, causing Valerus to look his way. One single tear glistened down Gaius's face, catching the sun perfectly before setting on his chin.

Valerus said nothing; there was nothing he could say. He followed the gaze back over the bay and the ships heading for the opposite coast, their sails white in the sun.

Finally, when Valerus could not longer take the pain that was welling up, he turned to Gaius fully. "Why didn't they let me take her?" he asked, tears coming to his voice.

"They did the right thing," Gaius muttered without looking his way.

"At least I could have brought her back."

"And do what?" The young man shook his head and looked at him. "My uncle was also left on that shore."

"She was dead, what harm could it do?"

For a second Gaius was silenced by the tears and hurt in his voice before explaining, as gently as he could. "How many people were on that beach, Valerus?" Valerus did not reply so the man answered for him. "Hundreds, even thousands. They were all as desperate to get away as the person next to them. If you or my uncle's tenants had taken a body aboard, it would have struck a riot. Focus on the living. There is nothing for the dead in the realm of the living."

Valerus was clenching his eyes shut, as if trying to block out his words. Tears were squeezed out of him as he ran his hand through his hair. He felt how it had been cleaned from the mud and ash that had stained his hands when he had last seen the woman he had loved so dearly.

Gaius looked back across the bay in a gesture of hope. "There are many rescue ships coming in. I will go personally to the shores of Stabiae and return the bodies. Would you like to join?"

Valerus looked across the bay, feeling the bile rise in his throat. He shook his head. "I never want to go anywhere near that mountain again."

⁂

Valerus, Gaius, and Gaius's mother dined alone that night, reclining and sharing wine. Valerus had never felt less like eating. He was hungry; his body craved something with which to retain the purpose he once had, but his thoughts wondered as to why. What was there left for him? The devastation of the cities around the mountain had left him poor, homeless, an orphan, and, worst of all, alone. What did he have to live for? There was nothing left other than the darkness Vesuvius had first brought down on him nearly two days ago.

"Are you eating that?" the older woman asked from across the table.

Valerus looked blankly at the apple he had been holding in his hand for the last few minutes as he wondered through his bleak and empty future.

He tossed the fruit on the floor and let it roll beneath the table. Then he got up and left the coenaculum without the exchange of a single word.

Valerus was given the room which was saved for aristocrats and high nobles from Rome. By the look of it, Pliny must have been visited often.

The view was to the south, but craning out the window he could see the dark lining of Vesuvius. Across the dark bay were the small flickering lights of ships.

It was such a strange sensation to think it had all happened in a little more than a day—all of it. Two days ago Flavia was still with him and the future, though they were fugitives, had never been brighter. It made him want to laugh yet curse the petty problems people immersed themselves in on a daily basis.

A light fell across the room as Gaius came in, joined him at the window as he had done before, and smiled when a breeze blew in from the south. "Smell that, Master Valerus," he said as he inhaled deeply. "Clean air. Fresh from the sea."

The man did not comment.

"I must live up to my uncle's wishes now," Gaius said. "His will announces that I have been given his personal galley, his home, title, slaves, and most possessions. Yet, more importantly, I have been given his name. My uncle has become my father through death." The two men caught each other's eyes. "I gained something great through the destruction: a family."

For the very first time, Valerus smiled sadly before looking back out over the ocean. "I gained nothing," he muttered, his smile swallowed by the reality of his words. "I only lost everything."

"I cannot believe that," Gaius snapped and turned to him. Valerus regarded his expression and noticed that the young man was serious and suddenly appearing terribly aggravated by his words. "Lost everything? Even love? Even the memories you have of her and the experiences you shared?"

Valerus drew to face him fully.

"You loved a woman who returned it," Gaius continued. "You escaped a disaster not even the gods could control."

"It was a punishment." Valerus shook his head. "Why spare me other than wanting me to suffer the loss of everything that I lived for?"

Gaius drew in his breath and sighed. When he spoke again, his voice was much more subtle. "My father did not believe in the gods," he said sheepishly as if confessing it for the first time. "He believed in facts, life and death, and the chance of coming upon each of them. They are not rewards or punishments. It's merely what we call *life.*

And what does not kill us makes us grow. Death is for those who have nothing left to learn."

"Are you insulting the dead?" Valerus asked, aghast.

"Of course not—on the contrary. We who stay behind remain students." He smiled, as if pleased to say the following words. "My father has become the teacher … as has Flavia."

Valerus shut his eyes to draw in the man's words, wondering how Gaius could place words so well that they actually felt to be healing some of the wounds. Valerus forced a smile on his face when he spoke again. "I have always been the student. Since the day we met, she was tutoring me."

Gaius gently clasped Valerus's shoulder. "Have a good night's sleep, Valerus. You will see that in the morning it will all be a little clearer."

August 26

Not necessarily. Valerus's thoughts were the reason for his nightmares and the empty peace that fueled him through the night. Before first light he got dressed and left, taking to the streets and wandering through unfamiliar territories.

The smell of bread was picking up and bakeries were lifting their windows. It was amazing how the world appeared able to continue as it always had.

Not for Valerus, though. He wandered aimlessly, thinking of what Gaius had told him and wondering what he had from Flavia that still drove him to survive—to exist. What was his purpose now? Fighting? Standing before the emperor? That felt so fake and ruthless after what he had felt in Flavia's presence. His fear now was that nothing could ever come close to the life and love he had had.

Dawn rose and the sun filtered across the streets, warming the flagstones and bringing light to the city. People began to line the bakeries while others accompanied their families to a fine breakfast.

It was then that he saw a familiar face; Lucius was seated alone at a table outside a bakery, glancing into space over his uneaten breakfast of fresh bread and eggs. Valerus watched from across the street, aware of the mixed emotions that came over him. In one part, he was pleased to see a familiar face and know Lucius had made it from Herculaneum where everyone else had perished. He wanted to join him at his table and recapture old memories from a time when he was still happy.

But another part rebelled. He remembered that it was Lucius who had given him away to the authorities; whether willingly or through torture. A thought that plagued him was that he knew Flavia and he would have made it from the city long before the eruption, long before the guard knew their location, if it had not been for his old companion.

He made to walk past, stopped, and turned again. Lucius was looking his way now but said nothing and made no reaction, obviously conquered by the same divided emotions, mostly shame and a lot of regret.

Valerus could not walk away. The two of them had been childhood friends and Lucius had literally saved his life before. Perhaps his deed balanced it all out.

With a faint, sad smile, Lucius gestured to the empty stool by his table. Returning it and saying nothing, Valerus accepted and sat down opposite him.

It was earlier that afternoon when Gaius and the sailors brought Pliny as well as Flavia's body into Misenum. Valerus stood over her as she was laid on the dock near his feet and had trouble recognizing her. They had cleaned both casualties but she was pale and lifeless and when he touched her brow she was icy cold. Dirt and ash were still trapped between her stiff fingers and toes and Valerus had to look away. He could not stand the thought of it being the last image he would have of her.

Pliny seemed so at ease in death; there even appeared to be a smile on his face and anyone else would have thought he was merely sleeping.

He looked back at the woman; dried from his tears, he could not shed a single one. In a strange way he was happy for her, knowing that her journey forward was going to be a lot easier than his.

Her hair was still wet and clung to his fingers when he touched it. His hand ran down the side of her face to her shoulder where he noticed the green pendant still hanging from her neck. He felt like a tomb raider, a looter, and a thief when he snapped the tiny string and clenched the small shell in the palm of his hand. He pressed it to his brow and made a silent prayer to every god he thought would listen. After the disaster, though, he doubted that there were any gods at all. He wondered what Flavia's belief had brought her in the end and discovered that she at least had been spared the heartbreak. What had the gods done for *him*?

They had brought Flavia into his life, and that was more than he could have asked for.

Chapter 54

August 27

Valerus was sitting by the docks, carving a piece of wood absentmindedly as he watched a few more remaining ships come in from Stabiae, most bearing bodies. His mind went back over the days before and after the eruption, unable to believe that his life had changed so dramatically after just two days.

Some wood shavings fell on his legs while others were blown across the beams.

He thought of Flavia and tried to find the legacy she had left him, as Gaius had convinced him she had. What legacy? She had been a slave—a Christian slave—who no one wanted other than him. He had done everything in his power to keep her alive and all of it had been in vain. Thinking of her God as well as all of his, Valerus could not help but feel robbed.

He looked down at his small carving; he had carved from a cube of wood a tiny cross that fit into the palm of his hand. Why he as a Roman made a miniature instrument of Roman torture he had no idea. Perhaps, he thought, it made him hope she too would come back as He once did as the stories told. Or, more so, it reminded him of the things Flavia had believed in and what she had dedicated herself to. Valerus knew that he could never believe the things she had. For the moment, he did not believe in any god and felt no need to worship or praise gods after what they had done. Yet there was a certain sense of peace in this, he realized, like a simple truth that stood between his gods and Flavia's deity. In a strange sense, he felt free.

A helmsman called out to a companion and Valerus was pulled out by his voice. He looked out at the ship and then farther out over the bay that stretched behind them. The water was shimmering in the glow of the sun and the tiny cross felt heavy in his hand. Suddenly the possibilities appeared endless.

Flavia *did* leave him something—something far greater than memories.

Gaius Secundus was at work in his study, doing anything to distract himself from the loss of a few days back. Like Valerus, he had not stayed for the burial of his loved one and was avoiding his mother when he heard her coming back into the house. He organized for a surgeon to remove Valerus's stitches during the coming week then turned to the will of his uncle. He made himself appear far busier than he was when his mother looked into the room.

For most of the time, Gaius wrote poetry, mostly of love and the pain thereof. He documented what he had seen from the mountain along with what the helmsman and Valerus had told him. Also he recorded his own hopes and fears regarding the disaster and the pain he had felt when knowing that his uncle had never made it to Herculaneum nor had Lucinda who had undoubtedly perished on the beach.

He took a few minutes to cry before pulling in his law books and the writing work his uncle had left for him. There was a lot to do, which he needed to focus on.

It was only some time later when he felt another presence. On looking up, he saw that Valerus had walked in, without requesting his presence, and was in the process of taking up the seat opposite him.

"Master Valerus," Gaius said sarcastically as he gestured to the taken seat, "take a seat."

Valerus leaned over his way. "You said your uncle left you his personal galley, correct?"

The young man nodded solemnly.

"I want it."

The statement shocked Gaius so much that his jaw dropped open and for a few seconds he couldn't find any words to fit his thoughts. Finally he managed to bring out a few weak words. "The galley? Why?"

"What are you going to do with it?" Valerus asked him. "You are not a sailor."

"Neither are you."

Valerus gave the smile of a man who knew it to be true but did not seem to make it an obstacle. He set his palms flat on the table and noticed that under them Gaius had rolled out a map of the empire, stretching out from Persia to the Atlantic. With care he brushed the surrounding documents away and pointed to the small speck that was Rome and ran his finger to the far tip of Hispania. "How long to Cadiz by ship?"

"It all depends on the wind, Valerus." Gaius shook his head. "Depends on the gods."

The man smirked and looked down at the map again. Gaius followed his gaze before looking up at his tortured, focused expression again. "Where exactly do you want to go?"

Without looking up or taking a second to reevaluate his decision, Valerus ran his finger westward, to the end of the map, and then along the hardwood to the edge of the table. Only then did he look up. Gaius stared at him, unable to believe it.

"The end of the world? You want to sail over the edge?"

"Is there an end to the world, Master Gaius?" Valerus asked with a faint knowing smile. "Are you certain that the earth drops away at the end of the map?"

The young man looked down and then up again. "You think there might be something else instead?"

"Flavia believed it. And she got me to believe it as well."

Gaius saw the look in his eyes; the look of a man who had lost everything, from his home and family to his loved one and his future. What did he have other than a fantasy?

And yet Gaius could not do it. There were laws and he had dedicated much of his life to learning them. Slowly he shook his head. "I can't give you my uncle's galley." Valerus did not move or make a sound as he spoke. "Besides," Gaius said as he felt forced to make an excuse to satisfy the look on his face, "you could never man a galley like that yourself."

"Lucius is prepared to join the venture. His mother was killed in Octavianum along with the rest of the city. How long will it be before the senate begins searching for him again? He could use the low profile."

"Even with two people you could never even get out of the bay. You will need at least twenty slaves, if not more, to properly maneuver, and I cannot give you any of the slaves. Some are worth their weight in gold."

"Lucius already got eight slaves for the price of twelve sestertii. He's sure to make twenty in the next week."

Gaius was genuinely surprised by it. "Where did he get those?"

"Sleatus Markets."

Gaius covered his face with his hands and shook his head. "No Valerus … no. They are the worst. Criminals, thieves, slaves worked half to death by previous owners."

"That's right. Whipped, beaten, teeth rotten … half-starved. A trip like this can only be an improvement … an act of mercy because they will be looked after well." He swallowed whatever emotion was coming up and added softly, "serving …"

The silence that fell over the study was one neither of them were accustomed to. It swallowed every sound from the outside world of birds and crowded streets; for that moment there were only the words Valerus had said that hung in the air.

For a long time, the two men stared at one another. It was only when a slave came to clean that Gaius had to break the silence. "You cannot sail, Valerus, and I cannot give you a galley."

"Tell the senate it never made the onslaught of Vesuvius. No one needs to know."

"You are asking me to give up my uncle's legacy?"

"Are you asking me to give up an entire new world?"

Gaius heard his uncle speaking through Valerus in that moment—the explorer side of Pliny. The young man thought how his uncle would have taken part in such a venture without a second thought. Why he had never thought of it himself he could not imagine. He remembered the last image he had of Pliny, how he had raced to a place from which everyone was so fearfully leaving.

His uncle's legacy? Perhaps Flavia and Pliny were connected in some strange way; they had, after all, both become teachers. Maybe it balanced each other out: the galley and the faith—the idea and the means. Yes, the world suddenly became a little clearer, and Gaius felt inclined to ask one more vital question. "When do you hope to leave?"

September 6

Valerus did not know how he got through the days that followed, but somehow it all seemed to work out. One galley, one experienced helmsman, and a crew of twenty.

The sun had not even risen when Gaius accompanied him out to the docks where Lucius was waiting. Valerus went forth and grasped his companion's hand. "Are you sure you want to do this?" By the tone of his voice it was not the first time he had asked it.

Lucius replied with another question. "With my mother gone, what have I got left here?"

"A future."

For a few seconds, Lucius thought about this before smiling. "Maybe there is a future out there." He nodded toward the ocean. "A new world is bound to have promise."

"We may never find it," Valerus reminded him.

"I think we'll be lucky."

Valerus turned to Gaius and smiled as he took his hand. "I hate to see this as a farewell, Gaius. After everything you did …"

"I view this as my greatest contribution. I look forward to your return."

"*If* we return."

"You're right," Gaius said as he grasped his shoulder. "You would likely make a home across the ocean. Why return here?"

It would have been an opportunity to laugh or at least chuckle at the thought of not returning to the empire, but the air was quiet and solemn. The two men embraced one last time before Gaius stuck a stack of papers in Valerus's hands. "Don't forget to document." He smiled.

Valerus took the papers without a word and followed Lucius aboard. It was going to be home probably for the rest of his life.

Epilogue

March 23, 80 AD

They reached Cadiz when winter fell hard and took heed of the changing weather. Here they waited for the first signs of spring before beginning to stock up until the holds were filled to capacity. From this point they set sail again, despite the warning and condemnations of the locals when hearing their plans.

Now the ocean lay ahead, the ocean as none of them had ever known it. It was where the map ended and the line was drawn. Few had gone farther and none had ever returned. Valerus wondered whether he would return, even if they did find what Flavia so much believed was there.

In the darkness of the night and under the reassuring glow of flickering stars, Valerus vaguely made out the horizon far ahead like a line drawn across the earth. Then for merely a second he knew—he believed with all his soul—that the world did not end. A life, maybe, but the world he knew had to hold further secrets and a promise for adventure.

He smiled for the first time in weeks when he felt the coolness of the green pendant gently tap against his chest with the rocking of the ship. Unconsciously he clenched it in his hand, thinking that the legacy which Flavia had left him could one day change everything—even the world itself.

Above him a shooting star darted across the heavens, and he took it to be a good omen.

And who knows? Maybe, by some miracle, he would make it.

CPSIA information can be obtained at www.ICGtesting.com
Printed in the USA
BVOW05s1924130214

344874BV00002B/3/P